EVEN IN THIS

DIANNA L. LANSER

"This page-turning debut novel will keep readers up at night as they follow Miah and Brandt's story of young love, a close-knit Australian family whose love for each other is tested, and the traumatic event that threatens to derail all their lives. Christian readers fascinated by true crime podcasts will be riveted by the hunt to bring a criminal to justice, but more, the rest of the story, and how God's goodness can be found even in the worst circumstances. Lanser's writing is beautiful, and she has done her homework on criminal procedure, trauma, and the complicated nature of healing."

LORILEE CRAKER, author of sixteen books, including the *New York Times* bestseller *Through the Storm* with Lynne Spears and the ECPA bestseller *My Journey to Heaven* with Marv Besteman.

"In her debut novel, *Even in This,* Dianna Lanser has told a story that is equal parts vulnerable and powerful, raw and beautiful, deeply emotional and profoundly hopeful. Lanser doesn't shy away from the harsh realities of the evil that people can inflict on each other. She also doesn't hold back when it comes to pointing to the ways in which we come to each other's aid and rescue. As I read, I couldn't help but be reminded that God works for the good of those who love Him."

SUSIE FINKBEINER, author of *The All-American.*

"Dianna Lanser brings readers from a secluded cattle station in the Australian Outback to the clear waters of Lake Michigan and beyond, as Miah sets out to reclaim her heart in the wake of great pain. With an emotionally charged narrative and sensory-rich scenes, this coming-of-age tale celebrates the healing power of gratitude, EVEN IN THIS."

JULIE CANTRELL, *New York Times* and *USA TODAY* bestselling author of *Perennials.*

"Dianna L. Lanser's book titled *Even In This* is a very enjoyable and interesting read. I appreciate her style and especially her respect for the cultural ways of the Native people of the Americas. Being a U.S. Marine Veteran myself, her sensitivity and honor for those who serve was greatly appreciated. I highly recommend her book."

DR. CASEY CHURCH, Pokagon Band of Potawatomi tribal member, pastor of Good Medicine Way in Albuquerque, New Mexico, and author of *Holy Smoke: The Contextual Use of Native American Ritual and Ceremony.*

All gratitude and honor to Jesus, the Substitute Sufferer.

With unending love, this story was written for my children:

Alicia – the Joyful Adventurer
Brandt – the Generous Giver
Andrew – the Gracious Accepter
Amy – the Compassionate Creator
Nicole – the Resourceful Defender
All you'll ever need in life is more of Jesus.

And dedicated first to:
My parents, Harrison and Peggy Bailey who are
in the presence of the Great Mystery.

And second, to:
My husband Brent, a man of the earth and
the God who created it.

And finally, to:
All those needing hope as they turn the corner and find
themselves walking through the valley of the shadow.

I acknowledge that the land on which I live is the
ancestral home of the Anishinaabe people, including the
Odawa, Ojibwe, and Potawatomi nations. I'm grateful for
the influence, wisdom, and goodwill of the people of the
Three Fires Confederacy, as well as their care and love of
this land. May Creator strengthen and guide them in their
ongoing struggles for sovereignty, justice, and respect,
and may I do my part to support their efforts.

PART I

In him we were also chosen, having been predestined
according to the plan of him who works out everything
in conformity with the purpose of his will. – Ephesians 1:11

*"Our life is very mysterious. In fact, it would be totally
unexplainable unless we believed that God was preparing us for
events and ministries that lie unseen beyond the veil of the eternal
world."* - L.B. Cowman

PRELUDE

Barcelow Downs, Queensland, Australia
September 1995

It's shocking what can come with the rising sun.

At the bluing of dawn's first light, the government people had come for Jannali when she was just a boori, a young one. They arrived with their growling automobiles and rigid pale faces and pulled her and the other Aboriginal children from their kin and the land as if they were bindi weed.

Joy can come in the morning too. Just when her fear and loneliness grew unbearable, joy had tumbled by on a breeze of forgiveness, catching on the gate of her picketed heart. Amazing thing, really. If joy found its way back to her unsuspecting soul, then wouldn't it return to the girl who dripped with sorrow beside her?

Jannali squinted into the warm rays of sunlight rising above the peaks of the Great Dividing Range and gathered Trace and Claire Bennan's only daughter to her side. If the girl held hope of handling trouble like an adult, she released it with a mournful cry and a stream of salty grief. One overburdened tear cut a straight path down the youth's cheek and glanced off the veranda railing before splitting wide open on the dusty red earth below. And over in the south paddock, the spring calves bawled for their breakfast, making matters seem worse than they were. Not that the girl's situation wasn't grievous. It's just ... she had a powerful imagination and a will to match. And, well, at least she had her family.

Choking back thoughts of her own stolen childhood, Jannali shifted her weight to her good hip and coaxed the girl, all fire and song, down onto the wooden bench with her. From the moment Claire Brennan had given birth to the squalling mite, Jannali knew there was something special about the child. A cloudburst during the dry season? Who could deny the sign? Certainly, the Brennan girl would walk a path to greatness, surpassing her twin and overtaking the rest of her brothers.

All one-and-a-half leggy meters of the eleven-year-old wriggled in the nest of Jannali's embrace before surrendering against her breast with a sigh. Except for the girl's tearful hiccupping, they both sat still until a breeze from the south awakened the faithful windmill, nudging it to pump life into the droughty cattle station. Only when the wheel began to turn with a low moan did the tween venture to test the bridge between her heart and voice. "Jannali?"

"Yes, Miah?"

"I ... I reckon you heard I almost killed Joshua and ... and I hurt Bradley's hand." The girl's confession seeped past the guarded threshold of her soul and then trickled down her face. "And my dad ... Oh, Jannali, he's ...."

"Shh, it'll come good." Humming a quieting tune, Jannali wiped her young friend's sweaty brow then finger-chased a tear down to those rosebud lips that, depending on the girl's mood, could bless with beautiful singing or accost with emotional preteen rants. "Guwiyang. Yabun."

"What?" Capricious as the Simpson Desert during the wet

season, the youth brushed back her tears and peeked through a tangle of straw-colored curls. "What does that even mean?"

Jannali couldn't help but grin at the girl's dark blue eyes brooding like the monsoon skies of the north country. "Guwiyang means fire. Yabun is song." She held her friend closer. "It's a mystery how fire and song can reside together in one girl's spirit, but they do. Somehow in yours, love, they do."

"If I have fire and song in me, then my dad's full of nuts and bananas. H-he wants to leave Amaroo Station—move me and my family to America. What will I do without you? Without Kylie and Caleb? My dad and his rich American friend, Mr. Ellison, have destroyed everything!"

"Not everything, sweet." Jannali pressed her hand over the girl's heart. "If you search deep within you, past the fire and song, you might discover there's room for joy to grow." She paused as a chattering flock of pink and white cockatoos flew by and settled onto the convenient branches of a nearby gum tree. "Change can be good, Miah. It's all a matter of perspective, a matter of choice. Come what may, I hope you choose joy."

CHAPTER ONE

Michigan, United States
July 2001

Choose joy? Didn't Jannali know joy can suddenly flit by and land in a girl's lap, even without her choosing? Or maybe Jannali knew, but because of her past, never allowed herself the luxury of instant joy—the kind that bubbles over when a friend's extravagant kindness humbles or when the beauty of a quickly snapped photo surprises.

Miah pulled the faded photograph of her older friend closer and studied the patient smile carved from those early years of sadness. Perhaps Jannali believed the bridge between sorrow and joy couldn't be trusted, and only on rare occasions did she muster the courage to cross over.

Maybe the boy in the beautiful snapshot felt the same way. Maybe his loss had been so great that now, as a young man, he denied himself the joy of ever loving again. She hoped not. One day she'd find him, a treasure hidden in the Big Horn Mountains to dig up, claim, and ... love.

Miah slid the picture of Jannali back into the clear acrylic frame, then dropped it in her lap. She reached over to her nightstand and took hold of the black-framed picture of the young cowboy she had snapped her first week in America. The heartbreaking scene always seemed to cut lines of guilt across her heart. Why did Jannali and the boy in the picture have to begin their stories with pain and sorrow while others like herself seemed to sing and dance their way through life with barely a sniff of trouble?

And why did the phone always ring just when she was enjoying a little peace and quiet? She pushed the photographs off her lap and onto her bed then raced across the hallway into Mum and Dad's room, snatching up the phone on the fifth ring.

"Hello, you've reached the Brennan's." Her foot tapped an impatient beat on the oak floor while irretrievable seconds spun away on her parents' anniversary clock. Pound to a penny, it was a telemarketer. Back home on Amaroo Station, the phone rarely rang, but here, in America, it never stopped. Everyone had something to sell: windows, carpet cleaning, educational books, and the worst were those political recordings. Mum and Dad couldn't even vote, for crying out loud.

"Hello." She sank onto the edge of her parents' bed and picked at the fray of her cut-off jean shorts. "Hello. Is anyone there?"

"Miah ..."

The two breathy syllables jarred her ear like a chord on an untuned guitar. And while instinct told her to hang up, experience reminded her the man would simply call back—at least that had been his pattern for the last month or so. "Who is this?"

The caller whispered her name again then left her guessing in silence.

"You're really ticking me off. If you keep calling, I'm going to alert the phone company." Her threat only seemed to encourage the heavy breathing and filth that began to sluice through the handset. "Listen, you ugly yobbo, do the world a favor and hang yourself already."

A low chuckle taunted her ear.

"Didn't you hear me? Rack off and never call this number again!"

"You're so sexy, Miah."

"Yeah? Well, you're so sick! And ... and I have four *very* protective brothers!" Truth be known, her oldest brother, Rob, rarely involved himself in her life. And while Drew, her flawless twin, made it his goal to live at peace with everyone, Brad and Josh, the two in the middle, would sooner tie her up with baling twine and drown her in the water hole. But she'd never let pervo man know that. "I'm telling you, mate, you really don't want to mess with me *or* my brothers."

Husky laughter preceded a string of vulgarities that polluted her ear like a sploosh of vomit.

"You disgust me! If I ever find out who this is, you'll never phone anyone again!" With a huff, she ended the call and slammed the receiver back into the charging base before the bloke could have the satisfaction of replying again. "What a loser! What a freaking loser!"

Exasperation hissed between her teeth as she trotted back to her room. How would she ever get rid of the freak? If Mum found out about the calls, she would put them all on the first plane back to Australia. And Dad? He'd do the opposite. He'd never let her leave the farm. Either way, she'd never get to see what might come of her music.

As if the phone were bent on provoking her, it sounded off with another annoying ring. "You've got to be kidding me." She ran back across the hall into her parents' room and yanked the phone to her ear. "I told you to rack off and never call this number again!"

"Miah Moo? Is that you? Is my favorite songwriter having a little trouble today?" A chuckle accompanied the baritone voice.

"C.J.! Hi! Oh, my goodness. I'm so sorry. I-I thought you were someone else."

"Ooh wee! I wouldn't want to be Mr. Someone Else! You was harsh, sister!" The popular deejay's laughter boomed through the receiver.

"I'm really sorry. It was an annoying prank caller. H-He made me so angry!" Her emotion escaped in a falsetto twitter.

"What did he say?"

"Just stupid stuff. C.J., promise you won't tell my dad? If he finds out, he'll pull in *all* the reins. If you know what I mean."

"Oh, ho! We can't have that. Not now, at least." Another round of C.J.'s chuckles served to calm her jittery nerves.

Not now, at least? What did C.J. mean by that? Could he possibly have news from Nashville already? Did she dare ask? No, that would be impolite.

"Speaking of the old cowpoke, is he around?"

"Well, he's certainly not in the house. He only comes inside to eat and sleep. And if it weren't for my mum, he'd bunk in the barn or pastures with the cattle."

C.J.'s deep belly laugh accompanied the bird song trilling through her parents' bedroom windows. "Well, can you let him know I called? I was thinking about getting the small group together this weekend or next to fix Marcus and Trina's lawn and put their fence back up. Between them having to replace their well, Bri smashing Trina's Suburban, and Marcus losing a patient, I thought this just might be the encouragement they needed."

"Aww, C.J., you're so thoughtful."

"If we don't help each other, what are friends for?"

"Well, you're an extraordinary friend, always thinking of others. And I'm so grateful for everything you and Mateá have done for me and my family.

"Thanks, Miah Moo. I receive that." C.J.'s chair squeaked under the weight of his ample frame, and his voice grew quiet.

"Hey ... I've got two minutes until I have to be back on the air." The chair squeaked again. "Mateá told me not to say anything until my friend has a definitive answer for you, but I thought you might appreciate a little news from the Smoky Mountains to keep you hoping. Are you sitting down?"

CHAPTER TWO

"C.J., don't fool with me."

"I'm not kidding. Are you sitting down?"

"Aye. On my parents' bed." Miah's left hand fairly trembled as she smoothed the summer-weight comforter. And right now, she needed all the comfort and all the familiar and steady she could get. "C.J., I just want you to know, no matter what your friend decides, I'm really thankful for all your help recording and mixing my music and giving it radio time."

"Mmm, hmm. Mmm, hmm."

"I'm so very grateful, C.J."

"I appreciate that, Miah." He chuckled.

"To be honest, I'm a little afraid too. All along, I-I've had a feeling about my music. I mean ... It's not mine. It's not me. It's God who's given me the songs, and I don't know if I'm ready for ... what may come."

"Mmm. Well, here's the thing. I'm so glad you recognize where your talent comes from, Miah Moo. God has definitely given you a gift, and He's gonna be with you and give you what you need, when you need it. And me and Teá, your family, Bri and her parents, and Pastor Bryce and Celia, we'll be here for you too. But if things happen like you and I think they're gonna happen, it'll definitely open a can of worms. Good worms though!" More laughter bubbled through the phone, challenging her insecurities.

"C.J., you're such a goof. So ... Did your friend get a chance to listen to the songs?"

C.J.'s joy settled to a hum. "He did. Mmm, hmm. He loved everything you wrote. I knew he would!" Laughter once again rocked her ear.

"Seriously? I-I can't believe it!" Her voice pitched toward the highest height of hope.

And like a switch, C.J.'s tune flipped from hyped deejay to responsible-dad-type figure. "Now listen, Miah Moo. This is not a done deal. Just because my friend likes your music doesn't mean the rest of the big guns at Smoky Mountain Music will. Understand?"

"Aye, I know. And even if they do like my music, there's the hurdle of my parents."

A deep rumbling chuckle agreed with her. "Oh, ho, ho ... It's gonna be some fun watching your daddy wrestle with God's will. He'll get there. Don't you worry, Miah Moo. He'll get there, all right. Okay, gotta go! Don't forget to tell the old man I called."

"I won't. Bye, C.J. Thank you!"

A breath of unbelief blew from her lungs as she fell back on her parents' bed. Could this really happen? Was there a teeny chance Smoky Mountain Music would offer her a contract? And if they did, would Mum and Dad ease up on the rules, let go of their caution and allow her to sign?

Blinking up into the beam of dust and mid-morning sun gilding her parents' bedroom, she reached out as if the answer could be fetched from the warmth and beauty dancing above her. At least now Mum seemed happier and more settled than when Dad first agreed to manage Mr. Ellison's organic beef operation.

Mum had fairly choked on her dinner—they all had for that

matter—when Dad suggested they pack up and leave Nana and Granddad's expansive cattle station. "America is the septic tank of humanity! And you want to take our five children there?" Mum argued.

After weeks of whispered midnight talks, Dad won Mum over, promising to move the family back to Australia at the first hint of trouble. However, there was no whispering the day Mum signed on the dotted line. "Trace Brennan, if anything happens to our kids, it's on you. It's all on you!" She had pushed her fists into his chest, and with tears flowing, fell into his arms.

Five frigid winters in Michigan had come and gone, and if Mum were honest, she would probably say their time in America hadn't been so bad. Hopefully, Mum's heart would continue to warm to their new life. Hopefully, Dad would lower his standard of vigilance.

"How's the nap, ya lazy layabout?"

A loud smack and stinging slap on her bare thigh ripped her thoughts straight off the wall of her brain.

"Jingoes, Brad! She sat bolt upright, rubbing the hot pain away with the coolness of her palm. "That! ... hurt." Her anger stalled out as tears itched to roll off the rims of her eyes.

"A little pain now or a bucket of pain later." Her brother backed away, keeping his smirk turned toward the pink handprint developing on her leg like a Polaroid picture.

"A bucket of pain from what?" She swallowed her emotion and then blinked up at Brad's smug blue eyes with a strong dose of practiced patience.

"From Dad, that's what. He wants you in the barn flat out, and he's madder than a cut snake."

"Why? What'd I do?" She nursed her leg with another gentle pat and then rose from their parents' bed.

"It's what you didn't do." Brad pushed his finger into her chest. "And when Dad finds out you've been loafing, he's going to spit the dummy."

"But I filled the mineral feeders, let Battle Chief out to pasture, locked the gate, turned the electric fence back on, and got the calving stalls so clean even I'd sleep in them. I followed Dad's instructions to a T."

"Life is such a mystery, isn't it?" He mocked her with a grubby little chuckle then ran out of the room, his curls sticking out like tiny brown horns.

"Jerk." Willing her anger and tears to stay zipped away where Brad could never see them, she stepped from the tidiness of her parents' room and crossed the hallway into the chronic messiness of her own bedroom.

Shoe boxes, photo albums, and stacks of pictures littered the floor while a selection of CD's, music books, her notebook, and Granddad's trusty Taylor guitar were strewn across the gray and white comforter making it appear like a crazy patchwork quilt. And the photographs she'd been looking at when C.J. called were ... gone. Gone like a dropped wallet in a poor man's path. And she had a darn good idea which beggar had nicked them from her bed. "Brad ..."

He'd been a burr under her saddle since the day she and Drew turned seven. Granddad had given her his old guitar and Drew, his drum set. Brad's jealousy and bullyragging grew and grew until the injustice of it all exploded from her when she was eleven and he was fifteen. He stole her journal, and when she stormed into the paddock, she spooked a horse that cut Brad's hand and nearly trampled her other brother Josh. The whole terrible kerfuffle happened six years ago, and while she had begged forgiveness from Brad, Josh, and Jesus, Brad was showing no signs of softening. In fact, he was getting downright mean.

With Rob graduated and married and Josh starting his second year at Michigan State, Mum said Brad was feeling a bit behind the game. A bit? That was an understatement, but it was his own fault, really. He could have been a senior at university this year. Instead, he'd backed out of freshman orientation at the last minute. A lack of confidence? A lack of direction or passion? Who knew?

One thing was certain, Brad was not happy, and once again, he'd deemed her a most convenient target for his anger. And now, somehow, she had riled Dad too.

She started across the room for her flip-flops then stopped short at the south window where the smell of fresh-cut hay and the familiar growl of a diesel engine blew in on the mid-morning breeze. Down on the drive below, Josh's black truck rumbled past the house followed by something new—the ning-ning-ning of a motorbike. The pickup turned and stopped parallel to the side of the big red barn—the barn where Dad and her fate awaited. Then like a horse out of the gate, Josh gunned his truck over the grassy berm and came to a screeching halt right in the middle of the basketball court where Drew and Brad were shooting baskets. "Oh, my goodness!" Shaking her head, she patted her heart with her hand. Josh was crazy. And Brad was ... mean.

She left the window and the shenanigans going on below and stepped over to her small writing desk. Maybe in a moment of benevolence, Brad had dropped the pictures of Grandmother Jannali and her American cowboy amongst the chaos of her desk. Pushing aside her journal, her 4-H project binder, and a stack of old school papers, she lifted her backpack—even peeked inside, and then checked the wastebasket below. Nothing. Where in the blue blazes did he put them?

Sighing, she scanned the rest of her room, then shuffled into her flip-flops, and made her way down the stairs of the rambling old farmhouse to the kitchen, the back door, and Dad's wrath.

CHAPTER THREE

"Hey, Miah, 'owyergoing?"

She spun around to find Josh's face pressed into the refuge of the freezer. Sweat rolled down his backside, soaking the waistband of his saggy jeans. "Hey, Josh. I thought you were outside."

He closed the freezer door then opened the fridge. "I came in to get a few Dews. You want one?"

"No thanks." She grimaced at the smell of him and then avoiding contact with his sweaty bare chest, she followed him out the screened door and onto the patio.

"I accidentally grabbed one Dew too many. Sure you don't want one?" Josh offered.

She nodded, paused, and then reached for the can. "Actually, I've changed my mind. If I give it to Dad, maybe he'll go easy on me."

Josh passed off the can then wiped the perspiration from his forehead back through his cropped, blond curls. "Why? What'd you do?"

"Not a clue. Brad just said he's angry." She took her frustration out on a lonesome stone, kicking it down the blacktop drive a little too hard. Despite all her wishful thinking, it took a bad hop and pinged into the back panel of Josh's truck. "Oops."

"Oops?" Shooting her the evil eye, Josh walked up to the fender and rubbed the spot with his finger.

"Sorry." She stooped to get a closer look and twanged an anxious beat on the pull tab of the Mountain Dew can. "Did it make a mark?"

"I don't see anything. Lucky for you."

A loud complaint followed by a burst of laughter came from the basketball court, drawing their attention away from the smooth, black paint. They both stood and peered across the bed of the truck.

"Who's that?" The back of one very suntanned basketball player went up for a rebound, ran past Brad and Drew, and then hustled to the line for a three-pointer.

"A mate of mine. He's studying Vet Med too. He'd been planning on a summer internship at an animal hospital. Unfortunately, something happened at the last minute, and it fell through. Now he's stuck here until the fall semester. I thought Dad might be able to hire him for a few weeks."

"He's so tan. Where's he from?"

"South Dakota."

"South Dakota? The ponytail's a nice effect. What'd Dad think of it?"

"He hasn't seen it yet. Don't let looks deceive you, Miah. He's top-shelf. Come here, I'll introduce you."

"DuCharme! Think fast!" Josh tossed a soft drink in the direction of the newcomer who swiveled and caught the can close to his side like an American football player.

His dark eyes met hers for an instant before she lowered her own to the cement court and waited for him to complete the long double-take she could never get used to. Awkward with a capital A!

"Hey, you must be Miah. I'm Brandt DuCharme."

"Oh ..." Quick smart, she switched the Mountain Dew can to her left hand, wiped her right hand on her shorts and accepted the offering of his outstretched hand. "Yeah. I'm Miah. Nice to meet you."

"Josh told me all about your music."

Josh talking about her music? To a friend? She directed her raised brows at Josh then stole another wary glance at his friend. Jingoes! He was so very good looking and ... could it be he was an American Indian? "Are ... are you a musician too?"

He wore a warm, humble smile and reached for his T-shirt that was hanging on the side mirror of the truck. "It all depends on how you define musician." Pulling the shirt over his head, he covered his broad chest as if it might be offensive to her. "I played the cello up until I graduated. It belonged to the school, so I had to give it back. Haven't played since."

Josh snickered and lobbed Brad and Drew a Mountain Dew. "The cello? You don't seem like a cello kind of bloke."

"First chair in the Prairie View High School Orchestra, bro."

"Ha! And I'll bet you were a dapper chap in your black tux and bow tie, weren't ya?" Josh knocked the basketball from Drew's hand and bounced it in the direction of his friend.

Brandt laughed and lunged toward the ball. He looked straight at her, nodded, and then bounced the ball in her direction. "You wanna play?"

Although his invitation made her think twice, Brad's scowl reminded her she had business to attend to in the barn.

"Thanks. I can't. I ... have to help my dad out." Locking eyes with Brad, she silently pleaded with him to be quiet about what was really facing her in the barn. "Nice to meet you. Maybe I'll see you around."

"I hope so."

She tossed the ball back then turned and walked away before Brandt could see the unmistakable blush of flattery on her cheeks. Could it be her imagination or had there been something more than politeness in his reply? She must be dreaming to think Josh's friend might actually be showing some interest in her. After all, he would soon be a sophomore at State!

Before rounding the corner of the barn, she couldn't help steal a curious glance over her shoulder. He stood there with a friendly nod and a ready smile, just as if he'd been waiting for her to turn around all along.

She fairly floated into the cool shelter of the barn, but for Dad's sake, wiped the grin from her face.

What were the chances Dad got busy with something else and forgot all about his reason for being angry? Miah scanned the open space of the barn where her family set up the auction ring every fall. Except for the Bobcat tractor and a pallet of sweet grain, this part of the barn echoed of emptiness.

She walked the length of the auction arena then went around the corner into the calving stalls. "Dad?" Only silence and the smell of fresh hay and disinfectant greeted her.

With two possible places left to check, she slid the metal gate open and entered the older section of the barn where the cows were brought in for artificial insemination. The wide south wing lay empty too. But, what was this?

She ran over to the big yellow fertilizer drum, which had been repurposed as a trash bin. There sitting on top of a rabble of broken-down shipping boxes, feed bags, and soiled gloves sat the pictures of her American cowboy and Grandmother Jannali! "Bradley Beelzebub Brennan!"

She set the can of Mountain Dew on the floor and dusted off the pictures, checking them over for damage. Her cowboy looked beautiful as always—perfectly candid, absolutely vulnerable in his quiet strength. How her twelve-year-old self had taken such a captivating picture with Mum's ancient point-and-shoot camera was a mystery.

Even back then, Brad didn't waste time declaring the professional quality of the photograph a fluke. Yet, it rivaled any picture she'd ever seen in *National Geographic*. A person could almost feel the warmth of the Wyoming sunrise as it broke through the morning mist and shone a golden spotlight on the subjects. The magical glow gave a glimmer of hope to the otherwise poignant scene.

As for her, the memory always played a haunting refrain through her mind, its sadness raising a thousand questions. Who was the boy kneeling at the grave site, and who was the man standing at his side? How old would the boy be now? Josh's age? Eighteen—almost nineteen, maybe? If Mr. Ellison didn't know who the two stockmen were, then where had they come from? And how far had they ridden their grazing horses to reach the overgrown cemetery near Mr. Ellison's Ranchester cattle station? Had they loved the people who were buried beneath those headstones?

Someday she'd settle down in the rolling hills of the Bighorn mountains and find her cowboy and the answers to her questions. She'd write down his story—perhaps even become part of his story. First, however, she needed C.J. to nick her a recording contract. Without buckets of money, she'd never be able to buy a big station in Wyoming. Nor could she support Mr. Ellison's nonprofit, Water Wins, and help provide education and equipment for Nigerians to drill clean-water boreholes. And then there was her desire to help people like Jannali who had suffered for the sake of "racial preservation" and governmental policy.

To be sure, her dreams were far-fetched, but it didn't hurt to move forward in faith, did it? After all, God was in the miracle-making business. And right now, she needed Him to work his magic and smooth things out with Dad.

With the framed pictures in hand, she waved a fly from her

face, then picked up the can of Mountain Dew and retraced her steps back to the auction arena and over to the newly renovated workspace and her doom. From behind the office door the radio played U2's "With Or Without You", and Dad joined in with his off-key singing. Hey, at least he sounded happy. She cracked the door open and peeked inside. "Daddy?"

"There you are." He swiveled his chair toward her, his blue eyes full of cheer. "I'd begun to think you got lost in your daydreaming again."

"You're not angry?"

He twisted his brow into a question mark which matched the shape of his lopsided grin. "Should I be?"

"No, it's just Brad said ... Oh, never mind." She squeezed the photos tight in her hand. Brad's schemes were not going to get under her skin.

"Well, little Miss Gullible, go get your mum. I think she's in the garden. And grab Drew on your way back. I have something I want to show you."

"What is it?"

"You'll have to wait and see." Dad waved her off with a smile. "Just go get your mum and Drew."

"Should I tell Brad and Josh to come too?"

"No, not unless you want to be thrown into a pit and sold as an Egyptian slave."

What did Dad have that might possibly make her older brothers jealous?

"Be quick smart now."

"Oh! I almost forgot. C.J. wants you to call him, and here, this is for you." She left the can of Mountain Dew on the desk and then checked her reflection in the blank computer screen before backtracking to the basketball court and the flattering attention of the fawn-eyed Indian. Careful to hide her eagerness, she slowed her pace as she came around the corner of the barn. "Hey, Drew. Dad wants to see you. He's in the office."

All heads, except Brad's, turned her way, making it easy to hide her irritation with him. As Brad slammed the ball through the hoop, she flashed a red-carpet smile in the direction of Josh's friend letting her eyes linger long enough to let him know she liked what she saw. As far as she could tell, he seemed just as pleased at the sight of her too.

If she didn't run the risk of her brothers catching onto their silent tête-à-tête, she could stand there all afternoon exchanging glances with Brandt ... Brandt DuCharme, a name befitting his ancestry and his good looks.

What would Grandmother Jannali think of him? More importantly, what would Kylie think? She'd write her sweet friend back in Queensland and tell her about the American Aboriginal who had just stepped into her life. Or ... maybe she shouldn't write to Kylie. Maybe she should keep Brandt's existence to herself.

If Brandt even glanced at Kylie, all hope would be lost of ever claiming his undivided attention. There would be no way she could compete with the blended beauty Kylie had inherited from her dad and granddad's striking English features and Grandmother Jannali's warm, Aboriginal tones. Yet, the lucky truth of the matter was, Kylie lived far away in Queensland, and she lived here in Michigan with Brandt, who was playing basketball on her court, with her brothers, and possibly working for Dad the rest of the summer. So yes, she would write to Kylie tonight.

Drew deflected Josh's layup straight into Brad's hands, and instead of waiting to see the outcome, she skipped past the truck and down the drive to the garden. When she caught sight of Mum's pretty face flitting over and around the raspberry bushes like a happy hummingbird, she couldn't help but giggle. It seemed their hearts were beating to the same light tune.

CHAPTER FOUR

"*I*f it were up to me, I would have waited the three weeks until your birthday, but Mr. and Mrs. Ellison had been adamant you have these now. So, happy birthday to both of you."

Miah turned the white envelope over in her hands and glanced from Dad to Mum, and then to Drew. "What are they, Dad?"

Drew didn't wait for an answer. Like an eager kid at the Dairy Queen, he licked his lips and ripped open the pale-yellow envelope Dad had handed him. "Drumroll please!"

She tucked her own envelope between her knees and paradiddled her fingers on the side of the file cabinet.

Slowly and dramatically, Drew pulled the cream-colored card from its envelope. "And the winner is ..." As he opened the card, a light blue paper rectangle fluttered to the floor.

"It's a check, Drew!"

He grabbed it off the floor, took one look, and staggered backwards, stepping on her bare toes.

"How much is it?" She couldn't stand the suspense.

"It's got to be a mistake. Did you see this, Dad?" Drew exclaimed.

Mum and Dad exchanged a chuckle. "We know. It's not a mistake though. Read the card, son."

Drew turned his back to the circle, soaking in every handwritten word on the card. Didn't he know his secrecy would be the end of her? "Drew, how much is it for?"

"Sweetheart, why don't you open yours now."

Drew let out a happy whoop. "I can't believe it! I don't deserve this!" He passed the card to Dad then turned his attention to her.

For once she wished she didn't have an audience. Slipping her finger beneath the sealed flap, she ran it along the edge until the envelope opened to reveal a small square of colorful fabric. She'd seen this card before. In fact, she'd been with Mr. and Mrs. Ellison at the Women of Hope showroom in Jos, Nigeria when they'd bought a box of the handmade stationery.

She pulled the card from the envelope and held it up for everyone to see. The miniature quilt block of brightly dyed fabric had been pieced and stitched together into a cross design and placed in the window of the card. Next to the window, a vibrant blue embossing spelled out the message of the card, "Happy Birthday," and its simple beauty brought back bittersweet memories of her visit to Africa.

"Oh, Miah. It's lovely."

She nodded in agreement. "It's from Nigeria, Mum."

"Open the card already!"

She laughed at Drew's impatience. "Hang on." Now with the attention landing on her, she wanted to savor the moment. She wanted to give the Ellison's the respect they deserved. She would read the card and *then* peek at the check.

Happy Birthday Miah Dear,

What a blessing it has been getting to know you these past five years. Mrs. Ellison and I find you a truly delightful and talented young lady. We especially appreciate the enthusiastic way you approach life. It's people like you who make the world go 'round.

Thanks for sharing your dreams with us on the long, hot ride to the East Kambari Area. We're so glad you've considered your plans in light of what God wants for you. Thank you too for sharing His love and your songs with the children there. Your musical abilities come directly from the Giver of every good and perfect gift. Keep using your talents for His glory!

Last night on our way to a meeting, Mrs. Ellison and I enjoyed listening to your CD. We realized we are indebted to you. First, for your inspiring music, (which rocks, by the way) and then for all the work you do around the farm. Every time we visit, you and Drew are working as hard as the boys who are getting paid. We know it's not a show. It's very clear, between the two of you, that you are experienced enough to handle the whole operation on your own. So, we'd like to settle our account—with the stipulation you use the money to make your dreams come true!

In the grip of His grace,
Ben and Maddie Ellison

Mr. Ellison's encouraging words were the only payment she needed. She could ride high on his praise for months. Of course, she wouldn't be in this hopeful spot without her parents' support and the generous radio and studio time C.J. doled out. All the same, it was a gift to have people of influence recognize her music for what she prayed it would be, and now they had given her ....

She turned the check over in her hand. "Twenty-five hundred

American dollars! I can't believe it!" Big tears welled up in her eyes and collided with the laughter tumbling from her smile. She held the check out and compared it with Drew's. They'd never had so much money in their whole lives!

She traded cards with Dad, and through her tears, read Drew's note from the Ellisons. Their words to him were just as sobering. For whatever reason, the Ellisons saw potential in them. She and Drew would not—could not—let them down.

"Drew, if we put our money together, we could afford to have our music professionally mixed and recorded! We wouldn't have to scam off C.J. anymore!"

The excitement in Drew's eyes flickered then dwindled like a campfire choked with green wood. He stared at the check in his hand and shook his head. "Miah, it's your music, not ours." He looked to Mum for help. "I mean, I'll play the drums for you as long as I can, but it's not my dream. I want to be a pilot. I want to fly for the Royal Flying Doctor Service. Kylie's going to be a nurse and ... I want to go home. With this money, I could start flying lessons right now." Enthusiasm brightened his eyes once again. "Who knows? By the time I graduate next May and enroll at Queensland Aero Club, I could already have my private pilot license. I'd be so much closer to getting my commercial license."

His face wore a big apology, making her feel like a selfish goon. She knew flying had been his dream ever since he'd peeked inside the King Air that landed at Barcelow Downs and flown Kylie's brother, Caleb, to the hospital in Longreach. On the other hand, she hadn't heard Drew talk about it since they'd moved to America—at least not much anyway. She thought his dream had fallen by the wayside, like their oldest brother Rob's had.

And what did Kylie wanting to be a nurse have to do with anything? Unless ... unless Drew and Kylie's close friendship had somehow developed into something more. But if fireworks had been exploding between them, how had she missed it? And why hadn't Drew or Kylie said anything to her or Caleb? They'd all grown up sharing everything from sippy cups and saddles, to books and boots, and especially secrets. Although she tried not to take Drew's rejection personally, it still hurt. It was so very disappointing.

"Drew, what does Kylie wanting to be a nurse have to do with anything, anyway?"

He merely shrugged and gave her a shy grin.

"Well, I guess I know what happened to all my airmail stamps and why Kylie seemed so eager to help you wrap presents at Christmas." With a playful smirk, she elbowed Drew into the open door. "And I think I have a good idea what you two were doing in the shed. I'd bet my check, you weren't fixing tack!"

Drew's face flushed with embarrassment. "Uh ... yeah. I owe you for the stamps."

"Dad ... Mum ... Did you know about this? You let Drew have a girlfriend and not me?"

Dad yanked on her ponytail. "You can have all the girlfriends you want, Miah Moo."

"You know what I mean." Thank goodness she had a big, fat check in her hand, because right about now, she could get a serious grump on. She was tired of the double standard around here. If she had to wait until her seventeenth birthday to date, then Drew should too. Seventeen! That's ridiculous!

She sidled up next to Mum. "Dad, Mum had been fourteen when you told her you were going to marry her! All I want to do is go to a movie or concert with somebody. It's not fair!"

A quick wink to Mum accompanied Dad's smile. "I had to give Margaret and the honorable Judge Caelon McKinnon ample notice of my intentions, love. I knew it'd take years for the tall poppies to adjust to the idea of their privileged Scottish daughter marrying a no-hoper Irishman from the Outback."

Mum leaned back against the desktop, her gracious smile

neither affirming nor denying Dad's explanation. "Miah, your dad and I lived a thousand kilometers from one another and only saw each other once a year at the cattle exhibitions in Brisbane. We weren't dating. We were writing—just like Drew and Kylie." Mum studied Drew as if the untold shed story left some doubt in the back of her mind.

One shouldn't be so nit-picky, yet wouldn't it be something to unravel any hidden knots in Saint Andrew's perfectly woven character? "Oh, you're too right, Mum. Drew and Kylie were probably just writing in the shed. Nevertheless, in light of this latest development, a question crossed my mind. Could they have been pashing on each other?"

Drew threw daggers from his blue eyes and then snatched his card from her fingers.

"Drew, I'm sorry. I'm glad about you and Kylie. It's just so aggravating having to live by a totally different set of rules than you."

Dad shook his head. "Nothing could be farther from the truth, Miah." Your mum and I have the same expectations for all of you. We didn't know how Drew felt about Kylie. You can be sure, the next time they're together, Mr. Barcelow and I will set up some firm boundaries for them."

"Good." She folded her arms across her chest. "And since you have the same expectations for us, I guess you won't mind if I make an appointment to take my driving test. Drew's had his license for six months."

Dad exchanged a pathetic look with Mum, exasperation powering a sigh deep from his lungs. "Haven't we discussed this before? You're twins, not clones. In case you haven't noticed, sweetheart, you're different in every way, especially in how your brains are wired. When you're on the road, you've gotta stay focused on one thing and one thing only—driving. Not on the people in the car next to you, not on the radio, not on the scenery."

"I do stay focused!"

Dad raised his eyebrows toward Mum. "You wanna back me up a bit, Claire?"

"I thought you were doing just fine, Trace." Mum's cheeky grin mellowed to a softness, matching her kind eyes. "Sweetheart, your dad and I know you try to stay focused, it's just sometimes we wonder if you understand how dangerous it is out there."

"Your mum's right, Miah. It's like sending you out in a ring with an unbroke horse. We want to make sure you're absolutely ready. We'd like you to have more driving time and experience."

"How am I going to get it when you're always busy working? Dad, if I had my license, I'd use this money to buy a car. I could give music lessons. I've had so many people at church ask me to teach their kids."

"Why don't you teach them here?"

"The piano's in the busiest part of the house, Mum! It'd be too distracting."

Drew winked then gestured for them to wait. "I just had an idea I think you might like, Miah."

Drew stepped out of the office and offered a "what's up, mate" to someone or maybe three someone's who'd been hanging out much too close to the office door.

A combination of unbelief and shame torched up her neck as Josh's voice crossed the threshold and entered the office. "We were just showing DuCharme around and—"

"And enjoying your conversation." Brad's sarcasm-coated snicker confirmed the reason for her dread.

Oh, jingoes ... She would die a thousand deaths if Josh's friend heard every pitched note of her infantile whining for dating and driving rights. And Mum and Dad were oblivious to the humiliating situation. They stepped past her and followed the boys' voices out into the wide, vacant space.

Drew didn't seem to care either. Without skipping a beat, he tapped on the newly installed office wall and spoke up as if he enjoyed the added attention of Josh and Brad and their friend.

"Dad, what if we put up a couple soundproof walls next to the office and make a studio? There's at least fourteen feet of unused space here. We'd have to do something creative with the heating system so noise wouldn't travel through the ducts, especially if I put my drum set in here."

Dad's voice echoed back into the office where she'd hidden herself and her shame behind the door. "I think you've got something, Drew, but first I believe a couple of introductions are in order."

"Oh. Oh, right." Josh cleared the usual swagger from his voice. "Dad, Mum, this is Brandt DuCharme—a friend of mine from university. He's studying Vet Med too. And, Brandt, this is my dad and mum, Trace and Claire."

"It's nice to meet you, Mr. and Mrs. Brennan. You have a great family and an awesome operation here. Josh has told me all about it and has promised to show me around."

Jingoes! Josh's friend greeted Mum and Dad with the same kindness he'd shown her! How could she have been so vain? Brandt DuCharme wasn't interested in her. He was just a nice guy—to everyone, even whiny, self-indulged, almost seventeen-year-olds.

She crept out from behind her hiding place and hesitated at the doorway before quietly joining her family in the open space of the barn.

"What were you doing, sweetheart? Have you met Josh's friend, Brandt?"

She shrugged, nodded, and then gave Brandt a polite smile, because, hey, she could be polite too. When he returned her smile with a playful pout, she couldn't stop herself from volleying back with a shake of her head and a genuine grin. His confidence was infectious, his kindness inviting, and his eyes were ... endearing? Captivating? Beautiful? Yes, all of the above.

"So, what do you think, love?"

"A-about what, Dad?"

"About Drew's idea—using the leftover materials from the office expansion and building a studio right here, next to the office. If you and Drew are willing to put in the elbow grease, then the space and materials are all yours. So, what do you think?"

She tried to imagine sitting in her own private studio where she could practice, write, and ... teach. What she envisioned, she liked. She liked it a lot. There was only one problem. "I love the idea, but the thought of putting a baby grand in a drafty barn goes against any kind of logic. No, there's no way."

She stole a quick glance toward Josh's friend. He cocked his head with all that lovely black hair and smiled as if her opinion was the most interesting thing he'd heard all day.

Then Mum nodded and offered her two cents worth. "I agree. And anyway, I would miss hearing Miah playing in the house."

Drew shrugged. "Can't you use the keyboard or buy a used upright, Miah?"

"Hey! What's so interesting about a bloomin' barn wall?" Like marionettes controlled by the same hand, they all turned in the direction of Rob's cheerful voice. "You look like you've just seen a miracle. Did the image of Jesus suddenly appear on the wall or something?"

With her usual grace, Mum ignored Rob's wise crack. "What a nice surprise! G'day, you two!"

"Hi, Mum." Stepping around the power washer and its coiled hose, Rob took his petite wife's hand and led her over to where they'd all been imagining four finished walls and a carpeted floor.

"This *is* a nice surprise." Dad reached over, giving Amy a big sidearm hug. "Hi, love! You're especially beautiful today, and your husband doesn't look too bad either." He clasped Rob's hand with a single, brisk shake. "I know you don't usually dress up to visit your mum and dad, so where are you two going in such finery?"

"Actually, we're getting back." Rob perched his grin above Amy's long auburn hair, making the couple resemble a happy totem pole. "And we thought you'd all like to know, we've just been to the doctor and seen the visage of our own little miracle!"

CHAPTER FIVE

"This week may you live in the strength and knowledge of God's love. Go in peace."

Once again Trace's friend and pastor, Bryce Harrison, had delivered a relevant message, and for the third time this morning, joy bubbled from Claire in the form of a pinch to Trace's arm. Actually, she'd been giddy all week and had reasoned it would only be proper to share good news with friends by treating them to a barbecue. He couldn't agree more. After all, it'd been their friends who made life in America bearable for Claire, and now with a grandbaby on the way, she'd miraculously admitted their move from Australia had been a good thing. Indeed, they did have something to celebrate.

"Trace!"

He scanned the throng of people filing out of the auditorium and searched for a pair of eyes eager to connect with his. Finding nothing, he glanced back over his shoulder toward the front of the large hall and tried to listen for his name above the din of voices and walk-out music.

Up on stage, Miah met his eyes and smiled as the worship

team rocked the beat of one of the latest praise songs being played over the airwaves. The band members were definitely in their element and having fun.

Miah and Drew usually played in one of the smaller venues; however, with some of the more veteran musicians on holiday, they'd been given the opportunity to play in the televised auditorium for the first time. Even more surprising, Jeremy had suggested Miah sing one of her originals. And today, the church had shown their approval with an enthusiastic round of applause.

"Trace!"

This time the voice came from the left.

"It's Nathan. Over there." Claire nodded toward the far end of their row.

One section over, Nathan Haskin's blue eyes twinkled, adding a sparkle of kindness to his already friendly face. The older man waved, gesturing to meet up in the Atrium and then went back to his work, checking the emptied rows of chairs for discarded programs, coffee cups, forgotten Bibles, and misplaced pens.

Trace felt for Claire's hand, giving it a squeeze. "Nathan's one in a million."

"Too right. The crazy thing is, he reminds me so much of your dad. It's no wonder you and Nathan make such a good team."

He returned Claire's smile and tugged her hand again. She would never understand how much her encouragement meant to him, especially when it came to sitting on the board of a monstrously large church. Why he ever let Pastor Bryce talk him into accepting the nomination, he'd never know. He wasn't elder material. He was a cattleman and a well driller with lots of shortcomings of his own. He certainly didn't qualify as a shepherd of hurting and broken people.

At the urging of Claire and his friends, he whispered a prayer for help and put his hat into the ring. To his surprise, the role had turned out to be a good thing. With Nathan as his mentor and partner, he'd been challenged to pursue a more vital relationship with the Lord. Not only were he and Nathan seeing changes in the lives of the people they were ministering to, but he had also begun to experience a purposefulness in his own life. And isn't that why he had left everything behind and come to America in the first place?

"Trace, there's C.J." Claire motioned toward the back of the auditorium. "Are he and Mateá able to join us for tea today?"

"Oh, jingoes. I forgot to ask him yesterday when we were at Marcus and Trina's." He turned and searched the aisle for Rob and Amy who moments ago had been right behind them. Seeing them stuck in a slow-moving current with Josh and Brad, he mouthed his silent message. "We have to talk with C.J."

After receiving a nod from Josh, he pulled Claire aside and ran up the four steps into the large, two-tiered tech booth where cameras, computers, and boards with all kinds of knobs and sliding switches filled the long desks. He found C.J. stooped below the table, fossicking around a traffic jam of black wires and silver plugs.

"Hey, mate! You find what you're looking for?" Trace reached around a camera tripod and grasped the hand of his friend.

"Hey, hey, Tracey!" C.J. let out one of his hearty laughs, revealing his professionally whitened teeth, shining like heaven's glory against his dark brown skin. "Miah did good today! She did real good!"

"She did all right, didn't she?" He slapped his friend on the back. "Hey, thanks for arranging the workday at Marcus and Trina's yesterday. It was a good thing—just what they needed."

"Aww... man. It was worth every blister to see Marcus' face when he got home last night, wasn't it?"

"Too right, mate. And if you want to see his face again today, we're hoping you and Mateá can come over for lunch. We've invited the rest of the small group too."

"We? Where's the pretty part of we, anyway?" C.J. stood and peeked his head over the half wall of the booth and waved. "Hi, Claire!"

"Hi, C.J."

"So, do you think you and Teá can make it, mate?"

"You know it, bro'. You know it!" C.J's happiness boomed again.

"All right then, we'll get the barbie fired up!"

"Oh ho, I can hardly wait!" Good nature rolled from his friend's belly like the peaceful rumble of distant thunder. On the radio, C.J.'s trademark laughter brought joy and comfort to the tens of thousands who tuned in. To his friends, his laughter so effectively communicated his love.

The popular deejay dropped a big arm across Trace's shoulder. "Man, Teá's had me eating girlie salads all week. If I don't get to eat a steak today, I'm gonna die. I tell ya, I'm just gonna die!"

Trace connected with Nathan and set up a mentoring meeting for Thursday, but now, somehow, he had lost Claire in the crowd. Where could she have disappeared to? He scanned the area for her blond curls and the purply pink sundress she had bought just yesterday.

He checked her usual spot at the coffee bar and then glanced up at the bridge. Bingo! In fact, the whole family had gathered up there.

Trace weaved through the crowd, offering smiles to everyone he met on his way to the steel-girded loft. Could that be Ryan

Ambrose? Trace maneuvered himself around a small circle of talkers to see more clearly. Yep, that was him all right. Trace would never forget the younger man's face or his build. Ryan Ambrose had the looks of a man's man—and a ladies' man—which is what may have attributed to his trouble in the first place … and the second place.

If fidelity was a problem for the bloke, honesty was not. Ryan Ambrose would be the first to admit he had an insatiable appetite for the opposite sex. Broken and desperate after an unwanted divorce, Ryan had come to the church, seeking a way out of his addiction. He said he needed help to end the cycle of physical and emotional affairs that had destroyed his wife's trust. But for some reason, Ryan Ambrose had made himself scarce lately. Trace hadn't seen the sport in weeks.

Breaking his stride, Trace grabbed hold of his new friend's shoulders. "Hey, Ryan!" When the much younger man turned, a shadow of regret doused the initial spark of recognition in his eyes.

"Hi, Trace."

"Ow've you been, mate? I thought you fell off the face of the earth—didn't return a single one of my phone calls." He gave his friend a reassuring smile.

"I know. I'm really sorry. Between work and trying to do the right thing on the home front, things have been pretty busy lately." Ryan's eyes shifted to the boy standing at his side.

Picking up on Ryan's clue, Trace turned his attention to the youngster. "You must be Bailey." Teen-aged skepticism dominated the boy's features; even so, after a second's hesitation, Bailey accepted his hand with a half-hearted shake. "Your dad has told me all about you. He's really proud of you—quite an athlete I hear." The boy shrugged and stared at the floor.

"Bailey, this is Mr. Brennan," Ryan offered. "He's the man who's been helping me." The kid wasn't impressed. Clearly, he'd been wounded by his parents' breakup. "You know the pretty girl who was singing up on the stage today? She's Mr. Brennan's daughter."

The boy finally looked Trace in the eye. "She's got a good voice."

"Thanks, Bailey. I'll let her know you thought so." Trace turned his attention back to Ryan. "Listen, mate. I'm here for you."

"I know. Thanks, Trace."

"Okay. Well, call me when you get a chance."

Ryan nodded. "Your number's right up here." He pointed to his temple.

"Good on ya. Nice to meet you, Bailey." He gave the boy a friendly pat on the back and continued making his way through the crisscrossing maze of people. When he reached the other side of the atrium, he climbed the stairs to the wide bridge which connected the east middle school wing with the smaller worship venues on the west side of the huge building.

If the bridge wasn't taken over by the preteen crowd, it provided a fun place to sit and have a cuppa. It also offered a great vantage point to locate misplaced friends and family who might be milling around in the crowd down below. He didn't have to play the search game today; he knew exactly where his loved ones were.

Jogging up the last three steps, he kept his eye on the goal. Hopefully no one would leave the family circle until he could enjoy at least a minute or two with them all.

It seemed the older and more independent the kids became, the more he loved seeing them together. When they were little, he could only tolerate a couple kids at a time and preferred being with them one on one. Their constant bickering rustled up his own propensity for anger. He never thought he'd see the day when the kids could actually gather together with some semblance of peace. In fact, he should count it a miracle.

He should be counting his blessings as well. Rob, his loyal

and steady firstborn, had been hit hard by their move to America. Thankfully, he had navigated those rocky university years with resilience and grace. And just when Ben Ellison had been quick to employ Rob's giftedness and state-of-the-art knowledge in his organic beef operation, petite Amy Meyer had come along and given Rob an even stronger sense of purpose.

And then there was Brad. Like Rob once did, Brad was struggling to find his place in this difficult new world. "Oof. Excuse me, mate!" Trace braced himself from toppling the young man who seemed to come from nowhere. "I didn't see you there! You all right?"

The pierced and goateed stranger remained silent and poised like a mannequin while his dark-rimmed eyes bored a hole in the crowd in front of them.

"I'm Trace Brennan. I've seen you around, but I don't believe we've formally met." Although he thrust a welcoming hand forward, the chap kept his hands firmly planted in the pockets of his long, black coat.

With all the charm of a glinty-eyed owl, the kid, who appeared to be the same age as Brad, returned the hospitality with a patronizing, slow blink. "I know who you are, Mr. Brennan." The young man gave the slightest nod and then returned his steady gaze to the object of his trance-like attention.

Trouble fairly leached from the guy. His long hair had been dyed the deepest black and was gathered in back for all to see the satanic tattoos graffitiing his neck. The kid definitely meant to stir the spiritual waters. "So, uh ..." Trace fished for a name, except the sport didn't bite. "Do you come here with your family?"

"No. I come by myself ..." The stranger's dark eyes remained transfixed on the crowd in front of them. "... to pray."

Somehow Trace got the feeling he and devil boy didn't necessarily pray to the same god.

"I used to simply pray. Now I come to worship." The kid

turned to face him, and this time his lips curled ever so slightly. "You have a beautiful daughter, Mr. Brennan."

He followed devil boy's gaze to where it'd been aimed—right on his family, scoped in on his precious little girl who laughed unaware in the middle of the family circle.

CHAPTER SIX

nger erupted in Trace's throat like burning acid. Guest or not, this kid's defiance wouldn't be tolerated. "If you *ever* act inappropriately toward her, I'll have you kicked out of here so fast, your tattooed neck will spin."

Devil boy remained as cool as a cadaver. The bloke's words were slow and measured, completely in control, absolutely condescending. "How do you define inappropriate, Mr Brennan? One might think *you* are being inappropriate, right now." The boy opened his coat, revealing the silver hilt of a dagger, then businesslike, he pulled out a black, leather-bound book embellished with stickers promoting the same, strange symbols tattooed on his fingers. "If you'll excuse me. I feel the need to pray. Good day, Mr. Brennan."

He had half a mind to chase after the bloke and take him on a friendly guided tour of the locked west wing which housed the administration and counseling offices. Surely the young man would be surprised to learn right now, behind closed doors, twenty to thirty people had gathered to pray for every soul who entered Open Door Bible Church, including the likes of devil boy himself. The kid's one single prayer had no power over the prayers being raised in the west wing—no power whatsoever. Let the bloke believe he was intimidating. Richard Ferris, head of security, would be hearing about this encounter.

Trace glanced up at the red light of the security camera at the same time a quiet, familiar voice tapped on his heart.

Trace, weren't you just numbering your blessings? Haven't I blessed you to be a blessing, given you grace upon grace?

Yes. Thank You, Lord. But ... The kid threatened my daughter.

He said she was beautiful.

But, Lord ... Could it be possible he had misinterpreted the young man's intentions? Somehow read him wrong? Maybe he should try and make amends. Trace searched the crowd, but the young man had already slipped away into the crowd. *Lord, if I was too quick to judge, forgive me. Help me to be more understanding and loving, especially toward those who are different than me.*

"Dad!" From across the way, Drew's enthusiastic greeting broke into Trace's prayer.

Trace approached the family circle and returned his son's excitement with a tempered pat on the back. "Hey, Drew. You did a great job on the drums today."

"Thanks! It was fun being in the big room."

"Oh, my goodness! I can't believe it! It's Andrew and Miah Brennan! Can I have your autographs?" Brianna Bakhuyzen, Miah's energetic and zany friend bounded into the circle waving a pen and church bulletin in the twin's faces, nearly knocking them over with her theatrics. "You guys did such a great job!" she cheered.

Laughing, Miah caught her friend in her arms. "Bri! You are so embarrassing!" Miah laughed again then sported a cowering glance over her shoulder as if to assure herself no one outside of the family had witnessed her friend's outburst.

Rob and Amy shared a look, Josh and Drew took a startled step back and Brad donned a disgusted smirk. "Dang, Bri. Your excitement is a bit over the top, don't ya think?" he grumbled.

With the same confidence she had greeted Drew and Miah, Brianna leaned a shoulder toward Brad. "It wouldn't hurt you to show a little support for your sister, Brad." Two dimples marked the boundary of her cheeky grin.

"So true." Right away Amy put her hand to her mouth as if surprised by her boldness. Then smiling softly, she reached over and gave Brad's arm an apologetic squeeze.

"Miah doesn't need my support. She's fully capable of taking care of herself. I have a mangled hand to prove it." Brad rested his right hand within the fold of his left palm for effect.

"Don't you mean your hand was lacerated six years ago? Brianna looked to Miah for confirmation.

Always the peacemaker, Claire cleared her voice and gently steered Brianna toward a less sticky subject. "Bri, are you and your parents coming for tea today?"

"Oh!" Brianna's brown eyes grew wide. "I almost forgot! My mom wanted me to tell you my dad's on call and had to run up to the hospital for a bit. He didn't think it would be long. And ..." She drew closer and whispered. "Pastor Bryce and Celia might not be able to make it at all." Her eyes lowered. "Celia was... was spotting a little."

"Oh, no. I ... I didn't know she was expecting again." Concern skittered across Claire's face as she reached for his hand. "I wonder if they need us."

Brianna shook her head and whispered beneath the other kid's soft chatter. "Pastor Bryce said she's only six weeks along this time. He was going to call my mom with an update after they talked to the doctor."

"If she loses another baby, Rob and Amy's news is going to be so very hard for them to hear," Claire whispered. "Oh, my heart hurts for Celia and Bryce."

Miah nodded her agreement. "It's got to be so painful for them. But maybe this time the baby will be okay."

Josh's voice rose above the group, ending the girls' conversation. "Mum! I'm starvin'! Let's get moving!" He gestured to herd the family toward the stairs and the atrium below.

Before Brianna and Claire stepped away from their small circle, Miah leaned into Brianna and whispered something in her ear. Then raising her brow in a hopeful arc, she directed a hushed plea in Claire's direction. "Mum, promise to talk to Dad?"

The two friends were always up to something, and he couldn't resist the temptation to play along with their cagey game. He moved into their private huddle and lowered his voice too. "Talk to Dad about what?"

"Mum will tell you. Won't you, Mum?

"So ..." Trace took Claire's hand as they left the coolness of the church and walked into the heat of the mid-morning sun. Only ten forty-five and already the air felt thick with summer's humidity. Today would be a scorcher.

Claire shielded her eyes and searched the busy parking lot for the truck. "So what?"

Uh-oh, avoidance tactics. Not a good sign. "So, what were you supposed to talk to me about?"

She shook her head. "Trace, I really don't want to get into this. This is strictly between you and Miah." She sighed. "I don't know why she tries to drag me into her scheming."

"Maybe it's because she's stubborn and won't take no for an answer—just like her mother and old Nehemiah himself."

Claire rolled her eyes at his nonsense.

"What? You're the one who insisted on biblical names for the twins. Out of all the saints in the Bible, and you name our five-pound, four-ounce baby girl after a strong-willed, wall-builder who rips the hair out of people's heads? Maybe you should have put more thought into Miah's name, love."

Claire met his grin and obliging nudge with a sedate smile.

"You really don't want to discuss this, do you?"

"No."

"Well, at least give me a hint of what Miah's going to hit me up with."

The heat seemed to melt Claire's pretty smile into a blended palette of meekness and uncertainty. "Trace, she only wants to go to the Dustin Rhodes concert with Brianna ... and a couple boys from church."

"I reckoned it was something to do with boys. The funny thing is, Josh's friend—you know, the Native American kid, DuCharme? Just yesterday he asked if he could take Miah to the very same concert."

Claire looked surprised. "What did you tell him?"

He huffed. "What do you think I told him?" It was obvious Claire didn't appreciate his brusque reply. Despite the heat, he humbled his posture and stuck his hands in his pockets. "Are Marcus and Trina letting Bri go?"

"I think so."

"I bet they don't know about the boys."

"I'm pretty sure they do, Trace."

"Well, Bri's older."

"Not by much."

Whew! Things were really heating up. The truck would be a sauna inside. "Who are these blokes anyway? Do you know them?"

"One is the boy who sometimes plays bass in the Loft with Miah and Drew. Timothy Nguyen. He seems like a sweet boy."

Trace scowled. "He's a freshman at GVSU, Claire. Absolutely not! What is it with these blokes? Aren't there enough girls at university?"

"Of course there are, but do I have to remind the "Midwest's Top Beef Breeder" he's also produced an extraordinarily beautiful and talented daughter?"

No, she didn't need to remind him. Devil boy had done a thorough job of that already. "All the more reason to stand firm on my decision."

Claire's lips became a terse line of self-control.

"What? You want her to go?"

"I don't know, Trace. I don't know what the right thing is. At some point we have to let her grow up. We have to trust her judgment. If we don't, she's ... she's going to—"

"Turn into a renegade like her mum?" He held his wife's hands. "She won't, Claire. Miah may have a hot head at times; even so, she's always done the right thing. She's a good girl."

There were tears in Claire's eyes. "So was I ... until my parents tried to keep me from what I knew was right. Trace, we're cut from the same cloth, Miah and I. I don't want to drive her away."

"We won't."

Claire wiped a tear from the corner of her eye. "All I know is how determined I became when my parents tried to keep me from you and your family. I knew they were wrong about you, about me. If your dad hadn't interceded, I would have run away."

"The circumstances were way different, love. Your parents knew my parents. Your mum and dad were simply hung up on the status and image thing. We don't know these blokes from Joe Bloggs. For all we know, they could be up to their eyeballs in porn, alcohol, drugs, gambling—who knows what. Just because they go to church on Sunday doesn't mean they don't fill their minds with crap the other six days of the week."

He held her face in his hands. "Claire, I'm thankful you're finally feeling good about our move. I'm thankful you want the kids to build friendships and put down roots. But, you were right from the start. There is need for caution. One thing I've learned from being an elder, this church is filled with some really messed up folks—people who've lost their way. Some are truly looking for a way out of the trap they've set for themselves. And some are playing a deceptive game to appease the ones who care about them. I don't want Miah getting caught in their snare, and I would dare suspect, neither do you."

CHAPTER SEVEN

*E*ven above the noise of her sanding, Miah could hear Brandt DuCharme's motorcycle as it screamed onto Somerset Road, two kilometers away. If the old, salvaged machine were a blender, Josh's friend would be running it at a breathtaking liquefy. At a kilometer away, he'd turn onto the gravel road and slow the engine to grate, putting him about ninety seconds from the barn and her dirty, chalk-covered face. Jingoes!

Miah shook the drywall dust off her hands and brushed it from her T-shirt and shorts as best she could; still, it left a leprous paleness to every inch of her skin and clothing. Maybe Brandt would go right out to the fields. No, he wouldn't. He'd go into the office, find out where he'd be working, and fill out his timecard. Then on his way to the older part of the barn, he would search for her. And when he found her, he'd say her dad was a mean, old ogre who refused to let her have any fun. Ever.

The worn-out bike motored up the driveway, all the way to the barn, and then it cut out with surprising, abrupt precision. Before she could steady her quickening heartbeat, the metal door squelched against its snug frame. Then Brandt's boots made crunching noises on the cement floor of the barn as he walked toward the office.

Soon his tanned and callused hands would rattle the metal timecard rack and then send a pen clattering back to the desktop. She stood still, smiling at her ability to predict his every move. Next, there would be a shuffling of papers, some silence as he read the work order, and finally more crunching and popping on the cement floor. Oh shoot! He was coming!

Flipping the sander over in her hand, she pretended to be busy changing the screen.

"Morning, Miah!"

"Good morning!" She turned his way and tried to cover her self-consciousness with a warm smile.

"This is really coming along." Josh's friend stepped into the studio and scanned the space with such confidence it fairly burst from his broad chest. He didn't seem at all set back by Dad's rejection or her resemblance to the white witch of Narnia. He walked right up to her and chuckled. "Look at you. You're covered with this stuff!" His finger drew a squiggly line through the chalky dust on her arm then tapped the tip of her nose.

While his playfulness and self-assurance were exciting, she wasn't sure how to handle them. She wasn't even sure what to call him. Dad and her brothers called him DuCharme, but that sounded too chummy, and the name Brandt was so ... intimidating. Maybe it would be best to remain silent and watch him—follow his lead as if they were dancing. Yeah, as if they were dancing.

In one practiced move, he pulled an elastic from his long black hair then combed it back again with his fingers before retying it in a ponytail. "You must have been up at the crack of dawn to get this much work done."

She nodded and tried not to stare at the flexing of his biceps. "My dad's alarm goes off at five-thirty. He pretty much controls everything around here."

He smiled. "Including his daughter?"

"Especially his daughter." With the toe of her boot, she drew a smile on the dusty floor then shook her head. "I'm really sorry, DuCharme." There, she said his name—sort of.

"No problem. It's not like you didn't warn me. He only wants to protect you. You're his only daughter and ..." He paused until she peered into his soft brown eyes. "You're very beautiful."

Despite the heat radiating up her neck and into her cheeks, she managed to meet his kind words with a shy smile.

"Hey, we may not be able to go to the Dustin Rhodes concert, but your dad didn't say anything about not working together." He reached for her hand. "How about helping me clean the A.I. barn?"

<hr>

"Miah!" Brandt called to her above the hum and whine of the Bobcat's motor and hydraulics. With shovel in hand, she backed out of the stall and walked over to where he sat at the controls, lifting another bucket load of manure. Could it be he finally wanted to take a break? Jingoes, he was about as driven as Dad. He'd barely said two words to her since they'd started working. No one could blame him. What with the Bobcat's grumbling and whirring, they couldn't carry on a normal conversation even if they wanted to.

"You wanna trade spots for a while?"

"No, I'm fine," she shouted back.

"You sure?"

Nodding, she blew a stray curl off her beaded brow. Between the layer of drywall dust and the stench of manure and sweat, she could hardly stand herself. No wonder he didn't seem eager to engage in a close, meaningful conversation. She turned back toward the stall.

"Hey, Miah! Just in case you were wondering, the view's

really nice from here!" Brandt smiled as his gaze settled on her bare legs. Then throttling down the Bobcat, he motioned to the front of the barn. "Where do those stairs go?"

She turned to where he pointed. "To the loft."

"The loft?"

Surely, he knew barns had lofts. Didn't he say he had farming experience? "Yeah, you know—where the hay and straw are stored." She couldn't help giving him an idiot look.

"You carry it up those stairs?"

She laughed at his naivety. "No, we use an elevator."

"Why do you have stairs then?"

"So we can stack the hay." How could he not know how to put up hay? And he was going to be a veterinarian?

"So, you've been up there?"

"Aye. Lots of times."

"Well, what's it like?"

She shrugged. "There's hay for the horses. And by the end of this week, there'll be even more."

"Still, what's it like?"

"I don't know. It's hot and dusty."

A mischievous smirk pulled at the corner of his mouth. "And quiet and secluded? Don't you wanna show me?"

Her chalk-covered cheeks turned red hot when she realized the purpose of all Brandt's questions. He was nothing but a big tease! Well, two could play at that game. She bent, and with her gloved hands, picked up a dried clump of manure and flung it dangerously close to his face.

He looked as surprised as she when it smacked onto his shoulder and rolled down the front of his T-shirt and onto his lap. "Yo! What gives?" He jumped from the tractor, chose a ripe morsel of cowplop, and chased her into a stall.

Her laughter stopped as quickly as it started, and she pointed a warning finger in his direction. "Brandt! Don't you dare!"

Where her laughter stopped, his rose and rolled around with

his tongue and cheek. And his eyes began to dance a shifty jig. "You gotta pay to play, you little vixen!"

Her shriek betrayed her cheeky giggling as he lunged toward her, flinging the moist nugget her way. She screamed again, dodging the piece of dropping, and then she threw the handle of the shovel toward his chest. When he knocked it away, his next step forward put his foot square in the middle of the wide, slippery scoop. Falling forward, he couldn't catch himself, and all his weight smashed into her, pinning her against the concrete wall.

His face leached a small hint of pain then filled with concern. "Are you okay?"

She could only nod. For one short moment his eyes belonged to her alone. They were deep and kind. And they were beautiful.

"Are you sure?"

She nodded again, wanting the moment to last a while longer. All was right in the world. Even the tiny sparrows in the rafters above their heads thought so. They chirped a gleeful melody, joining in with the hopeful song playing in her heart. But then they suddenly flitted away in alarm. Which could only mean one thing! Someone was coming!

Brandt pushed himself away from her just as Dad blasted her friend's name like profanity across the thickening air of the barn.

"What in the bloody bells is going on here?" Picking up the shovel, Dad wielded the handle like a copper's night stick and glared into Brandt's innocent eyes.

"Dad ... It's not what you think." She levered herself away from the wall and moved in front of Brandt to protect his character and good name from Dad's wrath.

"Don't tell me what to think! Get in the house, Miah!"

CHAPTER EIGHT

Seven-twenty. Miah turned her eyes from the clock on the oven to the kitchen window. She peeked out and checked on Brandt's progress one more time. He'd nearly emptied the second load—maybe another ten, fifteen minutes at the most. Hadn't he paid enough for their impulsive, careless game?

A fresh flood of regret stung her eyes when Brandt appeared at the barn door and grabbed another bale of hay from the wagon. In the last half hour his stride had become slower, stiffer, like Granddad's. Jingoes. Dad could at least have given him some water.

Well, the minute Brandt racked the last bail, she'd sneak him a fizzy drink and a leftover roast beef sandwich from the fridge. Then she'd run out the front door and try to catch him on his way down the driveway. She couldn't afford to miss him. This might be the last time .... He had to hear how sorry she felt ... how she felt about him.

It didn't help to empty the dishwasher. The minutes ticked by slowly and the clinking of glassware only reminded her of the uncomfortably quiet dinner and the meatloaf Dad had forced her to choke down. "Your mum has gone through all the work of preparing it. You're going to eat it," he'd said.

Her brothers knew the sketchiest of details and surely tried to imagine why Brandt hadn't been invited to tea and why he'd been told to put the hay up by hand. No doubt they'd been playing out a sordid scenario in their minds all through dinner. However, Josh would get the square story from his mate soon enough. And while Drew would give her the benefit of the doubt, Brad might take advantage of the unfortunate situation and blow it into epic proportions.

At the pumping of the motorcycle's kick starter, she rushed to the fridge, grabbed a Pepsi and sandwich, and then ran through the lounge room. Bursting through the screen door, she ran down the five wide steps of the veranda. *Please God, let me catch him!* The summer-dried grass poked at her bare feet as she ran across the lawn to the end of the driveway. Don't peel out, Brandt. Please, please go slow. Oh, snap! Mum was in the garden!

Brandt rode down the drive toward the meticulous rows of produce and stopped right in front of the beans where Mum worked. No! He wouldn't! A slurry of embarrassment flooded into her cheeks when he got off his bike and walked straight down the fertile, brown path to where Mum straightened from her kneeling position.

A blue jay jeered from atop a nearby maple tree, making the situation even more awkward. Then Brandt shrugged and slowly shook his head, most likely offering another apology. Mum took a turn at her own humble gestures, without a doubt, graciously extending him forgiveness. Their conversation ended as quickly as it started, and he turned to leave. And when he turned, he saw her waiting at the postbox. She was sure of it. Mum noticed her too, hesitated for an instant, and then went back to picking beans.

Brandt kept his eyes forward even as he tipped his motorcycle upright and off its stand. Would he know she wanted to talk with him? She moved to the center of the driveway, and when he pulled up next to her and cut the engine, she hadn't readied herself for what she saw. The tears she'd been trying to hold back slipped down her cheeks.

"Miah, are you okay?"

She nodded. "You're not … I-I'm sorry. I'm so sorry." His eyes were red and puffy from the exertion of his work. His dark, ruddy skin was drenched with sweat and speckled with scratches and bits of chaff from handling at least one hundred bales of hay. And his palms were one fiery blister.

Dad had gone too far, way too far. She should have known he'd find a way to beat the snot out of Brandt without laying a hand on him. "I hate my da—"

Brandt silenced her lips with his torn fingertips. "Don't say it, Miah. Don't even think it. He's a good man, and he cares about you very much. You don't know how lucky you are." He swallowed and looked away, and she thought the dark brown centers of his eyes might melt into the shimmery light collecting at the rims of his lashes. "You don't know how lucky you are."

Something lay beneath the soil of his heart, something raw and buried deep. A secret? An untold story, like her cowboy's? Her tongue tasted the trace of salt Brandt's touch had left on her lips. "I'm sorry." She apologized for the pain of his past and for the pain he'd endured today. "Will you be coming back?"

He denied his emotion with a chuckle and shook his head. "No. I pretty much blew it. I'm done."

"Maybe my mum or Josh can talk to my dad."

"No." He wagged his head again and stared far down the gravel road. "How could I have been so stupid?"

"You're not stupid. I'm the one who threw the first handful. I'm to blame."

"No … No …" A curse hissed between his teeth as he bent

forward and squeezed the bike's hand brakes in frustration. "I'll never get to see you again."

"Well, you could always come to the fair. It's in a month—August six through eleven. I'll be there all week and even have a concert on Friday night." Silence passed between them as she searched for a better solution. "I know! You can come to church! My dad can't stop you from going to church!"

"To church?"

She nodded. "Yeah. This is a free country, isn't it? And there's free coffee and cookies! College kids like free things, don't they?"

He laughed out loud. "I guess they do." The torn vinyl seat squeaked as he settled back and rubbed his sore hands on his thighs. "Miah, I haven't been to church since ... since I was a little kid."

"No worries. Living in the Outback, I'd never been to a real church until I moved here. No one will count it against you." She tugged on his sleeve. "Come on, you'll like it. There's really good music!"

"So I've heard." One of his bloodshot eyes gave her a wink.

"You'll come then?"

He leaned forward and rolled his head in a slow, noncommittal sort of way.

"Josh can give you directions," she coaxed in a sing-song voice.

The yellowing sky and the maple branches above their heads seemed to join in Brandt's good-natured chuckle. "I never thought I'd say this; I guess I better get my Sunday school shoes shined up."

"No worries. You can wear your jeans and boots. People come just as they are. Really. There's even a bloke who comes all dressed up like Satan himself."

"Horns and a spiked tail?"

"Well, not quite that extreme. Long black coat and hair to

match—kind of like yours. But he has piercings and satanic tattoos down his neck. He stares at me. It's kind of creepy."

"Dang. Does your dad know?"

"No. He'd have a fit."

Brandt threw his head back with a hearty laugh. "Somehow, I believe you."

"Yeah. Sorry."

He shook his head. "You should tell your dad."

"The bloke isn't so bad. It took a while, but I finally coaxed a smile and his name from him—Adam Chisholm. It fits him." Her giggle played in harmony with Brandt's chuckle. So ... can I tell Josh to call you about church?"

He conceded with a nod. "Sure. I wanna see this devil guy."

"Yay! The day is finally redeeming itself! Oh, here. This is for you. You must be starving." She held out the soft drink and sandwich.

"Thanks, Miah. I think I'll just take the Pepsi. My stomach's a little iffy right now."

"Why don't you keep the sandwich for when you get home? It's my mum's roast beef. Do you think it could fit in this storage compartment?"

"Yeah, it might."

She helped him arrange a few small tools, a flashlight, some fast-food napkins, and a beat-up DVD case. "What's the movie about?"

He snatched it from her hand, but not before she could see the shocking scene on the cover.

Descent to Desire. Could he be for real? She should have been polite and looked past the picture of the girl and her dreadful situation. She couldn't though. "That is so disturbing!"

Brandt held his forehead in the blistery palm of his hand and sighed as if he'd literally stacked the last straw. "I'm not making a very good impression, am I? The movie had been meant as a joke, Miah."

She looked at him doubtfully. "I don't find it funny."

"I won it at a friend's bachelor party. We played eighteen holes of golf, and I lost."

"I'd hate to know what the winner got."

"He only got bragging rights. Josh was there. You can ask him. I choose my friends wisely, Miah." He opened the case, being careful not to reveal the cover again. "Look, the DVD doesn't even work. The best man deliberately scratched it up. I ... I forgot I even had the stupid thing."

She peeked a wary eye his way. Despite seeing broad scratches all around the disk, a shadow of doubt darkened a small corner of her mind. What if Brandt was into porn? Besides Brandt and Josh being friends, what did she know about him anyway? Not much. She didn't know anything about his family or his background. One thing she could bet on; he had a story. A regretful story? Maybe. A painful story? Most likely. And a story probably written without the presence of a vitally important character—the Hero, the One who could keep them all from falling.

"You don't believe me do you, Miah?"

She shrugged.

His eyes tried to convince her. "Wait a minute." He dug around and pulled a lighter from the compartment then yanked the movie's title page from its plastic case. The paper slowly caught fire and when it became engulfed, he dropped it to the gravel road. The flames lapped at a young girl's beauty, making her look even more fearful and agonized. When she had been consumed and been given rest from her torturers, he ground her ashy remains in the road. "There, now it's harmless."

She should have defended the girl. Anything so evil could never be harmless; still, the image left her speechless. And while she couldn't help pity the girl and wonder what circumstances led her to prostituting herself, Brandt snapped the blank case shut with finality as if the girl's predicament was not his problem. Then he raised his eyebrows like he expected a round of applause. However, she could only muster a half-hearted attempt to disguise her disappointment in him.

"I'm telling you the truth, Miah." When she didn't reply, he tucked the case back into the storage trunk next to the sandwich and then pulled his helmet off the handlebar. His ponytail splayed across his back as he rested the helmet on the seat between his legs. "What can I do to convince you?"

His question hung in the quiet space between them. When he finally moved, he stretched his blistered hands across the hundreds of tiny, airbrushed stars covering the glossy, black background of his headgear.

The diamond-like stars were brilliantly distinct and thoughtfully arranged—like the constellations over Amaroo Station. They made her think of the constant, unwavering love of her family and friends back home in Australia. Just like the stars, her loved ones were trustworthy and faithful. They were part of her heritage. And she was thankful to be covered by the gracious canopy of their wise counsel and God's guiding hand. Both had saved her from a world of hurt and many foolish mistakes.

If she could wish on one of those stars right now, she'd wish she could be as sure about Brandt as she was of God and her family. She'd hope upon hope that Brandt would prove to be as good and honest as he wanted her to believe. And then she'd ask God to give him the love and guidance he seemed to long for and need.

She reached out and smoothed a finger over one of the brighter stars. "They're beautiful, Brandt. The stars are beautiful."

The warmth of his hands covered her own hands. "You're beautiful, Miah. I hope you can trust me."

CHAPTER NINE

Monday, August 6, 2001

The loudspeaker squelched, and the announcer's voice cheered across the arena in Ring B. "I hope everyone's enjoying their time at the Crandall County 4-H Youth Fair!" A smattering of the spectators in the stands responded with applause and a few even yelled an enthusiastic "Yeah!" The rest were chatting and laughing with friends or trying not to lose their patience in the heat of the noonday sun as they juggled two or three whining kids and an armful of lemonades.

"Okay! We're ready to begin the Senior Advanced Reining Event. Each 4-H rider will complete the riding pattern laid out in the horsemanship handbook. The judges will be looking at three things: control, execution of maneuvers, and attitude of the horse. Our first rider is number 3665, Stacy Church, riding Athena. Rider number 3624, Miah Brennan, is on deck."

Miah took a nervous breath, adjusted herself in the saddle, and then wiped her perspiring hands down her horse's neck, ending with an encouraging pat. She watched the first rider move her beautiful palomino mare through the initial part of the reining pattern effortlessly, which didn't help Miah's confidence. She hadn't prepared her horse for the fair as much as she had hoped to. She had instead given priority to putting the finishing touches on the music studio, training her steer for the show ring, and getting used to having Brandt DuCharme back in her life.

She still couldn't believe Brandt had shown up at church following the whole manure fight and DVD thing. Week after week, he kept coming back, and each week he would sit next to Josh and join in their family and friends' conversations after church. Then two Sundays ago, the day before her seventeenth birthday, Dad shocked her by inviting Brandt to join their small group for tea.

All afternoon she had watched Brandt from afar. In the guise of grooming and saddling the horses, she and her friend Bri watched him barely survive a grueling match of Australian football. And then as he showed off his riding skills in an impromptu rodeo, they pretended to be busy entertaining C.J. and Mateá's little girl, Aspen. Finally, when Brandt carried a fishing pole to the end of the dock with Josh, Dad, and Pastor Bryce, she and Bri had found a quiet spot under a nearby willow to solve life's most pressing questions—like what swimsuit Bri should wear to the youth group pool party.

At first, the fisherman's rowdy banter boomed across the large pond, then after some time, their voices settled into a quiet prose as reflective as the smooth black water. She and Bri were left to rely on their imaginations alone to interpret the anglers' body language and topic of conversation.

She couldn't remember if it had been the unexpected moan or the peculiar shuffling of bodies that brought Bri's hilarious account of her grandmother's run-in with the law to an abrupt halt. Whatever the case, they both stared at the end of the dock where Josh, Dad, and Pastor Bryce gathered around Brandt's broad, heaving shoulders. His unashamed sobbing caused a tightening in her own throat.

She had wanted to run over there and comfort him, to wipe away his tears, but Dad and Pastor Bryce had prayed people through their pain hundreds of times. Brandt had landed in capable and caring hands.

In the evening when Brandt had climbed on his motorbike to leave, he still seemed troubled. He'd barely glanced her way when she waved goodbye. After he left, Josh hadn't exactly been a plethora of information; he'd kept his mouth sealed tight like a jar of Mum's green beans. When she pressed him, he admitted Brandt needed to work through some heavy things. Then he dismissed her with a shrug. Something like compassion must have worked at Josh's conscience because seconds later, he'd called her back and assured her Brandt would be okay—he'd put his life in God's hands.

Later that night, she'd been filling her journal with all kinds of speculations when Dad knocked on her door. He had looked so serious as he crossed the room and sat on her bed. He didn't give her a lot of details either. Instead, he cautioned her to guard herself, to not rush into things with Brandt. He had told her what Brandt needed most was a circle of friends, not an exclusive relationship with a girl to distract him. "He needs people in his life who can help him grow strong in his brand-new faith. Are you able to help him stay focused on the important?" he had asked.

She had said she could, but deep down wondered why she couldn't do both—be his girlfriend and help him grow in his faith. What would be the problem with that?

Great job, Stacy and Athena!" The announcer's voice blared from the speaker, interrupting her daydreaming. "The next rider is number 3624, Miah Brennan, riding Jazz. On deck is rider number 3627, Etanya Williams riding Fargo."

"Well, ready or not, Jazz, here we come." The gate opened and she waited for the first rider to walk her sleek palomino out of the arena. Jazz danced and whinnied at the sight of the pretty mare. "It's time to focus, Jazz. Eyes front and center." She gave him a kick and then another before he moved through the gate. He trotted to the center of the arena where she reined him to the left to face the judge. After settling herself in the saddle, she gave the judge a nod and waited for his signal to begin the riding pattern. At the short whistle, she barely touched the rein to the right, and Jazz responded by walking in a small circle. Once the circle was completed, he picked up the pace and ran around the two larger circles.

Back at the center point, she tapped the lead to the left and Jazz repeated the three left circuits beautifully. At the center again, she reined Jazz to the right, and he ran with speed past the east end marker. When she pulled the rein to the left, he performed a left rollback perfectly then ran in the opposite direction at full gallop. But instead of pointing his nose straight toward the west end marker, he turned his nose to the right and ran like lightning toward the entrance gate. What had gotten into him?

She pulled hard on the rein to direct Jazz back on course, but he reared, came down hard, and then kicked his back legs behind him. When he took off running for the gate again, she didn't even try to stop him. It was over, and all she wanted to do was hide under a rock.

Ethan Turchetti, the gatekeeper, was quick to climb the metal rungs to make himself even taller. He waved the horse off with his hands high in the air for all the blooming crowd to see. Thank goodness Jazz saw him too—the horse never would have jumped the gate. Within a foot of their doom, Jazz skidded to a halt and launched her head-first over the top bar. She somersaulted and landed on her back in a plop of horse manure.

Ethan scrambled over the gate and grabbed Jazz's reigns. "Are you all right, Miah?"

She sat up and tried to get a breath in.

"Help her up, Rory," Ethan said, directing one of his young

disciples. The wide-eyed kid was part of a mob of junior high school boys who followed Ethan around like he was Jesus himself. With guitar in hand, Ethan would sit atop the stacked hay in the bed of his pickup truck and call all young male 4-H'ers unto himself, teaching them to do good—amongst other things, like listening to the right music, wearing the right jeans and tilting their cowboy hats just so, all with the goal of impressing the girls. Yep. Ethan Turchetti was king of the fair. Tall, good-looking and a personality as big as the arena she'd just been thrown from. Jingoes ....

She unsnapped her riding helmet then levered herself up without the help of the boy's hand just as the announcer added insult to her injury. "Rider number 3624, Miah Brennan, has been disqualified. Next rider 3627, Etanya Williams, please proceed to the center of the ring."

"Open the gate, Rory, my man," Ethan directed again.

The boy hustled to swing the metal gate wide, and after Etanya rode her horse past them and into the arena, Ethan brought Jazz through to where she stood, sweaty, dirty and shaken as she was.

"Are you okay?"

She nodded, and Ethan ordered the boy again. "Rory, walk the horse around the cool down area for Miah."

The boy's eyes grew and his jaw dropped. "No way!" He shook his head. "I'm not getting ten feet near the monster!"

"I'm fine." She took the reins from Ethan. "Thanks." She tugged on the reins, and trying to regain some dignity, she bowed and waved as she walked Jazz through the small crowd of gawkers.

"Hey there, buddy 'ole pal! Are you okay? Oh, my gosh! I couldn't believe my eyes! One minute you were stealing the show, and the next minute ... you were the show!" A rippling stream of laughter tumbled from Bri's mouth as she ran up behind Jazz.

"Brianna ... no bubbling. Not now. And how many times have I told you not to run up behind a horse, especially this idiot."

Bri trotted up to Jazz's face and nuzzled his long nose. "He's not an idiot. He just wanted to join in the frolic of the fair and play with that pretty mare, Goddess Athena. Didn't you, Jazzy Wazzy?" Bri's voice dripped with sweetness, and then with a wink of her mocking eye, she screeched and cackled like the wicked witch of the west. "Oh, but you're not a stallion! You're a *gelding*! Girls like Athena, don't give a hoot for boys like you!" Bri roared again at her cleverness, and Miah couldn't help giggling too.

With all the drama God had packed in her DNA, Bri sucked in a gasp of air. "And speaking of stallions. Look who's talking with Brad and Josh!" She nodded in the direction of the huge John Deere tractors and combines displayed near the main concourse. "Jared Nicholson!" Smacking her hand over her heart, her words came out all energetic and squeaky. "It's. My. Lucky. Day!" She gazed into the cloudless sky as if she were thanking the heavens above, and then her voice grew serious, but only for a second. "Miah, if you're sure you're all right, I'm going to go over there and cast some bubblin' Brianna Bakhuysen charm and see what I can catch!" And off she went with a Hollywood wave.

Miah grinned and shook her head at Bri's nonsense and then tugged on Jazz's reins. "Okay, numbskull, let's get you cooled down and back in your stall. What were you thinking back there, anyway?" She walked Jazz around the cool-down area for a couple of circuits and then led him back to the third of four barns that housed the hundred plus horses competing in the Crandall County Youth Fair.

Each open-ended barn held sixteen stalls on either side of a wide cement aisle where fairgoers could walk and view the horses, awards, and themed decorations, which represented each

4-H Club competing in the fair. Her club, the Somerset Stars, focused on western riding and was made up of girls like herself who had to work for a living—unlike the girls in the English riding clubs who were backed by rich mums and dads.

"All right, Jazz, here's your home away from home." When she pushed the sliding door open, the horse shied, backing into a man who had been following much too close behind them. The man fell against a metal wheelbarrow, which careened into the portable, tack cabinet with a loud crash. Just as the bloke righted himself, Jazz let loose a swift kick, which thankfully missed the target. But then he spun around to face the clatter, taking her with him. Still, she held tight to the reins. "Whoa... Whoa. It's okay, Jazz."

The man, all red in the face, let out a string of expletives, and her own face burned with the embarrassment of it all. "I'm so sorry! Are you all right? My horse, he's not himself today. I ... I'm really sorry."

The man swore again, then with a big scowl on his face, he adjusted his ball cap square on his dark brown hair.

"Are you okay? I'm so terribly sorry."

"Yeah. Yeah, I'm all right."

The man didn't appear to be hurt, just peeved, and truthfully, she was too. Who in their right mind would tailgate a horse? Jingoes!

"Where's the accent from? England?" the man asked, brushing himself off. "I thought you Brits are supposed to be good with horses."

She tried to hide the irritation rising within her. Didn't the man have any proper sense of boundaries or tact? "No. I'm not English. I'm from Queensland ... Australia."

"Australia? You're a long way from home, aren't you?" The man chuckled and ran his hand down the side of Jazz, making the horse flinch.

The guy lacked any fear or respect for horses—he obviously

didn't know a single thing about them. "Yeah, my dad moved here for work—he's a stockman and a boreman." She pulled the horse closer and loosened his girth strap, and the man just stood there staring at her. Was he waiting for her to say something else? "So, uh. Where are you from? From the city?"

He finally turned his dark, skeptical eyes away from her and squinted down the aisle toward the west end of the barn. "I guess you can say I'm from here, there and everywhere." His laugh made his groomed mustache spread wide across his face. Then turning his attention back to her, he asked, "Have you ever been to the state of unconsciousness, Miss Australia?" He laughed even louder and nudged her with his elbow as if they were chums sharing a beer.

What kind of question was that? And how should she respond? She took a step back toward the stall and simply gave the man a half smile.

"Hey, Miah."

Oh, thank goodness. Drew and Dad walked toward her from the same direction the man had been staring. "Am I glad to see you two! Jazz has been totally berko today. He threw me during the reining event—"

"Huge disappointment." Dad interrupted.

"Well, there's more. When I tried to get him into his stall, he backed up into this man and knocked him down. And then to make matters worse, Jazz kicked at him."

Dad looked with concern toward the man. "Are you all right, mate? I'm truly sorry for the trouble."

"Oh, yeah. I'm fine. Totally fine." The man spread his arms out and glanced down at his big, tall self as if to prove the state of his good health, and then he looked at Dad. "Your daughter, well, I'm assuming she's your daughter, was just telling me she's from Australia."

"Aye. Queensland. Have you been there?"

"No, but I do like to travel."

It seemed like Dad and the man would get along just fine without her, so here was her chance to escape.

She turned to Drew and whispered beneath Dad's conversation with his newly found friend. "Will you take care of Jazz for me? I need to change my shirt before we show our steers. Jazz catapulted me into a pile of manure."

Drew nodded then spun her around to see the soiled spot on her bedazzled, hot pink and black, western show shirt. "Are you okay? You took a nasty fall."

She rolled her eyes and shook her head at the thought of the embarrassing scene. "Yes, I'm fine. But thanks for caring."

He nodded again. "We have thirty minutes before we have to line up to show the steers, so you better put some oil in it."

"Thanks, Drew. You're the best. I owe you one."

"Well, actually, I was going to ask you if I could get out of tearing down the set after Friday's concert."

"Sure, but why?"

"Wouldn't you like to know." His smile slowly spread across his face like the dawn.

CHAPTER TEN

Friday, August 10, 2001

From off stage, Miah squinted past the glare of the bright lights, searching the crowd for some familiar faces. There they were, front and center, sitting shoulder to shoulder in the stifling heat of the huge circus tent. She elbowed Drew to check them out. From this angle, they were a lucky-looking group, all talking and laughing and sipping on the tin mugs they'd bought from Bayou Billy's Old-Fashioned Soda. One, two, three, four, five—five rows of friends and family had come out to the county fair on a hot, sticky night to show their support for the band, Odessa.

Actually, she was the lucky one, or maybe blessed would be a better word. Besides the debacle at the reining event, life had pretty much presented itself as perfect. In fact, for the past four or five weeks, it seemed as if the very face of God were shining down upon her. Between the generous radio time C.J. had been giving the band and the unbelievable email she'd received from Smoky Mountain Media requesting additional demo tracks, she could hardly contain her gratefulness.

Then just last night, she'd received another blessing. Her steer had won Grand Champion! And to top it off, this afternoon when everyone was cooling off at Stoney Lake with some competitive chicken fights, Brandt lured her away to the woodsy island where he'd stolen a kiss, putting their relationship in a whole different category—in her mind at least.

In terms of her songwriting, she certainly wasn't lacking for inspiration. She'd literally filled a journal with some great lyrics and thoughts for new songs. And it all began the day she'd received the Ellison's check and first gazed into Brandt DuCharme's storytelling eyes.

Never in a million years could she have dreamed Brandt would become a main character in her own story. Still, there he sat, sandwiched between Dad and Bri's dad, the great and wise, Dr. Marcus Bakhuyzen.

She peeked around the long, vertical 4-H banner, catching Brandt's attention. He smiled and gave her a thumbs up, looking remarkably comfortable with the seating arrangements. No, she never could have imagined things working out the way they had. It appeared as if God took great pleasure in throwing her one big surprise party after another.

She returned the smile and thumbs up to Brandt as the emcee stepped onto the stage and wiggled the mic off the mic stand. "Welcome to the big top everyone! My name is Matt Bowman and I'm your host this evening. We have some great entertainment lined up for you tonight, but before the band takes the stage, I would like to invite you all to tomorrow night's rodeo. It starts at seven p.m. sharp in the Brian Russel Memorial Arena, and we have some incredibly talented riders taking part. You won't want to miss the thrills and spills."

The emcee began his transition to their introduction, and a collective, nervous sigh hushed through her huddle of friends and fellow band members as they took their places. Even her stomach twanged with anxiety, or could it be hunger?

She really should have made time to eat dinner, but prayer had taken priority. The band had met thirty minutes before set up to ask God to take control of everything: lights, sound, instruments, their words, their voices, their attitudes. Most importantly, they asked Him to open the hearts of the people who might happen to wander by and listen.

She looked to the back of the tent where C.J. stood ready to man the soundboard. Behind him, the dizzying carnival rides zinged, whipping their bright, blinking lights and riders around like a psychedelic dream. Shouts and laughter from the midway collided with the shrieks and screams from atop the Zipper and the Sea Dragon. *Please, God, fade the electric commotion buzzing around back there, and allow the audience to hear Your message of hope we want to share.*

"And now, without further ado, please give a warm welcome to the band, Odessa!"

Right on cue, Drew started in with a knee-slapping rim tap, setting the beat for Jason's pure Tennessee accent. If anyone's voice could draw in a crowd, Jason's could. And the song? Well, any red-blooded American would be compelled to stop in their tracks and sing along to "Thank God I'm a Country Boy." Even before the first word came out of Jason's mouth, the crowd picked up the bluegrass beat with the slapping of their own hands and knees. Jason laughed into his microphone and gave a hearty whoop, sounding like John Denver himself. "All right! Here we go!"

At the chorus, the band joined in with instruments and backup vocals. Zach carried the beat on bass, Alicia played the fiddle, Jason picked away on his banjo while singing lead, and she added rhythm with her acoustic guitar. The audience seemed to love it, and the people passing by were doing exactly what they were supposed to—stopping, then staying.

When Jason brought the song to a happy ending, Brooks led them into something just as fun, "What About Now," by Lonestar. Alicia followed Brooks' piano intro with her electric guitar and after four measures, Jason and the rest of the band picked it up.

By the end of the song, they really had the crowd's attention. Now, if she could only keep it with Lee Ann Womack's, "I Hope You Dance". As she stepped up to the mic, Brooks did his magic, directing a full, rich orchestra from the eighty-eight keys on his Yamaha keyboard. In spite of the crowd, she couldn't help but direct the song's hopeful message toward Brandt. When she got to the end and sang about giving faith a chance, Brandt looked as if he truly understood the intent of her heart. And it seemed as if the audience did too. They responded with an enthusiastic round of applause and cheers.

As the hoots and whistles died down, and before the band transitioned into the next part of the set, she took a minute to thank the crowd and introduce the members of Odessa. Then as the band played through the prelude of her first original, she slipped in an advertisement for their CDs and mentioned they could be heard on WLYF 88.9, hopefully increasing C.J.'s already large, devoted following.

During the next three songs, the band acquainted the audience with a rock beat praise and worship sound, which didn't seem to deter the crowd's enthusiasm. Of course, an eighth of the people sitting under the tent were friends and family. Most likely, their exuberance is what captured the attention of the four or five rows of bystanders who gathered around the perimeter of the tent. And there, way in the back, standing straight and unmoving as a tent pole, Adam Chisholm stared her down with those dark, zombie-like eyes of his.

Lord, soften Adam's heart. With Adam's unyielding eyes on her, she traded places with Brooks and stood at the keyboard. Slowing the tempo of the set, she shared a little background of the next song, her favorite. "All the songs I've ever written have come straight from my heart, however, this one still cuts me to the core and probably always will. The words and melody were written in a day, not in a week or weeks like some of my other songs. It came to me when I was a frustrated, eleven-year-old girl trying to measure up to God's perfect standard and always failing miserably. In fact, the day I wrote this song, I nearly killed my brother with my anger.

"It wasn't until my dad helped me understand the invisible Creator God's great love for me that I could do the one thing God desired of me, which was to believe His Son's death on the cross had been payment enough to make amends for my caustic temper. Because Jesus laid down his life for me, I could trust His love. I believed He would never condemn me or never stop His relentless work of changing me."

She toggled an E no three chord in the left hand, then moved to A no three and back to E no three. At the same time her right hand stayed at the simple E no three, chiming in on beats one, the "and" of two, and three. The simple melody created a dramatic sound and threatened to tighten her voice with emotion. Taking a deep breath, she lifted her eyes above her friends, above Adam, above Dad. If she dared look at Dad, she'd choke up for sure.

I poured. You drank the bitter cup.
I watched Your blood spill out.
When Your eyes looked through me,
they pierced me with Your love.
My shame I swallowed, I had to turn away.
You were doomed, forsaken, there was nothing left to say.

Born from heaven's light into a darkened world,
Creator God, Eternal king,
Did You know Your destiny?

Just have a little faith, You whispered on the tree,

Hear with your heart and trust Me. My love will set you free.
Maybe I'm mistaken or what they say's not true,
'Cause if You're the God who really sees, You'd know what I did
to You.

Sent from heaven's light into a darkened world.
Spotless lamb, Unblemished One,
Why would You die for me?

Inside my soul it's dirty, my mouth speaks what's unclean.
I've burned bridges, thrown sticks and stones and yeah,
made sweethearts bleed.
It's not that I don't want You or fear to try Your love.
I have this ugly stain, I doubt You'd want to touch.

You gave up heaven's light for a darkened world.
Blessed Redeemer, Savior and Friend,
Could You die for me?

You draw me close. I see Your scars. I tremble and I weep.
Oh Jesus, I do love You. Is there one drop left for me?
I've changed my mind. Please change my heart and
wash me with Your blood.
'Cause all I am and hope to be, I'm ready to lay it down.

Jesus, You are heaven's light for a darkened world.
Rock of my Salvation, Lover of my soul,
Please, please die for me...

Glory! Glory! You reign victorious.
I'm bowing on my knees
And singing praises to the Lamb,
Yeah, Your blood has made me clean!

With every measure of the final chorus, the song gained momentum until the crowd picked up the beat with the clapping of their hands. The band had to repeat the chorus three more times because, crazy enough, the people didn't want to quit!

But what about Adam Chisholm? How was he feeling about all this? She searched the fringes of the crowd for his black-rimmed eyes and shiny, silver piercings without success. He'd disappeared into the dark ... where he probably felt most comfortable anyway.

A medley of relief and disappointment played across her heart, but the band had a set to complete, and the crowd certainly deserved to be rewarded for their enthusiasm. Odessa would make the final song something their loyal listeners could really dance and sing to—Matt Redman's "Undignified."

The fourth time through *"Na nana na, Hey!"* the heat, humidity, and her hunger were taking its toll. She seriously thought she would toss her cookies. And poor Drew was soaked in sweat. His blonde curls were now spiky tufts, making his hair look like perfectly baked, golden meringue topping. Still, the band gave it their all and continued to play and sing as if they were celebrating with King David himself.

When the song came to an end, the crowd cheered, making it clear they wanted more. Unfortunately, the band couldn't do anything about it; they had to have the stage cleared by nine-fifteen to make room for the karaoke contest.

After shouting a hasty thanks and extending an invitation for everyone to visit their promo table, she handed the mic over to the emcee. He raised another round of applause for the band as everyone but Drew began pulling plugs and packing up their instruments and equipment. Drew, however, jumped off the stage and headed straight for Dad. What was he up to? They exchanged a few words and then Dad passed his cell phone off to Drew. Drew smiled, gave Dad a thankful pat on the back, and then took off, most likely, to a quiet corner of the fairground.

Pound to a penny, her introverted brother had conveniently arranged a phone "date" with Kylie back home in Australia in order to avoid the post-concert small talk.

Grinning, she went back to her work until family and friends began taking over the teardown process, allowing her and the band to greet their old friends, chat with new ones, and try to hawk a dozen or so CDs.

The meet and greets were the best part of giving a concert. She especially got a kick out of the little girls who would swarm around the table, usually buzzing with questions about the "cute drummer." While Drew had no problem talking with the preteen crowd, the high school beauties would make him blush and twist his tongue into a knot. And since the big top was fairly thrumming with lip-sticked, teenaged girls hoping for romance, it made sense why Drew wanted to bow out of the after-concert conversations tonight.

Just like she expected; the first three people to buy a CD were little princesses who had somehow persuaded their parents to break a hard-earned twenty.

"How much are the CDs?"

Before turning to the impatient man inquiring about their CDs, she thanked a wide-eyed middle schooler and handed four dollars change back to her mum.

She forced herself to smile despite the man's rudeness and her own weariness. "They're sixteen dollars." She'd seen that critical scowl before, but where?

"Sixteen? You think you're worth it?" Although the man's lips curled up at the corners, his eyes withheld any sign of emotion.

She offered another friendly smile, hoping to win his confidence. "I may not be worth it, but the music is."

He pulled out a bundle of cash from his pocket and threw a bill down on the table. "You got change for a hundred, Miah?"

"Uh … I think so." Either he remembered her name from the

introductions in the middle of the set, or they had indeed met before. But the only memorable person she knew who carried around such large amounts of cash was Mr. Ellison. "You don't happen to go to Open Door do you?"

"Open what?" His dark brown brows buckled, creating a severe fault line above the bridge of his nose.

"Open Door Bible Church. I'm trying to figure out how I know you. You look really familiar."

He slid his grin to the left. "Well, I should. Your stupid horse nearly killed me earlier this week. Don't you remember?"

She tried not to balk at his sneer and over exaggeration. "Oh! Of course. Sorry ... Lights and shadows play tricks." Embarrassment added another ten degrees to her hot, flushed face.

"I figured you didn't recognize me." The man stroked his bristly jaw and finally gave her a sincere smile. "I'm on vacation, letting the beard grow, you know. So, are you going to give me my change?"

"Oh, right." She thumbed through the envelope for four twenties and four ones then stole another peek at the man's face. His wavy hair is what she hadn't noticed before. He must have been wearing a cap during their strange, unfortunate encounter in the barn. No matter, it was him all right. He had the same perfectly groomed mustache, the same straight nose and skeptical brown eyes. Definitely a jumped-up Yankee. At least that's what Drew had called him, and Drew had always been a good judge of character. "Here you go. Eighty-four dollars."

The man held his hand out flat, making her count the change back to him. She looked up only to catch his eyes moving over her body. What a creeper. What a creepy, jumped-up Yankee.

With the last bill, he clasped his fingers around the tips of hers. "The song you sang, Miah—the one about the blood being spilled. Is it on this CD?"

"You mean the second to the last song we sang? 'Die For Me?' " She pulled her hand from his grasp.

" 'Die For Me.' " He contemplated the title with a slow nod. "Yeah, 'Die For Me.' "

She returned a quicker nod and pointed to the back of the CD. "It's on there. Track three."

"Good ... Good, Miah."

CHAPTER ELEVEN

*I*t didn't matter that she had eaten a heaping bowl of Mum's pasta salad and downed two cups of lemonade, she still felt shaky. A shower after the concert would have helped, but Brandt had been so worried about missing the line dancing that she only had time to run back to the camper, throw on a clean T-shirt, and run a brush through her hair.

Miah dropped the brush on the blue, upholstered couch and pulled an elastic from her wrist. Now where were her boots? Or should she wear her sandals? They would be much cooler. "Brandt, should I wear my boots or sandals?" The second the question left her mouth, regret painted her face a bright pink, the same neon color of her T-shirt. How could she be so stupid? He probably thought she was the most petty-minded girl on the planet. She smoothed her hair back and peeked out the camper door. Yep, those were his thoughts exactly.

Brandt rolled his eyes and shrugged. "I don't care what you wear, Miah. Just put a little hustle in it. I want at least one dance with you before I have to leave." He levered himself out of the lawn chair then jumped up on the metal fold-out step and grabbed at her waist. "Come on. I like you just the way you are."

Twisting away from his grasp, she hid her self-consciousness with a giggle then finished pulling her hair through the elastic loop. "Hang on. I need to find some socks." The aluminum door clicked shut leaving Brandt and his cheeky fingers on the other side of the screen. He looked quite dejected when she finally fished a pair of boot socks from her duffle bag and dangled them in the air. "Chin up, mate. The lost is found." She loaded her smile with cheer and shot it his way. " 'Ow 'bout doing me a favor, Brandt? Turn off the generator? I'll be right there."

"That's what you said five minutes ago."

"I know. This time it's for real." She pulled on her socks and grabbed her boots just when the generator cut out and engulfed the camper in darkness. Shuffling out the door and down the step, she felt her way over to the picnic table where she'd left the flashlight somewhere amongst the mess of wet beach towels, empty Coke cans, and crumpled chip bags.

"Looking for this?" A click produced a shaft of white light, illuminating the area beneath the vinyl awning. As Brandt played the beam of light on her feet, she steadied herself against the table and stooped to yank on her boots. Ever so subtly, the spotlight left the pink stitching of her western boots and began a slow ascent up the length of her body, making her feel naked under his scrutiny.

"Knock it off, Brandt!"

Except for a quiet hum of approval, he remained silent and kept the circle of light creeping up her thighs. As soon as the light reached her face, she flashed him the ugliest mug she could muster. He got the last laugh though. The lightning-like brightness of the halogen lamp hit her eyes, nearly blinding her, and then to make matters worse, he clicked off the flashlight, pitching her into a darkness thicker than Moses' ninth plague.

"Hey!" She blinked at the wall of blackness and patted at the now vacant space in front of her. "Brandt, turn it back on! I can't see a thing!" A second sweep of her hands came up empty too.

"Come on." She stood still, trying to detect his hiding place, yet any sound he might have made was drowned out by the exiting traffic, the distant midway music, and the paradoxical mixture of adult laughter and the whiny cries of tired children. "Okay, okay. Marco ..." She waited in vain for a "Polo" to volley back. "Brandt?"

A current of warm air huffed against her ear.

Despite the heat and humidity, a ripple of goose bumps ran down her arms as she turned to face the wispy puffs of breath tickling her neck. Before she could reply or catch her own breath, Brandt's mouth covered hers with an impassioned kiss. His hand came up and held the back of her head making her feel, if not trapped, at least cornered. "Brandt ..." She really needed some air! When she tried to make some space, he brought his mouth near again.

"It's okay, Miah." He scooped up her hands in his and dropped them around his neck, drawing her closer to the pounding in his chest. Her own heart beat a heavy rhythm—not out of passion, but out of fear. What if he took his desire too far? What if someone saw them—namely Dad!

"Brandt, we better go."

He answered her with another kiss, and his hands began wandering too freely across her backside. If Dad saw them, it would be all over for them. Brandt obviously didn't care. Without any hint of fear or hesitation, his breathy whisper fell hot against her cheek. "You are so sexy."

"What? No! No, I'm not. I'm hot, smelly, and sweaty!"

She didn't know if she should be thankful or embarrassed when a fit of laughter fell from the screened window of the Slater's camper, putting an end to Brandt's seduction and evoking a short string of curses from his lips. "Brook Slater and his obnoxious friends?"

Trying to catch her breath, she could only nod and endure

the humiliating kissing noises and dramatic cries of passion, playing like a mockingbird from her neighbor's camper.

"Should I go over there and teach those little squirrel baits the hard facts of life?"

Her words stuck to her tongue. "N-no. They're simply having fun. And … We deserve it." She turned and left Brandt standing there, because actually, she didn't care what he did, as long as he stayed ten feet away from her.

"Wait up, Miah!"

She didn't. Picking up her pace, she tried to ditch him amongst the hundreds of motorhomes and campers packed onto the green like cattle in a feedlot. She needed some time *and* space. She strode past Kortman's giant house on wheels and the Turchetti's bunkhouse camper where a mob of people were standing beneath the large awning, all talking and sharing a laugh or two. "Hey, Miah!" Ethan Turchetti waved her down. "Good job tonight! Are you heading up to the line dancing?"

She nodded and kept running. Six rows to go. Why did their campsite have to be way down by the river every year? It put her too far from the barns, the bathrooms, and—if she could find them in the crowd—too far from her family and friends.

Her hands tried to cool the burning in her cheeks, and she tried to bite away the tingling in her lips. What happened back there anyway? Why hadn't she been able to let go and lose herself in Brandt's kisses? Wasn't his attention and affection what she'd been dreaming of for the past five weeks? And really, her fears of having another run-in with Dad were only in her head. In all likelihood, Dad had occupied his own mind by leading Mum around the dance floor. So, what was her problem? Maybe Dad had been right. Maybe she wasn't ready for a boyfriend after all, especially one who seemed so … so experienced. Maybe she should simply stick with the fantasy she had going with her Wyoming cowboy. It would be far less risky.

Cutting through another row of campers, she turned left onto the single traffic lane for row F. At the end of the lane, the shuttle wagon with its team of horses was about to clip-clop by on its way to the livestock barns. If she hustled, she might be able to catch it.

She jogged around a truck's bulging fender and sky-high bumper only to be pulled to an abrupt, stitch-snapping halt. The sudden loss of momentum made her stumble back against the invisible fist clenched tightly to her most cherished University of Wyoming T-shirt, which now had a rip in the shoulder.

"What's going on, Miah?"

Like she imagined the final day of reckoning to be, a rush of dread flooded over her. "Brandt..." She turned, pushed his hand away, and wished with all her might for the wagon and team of draft horses to come back and save her from having to choke up an explanation for her sudden flight.

"Why did you run off? Didn't you hear me call you?"

She shrugged and nodded, hoping her gestures would be answer enough. How could she explain her reason for running when she hardly understood it herself?

Brandt's fingers drummed an impatient beat on the bumper of the big Ford truck while the rounded toe of her boot kicked out an S.O.S. message against the tire. Unfortunately, the sound effects did nothing to quell the awkward silence pushing its way between them.

Brandt ended the uncomfortable stalemate with a big sigh and filled in the blanks for her. "I came on too strong, didn't I?"

Where words should have been forming, a seed of emotion took root and grew in her throat. Then once again in his boldness, Brandt reached out to her, only this time his touch brushed against her cheek with gentleness. "I'm sorry, Miah."

"No." She shook her head and swallowed hard. When he bent to look in her eyes, she couldn't bring herself to let him see inside her heart, to let him see the lie smoldering there like a hot coal. She wasn't an expert in the game of romance as her flirtations led him to believe. Instead, she was a greenhorn, as inexperienced and fresh as a year-old filly. And for the time being, she didn't mind keeping it that way.

When she gathered the courage to meet Brandt's eyes, they were blinking down at her with all kinds of sincerity, waiting for her to speak. She had to say something. But what?

"Brandt ..." His name stalled out in her throat then seemed to stick tight to the roof of her mouth. She had to force herself to begin again. "Brandt, I ... I'm afraid I've been leading you on. I'm sorry. I'm not what you think." Her pinky fingers met then nervously entwined one another. "You see, I've never had a boyfriend before. You're my first." She paused, waiting for the implications of her confession to sink in. "And up until this afternoon, I'd never been kissed before."

The hot, sticky air draped over her like a heavy wool blanket, forming tiny drops of sweat above her lips. She wiped them away with a shrug. "I don't know. Maybe I'm not ready for all this. I mean, it's not how I imagined it would be." In the distance, heat lightning sparked and glowed inside mountainous clouds, giving her something other than her wringing hands to focus on. "I better go. Bri's waiting for me at the barn."

A hint of pain, or maybe anger, skirted across Brandt's sweaty brow as she turned to leave. "Wait a minute, Miah." He pulled back on her shirt again and then lifted his palms to the same height as his seemingly rising blood pressure. "I don't think this is fair—you flipping a switch and deciding we're done."

Yeah, it was definitely anger sharpening his features. It made him look like the warrior-chief she'd imagined to be in his ancestral past. She'd seen his dark intensity before. He was angry with himself.

"Can't we talk this out?" His dark eyes flashed like the silent lightning accentuating his unyielding silhouette.

"Brandt, I'm not like the girl in your DVD."

He closed his eyes and shook his head with conviction as if the memory of the girl's ravaged, naked body repulsed him too. "Of course, you're not! And I told you, I've never had anything to do with porn. Ever!" He paused. "I'm not stupid, Miah. I know exactly what you are. You're a treasure. Very special. And I ... I just got caught up in the beauty of you. I'm sorry. If you give me another chance, it won't happen again. I promise. Please, I don't want to lose you."

"Hey, you two! I've been searching all over for you. Where've you been?"

They both turned in the direction of Dad's voice. Brandt answered first. "Mr. Brennan! We ... we didn't see you there." He took a deliberate step back, putting an acceptable distance between her body and his.

"You're going to miss the line dancing. It's nine forty-five."

"Miah wanted to change her clothes and get something to eat. We were just on our way up to the barn." When Brandt's eyes met hers, they were still pleading for a second chance. Hopefully, Dad didn't notice.

Nope. Too late. Dad had set his concerned gaze on her, yet at the same time, directed his question toward Brandt. "You two weren't at the camper alone, were you, Brandt?"

"Uh ... No, Mr. Brennan. I waited for Miah outside under the awning, and Brook Slater and his friends were around."

At Brandt's half-lie, she dropped her gaze to her boots.

"Brook Slater?"

Brandt must have nodded in reply. This was not going to go well. Dad was hesitating way too long.

"Son, I'm sure you had the purest intentions when you walked Miah back to the camper; however, I don't think it's a good idea for you and Miah to be there alone, especially in the dark. I'd hate for you and I to have another unfortunate misunderstanding."

"No sir. It won't happen again."

She looked up in time to see Brandt lower his eyes to the ground in respect.

"All right then. Let's get up to the barn." Dad clapped his hands together in finality, and although his words spoke of satisfaction, his eyes lingered on hers making it clear he'd be waiting to hear her side of the story at a more appropriate time and place. However, in her mind, the story wasn't ready to be told, because thanks to him and his untimely interruption, the problem hadn't been fully resolved.

Resolution or not, it didn't seem to bother Brandt. He grabbed her hand and kept pace with Dad as if they were all going to live happily ever after. And they might, it just wasn't clear in her head yet. She needed some time to sort it all out. Perhaps it would help if she wrote it all down. She'd get through the line dancing, say her thanks and goodbyes to her friends, then she'd snuggle down in her bunk with her journal and Bible, and she'd work it all out. And maybe by the time Brandt came back to watch Brad compete in the rodeo Saturday night, she'd have the courage and the words to tell him exactly how she felt.

CHAPTER TWELVE

The lively country music poured from the Kuyper barn, drowning out the final ounce of good sense Miah had left in her head. She didn't want to be here. She needed a little peace and quiet to set things square in her mind.

As they approached the crowd of onlookers, she watched a bead of sweat roll down Brandt's temple. What kind of internal thoughts had set those dark eyes like flint? Had he been beating himself up over his lack of self-control or had he become frustrated with her prudish immaturity? Who could tell? Although he'd kept a sweaty grip on her hand all the way to the barn, not once had he turned her way. Instead, he'd seemed intent on helping Dad solve the debatable question of whether a Power Stroke or Duramax could actually outperform a Cummins Diesel. She doubted Brandt knew or even cared. He was probably being polite and biding time like her.

They reached the outside fringe of the crowd and Dad pressed ahead, excusing his way through the throng of head-bobbers and sno-cone eaters who were watching the dancers in front of them. She had expected to follow him; however, Brandt held her back, leaving her heart torn as Dad climbed up three rows of the spectator stands to the right and then crossed over to the other end of the barn alone. Dad didn't seem to mind. Staying true to his colors, he offered a quick smile and friendly nod to everyone he met along the way. He was a good man, and even if his timing could be considered inconvenient, he was a very good dad.

Oh, how she used to crave his attention. There'd been a time back on Amaroo station when she'd gladly forfeit a day of make-believe to take the endless truck ride into Longreach so she could have him all to herself. And after the musters, when he'd come home from a week of droving cattle, she'd dance circles around his tall, strong frame until he sat down his dusty self and pulled her onto his lap. But now, if she were honest with herself, she sometimes resented his presence in her life. When had her heart changed? Why had it changed? And how sad that she'd allowed it to happen. *I'm sorry, Daddy. I love you.*

Brandt pulled on her hand, reminding her it still melted within his grasp. Evidently, he'd determined they too should find an opening in the crowd. Once again, he led the way with boldness, communicating with the spectators by way of nods and a few taps on the shoulder. The music pounded and hammered as Leanne, the ageless blonde beauty, shouted into the microphone, instructing the packed lines of boot-scootin' fairgoers. It'd be nearly impossible to find a place to join in.

Miah scanned the area for an open opportunity and some familiar faces. There at the other end of the open-sided barn, by the big livestock fans, near Mum and Dad, a group of her friends were laughing and dancing. Bri's wide eyes sparkled under the lights and her dimpled smile spoke of dreams come true; Jared Nicholson was escorting her across the dance floor. No doubt, Bri hadn't given her a second thought, and it seemed as if no one else was missing her either.

With the exception of C.J. and Teá, and Rob and Amy, most of her friends and family had stuck around. Even Ethan

Turchetti and his crowd had made their way up to the barn. He gave her a wink despite Brandt having a possessive hold on her shoulders.

Maybe she could find some redemption in the evening after all. It might be exactly what she needed, a little mixing with her friends, a little dancing, and a little laughter to chase away the seriousness of the past ten minutes.

The block of line dancers took two slides to the left, toward her parents who stood at the other end of the barn. Not surprisingly, her parents had struck up a conversation with their neighbor. No way! It couldn't be! All her inhibitions dashed away as she reached up for Brandt's hand. "I can't believe it!"

He leaned over her shoulder, bending an ear to her voice. "What?"

"Over there, talking to my dad," she shouted above the music.

Brandt's gaze followed her nod and searched the crowd of bystanders on the west end of the barn. When it settled on Dad's trademark Akubra hat, Brandt shook his head and shrugged, his mind not registering the significance of her alarm.

"The bloke bought a CD from me. When I counted back his change, he grabbed my fingers and wouldn't let go. He's as jumped-up as a peacock in full feather!"

A grin preceded Brandt's huff as he turned his gaze across the dance floor. "You mean Jack Dane over there?"

"Is that his name? Do you know him, Brandt?"

He looked down at her with an incredulous chuckle. "I only meant he looks like Jack Dane.

She shook her head, making sure he knew she didn't understand.

"Jack Dane. The actor. And no, I don't know that guy." He shrugged again. "I've seen him around. I saw him watching a couple of your equestrian events. The speed and action competition. And he attended the Extreme Cowboy Event too. I saw him talking with your dad." He leaned in closer. "I think your dad's trying to *save* him."

She hissed a doubtful breath. "Good on him. But if you ask me, the bloke is too far gone. He's an egotistical, spoiled-rotten American. And he's strange. Even Drew thought so."

"Why, what else did he do?" Brandt yanked on her ponytail. "Try to drag you into a dark corner?"

"Close. He gave me a dirty look, and I don't mean unkind or muddy. And he had a roll of quid as thick as my wrist. He probably sells drugs or something. You should have heard what he said to me in the horse barn earlier this week."

She turned her attention back to the sharp-featured, pompous man Dad was addressing. Oddly, the man's dark eyes were not engaged in the conversation. Instead, they roamed amongst the crowd as if he were hunting for someone.

"So, what'd he say, Miah?"

She leaned her shoulder into Brandt's side. "Jazz had been skittish all morning, he even bolted and threw me over the fence during the reining event."

"What? He did?" His eyes reflected a swirl of unbelief and concern.

"When I was putting him back in his stall, he shied and back into the man. He had been following way too close behind Jazz —serves him right. Anyway, when the guy was standing up, Jazz kicked at him then spun around to see what he was kicking at. After the guy said some choice words and I'd apologized up and down, he asked me where I was from. I reckoned I owed him the same politeness. So, when I asked him, he mumbled something about being from 'here, there, and everywhere.' After he quit laughing at his own dumb joke, he asked me if I'd ever been to the state of unconsciousness. I truly didn't know how to respond. Thankfully, my dad and Drew came along and rescued me."

Brandt stared at the man, contemplating her story. His eyes softened, losing their unreadable intensity. "Everybody's got a story, Miah." He gave her hand a squeeze. "We shouldn't judge. We don't have a clue what he's been through, and by the looks of it, his life hasn't been easy."

It'd been less than two weeks since Brandt had prayed with Dad and Pastor Bryce on the dock, and already he was beginning to sound just like them. But she wasn't judging the bloke, she'd had two encounters with the Jack Dane look alike now, and he was definitely seedy. "Brandt, who is Jack Dane? Was he in *October Sky*?"

He turned to her with a playful smile, the same smile that had prompted their manure fight in the A.I. barn. He shook his head and pulled his grin toward her. "No, you wouldn't know him, Miah. A long time ago he starred in a horror flick, and then he played in a T.V. show called *The Dark Hall.* The last movie I saw him in, he portrayed the misunderstood villain, Gregory Bloodgood. It was a great story, just not the kind your mom and dad would want you to watch. You were probably only ten or eleven when it came out anyway, and it wasn't exactly a kiddie movie."

"You're not that much older than me, Brandt. If it was so bad, I'm surprised your mum and dad let you see it."

"Yeah, well." He sighed and moved his squinty gaze toward the far, wooden rafters of the barn. "My brother took me to the movies *a lot*. Sometimes it's safer in the dark."

What did he mean? From what or whom did he need safety? Another drop of sweat rolled down Brandt's temple and crossed over into his short, trimmed sideburn. "I thought you only had a younger brother, Brandt."

"I do. Jett. But Skye, my half-brother, he uh ... died when I was thirteen. He had just turned eighteen."

She wanted Brandt's sad eyes to turn from the triangle-shaped trestles and look into hers. Instead, they remained locked in the corner, in a memory that transformed his sadness into a glassy hardness.

"He didn't even get to graduate, Miah." The muscles in his jaw kept a slow, solemn beat. "And if my dad was the source of everything bad, Skye had been everything good. Unfortunately, the cops and Skye himself didn't realize his worth. He sat in jail less than an hour before he found a way to hang himself."

What could she possibly say to ease his pain? She gave his hand a squeeze and hoped he would know all the sympathy behind it. "Brandt, I … I don't know what to say. I'm … so sorry."

He nodded. "Thanks." His weak smile couldn't disguise the grief in his eyes. "Besides my mom and my little brother, Skye gave me hope, helped me walk the right path. When he died, I told myself, somehow, I'd get off the reservation. I'd get away from the crappy little town that hated us, and I'd make something of myself—for my mom, for Jett … for Skye. I'd show my dad he pegged me wrong."

Brandt pulled his hand from her grasp and all too intimately, wrapped his arms around her chest and chuckled. "If my dad knew I was dating a white girl, he'd flip and fall off the wagon. No offense, Miah. It's just that my parents want me to marry a Lakota girl. But I'm gonna make my own path—a good path. And now that I'm on my way, for the first time in my life, I feel like the Great Spirit is up there watching over me, helping me."

"I bet He was always there, even when you didn't feel safe. Maybe you just didn't know what He looked like."

"Your dad said the same thing."

"So, my dad and Pastor Bryce know this story?"

"And more. Come on, let's dance."

She certainly couldn't blame the twangy, country beat and all the fancy footwork for her anxiety. Both had done their best to draw her into their carefree, happy world. Try as they might, they couldn't stop her from mulling over all the details of her unfinished conversation with Brandt. Why couldn't she simply enjoy this moment and be as cheery and upbeat as Bri? Since when had life become so complicated?

She followed her family and friends out of the barn, and by habit, they circled up to say their goodbyes. Even now, at this late hour, Brianna still bubbled with energy.

"What a blast!" With her eyes shining eternally bright, Bri gathered her long, brown hair off her neck and tied it back in a messy bun. "I could line dance every night!"

"Not me." Dr. Bakhuyzen fanned his T-shirt away from his sweat-drenched skin. "Whew!"

"What's the matter, Dad? Are your forty-seven years catching up to you?"

"No, absolutely not!" Bri's dad tossed a smirk toward his daughter, defending the physical capabilities of his tall, middle-aged body. "However, some of us have to work at six a.m. tomorrow morning and pay for their children's upcoming college tuition. Don't you agree, Trace?"

"You've got the six a.m. right, Marcus. But I can't possibly foot the bill for six college diplomas. It's always been understood the kids would have to come up with tuition on their own."

"Well, there's a novel idea." Dr. Bakhuyzen pulled Bri to his side and gave her a squeeze. "So how about going to the hospital with your old man in the morning, Breeze? I'm sure we can find some kind of work to help fund your degree."

As Bri's eyes did a barrel roll, Dr. Bakhuyzen wrapped his other arm around his wife. "What do you think, Trina?

Pushing her short, dark hair behind her ears, Brianna's mum curled a dimpled grin toward her husband and extended a grateful hand to her friends. "I think we should discuss this on the way home. Trace, Claire, thanks for a fun evening. Miah and Drew, good job tonight."

Miah met Trina's kindness with a smile. "Thanks for coming out and supporting us."

"Our pleasure, Miah."

Dr. Bakhuyzen gathered his family then nodded in Brandt's direction. "Brandt, are you ready to head out too? Or are you going to stick around for a while?"

Brandt looked from Dr. Bakhuyzen to Dad before his eyes stopped to consider the brooding, southern horizon. "I should probably walk out with you. I doubt the rain is going to hold off much longer."

Dad spoke up after checking the end-of-day To Do list that was most assuredly pinned to the corkboard in his brain. "Miah, did you feed Jazz and your steer tonight?"

"Aye, right before the band played. I should make sure they have enough water though."

"Miah, if you want to check Jazz, I'll check the steers."

She nodded her appreciation to Drew as Brandt moved to her side and took a tight-fisted hold of her hand. He cleared his voice and spoke up. "On second thought, Doc, why don't you go ahead. I'll help Miah with the horse then head out. I parked in the field way over on the other side of Mill Street anyway."

Dad didn't make any apologies when he gestured toward his watch and gave Brandt a resolved nod. "Ten minutes, mate. Then I expect Miah to be back at the camper."

They all said their final farewells then split like a scrum of rugby players, and she remained with the uncomfortable task of having to address the fate of her relationship with Brandt. There would be no more dancing around the issue tonight.

Why hadn't Dad used his parental power to move Brandt along? He'd never had a problem withholding his authority before. If he knew Brandt's past and had warned her to take things slow, why didn't he do more to discourage their relationship? Oh, no mystery there! It's because he loves to fix things: pumps, trucks, windmills, fences, and his favorite of all—people's broken, pain-filled lives.

Hopefully Dad didn't expect too much help from her.

Because if he did, they were all in trouble. Sure, she could sing and tell her story in front of a crowd, no problem, but when it came to helping people smooth out their own stories, she just didn't have the experience—not like Dad.

Deep down, her heart longed to be courageous and caring and pleasing to God. She truly wanted to be the self-sacrificing servant Pastor Bryce said God sought out. Maybe her desire counted for something. Maybe God would take her willingness and use it to help Brandt write joy and goodness into his difficult story.

So, what should she do? Try to work this out? If she did give Brandt another chance, somehow, she'd have to remain true to herself and to the work God had begun in him. Somehow, she'd have to drum up the courage to tell Brandt his boldness scared her and even made her feel manipulated at times. Yet, who could say he wouldn't take offense? Would fire return to his eyes if she told him it was more important to grow his relationship with Jesus than to pursue one with her—that in the long run, it would benefit them both? Well ... maybe it was a risk worth taking.

CHAPTER THIRTEEN

The barn smelled of horses, sweet grain, leather, and hay. Its comforting smell made Miah want to curl up and fall asleep in the aroma of its familiar friendliness. If she closed her eyes, she could almost be a dreamy little girl again, living back on Amaroo Station with its treeless, wide-open spaces and paddock of drowsy horses that milled about outside their stilted house.

Nothing could unscramble a person's mixed-up thoughts better than spending time outside in the great Aussie bush. A girl could clear her mind quick smart if she needed to, or depending on her mood, she could fill it with all kinds of fantastic imaginings.

It took no amount of imagination to picture Brandt as a veterinarian. From the corner of her eye, Miah watched in secret wonder as he whispered into Jazz's curious sniffs. When it came to animals, Brandt had the same sixth sense her brothers had been born with. However, if he wanted to be respected amongst the older farm folks, he might want to lose the braid that snaked down his back.

As she raked the last bit of manure from Jazz's stall, Brandt looked up and indulged her with a shy smirk. On second thought, braid or not, as long as he wore a quiet smile, he'd probably do all right. His fresh grin just might set the wariest cow-cocky at ease.

Yet, what about his anger? She had seen it twice now, how it consumed the last fleck of light in his dark eyes. She didn't care to see it again, nor did she wish for anyone else to experience it.

Without as much as a nod or a glance her way, Brandt grabbed the water bucket and headed straight for the spigot, kicking up a surprising cloud of tension behind him. Had she somehow misinterpreted his smile? Had his grin merely been a heroic attempt to ignore the proverbial elephant in the stall?

When Brandt returned with his boots scuffing up behind her, she moved aside, careful to give him a wide berth. He stepped into the stall and plunked the bucket down, sloshing a conspicu-ously sloppy wave of water onto the freshly bedded floor. No doubt about it, something simmered hot beneath his collar.

"How is he for hay, Miah?" Before she could answer, Brandt moved with exaggerated purpose to the corner of the stall and tested the weight of the hay bag himself.

"I think he's good, Brandt."

He nodded in agreement as the southern windows of the barn lit up with the flash of white, electric energy. "We better get going. You ready?" Bridled impatience crisscrossed his forehead as he offered her his hand.

She wasn't sorry to admit she welcomed the impending thun-derstorm. With any luck, it would send them both running—Brandt to the grassy parking lot across Mill Street and she to the camper. Then maybe she'd have a whole rainy night to pray through her dilemma.

The moment Brandt led her out of the west end of the barn, the thick night air lapped up all her hope. What she expected to be a fast-advancing storm appeared to be only heat lightning meandering across the distant, tree-lined horizon. There would be no thunder, no rain, and no chance of getting out of her sticky situation.

Brandt tightened his sweaty grip on her hand and steered her around a group of pierced and tattooed teenagers before heading straight for the main concourse. Even at eleven-thirty p.m. people were scattered along the midway, milling around, either nibbling on one last tasty treat or caught up in conversation with a long-lost friend.

As they passed by the swine barn, an angry, persistent squeal rattled her ears and clashed with the crazy mixture of laughter, music, and general fair chatter competing for her attention. Brandt didn't seem distracted. He had set his course and was intent on getting there. In his haste, he ran shoulder to shoulder with a stranger who emerged from the shadows of the barn as suddenly as the flash of lightning that brightened the southern horizon.

When Brandt offered a quick apology, the man made it clear he'd staked his claim and wasn't budging.

"Good job tonight, Miah."

"Oh ..." The distinct, sweet-sour smell of liquor polluted the air between her and the unforgiving man, forcing her to take a step back. As she shielded her eyes against the glare of the large barn light, she found the man couldn't really be classified as a stranger. "Adam ... Thanks. I, uh, saw you in the crowd."

"Yeah. I enjoyed ... watching you." With a boldness encouraged by his intoxication, Adam Chisholm reached across Brandt's chest and stroked her arm in a manner as suggestive as his voice.

Standing taller and much broader than the bloke, Brandt squared his shoulders before leaning forward and jabbing Adam's chest with a two-fingered shove. "Back off, bruh. I don't wanna have to hurt a dude when he's faded."

Adam's piercings glinted in the light as he gave a low chuckle from his goateed face, took a step back, and opened his black coat.

Brandt seemed undaunted by the silver hilt of a knife, but despite the heat, a shudder of chills ran the course of her body. "Let's go, Brandt." She gave his shirt an encouraging tug. "Come on." She had to tug again before Brandt finally backed down. "We're sorry, Adam. I'll see you at church. Okay?"

She turned and hustled down the concourse with Brandt on her tail once again.

"Adam? Church? Is he the devil guy you told me about? If he is, you need to tell your dad about him. And if you don't, I will. He's trouble."

"He's harmless."

Brandt's eyes widened. "He's not harmless, and if you think he is, you don't know what's up, girl." Concern collided with Brandt's anger and took an uncomfortable seat between them.

"I should get back to the camper. Do you want to take the shuttle? If we run, we can catch it."

He shook his head. "There's too many people. Let's walk."

Jingoes, couldn't he see the mountain of misunderstanding rising between them? Didn't he realize nothing constructive would come from a late-night conversation? The emotional evening had drained all the care from her.

Somehow Brandt must have sensed her weariness; he settled back into his quiet brooding. When they passed the parked parade of John Deere tractors, he pulled her into the shadows of a huge combine and finally spoke up. "Miah, we didn't get to finish our conversation. Before I go I ... I need to know where I stand with you."

His voice hushed with unusual timidity. Could this be the same guy who had practically herded her out of the horse barn? Where had all his bad-boy confidence gone? She searched his dark eyes for an answer, only they weren't doling out any information. They were on hold, waiting for her.

"Miah …"

She nodded without thinking. "I know, I … I've kept you waiting." Her pinky fingers found one another and twisted and turned like minuscule twins in their mother's womb.

"Miah, I'm willing to change anything and everything for you. Please, give me another chance."

He shoved his hands in his pockets and stared hard at the ground, waiting for her to untie all the knots in her tangled-up tongue. Maybe if she conjured up some anger, then the words would fly, no problem. However, she didn't feel especially imaginative at the moment. She felt fickle and immature, and simply at a loss for words. She rubbed the tense muscles in her neck and looked around for another way out. "My ten minutes are up. We should keep walking."

With a brusque sweep of his hand, he gestured for her to lead the way. "If you're not gonna talk, I guess I can only assume you're giving me the boot and you're simply too nice to say so. Am I right?"

"No, I mean … I don't know. I don't know what to do." Her pinky fingers continued to roll about then finally settled down, embracing one another in a comforting hug. Why did this decision have to be up to her? Couldn't he see she was only a stupid, dreamy girl who merely loved the idea of being in love? She wasn't, and probably never would be, as experienced as the college girls he'd surely been used to dating. Dad had been right. Seventeen was not a magical number that could suddenly make a person think and act like an adult.

They stayed on the pathway, passing row after row of travel trailers on their left, while cars filing out of the grassy lot, passed them on the right. Another hundred yards and the traffic lane turned to the right then switched back to the north, leading the procession of cars and trucks out onto Mill Street, leaving her and Brandt all alone in the glow of the old, wooden welcome sign.

Although they only had a short walk to the boat launch and the last row of campers, it felt like the longest, most awkward two minutes of her life. And now irony was getting the last laugh, because just yesterday, wasn't she dreaming of standing right here at the riverbank, in the dark, with Brandt—the very place where probably hundreds of other girls throughout the years had received their first kiss?

At the time, it had only been wishful thinking. Even so, she'd written it all down in her journal, how she imagined it would go. First, they would walk hand in hand under the big oaks, saying nice things to each other all the way down to the river's edge. Then they'd skip some stones and share a couple laughs before they'd finally shed their boots and wade out to the big rocks in the middle of the quiet water where the frogs and crickets and the light of a big harvest moon would be their only witness.

Brandt must have spent some time dreaming too. Instead of the river, he'd chosen the island in the middle of Stoney Lake, at midday, in their swimming suits. His kiss had been just as sweet as she imagined it would be. But tonight at the camper, she'd gotten more than she'd bargained for and definitely more than what she'd been ready for.

Now all she could think about was how close she was to her camper, her bed, and her journal. Just a thirty-second jog down the two-track to her left and she could be scot-free. However, Brandt took hold of her arm and directed her down to the boat launch, closer to the riverbank. He obviously wasn't in any hurry to get home. He wanted some answers—answers she wasn't ready to give.

At first Brandt seemed content watching the moonlight on the river, then giving the gravel a tired kick, he bent to pick up a stone. "So, are you gonna make me drag this out of you? Or should I throw you in the river?" He smiled, then tossed the stone in the air, and caught it with the same hand.

When she didn't respond to his smile or his joke, his eyes

glazed and became as hard as the stone he jiggled back and forth in his hand.

"If this is still about the DVD ... Man, Miah! I told you, I don't mess with porn!"

"I know." His eyes were growing fierce again. Why couldn't God make it rain and rescue her from this difficult, one-sided conversation? She turned and blinked back the tears welling up at the borders of her eyes.

"Hey, I'm sorry, Miah." Brandt's voice softened again as he reached out to her. "I didn't mean to upset you. Just talk to me. Please." His eyes pleaded with her then turned back toward the southern sky where lightning flickered beyond the huge oak trees lining the riverbank. "Listen, I promise I won't drink. I won't cuss. I'll go to church with you every Sunday. I'll pray and read the Bible every day. And we'll take things slow. I'll do anything. I'll change everything for you, Miah."

"I don't want you to."

He tossed the stone back and forth in his hands, acting like he hadn't heard her. Then he shrugged. "Unless ... unless it's something I can't change." This time he looked at her without blinking. "I pinned it, didn't I?" His dark eyes fairly pierced her own before he wagged his head at her. Air huffed between his teeth. "Frick, I thought if I moved here things would be different. I thought *you* were different." He tossed the stone up, caught it, and then whipped it in the direction of the opposite bank. A thick tree trunk took the hit then deflected the stone into the black water with a definitive *kerplunk*. "You can't stand a native kissing those pretty, pink, English lips of yours, can you?"

What? She shook her head. "No ... No, Brandt. I think you're wonderful ... beautiful. You had it right the first time. You're moving too fast for me."

She stepped back, avoiding his angry glare. "I was nearly twelve and infatuated with the picture of an American cowboy, when I promised myself that if I ever fell in love, I would savor the experience—every part of it. I guess I hoped to have a couple days to enjoy the bliss of my first kiss and to dream about the next one. It's all too fast. I'm barely seventeen. You're in university. I didn't think it would matter, but it does. It's not the difference in our bloodlines. It's the difference in our ages *and* our expectations." She brushed the stray hair out of her eyes and away from her tears. "I'm sorry. I don't think I can be the girl you want or need."

Despite the darkness, Brandt turned his eyes to the place where the stone had made an angry splash in the river. His head gave an indignant shake as his reply grumbled across the water. "It's just like an Anglo to decide what the Oglala Lakota wants or needs."

Her jaw dropped in disbelief as his pumped with spiteful adrenaline. If he was looking for a fight, well, she could give him one all right! "Right now, I don't really care what you want! And tonight, at the camper, you obviously had no regard for what I wanted either! You took advantage of the dark and made me feel trapped. And you embarrassed me in front of Brook Slater and his friends—not to mention putting us both at risk of losing my dad's trust! Oh, and by the way, I'm not English. I'm just as Australian as you are Amer... Lakota.

He turned, facing the light of the eight-foot-wide welcome sign and crossed his arms. "How foolish of me to presume your ethnicity solely on your skin color *and* your MOTHER TONGUE!" The anger in his sarcastic British accent scorched the humid space between them.

All she could do was stand there and shake her head. "You have a problem, Brandt." She turned and started to leave only to have her shirt tugged on for the third time that night.

CHAPTER FOURTEEN

"**G**et your sticky mitts off me!" Miah spun around and slapped Brandt's hand away. "I know what's going on here, and I don't appreciate it one bit! Regardless of what they told you on the reservation, I'm pretty sure the whole cavalry and Wounded Knee Massacre thing ended over a hundred years ago. I. Wasn't. There! I'm sorry for all the injustice, mate, but I wasn't there. So, stop blaming me and let it go! Just let it go!"

She had really done it this time. Brandt's lips were drawn in a laser-straight line, and he stood there blinking back the anger igniting in his eyes. Stepping back, she watched his fury smolder. When it finally collapsed cold and unmoving on his defeated shoulders, his voice choked out a whisper. "There's the problem, Miah. It didn't end—at least not where I'm from. Instead of horses, the cavalry rides around in black and white squad cars and picks fights with innocent, eighteen-year-old kids. Before they arrested him, the cops beat my brother to a pulp." Brandt's eyes were as misty as the fog forming above the river's surface. "How am I supposed to let go of my brother's murder?"

The chirping and peeping of insects and frogs mocked the

silence between them. How could she have been so insensitive? "I … I'm sorry. I didn't know."

Brandt didn't show a single ounce of shame when he wiped away the lone tear trickling down his cheek. Before he could dry his hand on his jeans, she held it to her lips then pressed it against her own hot, regretful cheek. "You've lost so much, more than I'll ever be able to understand. I'm sorry. Is there any way you can forgive me?"

Another tear rolled down his face while a deep sigh cleansed the tense air around them. He nodded and retrieved his hand to wipe away the last tear. "I'm sorry too, Miah." He proved his willingness to forgive with a gentle brush of his hand against her cheek.

She reached up and covered his hand with her own. "Did you know my best friend, Kylie Barcelow, is a quarter Aboriginal?"

A reluctant grin pulled at the corner of his mouth. "This wouldn't be Drew's Kylie, would it?"

"Aye." She smiled and hoped he could tell how deep her regret went. "Her family owns Barcelow Downs. It's southwest of my grandparents' cattle station. I've known her and loved her my whole life. When Drew and I were born, my mum didn't have enough milk to feed us both. So Kylie's mum, Anna, helped nurse Drew and me. It's weird, I know. Then again, in the Outback, you do what you have to. I reckon I can credit my strength and health to Anna." She stood up straight and flexed her biceps. "It's all her Aboriginal milk flowing through my bones!"

Brandt gave her muscles a squeeze. "Did you get your beauty from her too?"

She brushed off his flattery with a smile. "Anyway, I spent most of my childhood either at Kylie's homestead playing around the feet of her mum and grandmother, or she and her brother, Caleb, hung out at our place. I love her family like my own. Kylie's grandmother is the kindest person on Earth. You would never know she suffered a lot of trauma in her childhood." She paused as Brandt leaned in with empathy.

"Years ago, when Grandmother Jannali was about five, the government took her and thousands of other Aboriginal kids from their families. They put them in mission schools or in foster families with the hopes of wiping out their Indigenous ways. They literally tore Jannali, kicking and screaming, from her mother's arms. She never saw her again."

"Miah." Brandt's eyes widened, and he clasped her upper arms. "Is this shocking to you?"

"Yes. Very. Isn't it to you?"

"No. Yes. I ... I mean. The same thing happened here in America. For about a hundred years, the U.S. government rounded up Native kids and put them in boarding schools. They cut their hair, changed their names, dressed them in white people's clothes. They forced us to abandon our languages and cultures and adopt Christianity instead. 'Kill the Indian, save the man' was their philosophy."

"I had no idea this happened in America too!" Pausing to grasp the magnitude of the crime, she locked his wrists in her hands. "It's unbelievable! It's so ... wrong."

Brandt's eyes were closed when he nodded his agreement. "Both my parents were sent to mission schools. To this day, my dad grieves the separation from his family and the abuse and loneliness he experienced. My mom's story wasn't as painful— she attended an on-reservation day school. But my great uncle— my dad's uncle, was sent away to a school in Kansas. He was only six years old. When he returned to the reservation at the age of twenty after fighting in World War Two, he was a stranger to the land and our family. It took years for him to recover the whole of who he was meant to be—Lakota. Then again, how does someone totally heal from such a huge wound?"

A high black cloud eclipsed the glow of the full moon,

casting a shadow across Brandt's questioning eyes. "How did Jannali deal with what happened to her?"

Miah bit her lip. What could she say to make Jannali's story sound believable? Attainable? "I don't ... She ... Somehow Jannali determined deep within herself to not let bitterness eat at her. I know you and I can't understand this, but somehow, she chose to rise above her situation. She didn't overlook the evil but looked beyond it and tried to imagine something better. She treated her pain as if it were medicine or ... or a force of motivation or inspiration to nurture healing and purpose. And you know what?"

Brandt's eyes remained steadfast on hers, waiting for an answer.

With mystery in her voice, Miah whispered. "Grandmother Jannali fell in love and married one of the pommies."

When Brandt's forehead buckled in confusion, she couldn't help giggle. "Pommy. A British immigrant—you know?" Clearly, he didn't understand. "Kylie's granddad was English, and a very good man," she explained. "He paid Jannali's way through nursing school. She had it in her heart to make something good of her tragic past—like you're doing."

Brandt peered across the river toward the distant storm and gave a thoughtful nod. Except now, the storm didn't look so distant. Instead of the southern horizon flickering with silent heat lightning, the whole sky became immersed in heaven's glory. She closed her eyes to the blinding light and waited for the first roll of thunder. So, it might rain after all.

Brandt had turned from the flash of lightning too, and now his eyes were on her, waiting for her to get to the point.

"I was eleven when my dad told us we were coming to America. I didn't want to move here. No one in my family did. We thought my dad had lost his mind. My mum was crying, and my brothers were livid. Rob started throwing angry words and furniture around. He threw my mum's yellow ottoman right through the screened door of our veranda. Out of fear, I ran down the steps too and didn't stop until I had reached Barcelow Downs, five kilometers away" She shrugged as her breath huffed through her grin. "Barcelow Downs is the *only* place to run to. There isn't another homestead for seventy kilometers. When I got there, Kylie's grandmum, Jannali, took me in her lap, tears and all, and told me a secret. Do you want to know what she said?"

Brandt kicked at the gravel, then showing her the intent, brown iris of his eyes, he nodded.

"She told me, 'Although we don't always have a choice about the things that happen to us or around us, we do have a choice about what happens inside of us.' And then she said, 'Choose joy, Miah. You can trust your daddy *and* your Heavenly Father. They both love you very much and have a good plan for you.' Brandt, I think you're taking the right steps. Just don't let bitterness trip you up and ... don't let me get in your way either. You're on a good path."

"You could never be in my way, Miah. I want to walk this path with you. You can show me how I'm supposed to make all this work ... with who I am." He shrugged with earnestness in his eyes. "I'll be honest, I'm torn between your way and the Lakota way. I didn't come to Michigan to run away from who I am. I only wanted to see if there might be a place for me ... out here." He searched the stormy sky as if God might point the way to a place of belonging, but then his eyes brimmed with tears again and he turned away.

"Brandt?" She reached out for his arm. "Hey, what's wrong?"

When he faced her again, his tear-filled eyes scanned the river beyond her, and he shook his head. "I don't know. Maybe you're right. Maybe this is a mistake—you and me." He took a deep breath and released it slowly between his lips. "One time when I was about ten, my mom took me to a church just outside the reservation. Jett wouldn't go. When my dad found out what my mom did, he laid into her so hard." Brandt sniffed back his emotion. "I hated him for it. But now I-I think I'm beginning to see why my dad treats my mom and me the way he does. In a weird, warped way, I think he's trying to protect us. He's just so … damaged."

She encouraged Brandt by taking his hand, but still, he wouldn't look at her. Instead, he stared straight across the water letting a river of glassy tears cut a path down his cheeks. "I don't know … Am I wrong to align myself with an institution that has abused, lied to and … and murdered my loved ones, my ancestors? We've experienced unspeakable atrocities—all by the hands of the whites—their law and their religion!" Bitter sobs exploded from Brandt's heart and skipped across the river, sinking hard into the muddied earth on the opposite bank. And all she could do was hold his hand in the paleness of her own, feeling responsible for all his losses.

A minute passed and then the sky sparked with white electricity, highlighting his dwindling tears, and somehow her voice found itself amidst the shadows of his quieting grief. "Brandt, I'm so sorry. I wish I could take your suffering away. I wish I could bring Skye back and erase your dad's painful childhood. I wish things were different. I wish history didn't happen the way it did. How … What can I do to help?" She searched the eddies of pain swirling around in his tear-filled eyes.

He shook his head. "I don't know, Miah. But I do know I have a lot of hurt—hate—buried here." He tapped on his chest. "And I don't want to take it out on you."

She moved close and leaned into his side, wrapping her arm around him. "And I don't want to cause you any more pain. I'm deeply sorry for the terrible things I said to you. You didn't deserve an ounce of my unkindness and anger. Please … forgive me?"

He turned to face her, finally looking into her eyes. "You know I can. But I'm not going to apologize for who I am." He shook his head. "No more. The Lakota way is a good way too.

When she nodded in understanding, he took her hand in his. "And somehow, I know your way and my way can fit together. I want it to fit together."

She didn't get the chance to agree. The sky flashed a brilliant warning of things to come, making her gasp. "Jingoes! The lightning is getting close! We better go before we're barbecued."

With a nod, Brandt scrutinized the sky. "Yeah. I think you're right." Then he closed his eyes to the light breeze now blowing across the river and stirring the humid air. "Miah, I think you're wonderful. You're smart, kind, creative and so beautiful. I-I hope you can see some good in me too. Would I be pushing things if I asked you for a kiss? One little goodbye kiss and I'd float all the way ho—" Before he could finish his sentence, a loud clap of thunder applauded his audacity and drowned out his last word.

***

Miah's fingertips lingered where Brandt's lips had whispered a promise of patience. And like the clouds quickly lowering the celestial ceiling down upon her, she felt as if she were floating too. With Brandt on his way to the parking lot across Mill Street, she was tempted to take her time walking back to her camper and enjoy the cooling air and the hushed sounds of the night, but if she dawdled too long, Dad would surely have some words for her.

She picked up the beat of her pace as thunder kept time to its own grumbling cadence. Then once again, lightning drummed up enough kindness to light up the crackly gravel lane spreading out ahead of her. There could be no doubt about it, the crunching and popping beneath her boots made the best music in the whole, wide world. On the other hand, a girl couldn't discount the midnight breeze hushing a love song past her ears … Or was that the sound of footsteps swishing through the grass on the other side of Mr. Slater's red Silverado?

Turning toward the river, she stopped to listen. She wouldn't put it past Brandt to sneak up on her for another kiss. He had before. "Brandt?" The wind blew across the lane, scooped up his name, and whisked it to the tops of the swaying oaks, leaving nothing but silence.

What if it wasn't Brandt at all? She'd die a thousand deaths if her brothers had been spying on her. Or what if one of the Slater boys had been using the river as a loo? Ha! The embarrassing situation could be worth a few laughs. A smile spread across her face then quickly disappeared when a twig snapped in the grass between her and the riverbank. Okay. Someone or something was definitely there.

Even though lightning flashed exposing a vacant riverbank, she couldn't deny what she heard. Could it be a skunk or raccoon? Maybe a deer? Well, she didn't want to stick around and find out who or what was sneaking around in the grass.

Her walk changed up to a trot as a deep roll of thunder rattled the ground beneath her feet. Yikes! The lightning was way too close! Lucky for her, the safety of her bed and her family were a mere eight meters away. And by all appearances, no one had waited up to welcome or scold her, whatever the case may be. Her family's camper sat dark and still in the crowded lot. Which meant there would be no writing in her journal toni—

If pain were a color, it'd be the blinding, fiery orange of molten metal, the same color that bounced off the backs of her eyes and burned through the roots of her teeth, all the way to the tips of her fingers and toes. And it was paralyzing. She couldn't move. She couldn't speak, even as the dew-covered law rose to catch her fall.

CHAPTER FIFTEEN

Trace woke to the sound of a loud rumble and lay there waiting for the first ping of rain to fall on the aluminum-clad camper. It never came. Instead, a pleasant breeze showed up and let itself in through the windows, cooling the air inside the efficient sleeping space.

He rolled on his side and brushed back the loose curls covering Claire's pretty face. "Darlin', did you hear the thunder?" He had to let her know. She'd be so sad if she missed it. Ever since he could remember, Claire had loved the sound of thunder. While he didn't necessarily understand the connection, he had his theory. Back home, during those years of drought, thunder meant the possibility of rain; rain meant pasture; and pasture meant fat cattle, which all converted to God's provision and peace of mind for his wife. "Claire. Sweetheart." Nope. Nothin' doin'. Sleep had taken her far away and wouldn't return her until morning. Even when he tried to pull her close, she didn't rouse.

A long strobe of lightning filled the camper as he tossed off the sheet. Surely Claire had thought to fold up the lawn chairs and take the beach towels down from the line, hadn't she? He really didn't feel like getting up to check, but if they wanted dry towels and somewhere to sit in the morning ....

He pushed himself up off the side of the bed and padded over to the screened door just as another flash of lightning illuminated the campsite. What in the world? The chairs were strewn helter-skelter all over the place. Had they all slept through a windstorm or had the Slater boys used them in some kind of crazy combat game?

After slipping on a pair of jeans, he snuck out the door and silently collected the towels off the line. Then folding up every last chair, he stuck them under the protective covering of the awning. Finally, turning to face the breeze, he sucked in the cool night air like a tall glass of water.

It didn't seem so bad—getting out of bed. In fact, he considered it downright peaceful and quiet, and thank the Lord, nice and cool. If he didn't run the risk of waking the family, he had half a mind to make himself a cuppa, pull up one of the chairs, and watch the fireworks.

In the west, lightning streaked across the sky then made a sudden, jagged plunge to earth. Wow! Absolutely awesome! Just like the dry lightning back home. Incredible!

The heavens proclaim My glory. The skies display My craftsmanship.

Indeed they do, Lord. And so do Your people. He had seen God's glory displayed in the life and work of his friend, Ben Ellison; in the dreams of all his Nigerian friends who were involved in Water Wins: Jeremiah, Marietta, Daniel, and the others; and in the hearts of all the people who helped lead the ministry at Open Door Bible Church.

He'd seen mountains moved and lives changed. He'd seen the impossible become possible: whole villages made strong from the benefits of clean water, education, and jobs; addicts rescued from the chains of pornography and drugs; broken marriages mended; excessive spending brought under control.

And it wasn't only the needy and struggling folks who'd had their lives transformed. He'd seen changes in himself. Where once he had a stagnant, almost irrelevant faith, he'd begun to see movement toward a laugh-in-the-face-of-death kind of faith. Where there had been an obsession with self, he'd now developed a desire to love and serve his neighbor. The changes were all a reaction to the abundant goodness of God's mercy and grace toward him and his family.

He'd been blessed beyond measure. But God help him if he ever forgot where it all came from. For he was nothing without the Giver. *Lord, keep me humble so I can be a worthy servant in your sight. If even the tiniest spot of self-reliance tries to worm its way into my heart, please make me aware of it. Give me the courage to cut it from my life like a cancerous tumor. And God, please protect my wife and my kids from it too. Help them to always trust You. Help them to walk in your way without any fear or doubt.*

Lifting his face and his prayers toward the magnificent lightning storm, he continued his petition with a specific request for each of his kids. He went right down the line, first remembering Rob and Amy and their baby yet to be born. He paused then left the electrically charged night air and moved inside the camper where he stood over Bradley and asked God to bless his love of the earth and his plans to start a tree nursery right there on the farm. Next came Joshua and his long, ambitious road through vet school.

After lingering a moment, Trace stepped to the back of the camper where the twins occupied the bunks. He prayed over Drew, the perceptive one, the one who had his heart set on flying for the Royal Flying Doctors. And then he finally came to Miah, his little girl, who didn't seem so little anymore and ... and who wasn't in her bed!

Thinking his eyes might be failing him in the dark, he leaned closer to the top bunk. Lightning flashed, confirming the truth.

Even so, he ran his hand down the length of her sleeping bag. It was empty, all right. And the clothes she'd worn to the concert lay right where she must have flung them on her bed. Where in the blue blazes could she be?

"Miah?" He quietly tapped on the bathroom door then swung the door open, sweeping the small room with his hand. Surely she'd understood when he told her to be back at the camper at eleven forty-five. Both she and Brandt had. Brandt had looked him right in the eyes and nodded. What time was it anyway?

Stumbling back to the front of the camper, he fished around on the countertop for his phone. Twelve forty-eight. One hour late. He might be able to give her fifteen minutes grace. But an hour? No way! He stood at the screened door and stared out into the dark, feeling like the most gullible yobbo on earth. What had he been thinking, letting her go off into the night with a six-one, ponytailed, motorcycle-riding, clay jar of testosterone? He could kick himself.

Well, at least they weren't pashing in Brandt's car; he didn't have one. Oh man, if the kid talked Miah into taking a ride on his dodgy old motorcycle, heads would roll. Maybe Brad or Josh knew something. "Brad." He shook his son awake. "Do you know where Miah is?"

"What?" Brad rolled over, making his annoyance known with a growl.

"Miah isn't in bed. You don't know where she is, do you?"

Groaning, Brad shook his head then buried it under his pillow.

This time Trace didn't bother to whisper. "Brad! Do you know where she is?"

"What's going on?" Claire pushed the sheet back and sat up.

"Miah hasn't come in yet."

Claire slid from the bed and ran through the exact motions he had just gone through, including the sweep of the bathroom. "Where could she be, Trace?"

His anxiety took the form of an impatient snap. "I don't know, Claire. If I knew, I'd be wringing her neck right now." He fumbled around on the countertop, knocking over a cup of water. "Sheeze, we need some light in here. Where's a bloody flashlight?"

"Cool it, Dad. She's fine." Josh moaned his way out of bed, grabbed a flashlight from his overhead cubby, and clicked it on. "She and Brandt probably went down to the river and lost track of time."

"Well, get your daks on Mr. Smarty Pants and help me go look for them." Lightning flashed again, reminding him of the risk in his plan.

Drew spoke up from the back of the trailer. "Dad, why don't you just call Brandt?"

Flipping open his phone, Trace began tapping through his list of contacts while Claire sat down and shared the edge of the couch with Brad. As the phone tried to make its magical connection, regret prompted him to reach out and hug Claire's sleepy head to his side. "I'm sorry, sweetheart."

"Hello?" A tired voice croaked through the receiver.

"Brandt, this is Trace. Hey, sorry to wake you. Miah doesn't happen to be with you, does she?" A long, disquieting pause hummed through the phone.

"What?" Brandt cleared his throat. "What time is it?"

"It's almost one. Is Miah with you, Brandt?"

"No ... No, Mr. Brennan. She's not with you?"

"No. It doesn't look like she ever made it back to the camper."

"What? Impossible." Brandt's voice came to life with concern. "I watched her."

"When, Brandt? What time?"

"It must have been around midnight—fifteen minutes late, I know. Even so, I watched her walk all the way to the camper."

"Where were you two?"

"We were talking down by the boat launch. I watched her from there."

"You saw her go into *our* camper?"

"I watched her walk as far as the red Silverado that's parked on the south side of the lane. She didn't have far to go. I figured she'd be fine. The lightning had become pretty intense, so I took off for the parking lot. I had to run all the way over to the field on the other side of Mill Street yet."

Trace turned his back on the anxious pairs of eyes watching him and paused at the screened door before stepping out under the awning. "Yeah, the Silverado is Mike Slater's." *Ten short meters from our camper ...Where is she, God?* Seconds passed before everyone joined him outside.

"She couldn't have gone up to the showers could she, Mr. Brennan? She had wanted to take a shower after the concert, only she didn't have enough time."

Claire came and stood at his side while the boys shined the flashlight in the direction of the river. "Not likely, Brandt. She knows she's not supposed to walk to the bathroom alone, especially at night. Some of those carnival workers have hungry eyes."

"I told her the same thing, Mr. Brennan. What about your truck? Maybe she didn't want to wake you and decided to sleep in there."

"Good idea." He snapped his finger at Brad and pointed in the direction of his own Silverado. Brad read his signal and directed the light into the truck's interior. He turned around with a negative shake of his head. "Shoot, she's not there. Had there been anyone else around, Brandt? Someone else who could have seen her?"

"No. I think everybody had taken shelter. The wind had picked up, and the thunder and lightning were getting too close for comfort. Is it raining there?"

"Not yet."

"Mr. Brennan, I hate to ask this. Could she have been hit by lightning or something?"

"No. If lightning had struck by our camper, we would have been shaken out of bed. The whole campground would have woken up."

"I guess you're right."

"Well, listen, Brandt. I'm going to check the bathrooms and the barns, just in case. And I'll see if the Slater's or Avery's heard anything."

"All right. Give me thirty minutes and I'll be there to help. Mr. Brennan, I think you should call the police."

"You think so?"

"Definitely. I wouldn't give it a second thought. There are some pretty weird dudes around. In fact, Miah and I had a run-in with a guy who looked like one of Satan's minions—goatee, piercings, tattoos—the works. Miah said he goes to your church."

The breeze picked up, cooling the wave of sweaty anger that broke out over Trace's body, and his sigh hissed across the tiny mouthpiece of his phone. "Adam Chisholm ... he's a dirty son of a—He's trouble. That kid is trouble. I had an encounter with him a few weeks ago." Claire's hands flew to her mouth as her wide eyes filled with fear.

"He's a piece of work, all right." Brandt's breath huffed through the phone too. "He tried to seduce Miah right in front of me. He was stone drunk. He couldn't have drawn his knife even if he wanted to. I-I'm sorry. I'm sure he's harmless, Mr. Brennan."

"It's okay. So, he flashed his knife at you too? It's an old stiletto, used in World War Two."

"Yeah? Well, he sure enjoyed showing it off."

Lightning flashed again, highlighting the whites of Drew's eyes. And Brad, in his usual practical way, pointed to his wrist, suggesting they were wasting precious time.

"Oh, and Mr. Brennan, who was the guy you and Mrs. Brennan were talking with tonight during line dancing?"

"Which one? I talked with a lot of people." Thunder rumbled in the not-so-far-away distance.

"Right before the last song had been introduced, you guys were standing by the livestock fans. He had dark, wavy hair, a scruffy beard, full mustache. And he wore a black T-shirt."

"Artie?"

"Yeah, could be. Miah didn't know his name, but she said he grabbed her hand at the promotion table and wouldn't let go. I guess he said some pretty weird things to her a few days ago too."

"Are you serious?"

"Totally. It sounds like he's had his eye on her all week. I wouldn't wait another minute, Mr. Brennan. I'd call the cops."

"All right. I'll give them a call. Drive careful, Brandt."

"Yep."

He'd seen that look in Claire's eyes once before—when Josh had become so sick, he passed out cold right on the bathroom floor. Sheer panic would be the proper label. "Claire." He held her face in his hands and willed the fear in her to subside. "It's going to be all right. Miah probably got an idea for a song and is up at one of the barns working it out on my dad's old guitar. She's going to show up."

Claire nodded and blinked back her tears.

"No worries, now. No worries." Her body melted into his as he tried to bolster her courage with a big bear hug.

"Dad, who is Adam Chisholm? Is he the one who has the stiletto?" Drew's saucer-sized eyes were filled with questions. Questions he didn't feel like addressing at the moment. "Drew, I'll explain later. Why don't you go check inside the camper one more time? On second thought, come here, sports." He motioned with his arms to have his family gather in a small, unbroken huddle. "Let's pray."

Before lifting his petition to the flickering heavens, his family came close and bowed their heads. "Father God, it's easy to jump to scary conclusions, especially on a dark, stormy night. But the lightning also reminds us of your power and your ability to see what we cannot. God, you see Miah right now. Please point us in her direction. Help us to find her safe and sound. Help us to not be afraid. For Jesus' sake. Amen?"

A round of amens echoed his own. "All right. Drew, quick check the camper. Then you boys take my truck and check the barns, tents, and bathrooms. Mum and I will call the police and wake up some neighbors. Brad, do you have your phone?"

He nodded.

"Call us if you find her."

CHAPTER SIXTEEN

Tears bled from Miah's eyes and a low moan nudged her from the thick fogbank of unconsciousness. She lifted her head only to let it drop in her hands. Oh, the agony ... It felt as if she were shrinking—like her head might cave in on itself. And if it wasn't for her constant swallowing, her brains were going to squeeze right through her nose. The pain registered out of this world.

"Hurry, Granddad." Oh, how much longer to Barcelow Downs? She couldn't stomach any more of this jostling around in his old Holden Ute. Still, Grandmother Jannali would know what to do. Surely she'd be able to soothe the sharp, electric spasms shooting through every nerve in her body. "Hurry, Granddad! Hurry!"

A brilliant flash of lightning filled the truck and shot another bolt of pain straight through her eyeballs right down to her stomach. "Stop the Ute! I'm going to throw up!" He didn't stop. Instead, a man much younger than Granddad reached across the seat and gave her an angry backhand, spinning her head back into the floaty white space again.

Strangely, Granddad showed up on the other side of

consciousness. And just as she expected, instead of anger, compassion filled his blue eyes. Were those tears? *Don't cry, Granddad. Please, don't cry.* He shook his head and gently touched the soft spot where the lightning had entered her swollen skull.

Somehow, they had left the Ute and the bumpy two track and had been transported to the comfort of her grandparents' veranda. She had indeed shrunk! She'd become small enough to sit on Granddad's lap and rest her aching head against the reassuring rhythm beating inside his chest. He held her for the longest time, rocking her in the old wooden chair like he used to when she'd been only two or three. "Miah." Granddad's voice brushed across her ear as a whisper. "I need you to listen to me. Listen well now."

She lifted her head and met Granddad's eyes.

"There's going to be a storm, love—a very severe storm. And you're going to have to be strong and courageous if you want to weather it." She turned and gazed through the screens, searching the endless, crystal-clear blue sky.

"Look at me, dear. While it's storming, you'll want to keep your focus on me at all times. If you take your eyes off of me, it may be difficult to find me. Rest assured, child, I will never leave you or forsake you. You have my word."

Granddad paused and held her head to his chest. "Now, it's very important to stay calm through it all. There can be no screaming or crying. If you keep quiet, you'll be able to hear my voice above the tempest. And you must do exactly as I say. Do you understand?"

She nodded. "Granddad, can't you stop the storm? You have the power, don't you?"

He patted her back with a steady, gentle beat. "I do. However, if you trust me, it'll all come good, Miah. You're a brave girl, a battler. And one day, if you stand strong, you'll be more than a conqueror. You'll bring glory to my name." He sat her up and turned her face toward his. "There's one thing I don't want you to ever forget." He paused and waited for her to peer into those eternally kind eyes of his. "No matter what happens, Miah—remember, I love you. I love you with an everlasting love. And nothing, not even trouble or hardship or persecution or famine or nakedness or danger or sword, will be able to separate you from my love."

"Where is he, Claire?" He didn't need her to answer as much as he needed to voice his frustration. Trace held Claire's back tight against his chest and looked over the top of the deputy's car, past the grassy lot, and up onto the Mill Street bridge. Surely Brandt's bike would crest the hill and whine across the bridge any minute now. They'd been waiting not thirty, but seventy-five, nail-biting minutes. He and Claire weren't the only ones who were getting antsy. Much to their dismay, the police had merely made some indifferent scribbles when they'd told them about the encounter Miah had with Adam and Artie earlier in the night. Instead, they seemed much more eager to locate Brandt and talk with him. If the kid didn't show up soon, they'd track him down as if he were America's most wanted. It wouldn't go well for him at all.

He glanced over at Brad who met his eyes with an anxious frown that mirrored his own impatience. Aside from pacing a hole in the ground, what else could they do? They'd been questioned and questioned some more. And despite the lightning and spotty rain, their friends had already scoured every inch of the barns and the fairgrounds. They'd searched everywhere except ... *O God* ... He tried to shake off the disturbing thought as a deputy turned away another group of well-meaning campers from searching the riverbank and the gravel lane where Miah had last been seen.

The police said no one should go beyond the large welcome

sign until the investigators and the K-9 team arrived. And they'd made the camper off-limits too. They'd stressed the importance of leaving everything as it lay, just in case Miah had left a clue to her whereabouts. Still, nothing looked out of the ordinary to him; except that his beautiful daughter was not in her bed. *Miah, where are you?*

He couldn't stand this helpless feeling any longer. Maybe he'd try Brandt one more time. Pulling his phone from his hip, he hit redial as Claire gave his arms a squeeze. "I hear him, Trace. He's coming." Sure enough, seconds later Brandt's bike roared down the hill and across the bridge. The kid didn't even bother to break at the train tracks. Once he turned onto the dirt road, Claire released a sigh deep enough for them all.

Three more vehicles followed Brandt into the fairgrounds—two from the north and one from the south—an unmarked Crown Victoria and two SUV's, probably carrying dogs. Trace pulled Claire along until they reached Brandt's hot, ticking bike. He knew he wouldn't have to say a thing to Brandt, the anxiety in their eyes would tell him the whole, short story. Somehow words choked from Trace's throat anyway. "She hasn't shown up yet."

Brandt's tired, bloodshot eyes blinked twice before they transfixed themselves on the gravel lane behind them. Then, as if his helmet became too heavy a burden, his head dropped and hung from his slumped shoulders. When he looked up, his face had turned the pale color of fear. "She has to show up, Mr. Brennan."

At this point, Trace could hardly drum up any compassion for Brandt. The kid had kept them waiting on pins and needles for nearly an hour and a half! "What took you so long, Brandt?" He didn't let the trembling in his voice stop him from continuing with the barrage of questions that had been pent up inside his head for way too long. "Why didn't you call? Didn't you know we'd be thinking the worst?"

"I hurried as fast as I could." Brandt peeled his helmet from his head. "My bike ran out of gas about a mile and a half from the only open gas station I could find. I should have called from there. I ... didn't think of it. I'm sorry, Mr. Brennan. Then to top things off, I got a ticket on I-96. A state cop pulled me over right past the Ionia exit. I swear he ran my name through every frickin' network they have."

What could he possibly say? He had to believe the kid, and certainly his story would be easy enough to confirm. "Well, I'm glad you're here safe and sound."

The boys walked up to join them, and Josh gave Brandt a solemn, "Hey, mate."

Brandt returned a somber nod, and then his nod turned into a sad, slow wag. "I should have walked her all the way to the camper. I'm sorry. I'm so sorry."

Footsteps swished through the wet grass behind Brandt. "Mr. and Mrs. Brennan?"

Trace's first thought was reporter. However, when the petite, pleasant-looking woman standing before them introduced herself, she dispelled any doubt of her authority and her capabilities. "I'm Nicole Krueger. I'm an investigator with the Crandall County Sheriff's Department, and I've been assigned to do everything I can to help you find your daughter." Without hesitation, she turned to Brandt. "Are you Brandt DuCharme, Miah's boyfriend? I understand you were with Miah last. Am I right?"

Clearly Brandt had been shaken by her military-like demeanor. He swallowed and blinked toward Josh before he finally answered her. "Yes. To all three."

"I'd like to talk with you first then, if I may?" She didn't wait for Brandt to answer. Instead, she turned and motioned for him to follow her.

Brandt had the look of a caged tiger cat. He didn't budge from the family circle.

Josh gave him a reassuring nod. "It'll come good, mate." Even so, Brandt didn't move.

The investigator turned back toward him, her light blue eyes scrutinizing the motive for his hesitation. "Are you coming, Mr. DuCharme?"

"No." He shook his head. "I want a lawyer."

She lowered her questioning brow. "I'm not arresting you, young man. Unless of course, there's a reason you think I should. Is there, Mr. DuCharme?" Her glacier-colored eyes didn't let up; they seemed to peer deep into the crevasse that scarred Brandt's fragile heart.

Someone clasped her arms and rudely pulled her from her painless pit of oblivion, and whoever they were, they didn't seem too concerned a lightning strike had split her head in two. Without any hint of compassion, they yanked her to a sitting position and dragged her from the car. The car? The last thing she remembered, she'd been bumping along in Granddad's Ute, and then ... Oh, dear ... The man. The angry, impatient man ...

She fingered her throbbing cheek and the tender knot on her brow. Why would he do such a thing? "Please, help me. My head ... I've been hit by lightning." She leaned into his chest as he steadied her, but his grip felt anything but kind. He squeezed her arms tight and moved her away from the car. When he slammed the door, a wall of black extinguished the light, and her eyes went crazy searching for a focal point. It was way too dark ... And the man much too quiet. This could not be good.

Strangely, rather than fear, sadness overwhelmed her like a tidal wave—the same consuming sadness that once bowled her over when Kylie's granddad passed and when Dad announced they'd be leaving Amaroo Station. Both times small seeds of hope had taken root and anchored her despite the distressing reality. Not this time though. Instead, her insides rattled the cold sweat right out of her bones onto her skin, and her aching head pounded the grief straight through her teeth and out her mouth. "I'm going to throw up."

The man clenched her neck and forced her to the ground where he held her face inches from what smelled like oil, dirt, and old, musty wood. Lightning flashed and proved her nose right. Her stomach spewed the half-digested remains of Mum's pasta salad and lemonade onto an aged, wide plank floor blackened with large rings of oil stains. The mixture of sweet and sour smells threatened to make her stomach revolt again.

"Are you about finished?"

So, the man did have a voice, and not surprisingly, it matched the cruelty of his hands. Nodding, she made a move to stand and tried to sneak a peek at the pitiless person who pushed her along, but darkness masked his face and their surroundings. They were definitely inside a building. An old barn is what she'd guess—a small barn or equipment shed. The wooden floor sounded sturdy, yet it echoed of another level below their feet. If only she could see the layout, then she wouldn't hesitate to scratch his eyes and bolt.

As if he could read her thoughts, the man's grip on her arm and neck tightened. "You can scream if you want. No one is going to hear you."

Funny, the thought of screaming never entered her mind. Somehow, she knew they were hidden from the rest of the world —from Mum, Dad, her brothers, her friends ... from Brandt. Swelling tears clogged her throat while the burn of stomach acid inflamed the back of her nose.

The stranger shuffled her along the length of the vacant open area then paused to lift what felt and sounded like a heavy, wooden trap door. His hands worked together, one lifting, one squeezing her neck so tightly stars appeared before her eyes. "Watch your step."

Maybe the man had a heart after all. He loosened his grip and paused before pushing her leg forward with his own. Her boots clunked out the exact opposite beat of his own steps as they descended into an even darker, much cooler space. A tomb-like space. No, the man wasn't kind at all. And she was in trouble. Grave trouble.

"Move it." He kicked at the heel of her boot as if he were squaring up a steer in the show ring. And like a frightened beast would, she pressed into his chest refusing to take another step. Spitting an obscenity in her ear, he squeezed her upper arms and rammed his knee into her thigh. "I said, move it!"

Her leg buckled in pain, even so, she couldn't go down the stairs. She wouldn't go down the stairs—not without a fight. In one desperate move, she raised her arms to slide out of the man's grasp, and at the same time, she reached back over her shoulders, clawing for his eyes. For an instant, his fingertips dug deep into her biceps, and then he sent her tumbling face first down the rest of the stairs. *God, help me! Please, help me!*

The man rushed her, and with an angry grip on her T-shirt, he yanked her off the floor and slammed her against a hard, cement wall. A strobe of light pierced the darkness, illuminating his devilish glare. "Try that again and I'll kill you!" He shook her once more for emphasis. "I'll kill you!"

His alcohol-saturated breath hit her busted and bleeding nose but the hitch in her neck wouldn't let her turn away. *Heavenly Father, please ... see me.*

When the man finally released his grip on her, she fell back to the gritty, damp floor in a half-coherent heap. Despite the ringing in her ears, a string of American-made slurs and the angry slam of the trap door accosted her hearing. And then trembling and hysterical sobbing took over her body with a will of its own.

Miah, you must stay calm. There can be no screaming or crying. Remember, I am with you, My dear. Although she tried to obey the voice in her head, she just couldn't stifle her choking tears.

The man stomped down the stairs. "What's the matter? Are you afraid?" His laughter sounded as manic as her crying. He came closer, stooped in the blackness, and felt for her face. Grabbing hold of her jaw, he wagged it back and forth. "You're not as exempt as you thought you were, are you?"

He gave her cheek a condescending pat before he stood and walked across the small room or ... or cellar? No, it wasn't a true cellar. Lightning flashed again, pointing out a small window at the top of the wall where the concrete ended and the wood frame of the barn began—like the windows in her basement at home. Home ....

Once more the sobs started to gain momentum. Would she ever see her family again? Were they even missing her yet? *When I am afraid, I will trust in You. O God, please see me. Please keep me safe.*

CHAPTER SEVENTEEN

It seemed as if the investigator had the whole provocation planned out even before she introduced herself. Trace knew she was simply doing her job and watching out for Miah's safety, but couldn't the woman lighten up? Brandt would never hurt Miah. He was a good kid—maybe a bit self-assured at times. Still, he'd proven himself a good kid. And considering what had happened to his brother, Skye, who could blame him for being on guard?

In all her commanding presence, Sergeant Kruger stood straight as a sentinel at her post, staring Brandt down, waiting to see what he would do with her bold allegation. And Trace couldn't help feeling sorry for the poor bloke; the kid had to be shaking in his boots.

Regardless, Brandt didn't show any sign of weakness. Pulling his broad shoulders back, he answered the investigator with all the respect he could muster. "No. There's no reason you should arrest me. I haven't done anything wrong. I would just prefer to talk with you right here, by my friends."

"I don't think that would be in anyone's best interest, especially yours and your girlfriend's. I'm going to have to ask you some very personal questions about your relationship with Miah. It could get ... awkward." Her sternness melted into a soft, understanding plea. "Why don't we just step over here?"

When she made a motion to encourage him with a light pull on his elbow, none of them were ready for Brandt's heated reaction. Yanking his elbow from the investigator's reach, Brandt drew a finger and pointed it in her face. "Lady, I don't care how many badges you have in your pocket. If you touch me again, I swear, I'll knock your head clean off your shoulders."

Before Trace could shout a single "whoa!" all of the investigator's five and a half feet had brought Brandt down to his knees.

"On your face!" she barked as she maneuvered him onto his belly. Wielding her mace, the ice returned to her eyes. "Deputy!" She nodded for some assistance.

"Is this your man?"

"He's not a man. He's a cocky punk who has a problem talking to me in private. Help him up. I'll talk with him over by your car." She shook her head in irritation then turned toward them with an apologetic look.

"Trace ..." Tears accompanied the shock in Claire's eyes. "Help him."

"Sergeant Krueger, before you talk with Brandt, there's something I should explain.

It had taken five years of drought to teach him worry couldn't change a situation—only prayer and people could make a difference. That's why he didn't hesitate to call their closest friends. While his pastor, Bryce Harrison, helped him navigate the incident commander's briefing—*O Lord, please don't let Miah become an incident*—he'd seen Celia Harrison, Trina Bahkysen,

Teá Start, and even Miah's friend, Bri, huddle with Claire in a small prayer circle. Between the four of them, they'd be able to keep Claire strong.

Now he stood north of the boat launch away from all the emergency vehicles, simply watching, waiting for the K-9 team to receive their final instructions. In a moment of his own weakness, he raised his head and searched the fiery heavens for some direction ... some strength. *God, I am so afraid. Help me to trust in Your goodness. Please help me to be strong for Claire, for the boys, and especially for Miah, wherever she is.*

Somehow C.J. must have heard his silent request. He drew near, offering a strong arm of support. "Tracey, it's gonna be all right. I just know it. You gotta keep the faith, bro'."

Sniffing back his tears, Trace returned C.J.'s kind gesture. "Thanks for being here, mate. It ... it really means a lot."

"They're gonna find her. Don't you worry."

He nodded and tried to think about the good things: like how quickly the police responded and organized the volunteers to search the fairgrounds, and how the first wave of storms miraculously skirted around them. And then there had been the kind dog handler, Thomas, who removed all his concern about the light rain that had fallen. The man reassured him the rain would actually enhance the scent of Miah's trail. *Thank you, God.*

He could also count his blessings because Brandt and the investigator were able to get past their initial prejudices and find enough common ground to work together for Miah's sake. While Ms. Krueger hadn't disclosed the entire course of her conversation with Brandt, she did say the young man had been very cooperative and had even agreed to a polygraph test when she suggested it.

There were "too many disturbing questions left unanswered", is what she'd said. Like, why had their lawn chairs been strewn all over the campsite? Was there a reason Brandt had been so quick to implicate Artie and Adam? And where was the Jeep Brandt had driven to the fair earlier in the evening? This question bothered him the most. He didn't even know Brandt had access to a Jeep!

Then there'd been the offhanded remark the Slater boy made about Miah running away after Brandt had gotten all "kissy face" with her. And Ethan Turchetti agreed, saying Miah had run past his camper all upset. Hadn't he himself come upon them while they were in the middle of a tense conversation? He wanted to believe Brandt would never hurt Miah, but now after eavesdropping on the kids' chatter, it took all his will to keep his own doubt from turning to anger.

So he tried to focus on the remote possibility Miah had run into friends and decided to stay with them in order to avoid a lecture from him. However unlikely the scenario, it sure beat the disturbing alternative of Miah somehow being lured from the campground by Adam Chisholm or Artie ... Did the bloke ever offer his last name?

Anyway, despite his first impression, he should be thankful the investigator seemed competent and thorough. She'd said that depending on what the dogs uncovered and what she could learn from Adam, she'd begin to look into the prank phone calls C.J. reported Miah had been receiving. Why his friend and Miah had kept the calls to themselves was beyond comprehension.

Sergeant Krueger didn't seem to think it out of the ordinary. She'd continued to rattle off her thoughts, saying she had half a mind to investigate Drew's "Artie from Utah." After hearing what Drew and Brandt had said about the loner, the detective said it might be worth checking out. To be sure, chills had run up and down his own spine, and he'd been grateful Claire hadn't been around to hear the boys' stories. Oh, if Artie did anything to Miah ....

Drew had been wary of the bloke from the very beginning. He'd even gone so far as to check his license plate when he'd spotted him sitting in his car down by the mill. Thanks to Drew and his keen perception, they had some vital information if it turned out they needed it.

Why hadn't he clued into the guy's weirdness like Drew had? He thought the sport simply needed a friend. Except for a couple words spicing up his language, he didn't seem bad at all. He came across intelligent enough and had a respectable job. And the bloke actually liked talking about spiritual things. In fact, it had been Artie who kept bringing it up—not him. The more he thought about it, Artie had been very interested in Miah. He'd asked some polite questions about the boys, but the conversation always seemed to come back around to her. *O God, protect our little girl.*

"Trace ... Did you hear me?" C.J. nudged his side, concern dominating his kind expression.

"I'm sorry, C.J., what'd you say?"

C.J. laid an arm across his shoulder directing him back toward their circle of friends. "The sergeant's asking for you. She wants to talk with you over here, by Claire."

He followed C.J. through the wet grass over to where the women had gathered under the protection of a benevolent neighbor's awning. Claire gave him a brave smile while the detective's eyes held no clue as to her purpose for calling yet another meeting.

The investigator nodded a greeting, glanced at the threatening sky, and then tapped the ever-present black notebook in her hand. "I thought you might like to know Adam Chisholm is off the hook." She baited her forthcoming explanation with a long, impossible pause. "Apparently, he left the fairgrounds right after he talked with your daughter and Mr. DuCharme. A deputy picked him up at eleven-fifty p.m. on a DUI charge, ten minutes before Mr. DuCharme said he and Miah parted ways. Chisholm's been in the county jail since twelve-thirty a.m."

She sighed, stared at the ground, and then raised her surprisingly compassionate blue eyes to an indiscriminate spot within the circle of their friends. "I'm sorry. I hoped this investigation would be cut and dry and … impersonal."

What did she mean by that?

"We're continuing to run some checks on the man from Utah, but depending on what the dogs find, we may have to take Brandt in for further questioning."

So, what were they supposed to hope for? The possibility of Miah being taken by a stranger or someone they *thought* they knew? At the moment, he could barely stretch his mind around either option. It all seemed so unbelievable. Really, couldn't there be a chance Miah had indeed run into a friend and decided to stay the night with her? Yes, of course, it was a very real possibility.

The detective reached out and squeezed his and Claire's arms. "I'll keep you posted." Then she politely dismissed herself from the huddle.

While the rest of them stood in silent speculation, Marcus called out an obligatory thank you, which the investigator acknowledged with the wave of her notebook. If only her notebook held the answers to all the questions swirling in each of their minds. God did though. He held the answers in His mighty hands.

Trace searched the furious-looking storm clouds brewing in the heavens above them. *Please God, let Miah show up all sleepy-eyed in the morning. Bring her back to us.*

"Trace …" Relief spread across Claire's face as she nodded toward the small crowd of bystanders who had gathered around the aging, white welcome sign to wait for the K-9 team to begin their search. Rob and Amy had finally arrived—three-fifteen a.m. Considering they'd been startled from their sleep only a half hour ago, the kids had made good time.

He started to jog across the wide dirt road to get them,

however, Josh and Brandt had noticed the couple too. The two boys left their spot under the massive oak and headed for the welcome sign, marking the edge of the staging area. On their way, the two friends picked up Brad and Drew who had been milling around where the police were doing all their planning and organizing. He probably should have been over there too, but he'd answered enough questions and done enough conjecturing. He wanted some action and some answers—now!

From across the gravel turnaround, he and Claire watched the kids exchange greetings under the dim light of the modest billboard. He was thankful they had each other. Then he thought about his own brothers and wondered when and if he should put in a call to Queensland.

The young people talked for another minute or so, and then all six of them tried to cross beneath the yellow tape only to be stopped by a deputy. Brandt spoke up first, and then Josh put in his two cents. After some lengthy explanations and some finger-pointing in the direction of where he and Claire and the rest of their friends stood, the officer finally let the group of young people pass.

These kids were his daughters, his sons, his offsiders, and mates. He should be happy to see them, yet apprehension had a tight grip on his joy. Could he hold it all together for them? Could he be the rock they'd become dependent on? And could he keep his doubts hidden from Brandt?

In the way of a servant, Marcus Bakhysen stepped forward and interceded for him. His friend gave Rob and Amy a heartfelt handshake and a caring pat on the shoulder as if he were comforting the family of a dying patient. Then fielding their questions, Marcus quickly brought them up to date before they passed into the arms of their mother and then into his own.

It went well. He actually kept it all together. And even though the worry on his kids' faces tore at his confidence, their presence bolstered his hope. However, their arrival had the opposite effect on Claire. Tears broke over the rims of her blueberry-colored eyes and ran down her cheeks. He held her in his arms while the rest of their friends and family gathered around.

From a heart all too acquainted with hopeful expectations and dashed dreams, Bryce offered up a prayer of thanksgiving and petition—a petition for a good outcome, for courage and strength, for protection, for faith.

Surely there couldn't be a more comforting feeling than being surrounded by the love of friends; faithful mates who were willing to bear some of the weight of their fear. It gave him and Claire strength when they felt so very weak.

"Amen. Thank you. Thanks, you guys." Trace raised his bowed head and wiped the tears from his eyes. As he gave a grateful embrace to the friends who stood closest to him, he noticed Jerry, the operation manager, waiting respectfully outside their circle.

"Mr. Brennan, we're ready. Did you want to listen in?"

"Aye. Thank you. Claire, you want to come too, sweetheart?"

She nodded and wiped her eyes as they followed the operation manager over to the staging area where the tailgates of the two SUV's were opened up to serve as a makeshift command center.

Initially, when Trace had inquired about following behind the K-9 team, Jerry had discouraged him for reasons he hadn't considered—for reasons he didn't want to consider. Then after a moment's thought, the compassionate man had invited him and Claire to listen in while the search was coordinated from the staging area via radio.

Everyone who responded to their call for help had been nothing less than accommodating. There were a few standouts, like Thomas Borrink, the man who would be following Miah's trail. In the short time Trace had talked with the dog handler, he had somehow developed a special bond with the man. Despite the fact Thomas looked to be pushing sixty, he had a positive, energetic demeanor and seemed completely sold out to helping them. The man had said he hoped to be the one to find Miah and bring her home—and not for prideful reasons. Trace could tell the man truly cared.

Outfitted with reflective vest, head lamp, flashlight, and radio, Thomas and his bloodhound, Rex, stood ready at the river's edge. The kind man gave his dog a pat, then seconds later, let the eager hound's lead line out with a firm command to "check."

With his nose to the ground, Rex ran in a senseless course around a wide area, including the boat launch. After thirty seconds or so, Thomas called the hound back in and fitted him with his own dog-sized, reflective vest. After securing the lead line to a clip on the back of the harness, another man, Keith, attached a yellow glow stick to the side of Rex's outfit. Keith, as it turned out, would be serving as "flank" for Thomas and his dog. His job was to keep their way clear and safe.

The incident commander stepped up, and from a plastic zip-lock bag, produced Miah's olive-colored T-shirt, the one with the randomly placed square rhinestones and even smaller square sequins. She'd worn it to the concert already five and a half long hours ago.

Thomas took Miah's shirt and put it right in the hound's nose. "Got it? Got it, Rex?" With the next command, "seek," the bloodhound took off again, seemingly sniffing all about without any rhyme or reason. He even came all the way over by them, past the big leafy oak. Then suddenly, he turned back toward the river. For a split-second Rex paused and buried his nose in the dirt before making a beeline toward the gravel lane and their travel trailer.

The dog seemed happy and unaware of the dread paling Claire's face when he circled the grassy area in front of their awning then trotted, nose to the ground, past their camper, and continued further down the gravel lane.

He felt his own blood drain from his face. Miah never made it to the camper! Claire clutched his arm, and her breath stuttered as they watched the headlamps of Thomas and Keith disappear into the woods where the gravel lane came to an abrupt dead end.

For what seemed like an eternity, all those in the staging area remained unmoving. They saw nothing. They heard nothing. Then Rob showed up, worry lines creasing his forehead. "Any news, Dad?"

He shook his head in disappointment as the radio squawked to life.

"Base, do you copy?"

Jerry shot him a tentative look. "Go ahead, Thomas."

"The subject followed a freshly laid two-track for about twenty yards into the woods. A vehicle turned around back here and then drove out. At the turnaround point, we located an earring matching the description the subject had been wearing. We're still on her trail, heading back out of the woods."

"Ten-four. Thanks."

Jerry's eyes skipped past his own and met with the investigator's, where he seemed to blink out a secret message. She nodded then stepped over to one of the squad cars and spoke to a deputy. The deputy didn't seem alarmed but simply popped the trunk of his car and pulled out another roll of yellow tape.

"Jerry?" His voice caught in his throat. "What happened? What are you thinking?"

The operation manager shook his head and shrugged. "I'm not sure, Mr. Brennan. It sounds like Miah came back out of the woods. Whether she had been in a vehicle or on foot, I don't know. We'll have to wait and see what the investigators find. They'll be able to tell. There's bound to be some tire tracks and footprints."

"What if Miah got in a car? Can the dog still follow her scent?"

Jerry nodded. "Sometimes, Mr. Brennan. If the vehicle was made after nineteen seventy-eight it's required to ventilate with the outside air. Of course, it helps if a window or sunroof is opened."

"I see." His mind desperately tried to perceive why Miah would have gone into the dark woods in the middle of an electric storm and why she would have felt the need to sneak away. The only answer he could come up with was—she wouldn't. Unless perhaps, she'd been lured by the charm of a college-aged kid driving an open-air Jeep. Had she and Brandt taken a quick joyride that turned tragic and Brandt was afraid to admit negligence?

When the headlamps of Thomas and Keith came bobbing back out of the woods with a little yellow light leading the way, Trace shook the terrible thought from his mind. He gave Claire a reassuring squeeze and kept his eyes glued to the glow stick. Bouncing along the way, it kept on a straight path toward their travel trailer. Stop Dog. Stop right there. He didn't. His nose followed an invisible trail leading right through the group of bystanders and past the white and green welcome sign.

Where the dirt road split, the dog had to make a choice—continue going straight, under the bridge, and into the field on the other side of Mill Street, or take the right fork to the north, and head out of the fairgrounds. Rex didn't waver even for a second. He took the right fork as if he were following a trail of kibble.

At Mill Street, the search team stopped to wait for a late-night grain truck to pass, and then they crossed over to the southbound lane. Brandt broke from the small crowd, his hands slapping the top of his head in a show of unbelief. The kid looked so pitiful standing there all alone in the shadows. This time, try as he might, Trace couldn't drum up any compassion for the boy. Josh, being the better man, came to his mate's rescue. He slapped Brandt on the back and they both took chase after the bloodhound, only to be whistled back by a deputy. The two friends stood in the middle of the green, helplessly watching like everyone else as the trio of lights bobbled across the train tracks, over the Mill Street Bridge, and headed up the big, curving hill to … to only the Lord knew where.

CHAPTER EIGHTEEN

"*You have searched me, Lord, and You know me. You know when I sit and when I rise; You perceive my thoughts from afar. You discern my going out and my lying down; You are familiar with all my ways ... Where can I go from Your Spirit? Where can I flee from Your presence? If I go up to the heavens, You are there; if I make my bed in the depths,*" (*even in the basement of a barn, Lord*) "*You are there.*"

Whispering the one hundred and thirty-ninth Psalm seemed to help burn through the throbbing fog in Miah's brain. It gave her the peace she needed to stay calm, because every time lightning flashed, the man's menacing image came into focus.

He was sitting there on what looked like a low workbench, staring at her, taking long, slow drags on that infinite cigarette of his. She could put up with its thick stench as long as the fiery, orange ashes continued to give her a point of reference in the darkness of their concrete crypt. However, the perfumy smell of alcohol just might put her stomach over the edge again.

The fermented liquid sloshed up and down for the umpteenth time before its glass container finally clinked down on a hard surface. Then the man shifted, and his feet scraped onto the floor as he stood from his perch.

"Miah, are you awake?"

He knew her name? Without moving or breathing, she watched as the reliable glow of the cigarette moved upward, grew in intensity, then dropped to the floor in a shower of lava-colored sparks.

Dread seized her soul as the stranger's footsteps came close and stopped in front of her. "Are you alive?" For a tense eternity he simply stood there.

Had he lost her in the darkness or was he listening for signs of life? She couldn't hold her breath much longer.

"Miah." A boot nudged her rib.

How did he know her name? And what did he want with her?

He squatted down, and his stale breath hit her tender and swollen nose, dousing her stomach in a tsunami of nausea. Even though her gut revolted and the man's hot fingertips patted her neck for a pulse, she willed herself to lay still—dead still. *Hide my heartbeat, Lord. Hide my heartbeat.*

In the midst of her silent, desperate plea, doubt slithered in and hissed a terrible lie in her ear. *Your faith is a joke, Miah. It's dormant and insignificant, like a tiny mustard seed. It will never help you.* She fell for the deceit only for an instant. And the man found what he'd been searching for.

His fingertips left the pulse in her neck and lingered on the curve of her collarbone before they went exploring further down her chest—too far down her chest! Gulping air back into her burning lungs, she smacked his hand away and cowered closer to the wall.

"Oh! So, you are awake." His taunting laughter slapped against the cold slab walls as he grabbed at her arm. "Come here, Miah. I'm not going to hurt you."

"Who ... Who are you?" Even though her imagination had conjured up a sketch of the man, she needed to know the truth.

"I can't believe you don't remember me, Miah. I'm going to be your best friend." He dropped to his knees and fished around until his fingers found the button of her jean shorts. "You won't be able to live without me."

She lashed out in sheer panic. Her arms and legs flailed wildly in the dark, determined to protect her body, desperate to preserve her life. Even so, the man kept her near and subdued her with his angry strength. "Didn't I say I'd kill you? Did you think I was kidding?" While one of his hands pinned her wrists to the floor above her head, the other wrung her neck like a dishcloth. Blood rushed to her eye sockets as his voice growled a vicious threat.

Remember, Miah. Neither life nor death can separate you from My love.

"I don't want to die. Jesus, please. Save me." Her voice was not her own. It sounded heavier and garbled as if it were coming up from the waters of the deep.

I am your refuge and dwelling place; underneath are My everlasting arms. I am here, My beloved.

She tried to reach out for the comforting words, only the man wouldn't let her go. He kept tugging at her, pulling her back from her peaceful, dreamy descent.

"That's right, Miah. Pray and see if God will save you." The man's jeering, stinking laughter sounded as thick and warped as her own voice.

O Lord. Don't hide Your face from me. Hear my prayer, listen to my cry for mercy; in Your faithfulness and righteousness come to my relief. At first her tears caught in her throat. Then once they squeezed past the painful swelling, they tumbled over the rim of her eyes and down into her ears. "Please ... have mercy," she whimpered.

"Shut up! If there's no mercy for me. There's no mercy for you."

She struggled against his hold until a feeling of futility set in and deemed groveling her only option. "I ... I have money. You can have it."

An angry curse blasted her ears as the man's hand smothered her nose and mouth. "I said, shut your pie hole, Miah!"

Please forgive me, Lord, for my many sins. Please, don't bring me into judgment. For no one living is righteous before You.

Her lungs burned for their last breath while the evil mocker had his way. Yet God, in his mercy, let her escape the man's abuse. Her mind flew across the red sands of the Simpson desert, past the grass plains of the channel country, and then soared above the muddy Thomson River before it dipped low over the welcoming homestead of Amaroo Station and nestled her in her mother's embrace.

Peace and love were the only things she felt as Mum wiped away her tears. And while fear and sorrow faded into things forgotten, she became a little girl again, snuggling with Mum on their wide, screened veranda. For a while, they simply enjoyed the creaking rhythm of the wicker, rocking chair. Then Mummy's sweet voice joined the swaying beat with the comforting words of a favorite childhood song. "Jesus loves me, this I know. For the Bible tells me so. Little ones to him belong." Mum's voice cracked with emotion.

"Mummy, keep singing. Please keep singing." Mum smiled despite her tears and nodded. "They are weak, but He is strong. Yes, Jesus loves me. Yes, Jesus loves me."

"Again, Mummy. Sing it again." She listened in peace until pain so unbearable yanked her back to the reality of her nightmarish ordeal. "Oww ..." The taste of blood filled her first moments of consciousness. She lay there soothing the pain of her punctured lip with the tip of her tongue and tried to control her violent trembling.

Except for her breathing and the distant rumble of thunder, a deep settling silence fell over the tomb-like room. She might be alive, but she was not well. Her stomach heaved then began to pitch.

She rolled to her side and began to wretch when the man swooped in from the darkness, his anger flaring. "Come here." He covered her bloodied mouth with one hand while his other grabbed her waist and pulled her up the stairs, dragging her hobbled legs behind her. At the top, he shoved the trap door open and tossed her up the last two steps.

Landing in a stunned heap, her mouth twanged with salivation as she tried to retrieve her shorts from around her ankles. Unfortunately, the man didn't give her a chance. He hefted her past her original slew of vomit and past the car. Then his arm squeezed her belly hard as he paused to slide the barn door open. With a great heave, he sent her tumbling down a wet grassy slope, where she relieved herself of the panicky, churning in her stomach. Although the stomach acid stung the quickly swelling hole in her lip, the fresh night air acted like a balm to her soul. She buttoned her shorts then lay on her back, letting the cool sprinkles of rain wash away her sorrow and pain. *Lord, thank You for keeping me alive. Thank you for being here with me. Please show me the way out of here.*

Hope emerged as lightning spanned the heavens and reflected off a forest of trees. The small clearing and barn were surrounded by tall thick woods. If she had the strength and half a mind, she could run. Surely, she could find a hiding place out there. And in the morning, if the sky cleared, the sun could be her guide to the east, west, north ... south? Which way was home?

Footsteps swished through the tall grass. "All right, Miah. Let's go. I need some sleep." *O God, if there's a way to escape from this crazy man, show me. Please show me what to do.* She rolled to her hands and knees and crawled through the wet grass toward a lone juniper. As she prepared to bolt, the man's strong hand pulled her back on her heels.

"You're persistent, but not very bright. Didn't I say bad behavior won't be tolerated?" He spun her around and planted his fist square in her eye. Jagged streaks of red and white light bounced around inside her brain as the here and now vaporized into a deep, black hole.

A loud crack of thunder tore into her sleep, waking her to the roar of heavy rain pounding on the earth and barn above her. Instead of the dark of night, gray morning light tinted the small window, making the shadows less ominous. So, there would be an end to this everlasting night after all. Relief came in the form of a tearful sigh as the morning dawned dark and drear on the raised hackles of an angry storm. *God, please don't let this be a sign of things to come.*

Miah tried lifting her head, but pain blocked her effort. She hurt all over—her top, her bottom, and her in between. The chain binding her neck and hands to the bottom of the stairs rattled as she turned on her side. Squinting with her good eye, she could just make out the figure of the man. He looked quite harmless, sprawled out there on the workbench, oblivious to the storm raging above them. She knew better. In fact, if she were free, she'd make a straight track for the bottle he'd been nursing last night. She'd break it over his ugly, evil head, and then she'd slash his bloody throat—*if* she were free.

But she wasn't free. The weight of her chains made sure she wouldn't forget it. And her sorrow and deep despair magnified the pain scissoring through her body as she rolled to her back and prayed the desperate prayer of Jabez. *Oh, God, let your hand be with me, and keep me from any more harm so I can be free from pain.*

CHAPTER NINETEEN

Trace watched in unbelief as deep, soul-searing pain seeped from Claire's eyes. Her eyes weren't the only pair bearing the evidence of fear. Trace had seen it in the eyes of everyone who heard the Lieutenant's report. At first, the shock of Artie's past conviction for a sex crime brought everyone's efforts to a screeching halt. Then, like a seized pump being greased, hope kicked in and gradually put everyone back in operation—if only at half speed.

It seemed strange how each person had their own way of dealing with the dread of what might be, and it all unfolded as if in slow motion. Claire sank hard into his chest; the investigator turned her back to them and pulled out her phone; the operation manager cleared his throat; while Brandt continued to pace in an endless, nervous circle. Everyone else stood in some form of whispering huddle or comforting embrace. But Trace held it all in until the stress became too much and forced his heart to skip an essential beat.

This unreal situation was all his fault. He should have watched over Miah more carefully. He should have clued in on the oddness of Artie, or rather, R.D.—short for Ronald Duane

Maddox, as the police pointed out. And he never should have brought his family to this septic, wicked country. What had he been thinking? How in heaven's name had he believed the still small voice inside his head belonged to God? Claire had been right. His desire to get out from under their debt and away from a bloody drought had been simply that—desire—not some divine calling from the Invisible Orchestrator.

He wasn't angry at God. No, he wasn't in any position to be. His beautiful daughter could be crying out for His mercy right now. God alone had the power to make this whole thing turn out good, or with the stroke of His finger, He could change their lives forever. They had no choice except to trust the Holy One would keep their best interest in mind.

"Trace ... Claire ..." Marcus' sympathetic voice whispered behind them. "News10 is here. They're wondering if they could speak with you."

Claire's eyes wore no apology as she choked out a tearful reply. "I can't, Trace. I ... I'm a wreck."

"It's all right, sweetheart. Will you be okay with Trina while I go talk with them?"

Claire accepted Trina's comforting embrace and nodded to send him on his way.

"I'll be back as soon as I can, love." He hated leaving her, but the police had said it would be important to get Miah's story out to the media. The radio and TV stations were their best allies in helping to find Miah quickly. The more people who were exposed to her picture, the better chance they had of finding her.

Unfortunately, the severe weather rolling in had halted the bloodhound's search and would also be competing for news time. The National Weather Service had issued a severe thunderstorm warning about a half hour ago, around five-thirty a.m. With any luck, the news stations wouldn't be too occupied tracking all the storms to run Miah's video in a timely manner.

Time ... the one thing everyone seemed concerned with.

Everyone except Marcus. Trace's good friend had canceled several appointments at the hospital this morning to help him wade through the bombardment of attention. Marcus stood at his side during two other media interviews and had articulately filled in the blanks when emotion had choked his own thoughts and words.

"Mr. Brennan!" Trace turned to see the lieutenant trot after him. The tall, bald-headed man had arrived an hour after the bloodhounds had determined Miah's trail had indeed left the fairgrounds. He seemed to be a bit of a hotshot, a take-charge kind of guy who rattled the investigator's chain. Who could blame him though? With his line of work overseeing major cases involving violent crimes—*O God, please protect Miah*—he had to be somewhat case-hardened and brash.

Still, the lieutenant wasn't so sharp-edged that he didn't notice the blood rush from Claire's face when he had introduced himself, impressive title and all. The man had taken time to reassure Claire that Miah wasn't necessarily in harm's way. She just happened to be missing under suspicious circumstances, which also fell under the big umbrella of major case investigations. And now, since the police had followed up on Sergeant Kruger's hunch and had linked a Ronald Duane Maddox and his disturbing criminal record to Artie's, or R.D.'s license plate and silver Camry, the lieutenant's presence proved even more justified and welcomed.

"Mr. Brennan." The lieutenant braced himself against the wind. "A couple of tips. When you're speaking with the media, keep your statement brief and to the point. Talk about the pertinent information: what Miah was wearing; what she looks like; the birthmark on her arm. Don't forget to mention her accent. And show her picture. Show it a lot. Don't let them get you off track about how you and the family are doing. We all care, but we don't need to waste the precious thirty seconds they'll give you. This is about Miah. The longer her face is up on the TV screen, the better. And at this point, don't say anything about Ronald Maddox or the silver Camry, nothing has been substantiated. We have eight thousand dollars to offer as a reward for Miah's safe return. Do you have the Silent Observer number?"

"I, uh … No."

"I'll make sure someone passes it on to the reporter."

"Th-thank you."

"Oh, and, Mr. Brennan, as soon as you're done there, it might be a good time for a polygraph test, if you are still up for it. A deputy is giving Mr. DuCharme a ride into Grand Rapids right now."

He nodded. If it hadn't been for the guidance of Faith Tubergen, he would have been highly offended at such a request. Thankfully, the police had the foresight right at the very beginning to contact the National Center for Missing and Exploited Children. The NCMEC had in turn referred them to H.O.P.E and Mrs. Tubergen.

Although the older woman had driven through the wee hours all the way from White Cloud, her eyes sparkled with kindness when she'd finally arrived. He never would have guessed this zippy, grandmotherly widow had experienced the nightmare of her own daughter's abduction. Tragically, her eighteen-year-old daughter, Heather, had never been found. After years of working through her grief, Mrs. Tubergen decided to devote her retirement years volunteering her assistance to families who were walking the same agonizing tightrope as she and her family once had.

With a name like Faith, how could they not trust her? So far she had been a deep well of helpful information, and she'd promised to walk with them every step of the way. Right from the very start she had explained, while it wouldn't always feel like it, the law enforcement officers were their partners in pursuing a common goal. She stressed how important it would be to establish a relationship based on mutual respect and trust.

She had even suggested they volunteer early to take a polygraph test so the police could move more quickly onto other suspects. So, Brandt agreed to go first, and then Trace would head downtown too—as soon as this news interview was behind him—and after he made a call to his loved ones in Queensland.

How in the world would he explain this to his family? Except for his dad, they all thought he'd lost his mind bringing his family here. What would they think now? And what would Claire's parents say? The blue-blooded Judge McKinnon would jump in a plane and be here lickety-split, throwing his great name and power around without much effect. Even so, he had to let his family know—right after he talked with News10.

The day would be ending at Amaroo station with probably no rain clouds to be seen. In contrast, the Michigan morning had barely broken as dark gray clouds swirled above them, dousing everything with heavy buckets of rain. *God, please stop the rain so the search for Miah can resume.* Trace shook the rain from his jacket and then stepped up into Kortman's huge motor home where moments ago, Rob, Amy, and Claire had taken shelter from the storm.

He held Rob's cell phone high in the air and walked the length of the big bus, hoping to find reception. There they were —five bars. He plunked his weary body down in the driver's seat and leaned his head against the cool condensation fogging up the window. On the other side of the glass, lightning flashed, the wind blew, and fierce rain clawed against the pane as if it were an evil demon begging to take residence in his empty soul.

If he felt empty, how did Claire feel? Desperate? Despondent? At the encouragement of Faith Tubergen, he had tried to get Claire to take a nap. And as soon as he made these phone calls, he'd go back and lay down with her. He'd hold her until the police were ready for him to go downtown.

He stared at Rob's phone not sure how to operate the new-fangled thing, and in prayerful hope, his right arm covered his own phone where it rested on his hip. The police had told him to keep his line clear just in case Miah tried to call or ... or in case someone else, someone like Ronald Maddox tried to call.

As his finger pressed hard on the international prefix, his heart skipped another beat, and his hand shook like the hind legs of a newborn calf. How in the world were Mum and Dad's nerves going to handle this news?

"Hello?" Mum's perky voice sang into his ear.

"Hi, Mum. It's Trace."

"Oh, Trace! How are you? You'll never believe it! I just got off the phone with Anna Barcelow. She had called wondering how all of you were doing. She said she tried to call you earlier today after she'd suddenly got a strong sense to pray for your family. And here you are!" Laughter accused his ear. "Everything's all right, isn't it? How's the fair going?"

"It's been going fine. And you and Dad are doing well?"

Rob crept up and took a seat in the passenger side of the cab, offering another cup of coffee.

"Aye. We're all in full feather. It's been very busy here with the muster—hard yakka, you know. But it's been a good season. You're not getting sentimental and longing to come ride the dusty cattle track with us, are you?" Mum chuckled.

"Right now, I wish we were all back home helping with the muster." But actually ... We do need Anna's prayers. We need yours too, Mum. We're in ... a bit of a tough spot. I reckon Dad's out at one of the stock camps, isn't he?" He tried not to let his voice fall.

"What is it, love? What's happened?"

"Maybe I should talk with Dad. Is he there?"

"He's outside with your brother. Troy dropped off an empty

trailer. They're going to load cull cattle in the morning. I'll ... I'll go get him. I'll be right back, dear."

Mum's voice was a dead giveaway. She'd already become upset. And she would run right out to the cattle yard and alert Dad that something was very wrong in America. And after passing a few silent or not so silent questions between the three of them, they would all pace into the kitchen where Dad would pick up the phone with a tonnage of apprehension in his voice. *O God, help me break this to them gently. Please give me words of hope and not despair. Thank you for letting Troy be there with them.*

He covered the receiver with his fingers and directed his comment toward Rob. "Nana's getting Granddad. He and Uncle Troy are outside in cattle yard."

Rob nodded. "It's probably a good thing Uncle Troy is there."

"Aye. My thoughts exactly." Through the cell phone, he could hear the screened door slap against its frame, and then the voices he loved so dearly picked up definition as they drew near to the phone, which had surely been left on the big, mahogany kitchen table.

"Tracey?"

"Dad ... It's ... it's good to hear your voice."

"You too, son."

He let the silence linger too long.

"Trace? Is everything all right?"

"I ... I don't know how to tell you this. It seems so unbeliev-able. We can't ... find Miah. And uh, there's a chance she may have been taken by somebody—a stranger. We don't know right now. We're praying she'll show up real soon."

"What do you mean? Where, Trace? Where did this happen? Did you call the police?"

"Straight away, Dad—right when we noticed she hadn't come back to the camper. I woke up last night, and she wasn't in her swag."

"You're at the fair?"

"Aye."

"Was she with her friends? Certainly, they know something."

"Uh, yeah. With her boyfriend." That wouldn't settle well.

"A boyfriend? She's only a little girl, a beautiful little girl, Trace." Dad's silence fairly hinted of ... disappointment? Sadness?

"She's seventeen now, Dad. And the boy, he's a good kid. He wouldn't do anything to hurt Miah. I'm sure of it."

He tried to redirect Dad's concern by telling him how the bloodhound had followed Miah's trail into the woods and back out again and how they all watched the dog disappear over the big hill on Mill Street. He explained how the police were positive Miah had been in a car and how the dog handler had run a "skip trail" for almost fifteen miles straight south on Mill Street, otherwise known as M-50, until the road and the search had come to a dead end at Cutter Creek Road.

He told Dad how the terrific thunderstorm, which was beating upon them now, had blown in from the south and stopped everything just as morning had begun to dawn. However, he didn't tell Dad about the eighty-hectare cattle station, just east of Mill Street, which had plenty of space for someone to hide out. And to the west, there were hectares upon hectares of deeply wooded, state hunting land—a prime spot to dump a body. Of course, this information would not be helpful for Dad to know, nor had the police voiced any concern. His own morbid fears and speculations were simply taunting his imagination.

How could he not think the worst though? Shortly after everyone had been informed of Ronald Maddox's one-time felony conviction on a criminal sexual conduct charge, he and Pastor Bryce had overheard Sergeant Krueger speaking with a newcomer to the small battalion of law enforcement officers—a blue-jacketed FBI agent. Bryce had choked on a swallow of coffee, and his own knees had nearly buckled when they'd heard the words, "Ronald Maddox," "open cases," and "murder." He would never mention this to Claire, nor to his parents, and he almost wished he hadn't heard those startling words himself. At the same time, he should probably be glad Bryce didn't have to carry the horrible secret around by himself.

"So now what, Trace? Are the police investigating this Ronald Maddox bloke? And will the dogs be able to pick up Miah's scent when the storm lets up?"

"Yes, Dad. They're checking him out, and I'm sure as soon as it's possible, they'll resume the tracking."

"We should be there. I'm so ... I can hardly belie—Did you call the Australian Embassy? They'll get things moving. They'll move a mountain if they have to."

"No, I didn't even think of it. The police are doing a good job, Dad. But ... I'll call."

"Why don't you let me call, Trace. You've got enough to worry about. I'll check and see if they can arrange some reasonable flights for your mum and me. I'm sure the Judge and Mrs. McKinnon would want to come too. Did you ring them?"

"I'm going to ring them as soon as I hang up with you."

"How are Claire and the boys?"

"She's holding on. She's trying to get a little rest. We've been up all night. And Rob and Amy are sitting right here. The other boys seem to be doing fine too. We simply keep hoping and praying, you know. And we have a lot of good friends who are supporting us."

"Your friends from church? They're there?"

"Yeah, they've been here all night. Dad, listen. You don't need to come—not yet. You've got the muster to finish, and there's not much you can do but pray anyway. You can pray right where you are."

"No, we want to be there. Your brothers and Thom Barcelow can take care of things around here."

"All right. You do what you feel you have to."

The conversation came to an end with Dad entreating the God of Salvation with a heart-felt plea for Miah's safe return. Instead of bringing comfort, the prayer only magnified the weighty burden of guilt that had been pulling on him all night long. Oh, what he wouldn't give to undo the last five years. He'd welcome a hundred years of drought if they could all still be living in the protective isolation of Amaroo Station.

Why? Why did he have to bring his family here? All for the sake of doing something good? Of being part of something bigger than himself? If anything happened to Miah, he'd never be able to forgive himself. Claire and the boys would never be able to forgive him.

As if it were heaven's job to add to his heavy load, small pellets of hail mixed with the pounding rain and beat upon the RV's big windshield and his wavering faith. "Robbie ... Do you hate me?"

"What?" Rob turned from the hypnotizing, rain-splattered view. "Of course not, Dad."

"I'm sorry, son. I'm so sorry for bringing you here, for pulling you away from your dreams so I could have mine. I'm afraid it's turning into a horrible nightmare."

"Dad." A mixture of pity and grace showed up in Rob's eyes. "This is not your fault. You're not talking sense. Miah's going to show up. You've got to keep the faith."

"Rob, you ... you don't know what I know." His voice cracked under the pressure of his emotion. "I'm so afraid. I don't know what to do." He took a deep breath and apologized for the renegade tear escaping his right eye.

"It's okay, Dad. Don't lose heart. Our part right now is to believe God, to let Him be who He is, and to trust He'll do what is eternally best. Isn't that exactly what you told me when I put up such a big barney about coming to the U.S.? And you were right. We must believe God is working behind the scenes. No matter what happens, Dad, we have to trust God is working out His purposes for our good and for Miah's good. She's going to be okay. We're going to be okay."

"You're too right, Rob." He sniffed back another tear. "Thanks for setting your old man straight. I don't know what I'd do without you." A small, self-conscious grin pulled at his cheek, and a long-awaited phone call buzzed at his hip.

"Dad, your phone!" Rob's eyes reflected the same determined hope that rushed like a strong dose of adrenaline through his own body.

He yanked his phone from his belt. "Rob, I don't recognize the number? I don't know who it is!" In a flurry of nervous energy, he pushed the door open to the wind and rain and bolted for the staging area and the investigator. Rain and hail pelted his head as he shouted into the phone. "Hello!" Nothing but the ominous swishing of white noise replied to his greeting. Or ... or could that be breathing? "I said, bloody g'day! Answer me you beast!"

CHAPTER TWENTY

"For goodness sake, Trace. I can hear you already! What are you yelling for?"

"Ben?" No! The disappointment was more than he could take. Like the pouring rain, hope fell from his heart as his knees splashed down in a muddy puddle.

"Trace? Are you there, Trace?" His friend called out from the soaked cell phone as if he were a genie in a bottle begging to be freed. But he couldn't save Ben Ellison. He couldn't save his precious Miah.

Just when despair began to claw at his back, two sets of footsteps splashed up behind him. "Hey, bro'." C.J. joined him in the puddle and wrapped his big arms around him in a cloak of encouragement. "It's gonna be all right, man."

Rob crouched down and hemmed him in on the right. "Dad, let me take the call."

Trace's hand sat limp on his thigh, relinquishing the phone to his son.

"Hello?"

Ben Ellison's reply twittered above the roar of the rain.

"Mr. Ellison, this is Rob."

More energy chirped from the cell phone.

"Yeah, a lot of people say I sound like him." Still more chatter. "You've got a new number? All right. I'll let my dad know."

As Ben's voice chortled on, C.J. tugged at his shoulder. "Let's get you out of this rain, buddy." He didn't resist C.J.'s compassionate suggestion. He needed someone to pick him up and carry this heavy weight for a little bit.

"You're coming in tomorrow, did you say? Uh ... no worries, Mr. Ellison. I'll make sure someone's there to meet you. 2:15 p.m., Delta flight 4716. Got it." Rob paused as if etching the details on his brain. "I'm sorry, what'd you say? My dad? Well, uh ... Actually, he's right here."

He waved Rob off. How could he explain this nightmare to Ben without blubbering into the phone like an idiot?

"Mr. Ellison? Just a minute, okay?"

All three of them stood and sloshed back toward to the Kortman's big motorhome. Rob waited ten sopping wet meters before he handed over the phone.

Miah tried to focus on anything but the steady pattering of rain. The sound made waiting difficult. And the incessant dripping in the back corner of their underground cave wasn't helping either. She had to go—bad! Still, she would never dream of waking the sleeping dragon because that might be suicide. No, she could wait. God would help her wait. All through the long, soggy night He had been her help, *an ever-present help in trouble. Thank you, Lord.*

God's presence had been so constant; He even showed up in her fitful dreams. And every time she woke to the crashing thunder, He had filled her mind with calming thoughts. Every time her pain and fear became more than she could bear, His comforting voice sang Psalm 121 over her, steady as the falling rain. Surely, God would give her patience.

I lift up my eyes to the hills—where does my help come from? My help comes from the Lord, the Maker of heaven and earth. He will not let my foot slip—He who watches over me will not slumber; indeed, He who watches over Israel will neither slumber nor sleep. The Lord watches over me—the Lord is the shade at my right hand; the sun will not harm me by day nor the moon at night. The Lord will keep me from all harm—He will watch over my life ...

Thank you, Jesus, for watching over me when I am so afraid. Please don't abandon me. Please help me find a way out of here.

For the hundredth time, she silently pulled at the plastic cable ties that bound her hands to the thick chains and bottom step. If only she could get her teeth on those ties, she'd gnaw her way through them, but another cable tie and chain held her neck in a choke hold, far away from her hands.

She eased her aching head back to the floor. Her nose and her left eye, which had completely swollen shut, pulsed with pain, and her right eye ... well, *thank you God,* it still worked. She squinted then stared at the planked ceiling above her. It looked much like the tack shed back home on Amaroo Station, including the silvery drape of cobwebs.

Amaroo station ... When would her parents make the call to Amaroo, to the family? Certainly, her parents were missing her by now. Wouldn't they ring Amaroo first thing? No, they would call Brandt, and when he didn't know where she was, they would surely call the police, wouldn't they? Yes, they would search the barns, the bathrooms, the entire fairgrounds, and they might even search the river. And then what? How would they ever find her? They wouldn't. They won't. It was hopeless ... unless ... unless she found a way to escape.

She pressed her fists into the persistent ache in her gut that had developed sometime during the sleepless hours of the night. While her mind had ridden the emotional rollercoaster of fear and hope, courage and despair, the pain had crept to her right side and now enveloped her back too. She couldn't stand it any longer. She had to relieve herself. But if she wet herself, she might miss an opportunity to run. She would have to wake the man. But how? What could she say without angering him? *God, please let this go good.*

"Mister ..." When the man didn't respond, fear pooled around her eyelids in the form of hot tears. She swallowed and tried again, this time a little louder. "Mister ... Please, wake up."

The man's right hand rose from its resting place and held his forehead. He cleared his throat then spat on the floor before swinging one leg off the bench and then the other. Sitting up with a curse, he propped his elbows on his knees and went back to cradling his brow with his hand.

Even sitting down, he looked monstrous—taller than Dr. Bakhuyzen—and dark hair with waves. Not black like Brandt's though. As fear trickled down her cheeks, she held in a whimper and watched the monster come to life. When he finally lifted his eyes to her pitiful state, he seemed almost surprised by her presence. Still, they were dark and full of malice—like she'd imagined.

"Don't you dare cry."

She sheltered her swollen, trembling lips within one another while the man's eyes bored into her with hatred. She couldn't take the tension any longer. "I ... I have to go to the bathroom ... very bad."

He stood and scratched himself. "I do too. You're going to have to wait." He picked up the bottle and peered through the glass before taking a long swig and swishing it around in his cheeks like mouthwash. In the distance, thunder continued to roll. He turned and glanced up at the small, gloomy picture of the outside world before clapping the bottle down on his makeshift bed. "The storm won't let up, will it?"

Concealing the fear that set her heart in a crazy pace, she

gave the slightest nod in agreement as he scuffed his apathetic feet toward her. She could finally get a good look at the beast—if she dared.

He paused and stooped over her. "Where'd your pretty face go, Miah? What a shame. You must be in a lot of pain."

Her breath stopped short. She knew those dark skeptical eyes! The carefully trimmed mustache! They belonged to the jumped-up Yankee from the fair, the man Brandt had called Jack something or other. Despite her battered features, recognition must have shown through her one good eye.

"So, you do remember me. It took you awhile, Miah." His lips curled in a sarcastic sneer, making it clear he enjoyed the power he had over her. Yes, she'd seen his wicked grin before—at the horse barn, at the promotion table, and at the line dancing. He must have been watching her, planning this all along.

He stood and trotted up the stairs leaving her brain staggering from its revelation.

The moment he shoved the trap door open and tramped across the planked floor above her, tears burst from her soul like a raging flood. *O God, why didn't you stop him? Certainly, you could have!* While the sliding barn door above her opened with a rusty protest, God kept silent. Even so, she kept on with her desperate inquiry. *Is this the punishment for my sin? Please, have mercy on me! Save me!* All too soon, the door screeched closed in its metal track, and hysterical fear tore at her last thread of rational thinking as the man's footsteps backtracked across the wooden floor. "Oh, God ... please."

My grace is sufficient for you, Miah. For My power is made perfect in weakness.

No! No, please I can't do this! I don't want to do this. I ... I don't know what to do.

Be still.

The trap door slammed shut, and she tried to blink away her tears as best she could, but she couldn't control the emotional hiccupping that interrupted her breathing. The man would know she'd lost it. He'd know she was so terribly vulnerable to his malicious jeers and hate-filled eyes. However, he didn't even glance her way. Instead, he clunked down the last steps, and then without speaking, he strode over to the long workbench and dug around in a backpack she hadn't noticed before. He cursed and dug around some more. Finally satisfied, he turned around and walked toward her wearing an evil smile.

His eyes leered at her body as he assumed a dominating position over her. Then sinking to his knees, the man proceeded to unfold the shiniest, pointiest knife she'd ever seen. She couldn't look. *O Father in heaven, protect me.* Suddenly, the knife tugged and snapped through the plastic tie, releasing her left wrist. Then another tug and snap gave freedom to her right wrist too.

The knife felt icy cold as it slipped against her neck. But no tug came. "Miah." She couldn't bring herself to open her eyes. Silence and the smell of alcohol invaded her senses as the man leaned in close, paused, then whispered into her ear. "Exactly how deep does a knife have to penetrate before it reaches the jugular vein? Do you know?" Her grimace only induced a round of oppressive laughter, followed by a sharp, freeing pull on her neck. He yanked her to her feet and growled with the voice of the devil himself. "Take off your boots."

He waved the knife when she paused. "Take 'em off or I'll cut 'em off. Even those socks."

When she straightened, he motioned for her to head up the stairs. At the top, before pushing open the heavy trap door, he ran the tip of the knife down her spine as a warning. "You run; I'll kill you. Understand?" She nodded while the stormy morning air plunged her skin in a cold bath of goose bumps.

The man prodded her across the plank floor, past her pool of vomit, now half dried, then past the car—a nice, silver car. At the wide, sliding barn door, she waited for his instructions. Would he somehow tether her, or would he brave the rain too?

"God, you are beautiful." With his head wagging and tongue clicking, he circled her, accosting her with his eyes. "How tragic for you and your daddy that our paths crossed." Then the man shoved the heavy door open with one hand. "Stay where I can see you."

She would have vomited right there except the prospect of thirty seconds away from the beast kept her moving forward. Without hesitation, she stepped into the cold pouring rain and padded down the grassy incline. Dirt and bits of seed and chaff clung to her feet and legs as she waded through the sea of tall meadow grasses.

"Stop. You've gone far enough."

Be not far from me, Lord. She knelt in the partial covering of the brownish-green prairie grasses and unbuttoned her shorts. Oh no. Not now. With all the discretion the man allowed, she quickly relieved herself and let the rain wash away her tears and the evidence of her untimely monthly cycle.

The shaking began when she made a move to stand, and by the time she returned to the man and the barn door, the trembling had become uncontrollable. The man didn't seem to notice or care. He grasped her arm and lead her straight back to the hole in the floor and the steps descending into hell. Only this hell was anything but fiery.

***

"You hungry?"

She shook her head. She lied.

The man shrugged, popped another powdery donut hole into his mouth, and chased it down with a gulp of bottled water. "Drink?" He raised the plastic container in her direction.

"No thanks." More than anything, she needed a warm blanket. Her shorts and T-shirt weren't enough to get rid of this teeth-chattering chill.

"You're such a polite girl. I bet your daddy and your Sunday school teacher taught you to mind your manners, didn't they? Follow the golden rule and love your neighbor as yourself." He smiled. "What? You're surprised I know all the magic words? Well, let me tell you, Miah. They're all a pile a stinkin' rotten garbage." He inspected his fingernail, bit it, and then spit the jagged fragment in her direction. "You people wear your polite smiles and hide behind those big, wooden church doors, pretending you're something you're not. But I know what you are, Miah. You're a liar. You're all a bunch of self-righteous liars. And your daddy's probably the worst of them all, isn't he?"

She raised her eyes to his shocking implication. "What?"

"You know what I'm talking about."

"No." She shook her head. "No."

"It's all right, Miah. You can tell me the truth. And the truth shall set you free!" His laughter mocked her as he brought the water bottle back up to his sneer. "At first they all deny it. But in the end, they finally admit to it with all kinds of healing tears streaming down their cheeks. You will too, Miah. You'll see. It'll make you feel much better."

Who is they? What is he talking about? *God, how am I supposed to respond to this crazy man?* "My dad is the most upright person I know. He wouldn't hurt a single soul."

"I know how it goes. You'll defend him to the very end. You all do. Don't worry, a little time with me, and you'll feel like telling the truth. Just you wait and see." He stood from where he sat on the steps and stretched his long legs. "Stay put. I'll be right back. Oh ... Here you go." The small bag of donut holes came flinging through the air and landed in her lap, raising a powdery plume to her nose.

The moment he climbed through the trap door, she ran to his backpack and began pilfering it for something—anything to help her. Surely he had a phone in there. What had he done with the knife? Above her, muted music played from the car radio.

"Hey, Miah. What's a good news sta——" By the time the man flew down the stairs, she only made it halfway back to her assigned space. "What do you think you're doing?" He grabbed her by the ponytail and yanked so hard that something snapped in her neck. Her feet followed the pull of pain all the way up the steps to the sporty, new sedan. Pausing at the open driver's side door, the man reached down, popped the trunk then dragged her to the back end of the car where he lifted the lid and packed her into the over-crowded storage area. Using the momentum of his rage, he broke off the glow-in-the-dark safety handle and dug the jagged edge across her chest before slamming the lid down tight on her feeble apology.

The pain went from hot to searing, and her scream came in the form of a stuttered, inward gasp. She pressed her T-shirt against her stinging skin, patting at the sticky blood seeping through the thin fabric. How could she have been so stupid? Once again, her impulsiveness had made her situation worse. How long would she be trapped in this darkness? Would she ever see the light of day again?

The car wobbled as the weight of the man's muscular frame settled into the driver's seat. Then the radio speaker scratched from a country song to an advertisement for auto insurance, then to static and next to a raspy, heavy metal number. She heard the man curse as another round of channel surfing began. It finally stopped at a newsy sounding voice. She knew that voice! Knew it well! It belonged to Kinley Wright! In a matter of minutes, C.J. Stardt, Kinley's partner in the "Right Start Morning Show", would wrap up the news spot with his "Good News" of the day. Oh, stay right there, mister. Please don't move the dial. If only she could hear C.J.'s voice, she'd have the hope and strength to hang on.

Kinley's matter-of-fact cadence slowed as she told the tragic story of two fishermen who were assumed drowned when their boat capsized off the shore of Grand Haven in the stormy waters of Lake Michigan. Then as if life magically goes on, Kinley's cheerfulness returned to intro Matt from the Weather Channel, and after Matt came Don Boyd with Blue Sky Traffic.

Next, it would be C.J.'s turn. Instead, Kinley's voice returned with an urgent reminder of the storm warning in effect until ten-thirty a.m. and a special emergency bulletin from "the Crandall County Sheriff's Department who is asking for help locating Miah Brennan, a seventeen-year-old female still missing under suspicious circumstances. She was last seen at midnight at the Crandall County Youth Fair, wearing a pink University of Wyoming T-shirt, jean shorts, calf-high western boots with pink stitching." Kinley's voice read on. "Miah is five six and weighs approximately one hundred and twenty pounds. She has long, blonde hair, blue eyes, a birthmark on her left arm, and speaks with an Australian accent. Friends of Miah are offering a reward of sixty-three thousand dollars for her safe return. If you have any information regarding the whereabouts of Miah, please call 911 or Silent Observer."

A loud whoop sounded from the interior of the car. "Did you hear that, Miah? You weren't kidding when you said you had money!" The man's laughter almost drowned out the commentary going on between Kinley and Steve, who was filling in for C.J., "who'd been with Miah's family all night." Steve took over the mic and went on to explain WLYF's close connection to the band, Odessa, and then led the large, devoted listening audience in a prayer on her behalf.

From the front of the car, the man continued to fling around his taunting abuse while she lay in her dark, cramped quarters, trying to soak up all the encouragement Steve's petition could offer. For the next three seconds, a piano played a very familiar tune, and she heard her own voice come across the radio waves. "Jesus, Son of Righteousness, dawning o'er the great divide. Rise with healing in your wings. Hold us closely to your side ..." And then, with the turn of a key, the music stopped, the car wobbled, the trunk lid clicked, and her good eye squinted in the sudden flood of gloomy light.

"Let's have some fun, Miah." The man sat down on the edge of the trunk and waved a cell phone in front of her face as if he knew exactly what she'd been doing downstairs. Raising his brow at her, he pressed three quick numbers and held the phone to his ear. "No emergency. I'm just inquiring about the reward for Miah Brennan, the girl who's missing."

He smiled and looked at her. "They're transferring me." While he waited, he kept his phone pressed to his ear and his eyes roamed the empty floor in front of him, then suddenly his head lifted to attention.

"Yes, uh. I'm calling about the girl who's missing. Miah Brennan." He smirked, then nibbled on his thumbnail. "I don't suppose a person could collect on the money if she were delivered in bite-size pieces, could they?" He ended the call and slapped his knee as if he were the most clever person in the world. "Idiots. Who do they think they are, trying to bait me."

CHAPTER TWENTY-ONE

Instead of letting her free-range like he had before, this time her ankles were chained to the bottom of the steps. He made sure she wouldn't have another chance to fossick around in his precious backpack. Although he had allowed her to relieve herself in the morning rain, she'd caught a persistent chill which only aggravated the ache in her gut and back. She couldn't get comfortable.

And neither could Duane—at least that was the name he'd offered. Ever since he listened to his voicemail, he'd been preening himself like a chicken with lice. He had shaven every last whisker off his ugly mug, including the dark, thin mustache. Then he set to clipping his fingernails. Even now he used the ever-present knife to clean beneath the remaining space between his fingertips and nails. Every once in a while, he'd pause to take a drink or a smoke, and when he did, he'd stare at her. He glared at her now as she pressed her hand into her aching side.

"Guess what I'm thinking about, Miah."

She dropped her hand to her lap. "I ... I don't know."

"Come on. Take a stab at it." He waved the knife through the air like a magic wand.

When she didn't answer, he looked her over with a crafty grin. "Come on, play along with me."

Emotion choked her throat, forcing tears to the rims of her eyes. She didn't want to play a game that might lead to more pain and humiliation. *Lord, what should I say? What should I do?*

Leaving his post, the man closed the gap between them and brought the knife close to her neck. "I said, play along with me."

Pray for those who persecute you, Miah.

Fear of Duane's knife forced her to look him straight in the eyes. "You're thinking about killing me." *I-I can't pray. This man is pure evil.* She took in a big gulp of air before turning away.

"Close!" His laughter bounced up the staircase as he plunked a foot down on the bottom step. Then leaning an elbow on his raised knee, he brought his clean-shaven jaw down to the level of her sore and swollen features. "Actually, I've been wondering how it is that you're still alive—why I didn't finish you off last night."

He's lost in bitterness and darkness just like you were, just like Brandt had once been.

She kept her focus on a little pill bug skittering toward the man's boot. Couldn't the innocent creature sense it was about to collide with an absolutely wicked force? *No. Duane is not anything like me. He's not anything like Brandt.*

"You know what I think it is?" He pulled his face away from hers. "I think I kind of like you." His freshly trimmed fingertips ran across her cheek and over the contour of her trembling lips. "You're so beautiful. You think you could ever go out with me?"

Rescue me, Lord! Then my soul will delight in Your salvation.

"I mean, if we met in a bar or something and I bought you a drink and asked you to dance, would you dance with me, Miah?"

She stole a quick peek at his eyes. They were totally serious. The pill bug ran into his boot, stopped, then changed direction and began crawling her way.

"Miah, would you dance with me?"

"I'm too young to go to bars. I ... I already have a boyfriend."

"I know. Let's say you were old enough, and let's say you dropped that pony-tailed Geronimo of yours. Then do you think you'd go with me?"

"I ..." She shook her head. "No, probably not."

"Why not? I'm pretty good-looking, aren't I?"

An incredulous smirk eked its way past her tears, and fortunately or not, he took her grin as a form of encouragement.

"So, I might have had a chance with you?"

She shook her head to set him straight. "No. I could never like you. You're a mocker."

"I'm a mocker?"

She nodded. "You mock everything I believe in, everything I love: my family, my friends, my faith. You are mean and hurtful, Duane." Zero emotion. She couldn't read a single thing on his usually skeptical face.

Finally, the man lowered his eyes then walked away as the little pill bug walked up her finger and onto her hand.

"I didn't use to be mean, Miah."

"I ... I can see that." She lied for the second time.

Bryce had been right. It did do them good to go home after the polygraph test. Taking a hot shower in the comfort and semi-privacy of normal and familiar surroundings is exactly what they needed. Claire appeared rested, if not relaxed. A set of clean clothes and a cup of hot tea definitely helped. Now, if only the storm would let up.

Rain ticked on the roof, counting off the seconds as Claire lingered at Miah's chock-full bookshelf. Trace didn't mind waiting. Claire needed this time to connect with the spirit of their daughter. He watched his wife's fingers run across each colorful binding that represented the essence of Miah's character and personality. Of course, there were the classics: *Grimm's Fairy Tales, Little Women, Black Beauty*, and a few of her other favorites. The short, thick volumes sat alongside several books from the *Little House on the Prairie* series, and then there were the history books of the great composers, a Bible commentary, a dictionary, a thesaurus, and a collection of textbooks she'd brought from Amaroo.

In the middle of them all, Claire's hand stopped at the pink photo album taking up residence between a yearbook from Center Pointe Christian High School on one side and at least ten completed journals on the other. She pulled the album out and gave him a brave smile. He could tell she wanted to take them all, but the police had said only the photo album, nothing else. They still had to go over Miah's room with a fine-tooth comb.

Clutching the album to her chest, Claire stood at his side, and they both took a final glance around their daughter's bedroom before heading downstairs. The yellow walls, the white furniture, the rumpled comforter looked so ordinary, so content in waiting for Miah's return. He and Claire were not. They wanted Miah home now!

He held Claire's hand as they walked down the stairs, through the lounge room, and into the kitchen where the hub of their house had been taken over by strangers who wanted Miah home too. Two men were talking together by the table. Another sat at the computer, most likely copying e-mail files, and another was talking on their phone.

Trace let out a shaky sigh and met the eyes of the taller of the two talkers—the man in uniform. "We're heading back to the fairgrounds now. My son, Rob, and his wife, Amy, will be around the homestead if you have any questions or need anything. Help yourself to what's in the cupboards or fridge. Should be a few sandwiches and beers in there."

"Thank you, Mr. Brennan. I think we'll be fine. Just in case you didn't hear it already, you have a message on your answering machine."

"Thanks." He walked over to the kitchen counter and pressed play on the recorder. "G'Day, Claire! Or maybe I should say night. It's probably midnight over there in America. I hesitated to call and wake you all, and then I realized you're probably at the fair anyway." The kitchen brightened with Anna Barcelow's familiar laugh. "You may think I'm crazy ... No, you know I am." She laughed again. "Anyway, I was cleaning up the kitchen when I got this strong prompting to pray for you. It became so strong I had to stop right here and ring you. I hope everything's all right and you're having a wonderful week. Your friends over here in the Outback are thinking of you and praying for you!" A voice shouted something from the background. "Kylie says hello to Miah and Drew! Call us soon, won't you?"

Claire's eyes beaded up with tears. "They probably know by now don't you think? Surely your dad called them."

He only nodded then turned to the officers. "If you don't think you need anything, I guess we'll be going now. Thanks for your help."

For living way out in the back of beyond they were relatively close to everything: thirty minutes from downtown Grand Rapids with all its culture, art, and first-rate medical facilities; sixty minutes from the Lake Michigan shoreline; seven minutes from Open Door Bible Church, and twenty minutes from the Crandall County Youth Fair. He and Claire had definitely been blessed. And as they motored down Sheffield Road in his big 2500HD Silverado, he tried to count each one of those blessings, if only to keep himself from going mad with worry.

Claire must have been counting something too. Every second or so her fingertips tapped an anxious telegraph message on the bright pink cover of the photo album she held in her lap. He lifted the console and pulled her close to his side. "You all right?"

She turned her trance-like gaze from the green, rain-soaked countryside to his hand, reaching out to steady her own. "As more and more time passes, the greater my fear, Trace."

"I-I know. Me too." He gave her hand a squeeze and then turned on the radio. " 'Ow 'bout some music?"

They caught the end of Hillsong's *Shout to the Lord* before Kinley Wright's enthusiastic voice gave a reminder of the upcoming news report at the top of the hour.

"But first it's Nicole C. Mullen with *Redeemer*," the upbeat deejay chirped.

The faith-filled song did help move them a step or two away from the stinging tentacles of fear that threatened to paralyze their minds. For the moment, he and Claire would hide in the shadow of God's love and trust He was holding Miah in His hands.

The song's timely lyrics came to an end, and then its final notes faded into WLYF'S noontime news jingle. Next Kinley's rhythmic voice began her report, announcing the National Weather Service had finally canceled all severe thunderstorm warnings and watches of the morning. She kept her positive pace despite the "sixty percent chance of more storms developing later in the afternoon and evening as temperatures begin to rise once again."

Then her voice took on a very serious tone. "As a reminder, a child abduction alert has been issued by the Michigan Amber Alert Network. The Crandall County Sheriff's Department is searching for Miah Brennan, a seventeen-year-old white female, height five feet six inches, one hundred and twenty pounds." Claire turned his way, and her eyes grew wide with alarm as Kinley read on. "She has blonde hair, blue eyes, a birthmark on her left forearm, and speaks with an Australian accent. The teen was abducted from the Crandall County Youth Fair and was last seen at twelve a.m., wearing a pink University of Wyoming T-shirt, jean shorts, and calf-high western boots with pink stitching.

"Authorities are looking for Ronald Duane Maddox, a thirty-eight-year-old white male, height six feet three inches, two hundred and twenty pounds. He has wavy, dark-brown hair and was last seen with a trimmed mustache, stubbled beard, and wearing blue jeans and a black T-shirt. The suspect is driving a silver 2000 Toyota Camry sedan with Utah license plates, six zero three K U J. The car may have been in the vicinity of the Shaw Lake Unit of the Barbour State Game Area during the very early morning hours. Law enforcement officials believe this child to be in grave or immediate danger. Do not approach the suspect. If you have any information regarding the abduction, please call 911 or Silent Observer."

By the time Kinley's report came to an end, anxious tears were flooding Claire's eyes. Anger leaked out too. "Grave or immediate danger? Trace, did you know this? Don't you dare keep anything from me!"

"Claire, I ... I knew the police suspected Ronald Maddox. We both did. The police must have somehow confirmed Miah is with Maddox." His heart pounded hard in his chest as he pressed the gas pedal to the floor. "O Lord, help us." Within seconds they reached where Sheffield Road intersected M-50. He had to make a choice: turn left and head into Griffith and the fairgrounds or turn right and shoot straight for the state hunting land to find his daughter. *O God. What should I do? Please show me where Miah is. Please keep her safe. Thwart Maddox's plans.*

As the big truck tires spun to the right, the diesel engine growled into a fast and furious pace.

"Trace, you turned the wrong way!"

"No, I didn't. We're going to bring Miah home. Ronald Maddox is somewhere in the state hunting area. I just know it!"

Claire pounded a clenched fist on Miah's photo album.

"Trace, please! Turn this truck around right now! You're not being logical! We'll never find her on our own!"

"I can't sit on my hands any longer, Claire!" They flew past Sixtieth Street and two more farms before Rob's phone rang on Trace's belt. In one simultaneous move, he yanked it from his hip and pressed the talk button. "Hello!"

"Mr. Brennan, this is Nicole Krueger. There have been a few developments in Miah's case."

"You bloody bet there has! I thought Mrs. Tubergen told you we wanted to be contacted first before you released any information to the press! Why didn't you, Sergeant Krueger?"

"You heard the Amber Alert ..."

"Twelve o'clock straight up. My wife and I are emotional wrecks right now thanks to your oversight."

"I'm sorry, Mr. Brennan. A call came into 911 in response to your friends' generous reward. The FBI traced the cell phone number back to Ronald Maddox. We tried to phone him. He didn't pick up. We're pretty certain Miah is with him. We, uh ... Where are you? We should go over some things."

Like an unconquerable army, hundreds of wooded acres surrounded the covered front porch of the West Michigan Gun Club. If the handful of law enforcement officers who loitered beneath the damp overhang were discouraged, they didn't show it. Try as he might though, Trace couldn't keep despair from throwing punches at his once-immovable resolve.

Staring over the porch rail at the ground, he watched rain fall from the roof and beat a two-inch wide trench into the sandy gravel. That's exactly how he felt—weathered and worn—as if all his faith in mankind and the police were eroding away. But Claire seemed to be hanging on. Somehow, she'd found a small handhold of hope despite their frustrations.

Behind them, the heavy wooden door of the cabin-like clubhouse finally groaned open. While the deputies straightened from their relaxed poses, he couldn't muster any interest when the baldheaded lieutenant and Sergeant Krueger scuffed across the threshold. They'd been talking in the clubhouse way too long. Didn't they understand meeting after meeting wouldn't bring Miah home? Action is what they needed. Deploying teams of dogs to search the huge, wooded haystack would be their best use of time.

"Trace, it's the investigators." Claire tugged on his sleeve. He didn't move. He couldn't move. "Remember what Faith said?" she whispered. "They're on our side, Trace. On Miah's side."

He knew she was right. He just couldn't make her truth his.

"Mr. and Mrs. Brennan?" The lieutenant interrupted Claire's quiet prodding and didn't wait for them to turn around before he continued. "This is Special Agent Torres with the FBI."

"Trace." Claire's eyes pleaded.

With all the respect he could gather, he turned and stretched out his hand to the man whose presence had been elusive at best. Why had the lieutenant waited so long to introduce the agent? Had he been observant enough to know the special agent's blue jacket with the bold yellow letters read like an obituary to them? Had the lieutenant been trying to protect them from the truth?

Officer Torres' dark eyes bore an apology, and his handshake pumped with sincerity and compassion. "Good to meet you both. I thought it might be helpful for you to know there's a whole team of people working behind the scenes to find Miah. And in case you hadn't heard, we're gaining some ground—thanks to Sergeant Krueger who called us early on."

"No ... We didn't know. Thank you."

Claire's hand entwined his own as the special agent went on. "For the past five or six years, we've been trying to solve some cold cases involving the abduction of at least three teenage girls and possibly more. Each case has shared a few similarities. Although the states the girls lived in were different, the girls all came from very religious families ... like yours."

Officer Torres paused as if his words got lost in the forest behind them. "We've finally begun to see a pattern. In each case, Ronald Maddox had either been traveling through the girls' states or had been living within two hundred miles of where the abductions had taken place."

Trace knew the answer before the question came out of his mouth. "Did ... Were the girls ever found?"

The detective's gaze dropped to the cement floor, then with a regretful shake of his head, he raised his eyes to the officers who had gathered around them. "Not until it was too late." Claire's grip tightened around Trace's hand as Special Agent Torres continued. "Their bodies were found in wooded areas relatively close to where the girls were last seen—never further than thirty miles away. In each circumstance, however, the perpetrator wasn't too concerned about hiding his crime. It seems as if he were trying to make a statement. Which leads us to Ronald Duane Maddox."

The special agent settled into a more informal stance. "Back in nineteen eighty-four, after a controversial trial involving a religiously devout family in Utah, Maddox was convicted of first degree criminal sexual conduct. We think it may be possible he has some sort of vendetta to serve. After Mr. Maddox completed a five-year prison term ..."

This can't be true! God, please! Please don't let Ronald Maddox be linked to these cases. Surely the police are wrong, simply jumping to conclusions. In his conversations with the bloke, not once had Maddox mentioned his time in prison. In fact, he had bejeweled his background with stories of occupational success and adventure. But ... what if the only truth in his stories were his travels from state to state? And now that he thought about it, Maddox had asked some very odd and difficult questions: "You said God loves everybody equally. So how can you believe some people are going heaven while others are going to hell? What's the worst thing you ever did? Then what makes you think God's going to let you into heaven? Let's say I rob a bank and you rob a bank, what makes you think you're deserving of heaven and not me?"

And then there were the questions pointed toward Miah. "Does she believe like you? I bet you and her are very close, huh?" The questions were posed in such an easy-flowing, sincere way. Not once had he become suspicious. Oh, he'd been such a fool, such a gullible, stupid fool.

"... And so, Sergeant Krueger's suspicions about Maddox have helped put all the pieces together." Special Agent Torres paused as the lieutenant closed his phone and stepped back into the circle.

"And today, we're going to stop him in his tracks." The lieutenant's eyes flickered with promise. "The State Police are flying a helicopter in from Detroit. It's equipped with a thermal imaging device which detects variances in temperature within the forest, hopefully pointing out Miah's location."

Then Sergeant Krueger nodded and added. "Until then, Novak Aviation has volunteered their services to do an initial flyover of the area. They'll begin the air search as soon as they arrive. Their ETA is fourteen twenty-five" She glanced down at her watch and then at the deputies. "That's in ten minutes. For the rest of us on the ground, we'll be bringing in some fresh dogs and organizing a grid search. We'll have to work quickly. There's such a large area to cover, and time is not on our side."

CHAPTER TWENTY-TWO

*D*uane settled back on the workbench and ran the knife blade up and down the fabric of his jeans. "Nineteen eighty-four feels like a freakin' long time ago."

Seventeen years ago, to be exact—the year Drew and I were born.

"I had just graduated from the University of Utah with practically a free ride. Good grades. So when I landed the job of a lifetime, I did what any red-blooded, American kid would do. I bought myself a brand-new Pontiac Trans-Am." He took a drink from his beer then raised it in the air as if he were toasting his good fortune. When she didn't respond with the same enthusiasm, he shrugged and went on.

"Then I bought a house near the mountains. My neighbors were really religious like you, and they had a bunch of little kids." He grinned at the memory of it. "When I'd get out of work those kids would always come over and beg me to take them for a ride in my car with the T-top down. Ava, their babysitter and older cousin, would pile those kids in the back seat and off we'd go up into the mountains. Can you guess what happened?"

"You were in a bad accident?"

He looked annoyed at her. "No. Ava fell in love with me. She was seventeen. I'd been twenty-one at the time. How old are you, Miah?"

"Seventeen."

For the first time ever, his eyes were absent of any malice. "Mmm. Right ... Well, one thing led to another, and we ended up ... together almost every time she babysat. She needed me. She said I gave her freedom from the nightmare going on in her house."

His voice took on a sharp edge, as sharp as the knife cutting through the fray on the bottom of his jeans. "Even though her dad claimed to be some holy man in their church, her parents were always fighting, and every once in a while, he'd sneak into her bedroom."

When the knife slipped from his fingers, hit the floor, and spun around like a race car on hot bitumen, he didn't skip a beat. He picked it up and went right back to slicing off the faded denim. "Ava needed someone to love her. So I did. You can understand that can't you? You love your Indian, don't you?"

Unsure of whether his definition of love matched hers, she gave him a noncommittal nod.

"Her aunt and uncle couldn't understand it. They blew things out of proportion and dished the dirt to her parents, who had me arrested. When I told the cops what her dad had been doing, they didn't believe me—Ava denied everything. Thanks to her lies and her smooth-talking dad, I wasted five years of my life in prison. They ruined me. It took forever to rebuild my job, my reputation."

Duane finished off the shiny can of beer and crushed it in his right hand. "If I could get ahold of her, I'd cut her into a billion pieces. But she's gone—literally. The last I heard, her parents checked her into a mental hospital. She'd fried her brain with pharmaceuticals." He laughed. "It's kind of ironic, isn't it? Me, an engineer with a drug company? I guess in a roundabout way, she's getting exactly what she deserves."

He laughed again, and his eyes took on a wild gleam. Before folding the knife closed, he held it up to the ash-colored light and examined its razor edge with the pad of his thumb. "You're right, Miah. I am mean. I'm as mean as the devil's dog and just as crazy." He released a jagged sigh then stood and stared out the small, rain-speckled window.

Her heart pounded out a warning that her impulsive mouth didn't heed. "We're all a little mean ... and crazy." He spun around, glaring at her as if she'd rudely intruded on a secret confession. Thick, impenetrable darkness consumed his eyes; still, she didn't waver. "All I'm saying is, I understand your anger. I've been there. I'm no different than you." *Please, God. Don't let Duane take his anger out on me anymore. Please, work in his heart.*

Duane's slow, deliberate applause hit the slab walls, bounced back, and smacked her with a mocking echo. "Yee haw. That makes two people in the whole, wide world who understands. Save the sentiment, Miah." He dragged the backpack near him and started rifling through it.

"Who's the other person?" The ache in her gut began to throb, making its presence more than just an annoyance. She sat up straight and pressed her fist into the pain.

"Charis, my little sister. She's stupid. She believes in fairy tales like you, so she doesn't count either." He found what he'd been searching for, offered her a cigarette, and then pulled the tab on another beer. "We hardly talk anymore. I pretty much steer clear of my family. My dad's a workaholic, my mom's an alcoholic, and my brother ... He's just out there. When we were in high school, he took a swing at me for makin' out with his girlfriend, so I hit him back—one punch to the face. When my dad found out, he beat the crap out of me with the buckle end of his belt. I hate 'em both for wronging me." He tossed his head back and took a long swig on the can.

Pastor Bryce's voice whispered in her mind and came out her mouth in the form of a timid recitation. "When we've been wronged, hate can feel right, almost holy. In reality, it's poison."

The cigarette glowed with life and a second later, smoke billowed from Duane's nostrils. His dark eyes followed a sharp line that ran straight through her, and somehow it didn't bother her. Unspoken words, with all their hidden meanings, floated around the dim cellar and mixed with the bluish smoke. And she lay down, resting in the stillness, trying to get some relief from the incessant ache in her belly.

Within seconds, her slumbering took her back to a hot, dusty day on Amaroo Station. The red gravel gnawed at the bottom of her boots as she stomped toward the paddock. And blood whooshed in her ears so loud, she could only perceive her brothers' mocking laughter. The instant her hands hit the gray wooden fence her memory turned into a bad dream. The fence became an obstacle course of spider webs and black beady eyes, yet somehow, she made it up and over.

When her brothers continued to hide her journal behind their hands and innocent smiles, she grabbed for the nearest prod she could find—not a whip, but Duane's shiny knife. "I hate you! I hate you!" Her voice screamed above the roar in her ears, and the sparkle in Josh's eyes disappeared as she rushed him, knocking him to the ground and plunging the blade deep into his belly. The shock on his face was haunting, his pain so terribly undeserved. Right before his face went deathly white, her name rasped from his last breath.

"Miah."

She turned with a start. Strangely, Josh's voice came from the blue sky above them.

"Miah."

The slow, simmering pain returned, and she opened her healthy eye to Duane crouched low beside her.

"What makes you an expert on hate?" He pulled on her arm. "Sit up."

Blinking back the nightmare, she obeyed and hugged her knees to her chest. The lifeless image of Josh clung to her mind's eye like a heavy ball and chain. "I ... I have to fight my anger all the time. I've always had a bad temper—ever since I can remember. When I was eleven, I nearly killed my brother. Do you know Joshua and Brad?"

Duane shrugged.

"They stole my journal, and I got so angry, I went crazy. I threatened them with a horsewhip, cracking it right by their ears. Then I rammed Josh hard in the belly, knocking the breath out of him. And to make matters worse, I spooked a horse that cut Brad's hand and nearly trampled Josh while he lay on the ground unable to breathe. It could have ended up tragic. Thankfully, my dad saved us all."

She waited for Duane to say something, only he kept smoking his cigarette and staring straight ahead at the shadowy corner of their gray dungeon. Did she dare say more? She held her aching head in the palm of her head and sucked in a stuttered breath before speaking. "The only time I really lose it is when someone wrongs me undeservedly. And that's why you're angry at Ava, isn't it? She wronged you."

Duane was in the middle of a long, slow drag on his cigarette when he turned and glared at her. "Exactly."

Rocking back, she tried to avoid the cloud of smoke hanging in the space between them. "Most of the time when I'm angry, it's truly justified. And at first it feels good, almost euphoric, like I'm flying. However, if I don't resolve it, if I don't try to forgive the person who wronged me, I find I'm not really flying, but falling to a disastrous end—like what happened between me and my brothers."

Like a startled grasshopper, Duane's cigarette flicked through the air and landed with a hiss in the leaky, damp corner. Just as abruptly, he rose off his haunches and headed up the stairs. He climbed halfway up and then turned to face her. "You think I'm headed for a disastrous end?"

Her fear only allowed her the slightest shrug. She could never tell him her deepest prayer was for his demise.

He took four steps back down the stairs. His dark eyes were possessed with the ancient demons of bitterness. "If I am, I'm taking you down with me."

She nodded her understanding and secretly began to pray all the harder.

Once Duane pushed his way through the trapdoor, her silent tears fell like the raindrops trickling down the small, rectangle window. She mourned all the time and energy she'd poured into getting back at Josh and Brad when they were kids. She cried for not having another chance to tell them how much she really loved them. And she cried for not having a chance to say goodbye to the rest of her family: to her parents; to Rob, Amy and their baby yet to be born; to Drew. *Carry on for me, Drew. Love Kylie for me.* She mourned all her dreams never to be fulfilled: the songs yet to be sung; the cowboy's story yet to be written; the station in the Bighorns yet to be stocked. *God, I don't want to die. I'm too young. Why? Why now?*

Even though God didn't answer right away, it was okay. She felt Him there—as sure and steady as the massive, wooden beam keeping the ceiling from crashing down on her. His strong, pillar-like presence kept her spirit from collapsing into an emotional heap of despair.

And she imagined Him collecting each and every tear she shed for family and friends who would be left behind. Her loved ones were countless and all so very dear. Grandparents, cousins, aunts and uncles, schoolmates. *Kylie ... Brianna ... I love you all. And Brandt ... I'll never know what we might have had. Keep* the faith, my friend. *Father God, I can't do this. Please, if it's Your will, won't You save me?*

As if in answer to her prayer, the car radio above her broke out in an all too familiar tune. *No, not that song, Lord.*

The song, written in response to the aftermath of the Columbine High School Massacre two years earlier, filled the empty ceiling space between her and her captor. She listened until the tribute to a slain student's faith echoed the same question she'd asked moments ago. *God, won't You save me?*

Even before God's quiet voice entered her thoughts, she knew what His answer would be. *I have saved you, Miah. By My grace you have been saved through faith—faith in the shed blood of Jesus who paid the penalty for your sin.*

Not that kind of save, Lord. Save me from Duane!

She remained free of Duane's nervous fidgeting and autobiographical ramblings through two more songs, the three o'clock newscast, and another quick-passing thundershower. Through it all she continued her dialogue with the One who had the power to rescue her and thwart the plans of her enemy. Even when the trapdoor slammed shut and Duane's threatening footsteps clunked back down the steps, she kept her eyes closed and her silent lips moving.

Once he reached the bottom step, he paused, not making the slightest move. What was he doing? Staring at her again? Please, just move along. *Have mercy on me, O God, for in You my soul takes refuge. I will take refuge in the shadow of Your wings until the trouble has passed.*

"They know you're with me." He paused and nudged her rib with his boot.

I cry out to God Most High, who will send from heaven and save me.

"Hey! Did you hear me?" He nudged her again.

She ended her prayer with a desperate, inner amen then wiped a lingering tear from her swollen eye.

"Don't do that praying thing anymore. It really gets under my skin." He hopped off the last step and walked to the middle of the room. "You wanna dance? I feel like dancin'." Spinning around, he raised his eyebrows at her. "I know you can. I saw you on the stage last night." He pulled out the knife and walked back her way. Without any effort, the knife sliced through the thick cable ties, giving freedom to her feet. "Come on."

Her legs refused to cooperate when Duane yanked her to a standing position with one strong pull. Not to be discouraged, he drew her close, his arms wrapped tightly around her, forcing her to move with the motion of his body. His breath smelled of the same sweet-sour mixture as last night, and her stomach began to revolt at the familiar, drunken stench. "Come on, Miah. Move what the good Lord gave you."

Her whole being quaked within her. This was not going to lead to anything good. As her own breath stuttered, his grew heavy, and he forced her to the floor.

Tears left over from her prayer had barely a chance to subside when a fresh flood began to overwhelm her. "Duane, please ..."

"Oh, my G—" He stopped mid-curse, his eyes shifting at a frenetic pace. "Listen ... A helicopter!" Where fear should have crossed his severe brow, a mad look of amusement accented his features. "They're never going to find you ... alive."

They both remained still until the faint sound of the helicopter became a memory. It never even came close. Like Duane said—they were never going to find her.

The despairing thought escaped her mind in the form of a quiet whimper that startled Duane from his thoughts. As if he had forgotten his reason for pulling her to the floor, he stood and began gathering the emptied whiskey bottle, the discarded beer cans, and the crumpled donut bag. "There's one left. You want it?" He smirked at her revulsion, then stuffed them all into the backpack, including her socks and boots he'd confiscated in the morning. A "souvenir" is what he'd called them.

While he continued to dig around inside the bag, she considered making a run for it, only he moved near the steps, blocking her way. "You know, you're a pretty lucky girl." He stooped to gather the chains and all the broken cable ties then stuffed them in the backpack too. "I prolonged your life thirteen, maybe fourteen hours. You should be grateful." His eyes flashed with cleverness. "You ready?"

"For what?"

"I've arranged a little meeting for you. A face to face ... with God."

CHAPTER TWENTY-THREE

hile Duane secured her wrists behind her back, the helicopter took another sweep across a different, distant horizon. If the pilot continued on his current course, she'd never be found. *Please, God, send the helicopter this way.*

Duane chucked the backpack in the trunk of his car then dug around and produced a metallic case from the bottom of the packed compartment. After unsnapping and opening the lid and lifting a silver handgun from its foam bed, he looked almost apologetic when he glanced her way. Then rifling around some more, he pulled out a small, green and yellow box and began filling the gun's clip with what resembled shiny, miniature missiles. He shoved the clip into the pistol with finality then slammed the trunk closed. "All right. Let's take a walk.".

A walk? She stood there, surely looking incredulous. Was this to be her Trail of Tears, her Via Dolorosa? Dread seized her body, leaving her completely immobile. If Duane wanted her to move, he would have to carry her. *God, I can't simply give in, can I? What should I do?*

Duane gave her no time to wait for an answer. He took hold of her arm and pulled her to the barn door. Then pausing to tuck the sleek firearm inside the pocket of his rain jacket, he pushed the door open wide enough for them to slip through.

Even though the afternoon sky drizzled grayness all around, the natural light pained her injured eye. Still, she accepted this new scene and the fresh air as heaven's reply to her desperation. Embracing the sense of freedom the surrounding dense woods gave her, she drew in the sweet fragrance of the forest as if it were her last breath. The subtle, tangy smells of the living, breathing earth renewed her strength and revived all her senses, including the ache in her side and belly. "Duane, I have to go to the bathroom."

When he turned, his eyes glossed with indifference. "By the end of our little hike, you won't have that problem. Come on."

Thunder rumbled to their right, echoing the hard, frantic drumming in her chest. If only she could see what lay beyond the endless ramble of vegetation and legions of sky-high tree trunks. Somewhere she'd find a road with cars and trucks, cabins and houses, and ... help.

"Duane, I've been thinking. The police probably have these woods surrounded. If you pointed me in the right direction, I could walk out. I ... I'd tell them someone must have hit me on the head, and when I woke up, I found myself in this forest—alone. All would be forgiven. I wouldn't say a thing. I promise."

His brow burrowed deep into his dark eyes, dismissing her idea as if it were the most ridiculous thing he'd ever heard. "Move it." He shoved her in the direction he wanted to go—left, farther away from the muffled sound of the helicopter, into the densest part of the woods.

God, are you still there? Have you left me completely defense-less? Between the cacophonic fear blaring in her head and the drops of rain pattering through the thick undergrowth, she barely heard God's familiar, small voice.

Don't I always keep my promises, beloved? I told you I would never leave you. And neither have I left you defenseless. My word is living and active and sharper than a double-edged sword. It pene-trates even to dividing the soul and spirit. Use the truth of My word.

She wanted to trust the Father, to obey Him, yet fear of Duane's unpredictable anger left her mind paralyzed and her voice mute.

With no trail to mark their way, Duane led her in what seemed like a straight path beneath the dark-green, sopping canopy. Patches of waxy ferns slapped against her shins while reddish-brown brambles scratched at her elbows and tugged at her shirt. All along the anxious way, her bare feet tried to avoid the roots, stones, and broken sticks poking through the collage of hardwood leaves littering the forest floor. Then to top it off, the cold rain contributed to her discomfort by adding goose bumps to her chilled bones.

Despite the miserable conditions, Duane seemed to calm in the quiet of their footsteps, and miraculously, she did too. Her tears fell in silent resignation as she internalized all her regretful goodbyes. Surely this was the hardest part of dying: not getting to say I'm sorry; not being able to reassure her loved ones of the peace filling her now, of God's presence with her in these woods. *O God, please take me quickly. For the comfort of my mum and dad, don't let me suffer. And please ... somehow, let them know I love them.*

Thoughts of how it would all go afflicted her mind. Would she really experience a light at the end of a tunnel like she'd heard in so many stories of near-death experiences? She really didn't want to go it alone. Maybe an angel of light would come and carry her into the arms of Jesus or at least take her as far as the pearly gates and the Lamb's Book of Life. What if her name wasn't written there? She'd done a lot of bad things since she'd first put her faith in Jesus. What if He'd grown impatient with all her mess ups?

My dear Miah, you're forgetting how much I love you. I will never go back on my word. When I offered up Myself on the cross, I became the final sacrifice for all your sins. I am able to save completely those who come to the Father through Me. I live to intercede for you.

Thank You, Jesus. Thank You ... Without being conscious of it, an old hymn with its new tune left her sore, swollen lips and joined with the melody of the dancing, rain-soaked creation. *"Before the throne of God above I have a strong and perfect plea. A great High Priest whose name is Love who ever lives and pleads for me. My name is graven on His hands. My name is written on His heart. I know that while in heaven He stands, no tongue can bid me thence depart. No tongue can bid me thence depart."*

Duane's footsteps faltered in a thick mass of jack-in-the-pulpits. "Shut your trap, Miah."

How could she? She needed this so very badly. *"When Satan tempts me to despair and tells me of the guilt within, upward I look and see Him there, who made an end of all my sin. Because the sinless Savior died, my sinful soul is counted free. For God the Just is satisfied to look on Him and pardon me. To look on Him and pardon me."*

The rain fell harder, and when she paused to blink back the rivulets from her eyes, Duane stopped his plodding long enough to take in her body with his critical gaze. Her hair clung to her shoulders like long stalks of wet straw. Her favorite T-shirt was blood-stained, stretched, and torn—looking much like her face felt. And while her legs and arms were bruised and marked with hundreds of thin red stripes, her feet were now a solid, muddy brown.

Duane squinted in the driving rain too. "You're just so sure there's a God, aren't you?"

She lowered her eyes under his skeptical scrutiny. "I hear him speak to me ... in my thoughts."

"You hear God talk in your head?" He stepped close and rapped his knuckles on the top of her throbbing head. "Hello,

God! You in there? Sheeze. You're crazier than me!" His mocking laughter rose above the kettledrum thunder and the rain sluicing through the trees. "Here we are, two raving-mad lunatics standing in a downpour in the middle of nowhere. It can't get any better than this, can it?" He shook his head and started walking once more. When she didn't follow, he turned back and simply motioned for her to fall in step. "Come on. Entertain me some more."

God, please talk to Duane. Please help him hear Your voice. Help him know You are real.

"Sing, Miah."

She choked back her fear. "Wh-what do you want me to sing?"

"Is there more of that song? What's it called?"

"One more verse. Before The Throne of God Above."

"Sing it then." He grabbed her elbow and pulled her along.

She swallowed hard and closed her eyes.

"Behold Him there the Risen Lamb, my perfect spotless righteousness, the great unchangeable I AM, the King of Glory and of grace. One with Himself I cannot die; my soul is purchased by His blood. My life is hid with Christ on high, with Christ my Savior and my God. With Christ my Savior and my God."

He turned and glared at her. "Sing."

"That's it."

Drawing close to her face, he grinned and patted her shoulder as if she were simple-minded. "Well then, sing it again."

Again? He wanted to hear it again? *Please God, use the words of this hymn to soften Duane's heart.* While Duane yoked her neck with his big hand, she closed her eyes, willing her feet to be led by his hand and the worshipful melody.

All through her singing, Duane's strides kept pace with the mournful rhythm. The moment the final word of the song left her lips, he stopped in his tracks. "Okay, this is far enough."

She opened her good eye to a bowl-shaped wonderland of pine trees that kept out the chaotic bramble of the rest of the woodlands. A thick layer of soft, burnished needles cushioned the forest floor, and here and there, granite boulders of various sizes had been deposited by ancient glaciers. As morbid as her thoughts were, she couldn't help believe God had provided her such a beautiful final resting place. *Thank You, God. I know You are here with me.*

Duane scanned the natural amphitheater as if he were picking out the perfect seat. Then reaching into his pocket, he brought out the hunting knife. She watched in unbelief as he unfolded the blade and checked its condition with the pad of his thumb like she'd seen him do before. His eyes were glazed with evil when he turned back toward her and pulled her further into the center of the sheltered evergreen cove.

She shook her head in protest and emotion rose to her throat in a tangled mass of dread as she resisted his coaxing. "Oh ... no ... Please, Duane, not the knife. The gun. I ... I thought you were going to use the gun?"

His chuckle rose from somewhere deep within his depraved heart. "You took me seriously? I'm not going to kill you, Miah. I'm gonna set you free." While his mouth said one thing, his actions said another. He tightened the vise-like grip on her arm, dragged her near one of the larger, variegated boulders, and pushed her down on the cold, wet surface.

Above them the sky flickered, and seconds later, thunder boomed through the forest, making the rain fall even harder. Duane paced around the large rock like a nervous cat, his eyes unyielding as the driving rain. And she sat there shaking, waiting for the first blow to come. "You are the God who saves. Rescue me and deliver me in Your righteousness. Give the command to save me, for You are my rock and——" There it was. Pain. Small, pointed, and certainly not subtle.

The tip of Duane's knife threatened the curve of her back,

and his hot breath hissed in her ear. She stared straight ahead, afraid to meet the madness in his eyes. While his left hand steadied her shoulder, the dull backside of the blade zipped up her spine taking her breath with it. Then just as swift, the sharp edge came down, releasing her hands from their tight restraints.

He raced around to the front of the rock, his face inches from her own again. "You know I'm the one who decides whether you live or die, don't you?"

She nodded without meeting his eyes.

"Then why do you keep praying?" He pushed the point of the knife into the delicate skin beneath her chin, forcing her to look up into his sneer that demanded an answer. She couldn't reply. Panicky tears choked her throat.

"Answer me!"

Salty, liquid terror fell over the rims of her eyes when he yanked hard on her hair. Then as if he'd commanded them, fear and desperation coerced an answer to tremble from her lips "God ha ... has the power to save ... to bend every action to His will."

Duane's snake-like eyes glowered at her for what seemed like minutes. Then miraculously, he lowered the knife from her chin and strode over to a smaller, adjacent rock. Relief came to her soul in great gasps as he rested his soaked boot on the boulder's marble-like face. *O please, make him let me go, Lord.* Just when she thought Duane might scrap his evil plan, he slowly turned and took in her pitiful state through the relentless rain.

"Miah, do you know I've killed four girls just like you?" Without giving her time to process the shock of his confession, he flew back toward her. Inches from her face, his bitter breath and manic-looking grin released the most resolute heckle she'd ever heard. "If God didn't save them, why do you think He's going to save you?" He raised the knife to the bridge of her nose then ran the blade across her cheek and down the length of her arm. "Why, Miah? Hmm?"

A slow trickle of tears followed the path of the knife down her face. "Maybe it's not me God wants to save. Maybe it's you. What if God wants to rescue you ... from the darkness?" She continued her desperate persuasion. She had nothing to lose. "The God who made you, loves you, Duane. He wants your heart very badly. Just as badly as you want justice for what Ava did to you."

Her eyes pleaded with his, willing the meaning of her words to sink into his stone-hard heart. "Duane, please. Believe me ... N-nothing you have ever done c-can change the way He feels about you." She tried to check her stuttering. "All you need to do is believe it. Run away from the darkness."

He moved to her side, pulled her back against his thigh, and lifted the knife to her jaw. His hot breath growled in her ear. "I am darkness."

"N-no, Duane. Don't let your past define your future. B-because God doesn't." Duane's grip on her neck tightened, momentarily cutting off her ability to breathe and speak. When he finally moved, he lowered the knife to her chest which allowed her to continue. "He sent His son Jesus to act on—"

Duane pressed the tip of the knife into her skin and started to needle her chest as if he were a mad tattoo artist. Even so, she forced herself to go on. "Jesus acts on our behalf, like an attorney before a judge, only ... He doesn't plead our case, because—"

He stopped his poking momentarily and looked her in the eyes. "Like an attorney before a judge? Only he doesn't plead my case? Oh, I know that one all too well."

"H-he doesn't plead our case because He knows we're guilty, Duane. Doomed to die." She paused, trying to take her focus off the pain. "Instead of letting us die, Jesus accepted the conviction and served the sentence of our crimes himself."

Duane stopped his pecking and moved the edge of the hunting knife across her neck, squeegeeing rain and her tears onto her chest. "God doing my time for me ..." His eyes widened with a hint of mockery. "It sounds too good to be true."

"It is true. God loves you so much. But you have to stop what you're doing. Right now. And you have to forgive Ava and her dad. You have to surrender your right to get even because ... God did the same for you."

"So, I guess that means you have to forgive me too. Right?"

"Yes. I can forgive you. If you let me go, Duane. I'll forgive everything."

"Really? You could do that?"

"Absolutely."

"Even if I ..." Lightning flashed as he moved in front of her and pushed her down against the rock "... did this?" The blade of the knife blended in with the gray of the sky as Duane raised it above his head.

"Duane! No!"

CHAPTER TWENTY-FOUR

lthough the day had started out dark and stormy, it beat the oppressive heat of the last two weeks. And now since the bad weather had finally passed, Ryan Ambrose determined he wouldn't let a little drizzle and gray skies put a damper on his plans. No, he'd made a promise—and a promise was a promise. He'd learned that lesson two years ago. And every time it crossed his mind, he could kick himself. One too many flirtations and one fatal affair had been the death of his marriage. And now, Brenda had moved on. Remarried to an accountant of all people.

He shook the regretful situation from his head, then smiled at the twelve-year-old reason for his and Brenda's shotgun wedding. "You ready, bud?"

"Just about, Dad." His son gobbled the last of his burger and tossed the wrapper into the carryout bag.

"Make sure you grab your rain gear. We might just need it." Ryan let the wipers take one last swipe of the windshield before he cut the engine of his very "late" model Dodge Ram. Then leaning over the seat, he grabbed his own raincoat and a pack of reflectors. On second thought, he tossed the reflectors back on the seat. This outing wasn't so much in preparation for the hunting season; he simply intended to spend some quality time with his son.

Ever since he'd returned to church and sought help for his problem, he had resolved to do things right. No more getting by, doing the bare minimum out of some guilt-ridden obligation. No, he would love his son the right way and for the right reasons —unconditionally, and because Bailey was God's precious gift to him.

From now on he would live for the Father and for Bailey. Through his devotion to their son, he'd show Brenda how very much he regretted his sin. And maybe somehow, she and Bailey would be able to forgive him and come to know for themselves the mercy and grace he'd received through Jesus.

The screeching of the truck door drowned out his sigh as his feet splashed down onto the muddied turnout, marking the Shaw Lake trailhead. Well, if nothing else, they'd be able to see some good tracks today.

"Dad, should I bring Grandpa Ambrose's gun?" Bailey smiled at him expectantly. It seemed like overnight Bailey's round, little-boy face had been replaced by the square-jaw, teen-model look they'd seen in the storefront windows at the mall. No doubt about it, Bailey had been blessed with a winsome face. And in fact, people said he was looking more and more like his dad every day—thank you very much! However, with every blessing, there came a curse. And someday, maybe today, he'd have to warn Bailey how his eye-catching appeal might get him into trouble. Pride could take over and pull him down a path he didn't necessarily want to travel.

"Dad, what do you think?"

"Uh, I don't know, buddy. It's supposed to storm again this afternoon. I don't want his gun getting wet. It's the one thing of my dad's I really cherish. Why don't you just bring your twenty-gauge?"

Regardless of the fine mist stippling their faces now, they both knew that could change without notice—after all, they lived in Michigan. He pulled his arms through the sleeves of his rain jacket and tried to read the sky through the forest of trees. What he could see of the horizon looked moderately gray, which meant he and Bailey might get their entire hike in.

They planned to stay on the Shaw Lake Trail for only about ten minutes before deviating to the north and cutting their own path through the state game area. With any luck, they'd find their way to God's Soup Bowl. Then it'd be another five-minute hike due east and they'd be in deer heaven. If they were quiet, they might even catch a glimpse of some fox or turkey. And as long as Bailey had his shotgun with him, the boy might be motivated to keep his eyes open for some squirrel or rabbit.

While Ryan tossed his backpack over his shoulder, Bailey pulled on his own rain jacket, filled a pocket with shells, and then inspected the gun's empty chamber before double-checking the safety. He was a smart kid, always paying attention to the important details.

"All right! You got everything?"

Bailey looked up with a grin. "As long as you have the compass and snacks, I think we're good to go."

"Okay. Lead the way, buddy, and ... keep your eyes peeled for bear."

Turning around, Bailey gave him a no-nonsense glare. "Very funny, Dad."

"You think I'm kiddin', don't ya?" He let his eyes sparkle with mischief. "A good buddy of mine—well, you know Gary Foster —the guy who works for Somerset Township Fire and Rescue?" Bailey smiled and nodded, going along with the tall tale. "He said they got a call last week that a huge black bear tore into somebody's garbage dumpster before it turned on their Angus bull. Gary said the bear clawed the head off the beast as if it were a mushy banana or something—said he'd never seen anything like it before." They both broke out in hearty laughter that echoed all the way down the wooded path.

Yeah, this is the way God meant it to be. Father and son sharing a few laughs, enjoying the great outdoors, having a little adventure. Good things might happen out here. Forgiveness might be given. Respect might be restored. Trust might be built. And maybe, just maybe, Bailey might open his heart to spiritual things like God … and Jesus.

They walked along, commenting about the red squirrel and chipmunks rustling through the soggy leaves, and how the red-tailed hawk's cry stood out from all the other bird calls. And then they wondered what their chances were of running across some deer. After a while, they got quiet and let the dripping, pungent varied greens and browns of the forest entertain their senses. When the mist changed to drizzle, Bailey turned to look behind them at the concealed western horizon. "You think it's gonna storm, Dad?"

"I hope not. And if it does? We'll have a story we can tell for years to come." He paused to check their bearings. "Bailey, see the big oak up ahead on the left? We'll leave the trail there." After fishing in his pocket for the compass, he passed it off to his son. "Here, you can have the honors of keeping us on a straight course due north. We should wind up walking along the ridge of the amphitheater I told you about. It's really something to see. You're gonna love it."

Once they left the trail, Bailey did an excellent job keeping them on track, and like a good soldier, he kept morale high despite the rain beginning to fall at a steady clip. In between sighting some small game in his gun, Bailey provided the enter-tainment, gruesome as it was. The boy told story after story of the sometimes stupid and horrific ways people had succumbed to death. Where Bailey got his information was a mystery, but

Ryan did have to admit the stories were interesting. Thank goodness there weren't any tales of electrocution by lightning.

Just as the first rumblings of thunder rolled through the forest, Ryan noticed the landscape had begun to take on a new, familiar form. Instead of the thickly vegetated, black-soiled terrain of the hardwood forest, the topography now included more defined hills and valleys that were interspersed with glacial rocks and the stately presence of the white pine and its soft, aromatic, needle-like mulch. They were nearing God's Soup Bowl.

"There were these two guys who were totally wasted. They had this four-wheeled cart and were taking turns towing each other behind a big loader. Well, the guy being towed wasn't thinking and wrapped the tow strap all the way around his waist. That's when the unfortunate thing happened. As the guy on the loader went around a corne—"

He pulled on Bailey's shoulder and gestured for him to be quiet. "Listen." He smiled, envisioning a twelve-point buck or maybe a doe and a couple of fawns sniffing their way around the low brush of the evergreen forest. "Deer!" he mouthed.

Bailey's eyes got big. All his senses were clued into their surroundings. Standing still like the majestic pines around them, they listened hard above the steady beat of the rain. At first they heard nothing. Then finally they heard some rustling and ... someone talking? Who else would be dumb enough to be out in the middle of nowhere during a veritable downpour? Poachers? The DNR?

Tiptoeing up the lip of the bowl, Bailey hid behind a tree. Keeping quiet, he turned and whispered. "Dad, it's a man and ... someone or something else. I can't see very good. There's a big tree in the way."

Ryan silently left his spot to join his son. It felt a little odd spying on the man. If the guy proved to be a squatter or poacher, then he might not be happy to learn he had company. And most likely the dude carried a gun.

From Ryan's vantage point, the man seemed a bit agitated. He circled the ground as if something might attack at any moment. Could it be a badger? Or a rabid raccoon? In an attempt to get a better look, Ryan stepped to the left and hid behind another tree. That view wasn't much better. A huge greenish-gray rock eclipsed whatever was on the ground, occupying the man's attention.

"Dad, he's got a knife!" Bailey whispered. The boy moved to a tree on his right and stepped up on a conveniently placed boulder. "I bet he's gutting a deer."

"Shh. Listen." The guy had said something. Still, if he'd been gutting a deer by himself, who could he have spoken to? Himself? Could he be a nut case or something—a recluse or bum who lived under one of those rocks, only venturing out to kill an occasional deer for food? The man simply sat there, his shaven face barely visible behind the rock. No, he couldn't be a bum. He looked too put together, too clean.

Both he and Bailey watched and waited, intent on listening for the man's next move. They didn't have to wait long. The guy scooted back a bit and then his shoulders and upper arms pushed forward in a lunging motion. He was gutting a deer all right. "Poacher," he whispered in Bailey's direction.

Bailey's face had gone white like he'd seen a ghost. "Dad, it's … it's not a deer."

What else could it be? The only large game around here worth poaching was deer. Leaving his post, he sidled up next to Bailey on the rock. "What in the— Bailey, don't look!" He had to turn away himself. His mind could hardly grasp what his eyes had taken in. Two legs. Two human legs protruded from behind the rock! "Give me your gun, Bailey! Here, call 911. But be quiet." Adrenaline raced through his body and his hands shook like the first time he shot a deer. It made passing off the cell phone almost frustrating.

The whole forest seemed to shake too as thunder rumbled above them and made the rain fall even harder. "Shells! Give me some shells, Bailey!" While Bailey frantically fumbled in his pocket, Ryan tried to formulate a plan in his head. Nothing came. In faith, he maxed the gun out with three shots in the magazine and one in the chamber, and then he stepped from behind the tree. *God, help us do the right thing.*

"Dad!" Bailey's whisper turned him back. With the phone to his ear, fear filled the boy's eyes. "What should I tell them?"

"Tell them where we are, what you see, what I'm going to do."

Bailey looked toward the man sitting behind the rock and answered the voice on the other side of the phone. "Yes! Yes, w-we do! My dad and I are in the Barbour State Hunting Area, by God's Soup Bowl and ... There's a man ... We think he's killing someone, stabbing them. My dad has a gun, he's going to try and stop him."

Ryan nodded his approval and left Bailey to give his commentary. He tiptoed to the north following the rim of the bowl and edged up to a massive white pine. He crouched low, listening. Could that be a woman's voice? Creeping forward, he went over the edge of the bowl, crawled twenty feet or so, and hid behind a large boulder planted less than fifteen yards between him and the crazy man. Yes, the voice and those legs definitely belonged to a woman—an injured and bleeding woman!

Oh, God! What should I do? Steadying the gun on top of the rock, he clicked off the safety and took aim at the dark-haired man. Should he yell and let the man know of his presence? Or should he fire a warning shot and let the guy know what he was up against? *Help me, God.*

Strangely, the man didn't move. He seemed to enjoy

watching his victim suffer and writhe in pain. Ryan would have chucked the bile rising in his throat, but the man suddenly shifted and raised a large hunting knife above the woman's chest. *No! God, no!* Ryan turned his gun in the same rainy direction of his prayer and pulled the trigger.

The man nearly jumped out of his skin. Then leaving the knife where he'd dropped it, he scrambled to the nearest tree. Unfortunately, the psycho had a surprise of his own. He pulled a shiny handgun from his jacket pocket and took off running toward the southwest—right toward Bailey! *Oh, God, protect him!*

Ryan's whole being shook as he lowered his own firearm to his shoulder and kept the would-be fugitive in the gun's sight. Anticipating when the man would come out from behind the shelter of a smaller white pine, he made his shot sure. "Got him! Yes!" The man took a few stumbling steps, then fell to his hands and knees before he recovered and kept running with a gimpy trot. "Crap!" There had been too much distance between them. The guy's wounds were most likely superficial. Just the same, they would slow him up and make him identifiable in the very least.

Taking off in pursuit, Ryan ran parallel with the crazy freak. He had to keep the guy way east of where Bailey had been hiding behind the huge pine. Ryan kept one eye on the man's tall, limping frame while the other searched for the tree, the rock, and Bailey. *Where are you, Bailey?* Surely he should have reached his son by now.

"Dad! Over here!" *Oh, thank you, Lord.* The boy's voice had never sounded sweeter. Ryan sprinted the ten yards to the partial safety of their original lookout point and then let off one more very ineffective shot. The madman was too far away, and now a wooded hill stood between them and him, but ... What if the creep circled back and tried to finish them off with his ominous handgun?

"You all right, Bailey?" The boy responded with a nod then wiped away a tear before it fell over the rim of his eye. "Dad, t-take the phone. Please."

Out of breath, he nodded his understanding. "You did good, son." His hand trembled as he traded the gun for the phone. "There's one shot left in the gun, Bailey. Reload and watch our backs. Follow me."

CHAPTER TWENTY-FIVE

"Hello. Bailey, are you still there?" Ryan could hear the 911 dispatcher's voice even before he brought the phone to his ear.

"Hello. This is Ryan Ambrose, Bailey's dad. I don't know if Bailey told you. I, uh ... hit the guy with birdshot from about forty yards away. It wounded him enough to make him stumble and fall. Then he got up and ran away. He's carrying a handgun and heading due south from where we are on the west rim of God's Soup Bowl. Do you know where that is?" He didn't wait for the dispatcher to respond. "Almost in the middle of the Barbour State Hunting Area. The northeast portion of the south-west quadrant. The guy's wearing an olive-colored rain jacket and jeans, dark hair and he's tall. I don't know ... six three maybe and two hundred twenty pounds."

"Are you and your son all right, Mr. Ambrose?"

"Yes. The woman's gonna need immediate medical attention though. We're heading back to where she is right now."

"All right. Just ... please stay on the line."

"Yeah, we're not far from her now."

With his hand, he sheltered his eyes from the rain and

scanned the pine needle mulched floor of the amphitheater. There were so many rocks, and they all looked the same. *Help me find her, God.* His heart led him over to the left by a thigh-high rock where a dark pool of rainwater grew on the soft forest floor. Blood. He followed a rivulet of diluted blood upstream, around to the other side of the rock. The woman was nowhere to be seen. And the knife? He searched all around where he thought it'd been thrown. The knife had disappeared too.

He raised the phone to his ear. "The woman must have taken off. Probably scared to death. We're going to look around. She couldn't have gone far—not with the wounds she had." He motioned for Bailey to spread out and start searching for the woman. "She was stabbed a few times, at least. If we do find her alive, she's going to need help fast."

"An ambulance is on the way, Mr. Ambrose."

"An ambulance? I'm not an expert or anything, but I'm thinking helicopter-fast. In fact, I heard one way to the north."

"Actually, Mr. Ambrose, the helicopter is searching for someone." The Dispatcher paused. "Was the woman wearing a pink T-shirt?"

"She had on a pink T-shirt and jean shorts."

"Dad!" Bailey waved him over to where he stood and then pointed in the direction of a grouping of smaller trees and granite boulders. "She's over there."

Sure enough. A tiny portion of pink stuck out from behind the shelter of a rock. He spoke into the phone once again. "We found her. Hang tight a minute."

He and Bailey walked up the small embankment then stopped short of the naturally formed hideout. "Stay here, Bailey. Let me check things out first," he whispered. His shaking legs took him up the remaining three yards of the hill, and before approaching the cluster of rocks and small bush-like trees, he called out. "Hello. My name is Ryan Ambrose. Do you need some help?" When the T-shirt disappeared behind the rock, he glanced at Bailey then stepped up close enough so the woman could see him.

"Oh ... Dear Jesus ..." She wasn't a woman. She was a little girl. Well, a frightened teenager in tremendous pain. "It's okay, sweetheart. I'm going to help you." When he stepped closer, she moved further into her hiding place and threatened him with the hunting knife she held in her bloodied hand. She couldn't have hurt him even if she tried. Her whole body trembled like a leaf in a hurricane and her breaths came in tender, shallow gasps. Although her eyes rolled back in her head twice, she fought hard to stay conscious.

He crouched down and tried to look as reassuring as possible. "No one's going to hurt you anymore. The bad man's gone now, and ..." He raised his phone in view of her sight. "I have the 911 operator on the phone. The police and an ambulance are on the way. What's your name, darlin'?"

She didn't speak. Instead, a low moan of relief escaped her bruised and swollen lips. Then dropping the knife, raw emotion spilled from her black and blue, bloodshot eyes. "I want to go home," she pleaded through a pink, frothy foam that had formed at the corner of her lips.

"I know. I know you do. First, we should have someone attend to those wounds. Can you tell me your name?" He spoke as gently as he could despite the urgency of the situation. Her breaths were raspy and labored, and it seemed as if blood flowed from every part of her body.

"Here you go." He removed his rain jacket and placed it over her shivering body. "Why don't you tell me your name now?"

Pain showed up on her face as she coughed and finally looked into his eyes. "Miah ... Brennan."

"Miah? Is your dad's name Trace? I ... I know him. You lead worship at Open Door Bible Church, don't you?"

She closed her eyes to his questions and took in a shallow breath of air.

"Okay, Miah. We need to get you out of this rain and to a hospital. Would you let my son and I carry you out of these woods?"

She nodded and rested her head on the rock she'd been leaning against. "Thank you ... Thank you."

"I'm going to get my son and tell the 911 operator where to send the ambulance. I'll be right back. Okay?"

He hustled away from the shelter of rocks and trees, down to where Bailey waited wide-eyed and shaken. Ryan let his report to the 911 operator be his report to Bailey too. "Bailey and I are going to carry the girl out. I'm so afraid she's dying. Her lips are all blue and foam is coming out of her mouth, and ... and she's bleeding all over the place. Can you have an ambulance at the head of the Shaw Lake Trail in ten minutes? The trail is on the east side of Shaw Lake Road between Graves Hill and Harris Creek Road. I have my black Dodge Ram parked there. They'll see it."

"Did you get the woman's name?"

"Miah Brennan."

He ran back up the embankment with Bailey in tow. "Give me your jacket and brace yourself, buddy. This is not going to be pret—" Miah had moved to her hands and knees, and her body heaved as blood retched from her mouth and splattered to the ground. "Oh, no!" He covered his mouth as if to steady his own stomach. He couldn't bear to watch her die, nor could he let Bailey see it either. He backed up, sure he would lose it. Still, he managed to raise the phone to his mouth, gagging as he spoke. "She's puking up blood! Gallons of it! I ... I don't know what to do! Please hurry! Oh, dear God!"

Beneath his frantic ravings he could hear the dispatcher's voice calmly trying to take control of the situation. "Mr. Ambrose, as long as Miah is conscious and breathing, she's all right. I would advise you; do not move her."

"If we don't get her out of here, she's going to die!"

"Listen to me, Mr. Ambrose. Please. What I need you to do, if you can, is apply direct pressure to her wounds to stop the bleeding. Does she have any wounds on her chest?"

"Yes!"

"Okay. If you hear a sucking sound coming from the wound, cover it. Cover it with whatever you have: your hand, your wallet, a plastic wrapper. Just cover up the hole. Do you think you can do that?"

"Yeah, I'll ... I'll try." He turned to where Bailey had been leaning against a tree only to find his son had sunk to his haunches. "Bailey, are you okay?"

"Is she going to die, Dad?"

"I don't know, buddy. I ... I don't know. Why don't you stay here and ... and pray. If you believe in God, Bailey, pray for her."

He felt so guilty leaving Bailey alone with his questions, but he had to attend to Miah.

He stepped back into the small cove only to find her sad, bruised face had been emptied of all hope. Like Bailey, she knew exactly what was going on. She knew she was dying.

"Miah, the dispatcher said we need to stop the bleeding and cover this hole in your chest." Avoiding her heartbreaking eyes, he pulled the neckband of her T-shirt down and pressed his work ID over the blood-red wound that bubbled and gurgled with every breath she took. He tried to look past the dark bruises on her neck, yet try as he might, he couldn't stop himself from imagining what other kinds of torture the girl had been subjected to.

"I'm sorry ... I threw up on your jacket."

He shook his head and managed a smile. "Hey, it's no problem. Can you hold this card right there for me?" He paused and made sure she had the strength to keep his ID secure over the stab wound. "Good job, Miah." He smiled again, and she did too.

He gently lifted her chin to assess the inch-long cut on the underside of her jaw. "Your mouth—d-did your tongue ...?"

Nodding, tears grew on the rims of her eyes. And then sucking in a sob, she closed her eyes and let the salty grief tumble down her cheeks.

"You're doing good, Miah." He did a quick check of the wounds on her hand and the slash on the calf of her leg. "Y-You're doing great."

The barrage of pouring rain and the girl's labored breathing drowned out his quiet prayer as he pressed one of his socks into her belly. She seemed almost peaceful as she rested her head against the granite boulder and waited. Waited for what? Death? The paramedics?

He watched every minuscule rise and fall of her chest. Maybe it would be best if she did die. He couldn't imagine how she'd ever live with the psychological wounds she'd surely be inflicted with.

As if she read his thoughts, she took a deep breath and let out a mournful cry. "I'm so thirsty! I don't think I'm going to make it!"

Her sudden lament startled him. "Yes, you are. You're going to be fine, Miah."

"No." Her body shuddered. "Will you call my mum and dad? Tell them I love them. Tell them I ... I'm not afraid."

"Miah, you're not going to die—at least not if I can help it." He pulled the jacket up around her neck and scooped her up in his arms. "We're not waiting any longer. We're getting you to a hospital."

Claire's tears fell hard like the rain, and she tried to choke them back as she plodded through another thick patch of brambles. To her right, eight meters away, Trace pushed his way through a different tangled web of vegetation. Determined to find their daughter and bring her home, he trudged ahead, bracing himself against the rain and lightning. If only she could be as sure as Trace, then she could keep going. Then she could stop these crazy, morbid thoughts from poking holes in her fragile jar of hope. Swallowing her doubt, she forced Miah's name from her knotted throat.

Eight meters to her left, Brandt let out his own emotionally charged and desperate call. "Miah!" His voice rang loud and clear through the sodden woodlands like some primeval war cry.

If Miah were anywhere near, surely she would hear him. Surely the fervent strength in Brandt's voice would give her daughter the will to hold on. *Please, God. Let us find Miah ... alive.*

Since the police had lost Miah's trail a kilometer east of the north entrance to the state hunting area, they were sure Ronald Maddox had taken her here. "It matched his profile," she'd heard them say.

That's why Trace had insisted, against the police and Mrs. Tubergen's urging, to help in the search. They were all out here: the kids; their small group friends; and hundreds of others from church, school, the fair, and from who knows where. The kindness and concern were overwhelming. With this kind of support, surely God would turn this into something to be used for His glory. Wouldn't He? *Please, Lord, lead us to Miah.*

She turned an ear to the thump of the helicopter in the west. *God give them success. Help them see a sign or something ... anything!* And what could be keeping the helicopter from Detroit, the specially equipped one? They really needed it now. *Please, God. Send it quickly.*

Claire continued to pick her way through the dense brush, searching to the right, left, then straight ahead. As she turned back to the right, a dark red bramble grabbed hold of her rain jacket, pulling her back into its sharp clutches, "Ouch! Ow!" She stumbled backward and landed in the middle of the thick briar patch. If it hadn't been for the hundreds of thorns piercing her underside, she might have stayed there and let the rain wash away every last bit of angst needling her spirit.

"Mrs. Brennan!" Brandt charged through the thicket. "Are you all right?"

Wiping a tear away and struggling to get up, she accepted Brandt's offer for a hand up.

"You okay?" He repeated.

"Yes. Yes, thank you, Brandt." She stood and picked the thorns from her jacket while taking an assessment of her wounds. "Only a few scratches. I'm fine."

"Claire! Sweetheart, are you okay?" Trace had come to her rescue too. More than anything she wanted to collapse in his arms and let him carry this heavy load for them both. But she knew she shouldn't. Right now, he was as vulnerable as she—maybe even more so. She'd seen the guilt on his face. She knew he was ready and willing to take all the responsibility for this ... this unbelievable nightmare. If she ever voiced the unfair accusations that had been flinging around inside her brain, it would set a regrettable wedge between them for sure. *Please God, help me to not seek blame."*

She forced a smile past her tears and nodded her appreciation for Trace's concern.

"I've gotta get you out of this rain. I'm gonna call Brad and see if he's picked up Ben from the airport yet. I'll have him take you back to the gun club."

"No, Trace. I'm fine. Really, I'm fine."

Discounting the strength of her will, Trace pulled Rob's phone from the pocket of his rain jacket.

"Trace, please. If Miah is out here somewhere, I want to be out here too." She tried not to fume as he thumbed through Rob's contacts and raised the phone to his ear. "Trace, I'm not leaving." Planting her arms across her chest, she turned to Brandt for support. Despite his own strength and stature, Brandt only managed a helpless shrug.

"I guess you're gonna to get your way, Claire. I got Brad's voicemail." Trace folded the phone and took hold of her hand. "Well, for now let's walk together. Okay?"

She nodded her relief as Rob's phone rang above the hiss of rain.

"Ah ha! It's probably Brad." He opened the phone and brought it to his ear. "Hey, mate ..." She watched as her husband's countenance went from a confident I'm-in-charge look to a serious, concentrated expression. Then for a matter of seconds, his face turned hopeful before it finally settled into deep, troubling concern. "All right. We can be there in ten—no, five minutes!"

Trace folded the phone and pulled her in the direction they'd just come from. "Come on! They found Miah!"

CHAPTER TWENTY-SIX

Claire could hardly catch her breath. Heart-drumming anxiety left her feeling light-headed, almost panicky. Yet Trace and the police officer were there to catch her if she were to pass out. So was a whole campus of hospital personnel, for that matter. But she couldn't lose it now. Not after all the heroic efforts to ensure they would be here when Miah arrived.

She and Trace had sprinted through the rain and thick woodlands to meet up with a police cruiser that had whisked them past country and cityscapes in order to reach downtown Grand Rapids in record time.

Besides Marcus who had served as friend, doctor, and spokesperson, they'd beat everyone. They had arrived at the hospital before the other law enforcement officials, the media, and Miah herself. And now, all they could do was wait. What a horribly helpless feeling. If it hadn't been for Marcus and his steadying presence now, they'd be climbing these sterile walls.

For the past fifteen hours, Marcus remained an ever-loyal friend. Once they'd arrived here on his turf, he had gone right to work, pulling strings, which allowed her and Trace to wait here in this long, beige corridor. Right before heading down the restricted helipad concourse, Marcus had assured them that as soon as Miah arrived, she'd be brought through those double doors and down this same hallway where they were simply waiting ... simply praying.

What could be taking them so long, Lord? Was the helicopter having a hard time finding a place to land? Or ... or was there no longer a need to hurry? *Please, Jesus, keep Miah in Your care. Give me patience and calm my nerves.*

Trace broke his own silent vigil, checking Rob's phone for the third time. "It's been ten minutes, Claire. Don't you think they'd have Miah here by now?"

In answer to his question, the left door swung open, and Marcus strode toward them. His tall frame commanded respect while his kind eyes spoke volumes of compassion. "She's here—thirty seconds behind me. Trace ... Claire ..." His tan arms enfolded them both. "I just want to prepare you. She doesn't look like the Miah we know and love." What had Maddox done to her baby? What kinds of atrocities had her little girl suffered? "Look at me, Claire." Marcus bent toward her. "I believe everything can be fixed. All right? Remember that, okay?"

She and Trace had no time to respond. Both doors crashed open and a team of five or six medical staff hovered around a yellow, metal stretcher that seemed to move forward by its own will. As it came closer, Marcus coached them once again. "She's unconscious, but go ahead, let her know you're here."

At first, cool relief washed over her. As sad and desperate as the patient's condition appeared, it was plain to see, that this poor bloodied creature wasn't Miah. However, Trace, obviously influenced by the power of suggestion, wrapped his hands around the swollen and bruised face of the half-dead girl, then bent and whispered in her dirt and blood-caked ear. "Miah, Daddy and Mummy are here. Please hang on. Hang on, sweetheart. We love you, baby."

And then she saw it tangled in a clump of the girl's filthy, wet hair—the silver earring with three separate strands of shiny, dangling squares.

Dizzying, hot fear broke over her body as her eyes moved from the earring, past the girl's terribly puffed-up and discolored face, beyond the breathing tube protruding from her neck, all the way down to the girl's left arm, to an egg-shaped birthmark. Miah's birthmark!

"No! No!" A dark, brimstone cloud knocked her to the white tile floor, burning the incomprehensible truth into her mind. *Why? Why would you allow this, God?*

"Why? Why?"

"Shh ... It's all right."

A cool cloth touched Claire's brow, soothing the feverish panic that muddled her thinking. She followed the compassionate hand up to its owner.

"It's going to be all right, Claire." Faith Tubergen's caring blue eyes were filled with the surety of God's goodness even though, after thirty years, He had never answered the one question that kept this older woman waiting, trusting ... serving.

"Faith?" Claire sat up enough to accept the comfort Mrs. Tubergen offered. "Oh, Faith ..." Tears drowned out her words. "You're here? Thank you. It means so much."

"I'm glad I can be here, dear." Mrs. Tubergen continued to embrace her in a warm, motherly way—in a way Claire had never known from her mother, in a way she didn't really deserve. Her weak faith should have long ago disqualified her from this kind of unconditional love, but it didn't. Miraculously, it didn't. God saw fit to sink her knee-deep in love. Trace and the kids loved her. Trace's family loved her. Her friends loved her. In their strange way, her parents loved her too. Most importantly, God loved her. And whether Miah lived or not, like Faith

Tubergen, she would trust in God's never-wavering, never-failing love.

She sniffed back her tears and accepted the tissue Faith offered. "Where's Trace?" For the first time, she glanced around the small, lounge-like room.

"I'm right here, sweetheart." From behind her, Trace's reassuring hand patted her shoulder.

"I ... I passed out. We should go to Miah, Trace."

"She's in surgery, love. Marcus said it would take some time."

Faith smiled and nodded in agreement. "Why don't you rest now? There's nothing to do but wait anyway."

A light tap on the door interrupted the stillness, and then a nurse peeked in. "Mr. and Mrs. Brennan?" The young woman walked in followed by a train of disheveled Brennans, all with various expressions of shock and concern on their faces.

"When you're ready, I can walk you all down to the family lounge near surgery. I think you'll find it much more accommodating for such a large group." The nurse smiled, looking impressed with the number of family members able to gather in the small room.

Claire returned the smile and counted the living, breathing blessings, filling the cramped space. Each one, in their own way, filled her heart with courage: Trace, Rob, Amy, Brad, Josh, Brandt—yes, he belonged too, Drew and ... Miah who was with them in their thoughts and in their prayers.

***

"Dad ... Mum ... You made it. Judge ... Marjie ... Thank you for coming."

"Yes, yes. How is she, Tracey?"

"Asleep ... since yesterday ... five-hour surgery."

"Lost ... blood ... stomach... punctured lung ... oxygen levels ... fever..."

Untouchable as a breath, the voices whispered in and out like the winds across the desert highlands. Their hush sounded as familiar and comforting as the swish of tender Mitchell grass renewed by the rainy season, and it compelled her to stop and rest in the midst of the gentle tones. Miah sank deep in the verdant grasses, meaning to escape the storm and her pursuer, but a breathy gasp and a tug on her hand pulled her from her hiding place.

"Dear Jesus ... What did that monster do to my precious granddaughter? Be gracious to us, Lord. Be gracious to us all. Keep us from sinning while we await Your judgment to fall on the man who did this. Please help the police to find him. And please, God, heal Miah. Touch her body, Lord."

Granddad? Oh, Granddad ... You were right. The storm had been terrible—almost unbearable. I tried to stay calm like you said. Still, I cried. I couldn't help it. It hurts bad. So incredibly bad.

"It's Nana and Granddad, Miah. Can you hear us? We love you, sweetheart."

I love you too. We should hide ... In case Duane comes back.

"Miah, it's Mummy. Can you wake up? Grandfather and Grandmother McKinnon are here too ... all the way from Brisbane. Come on, baby."

Mummy! Please, we need to get out of here! Duane, he ... he may change his mind.

"It's all right, Claire. Let her sleep."

"Trace, why don't you take Claire and her parents downstairs for tea? Ella and I will sit with Miah."

"No, John. Trace, I can't leave. I want to be here when Miah comes to. She'll need me."

"Come on, Claire. You and Trace need a break. Let your mother and me get the boys and take you all out for some lunch. A different scene will do you good. John and Ella will call us if Miah starts to wake up."

Although the voices were beautiful, the peace and quiet were even lovelier. And so were the soft grasses. She lay back down in the patch of green and let the whispered conversation drift down the hall. The hall? She was so mixed up. Where was she? *Mummy! Daddy! Wait! Come back!*

"Ella! Quick! Fetch them. Miah's waking up!"

Ella? Nana?

"Miah, it's Granddad. It's okay, sweet. Don't cry. Granddad's here. Shh, now."

Gentleness wiped away her tears as strength clasped her left hand.

"'I will lift up my eyes to the hills—where does my help come from?' Come on, Miah. This is our Psalm. Can you say it with Granddad? 'My help comes from the Lord, the Maker of heaven and earth.'"

'He will not let your foot slip. He who watches over you will not slumber.' Her tongue felt thick with pain. Even so, she could move it.

"Come on, Miah. 'Indeed, He who watches over ...'"

'... Israel will neither slumber nor sleep. The Lord watches over you...'

"Can you open your eyes, darlin? We love you, Miah."

Yes ... Oh, I love you too. I didn't get a chance to say goodbye, to tell you how much I love you all. But I do. I love you all so very much. I'm sorry for all the bad things I've said and done—all my selfish ways.

"Miah."

Daddy. She wanted so badly to cross over into the land of the living, to the place where her loved ones gathered, yet obstacles of barbed-wire pain and black-as-death darkness made the elusive threshold impassable.

"Just as you left the room, tears pooled at the corner of her eyes. And she moved her lips ever so slightly. Didn't she, Ella?"

"I'm sorry, John. I didn't see it. I ran to get Trace."

"Well ... she did. She's going to be all right. I just know it."

Trace turned his eyes to Miah's unmoving body. *God, please let it be true.* He wanted to believe Miah would wake up, but what about the doctors' reports? Hadn't they said the extent and speed of Miah's recovery was left to be seen because of the critically low blood oxygen levels her body experienced? Hadn't they cautioned he and Claire about the poison that had entered Miah's abdominal cavity through the stab wound in her stomach? And he certainly couldn't discount the mysterious fever Miah had from the time she had been brought in. The doctors still hadn't been able to pinpoint the cause. So, how could he allow himself to believe his one and only daughter was out of the woods?

It seemed the professionals were either padding the fall or creating a large margin for fate. Even Marcus had wavered between truth and optimism. After observing Miah's lengthy operation, something akin to shell shock had widened Marcus' eyes as he emerged from the catacomb of operating theaters. When he walked down the hallway toward the lounge where they'd all been waiting, Marcus had stopped short and clung to Trina as if she were his last, desperate handhold on all God deemed good. He looked so vulnerable, so grief-stricken.

After a moment's time however, like an amateur magician, Marcus had turned from the large gathering. When Marcus stepped back around, he had put on his doctor face and assumed his familiar, confident posture as he finished his walk down the corridor and delivered a positive report to the waiting crowd. Nevertheless, something very distressful had rattled Marcus. He'd simply chosen not to share it. Fifteen minutes later, after the surgeons had echoed Marcus' cautiously optimistic report, he'd bowed out to get some much-needed sleep.

"Claire, how is she?" A man's voice whispered above the hum of machines and electronic equipment.

"Bryce ... Celia. Hi. No change, really. She's still unconscious. How did church go?"

Church? Oh yeah, it was Sunday. Trace turned from the reassuring blip of the heart monitor, accepting a quick embrace from his friend and pastor. "Hey, mate. Thanks for coming back."

"You've been in our thoughts all morning, Trace. We had a special prayer time for Miah—for your whole family." Bryce extended a hand to Claire's mum and dad, taking the lead in making introductions. "Your Honor and Mrs. McKinnon, I'm Bryce Harrison, and this is my wife, Celia. So pleased to meet you." He reached across the bed. "John and Ella, it's good to see you again."

Then Bryce turned his attention toward Miah who lay at his side, mercifully oblivious to her pain, to all the tubes and monitors, and the seven pairs of eyes watching over her. Bryce's hand white-knuckled the railing as if by strength alone he could keep his brimming tears at bay. "Trace ... Claire."

Regardless of Bryce having stood here last night, reeling from grief like the rest of them, the morning had yet to provide him, or any of them, with new mercies. *Lord, I'm so thankful You brought Miah back to us. Thank you for Bryce, Marcus, C.J.—all our friends who have stood beside us, but ... Where's the joy? Why all this pain? What good could possibly come from it?*

"You ... you may be all prayed out, guys." Bryce's chin quivered as he peered through his tears. "However, I ... I'd like us to gather around Miah. Let's thank God ... Healing starts with a grateful heart, and ... and healing is what we all need."

Holding hands and locking arms, everyone shuffled close to Miah's bed which gave Bryce time to collect himself.

"Father God ... we are undeserving of Your love and constant care. In Your infinite kindness and because of Jesus, our Substitute Sufferer, You have made a way for us to come before You with purified hearts. Would You, in Your goodness, meet us here and accept the offerings of our praise? There is no one like You, God. Only You can heal the sick and raise the dead. Only You can truly save the lost. Thank You, Lord, for bringing Miah back to us alive. Thank You for Your peace and strength, for helping Trace, Claire, and their family stay faithful through the past thirty-six difficult hours. Because You do not withhold any good thing from those who love You, we trust You to bring healing to this family in Your time and in Your way. In their suffering, give them hope, allowing them to look beyond their current pain toward something better. Thank You, Lord, for Ronald Maddox's surrender, for putting an end ..."

Ronald Maddox's surrender? Whoa! Whoa! Wait a minute! When did this happen? Bryce's prayer continued, and yet, Trace didn't hear a single thing beyond that shocking bit of news. He needed some answers, and he needed them now! Stepping away from the circle, he pulled Rob's phone from his hip and dialed the detective. She was going to have some explaining to do. He pushed open the door and walked into the hallway to wait out the one, two, three, four rings. "Come on, sergeant, pick up!"

"Kruger here."

"Detective, this is Trace Brennan."

"Mr. Brennan! How is Miah?"

"Ms. Kruger, did you find Ronald Maddox?"

"... Yes ... Don't tell me you heard it over the radio again."

He let his silence speak for his anger. "Not the radio. My pastor."

"You're not going to believe this. I called dispatch and asked them to have the deputy inform you. Deputy Wosniak—he had accompanied you. Isn't that right?"

"No. Deputy Cooper."

She cursed and then cleared her throat. "I'm sorry, Mr. Brennan. The way things went down last night, it got really crazy."

"Where is Maddox, sergeant? I want to see him."

After a long, deliberate pause, the detective replied in a carefully measured manner. "He needed some medical attention, Mr. Brennan. He'll be arraigned first thing Tuesday morning. You can see him then; however, he won't be allowed to talk with you."

"No. Not good enough." He gave his head an impatient shake. "I'm not going to wait until Tuesday. If he's here somewhere on this medical campus, I'll find him."

"I don't know what you're hoping to accomplish, Mr. Brennan, but He's not there anymore. He's in the county jail, and I doubt he'll be getting out before his trial."

"Good. Then I guess he'll never get out of jail. And if he does, I'll kill him! I'll string him up and stick him with a dulled Mayall knife! Pass that along to the bloody, son of a—"

"Trace ..." Reason whispered his name as an arm reached across his back and steadied his trembling shoulder on the left. "There's another way, son." Dad's sad blue eyes looked right into his shaken core.

Trace lowered the phone and choked back fiery tears. "Dad, I'm almost fifty years old. I don't think I need you as my conscience anymore." His blurred eyes challenged the love of his father as he brought the phone back up to his ear. "Detective, you can tell Ronald Maddox ..." *O God, I have been faithful! I have served you for forty years! I left my home and my country for you. Don't I deserve better? Why? Why are you making my family suffer like this?*

"Mr. Brennan, are you there?"

Sensing his crumbling resolve, he tried to clear the rubble of emotion from his throat. "Ms. Kruger." And while the battle for right and wrong continued, he knew his old nature would inevitably surrender. "I ... I'm sorry."

In the final conflict, mercy and condemnation collided within his inner being, rocking him forward into his father's grasp. "I'm sorry, Dad. I'm so sorry. I hate him! I hate Ronald

Maddox so much!" His sobs echoed loud and unashamed throughout the open corridor. "Why? How could he have done this to Miah? Why would God allow it? Isn't He supposed to watch over those who follow Him?"

"He does, Tracey. He brought Miah back to us, didn't He? She's here and she's safe. Even if God had let her die, He would still love us. He would continue to care. He would want us to trust in Him."

Dad's eyes looked as pained as he felt.

"Did God love His Son, Trace? Of course, He did. Yet he allowed Jesus to suffer and die, all for a greater good. Did Jesus deserve the pain and suffering of the cross? Absolutely not. He endured it because He trusted His Father to raise him again. And like Jesus' journey of suffering was a journey of trust, so is ours. So is Miah's going to be. Just like Pastor Bryce prayed, we must cling to a hope that looks beyond our current pain, to something better. Right now, we have to trust God is going to make something good of this. We need to trust Miah is going to be all right."

"How? How is she ever going to get over what that ... that beast did to her?"

The double doors to the ICU opened, and The Judge peeked his head into the hall.

"Trace! John! She's waking up!"

CHAPTER TWENTY-SEVEN

"Yes, four o'clock. See you then." Wagging his head, Trace closed his phone, then flipped his Bible back open to the first chapter of James. Miah had been conscious for only twenty-four hours; couldn't they give it a break? Ever since word got out that she'd awakened, there had been a steady request for interviews: the police, a hospital spokesperson, someone from the District Attorney's office, and now Ronald Maddox's lawyer wanted to stop in at four? Really? Was interviewing Miah truly part of their jobs or were these people simply using their authority to satisfy a personal curiosity about the girl who had "Survived a Night with a Serial Killer," as the paper had headlined?

It would be thoughtful if they could at least give her a couple of days. Miah needed some time to heal body, mind, and soul. And to be honest, he and Claire needed the same. They would need to develop the right frame of mind to hear Miah's entire story. Even though Miah seemed fairly strong and in good spirits, it tore him up to watch her force words past the breathing tube and out her sore, stitched-up mouth. And as precious as her tears were, he found it so difficult to watch them fall to her brave, battered smile.

With time, he knew all her cuts and bruises would heal. And the respiratory specialist had assured them once the breathing tube was removed and the swelling went down, Miah's voice would be as beautiful as ever. The wounds of her soul, however, might take a lifetime to heal. *O God, I don't understand....*

His thoughts returned to the ancient scripture laying open in his lap. *Consider it pure joy, my brothers, whenever you face trials of many kinds, because you know that the testing of your faith develops perseverance ...* How many times would he have to read these words before he could really believe them? His eyes left the pages of his Bible and stared at the monitors keeping guard over Miah's vital signs. Pulse: sixty-five. Good. Respiration: twelve. Good. Oxygen: ninety-eight percent. Good. Blood pressure: one ten over sixty. Good. Temperature: one hundred point three. Better. Much better. And thank the Lord, she was resting peacefully.

Closing the leather-bound book, Trace stood, leaned over the bedrail, and brushed Miah's brow with his lips. "Her temp's gone down a little," he whispered.

Claire licked another envelope closed, then nodded. Of course, Claire already knew Miah's temperature. Claire could do five things at one time: track a monitor, pray, sip her tea, keep people up to date over the phone, and write thank-you notes. She'd spent the last hour writing to a few of the hundreds of people who had been a huge help in their time of need. The outpouring of support had been astounding, and offers of help and promises of prayers from friends and strangers alike were still coming in. It seemed unthinkable how this wonderful community of people could attract someone as malicious as Ronald Duane Maddox.

Claire set her writing down and met him at Miah's bedside.

"One hundred point three. Her temp is so much better. But look. Her urine is still cloudy." They both studied the bag of yellow output as if it were the most normal thing to do.

"Aye. But the urologist said, once those antibiotics kick in, it'll clear up." He took hold of Claire's hand and gave it a squeeze. It puzzled him how three doctors couldn't figure out the reason for Miah's fever until she'd finally woken up and told them. Nevertheless, he couldn't complain, those doctors had literally saved Miah's life. Two times they had lost her heartbeat. Twice they had done everything they could to bring her back— which explained why Marcus had emerged from Miah's surgery absolutely unnerved.

Of course, hindsight is always twenty-twenty. If he had known what was going to happen behind the doors of the operating room, he never would have allowed Marcus in there with Miah. It had hit too close to home. So close, that neither Marcus nor Bri had been able to visit yet. When Trina came up to the hospital yesterday with C.J. and Teá, she said both Marcus and Bri were struggling. As badly as they wanted to see Miah, they needed a little time to debrief. And that's why they weren't there when Miah finally woke up yesterday. Too bad. The experience probably would have healed what ailed them.

It had been two in the afternoon yesterday when The Judge had called him and his dad back into the ICU. He and Claire, their parents, and the Harrisons all stood around Miah's bed and watched the miracle unfold. It was the most beautiful, gut-wrenching, ironically-Miah thing he'd ever witnessed.

Like usual, her waking up had been a drawn-out process. At first, she took in a deep breath. After finding how painful the simple act of breathing was, she merely shuffled a leg beneath her covers. Then she must have thought she'd try out an arm. To everyone's surprise, her left arm came up and took a wide sweep, nearly exposing herself. Quick smart, Claire readjusted Miah's gown and covers, all the while whispering words of assurance. Even so, Miah thrashed about obviously agitated by all the pain. It nearly tore his heart out. Then she began rolling her tongue around inside her swollen, stitched up mouth. Later, she told them she thought the stitches were dirt.

After several unsuccessful attempts at working the "dirt" out of her mouth with her tongue, Miah reached up, not too adeptly, and tried to scrape it out with her fingers. When the pulse-taker thingo kept getting in the way, her frustration came out in the form of a high-pitched cry, sounding much like a newborn foal testing its voice for the first time. Miah's pain-filled tears brought a flood of tears to Claire, himself, and everyone else in the room —even the nurse.

"Miah, it's okay. Mummy's here," Claire soothed. Then like a beautiful, blue butterfly Miah's right eye fluttered open—her left eye was swollen shut. She took in all seven pairs of eyes, then smiled through her tears. "A party?" she squeaked in her barely audible, scratchy voice. "A party?"

"A party. Yes, sweetheart, a party." Claire choked.

"Sing, Mummy."

"What? What shall we sing, Miah?" Claire asked despite her own tears.

"Jesus Loves Me."

And so, they did until everyone had received a hug—well, a partial hug. Miah couldn't lift her right arm. It hurt too much. Then the very patient but keen nurse deemed the "party" over and sent the visitors out to the lounge where the rest of their family and friends were waiting. Just in time too. Miah had hidden her pain for as long as she could. When everyone left, she'd broken down and sobbed. Grief poured from her soul like a violent rushing river, and then surprisingly, she clutched her lower abdomen and side.

It only took a minute for the doctor to diagnose the bladder infection and although Miah's fever had come down today, what with all her injuries, she was still so very sick—not in any condition to entertain more questions, especially from Ronald Maddox's attorney.

"Mr. and Mrs. Brennan? Hi. Kyle Buschke. Thank you for letting me talk with Miah. How's she doing?"

Kyle Buschke? Should she know that name? Although Miah wanted to open her eyes and see the face belonging to the kind voice, a steady drip of medication made dozing the more desirable option.

"Well, Mr. Buschke, let me put it this way, she's alive. And your client should feel very lucky she is."

Your client? Who was Dad whispering with?

"Yes, I know. That's why I wanted to talk with you ... and Miah." The man paused as if he had expected the I.V. pump to sound off like it did. He cleared his voice and waited for someone to reset the pump and leave the room before he spoke again. "Mr. Maddox asked me to speak with you on his behalf. I agreed only because I thought it might bring you and your family some peace."

This time Dad cleared his voice. "Whatever Maddox has to say, we'll hear it in court. He's a deceiver, Mr. Buschke. He's the devil himself, and I won't fall for his lies again."

"I understand. But there's not going to be a trial."

"Pig's arse, there's not!"

"Trace ..."

Mummy!

"We'll be waiving the preliminary examination. Mr. Maddox is determined to plead guilty at his arraignment in circuit court. That is, if Miah and you can forgive him."

Duane. They were talking about Duane. Forgive him? Oh, yeah ... She'd told him she could. Somehow, she had to forgive him if she wanted God to forgive her sins. That's how it worked, didn't it? 'Forgive us our debts as we forgive our debtors.' 'If you do not forgive others their sins, your Father will not forgive your sins.' But God wouldn't expect her to forgive a serial killer, would he? She could hardly fathom that God's commands about forgiveness could apply to the likes of Duane. But if they did, then, true to his cruel and manipulative character, Duane had her right where he wanted her; stuck between a rock and a hard place. Pinned—no, stabbed —to the proverbial wall.

"What? And if we won't? Then what's he going to do?"

"He could push forward with a trial and drag Miah through a lot of grief. Considering he has a prior conviction and has confessed to four other kidnappings and murders, he would most likely be extending his life by going to trial. But instead, he's seeking forgiveness in exchange for no trial. I'm not saying you should forgive Mr. Maddox or assuming you could. I'm merely delivering a message. Mr. Maddox said Miah had to forgive him. He said she'd know what he meant."

She knew what he meant all right. Every stab of his knife, every mocking inquiry about how far grace could reach had a purpose, had a pointed meaning.

"Oh, for crying out loud! What is he up to?"

"I don't think my client is up to anything, Mr. Brennan. I believe he's simply looking for some forgiveness. The man doesn't have anything else."

"And I'm supposed to care?" An uncomfortable silence filled the air, then finally, someone shuffled their feet.

"You're a Christian aren't you, Mr. Brennan?"

"Are you mocking me? Because if you are, we're done talking, Mr. Buschke."

"No. Not at all. Jesus calls us to forgive, doesn't He?"

"Us? Don't tell me you're ... How can you defend him? I

haven't heard an apology. I haven't seen any signs of repentance from your client! Give me some evidence, counselor!"

"Trace ... Please ..."

"Claire, it's fine."

"I do have a note from Mr. Maddox. I'd like to read it to Miah, if I could."

The man hesitated a long time. When he finally spoke again, he startled her from the cozy cocoon of Daddy's easy chair. She'd been writing something. No, she'd been reading ... a letter ... splattered with blood ... a letter from Duane.

"Mr. Brennan, Mrs. Brennan." The man's voice dropped to a hush; still, she could hear it. "In his letter, Mr. Maddox expresses how sorry he is for what he did to Miah. I believe he's sincere."

"There's not a sincere bone in his body! Ronald Maddox is a blood-thirsty killer. He murdered four people. And if it wasn't for Ryan Ambrose, he would have murdered one more!"

Ryan Ambrose? Oh, yeah ... Thank you, Mr. Ambrose.

"Ronald Maddox is a hurting and disillusioned man, Mr. Brennan!" The man's voice was full of energy. He paused as if to gather his emotion and stuff it back in his chest. When he spoke again, his quiet voice sounded much more controlled. "I'm sorry. I'm not here to argue. I simply wanted to deliver a message of goodwill."

"Well, we won't accept it."

Why was Dad being so rude, so unlike himself? If she could only break through the foggy curtain of her medication, she'd intervene for the soft-spoken visitor.

"Mr. Brennan, I don't suppose you're familiar with the circumstances of Mr. Maddox's prior conviction, are you?"

"Aye. Somewhat."

"I met Ronald Maddox seventeen years ago when he'd been a bewildered, twenty-one-year-old, wondering how he got himself into the sticky predicament of a CSC charge."

"CSC?"

"Criminal Sexual Conduct."

"Right ... With a seventeen-year-old."

"Yes. Ava Carpenter."

Ava ... seventeen.

"From what I could see, Ronald Maddox was a good kid who made a stupid mistake. He was unfortunate enough to have me, a public defender fresh out of law school, assigned to his case. As a new Christian, I wanted to use my faith to shed some light in an otherwise dark place. I had built a very trusting relationship with my client. So trusting, I believe Ronald had been close to surrendering his life to Christ."

Why, Lord? Why didn't he?

"His sister, Charis, had recently become a believer and seemed to have some influence on him. The softening of his heart happened even when it appeared the plaintiff and her father were lying. Regretfully, Ava's dad, who regarded himself as religious, appeared to be a horrible example of a righteous leader. Ronald claimed the man had been taking advantage of Ava."

Yes. That's what he told me too.

"After meeting the family, I believed Ronald. Ava's father wasn't like Jesus in any way. The man reeked of arrogance, domination, and hypocrisy; his wife and children lived in dread. Unfortunately, I assumed the jury would see his character as clearly as I did. I had been so naïve. If I had known then what I know now, I would have pushed Ava's father so hard, he would have confessed every last sin he'd ever committed. I would have demanded the truth from Ava Carpenter and dragged her shame all over the courtroom for everyone to see.

"I know it wouldn't have excused Ronald Maddox from what he did. However, it may have given him a sense of justice and of being heard and believed.

"If only I had done my job right, the story may have turned out differently. Maybe your daughter wouldn't be lying here right now, hooked up to all these tubes and machines. Maybe four other families wouldn't be grieving the tragic deaths of their daughters. And maybe Ronald would have turned out to be a well-adjusted family man. Instead, when I lost his case, the glimmer of light in his young eyes turned to cold, angry darkness."

I saw and felt the darkness.

"And despite all my visits during his time in prison, I couldn't break through his thick wall of bitterness. I feel so responsible for what happened. I let so many people down, especially Ronald Maddox. Mr. Brennan, I'm only asking you to hear his apology.

"I don't know what your daughter said to him, but Ronald confessed his sin before me, the chaplain, before God—and he wants to do the same before you and Miah. His final confession will take place in circuit court before the judge.

"Mr. Brennan, please. Bitterness is what drove Ronald Maddox to do what he did. Don't let it take hold of you too. You can make a difference here. Mr. Maddox has admitted to four crimes, which were unfortunately committed in states allowing the death penalty. I'm afraid his days are numbered. With the knowledge of your forgiveness, perhaps he can live them in the light of God's grace."

Dad inhaled as if starting to speak. He shuffled to her bed and rattled the bedrail with the weight of his grip. "You ..."

Was Daddy crying? Daddy ...

"Mr. Buschke, you don't understand what you're asking. It's too soon. Way too soon." Dad sniffed back his tears. "If Maddox walked into this room right now ... I would kill him." The room was quiet except for the hiss of oxygen. "I am so angry—so bloody angry and hurting. What will my little girl feel when she's fully aware and has to face the horror of what has happened to her?" Dad's weight left the bedrail and his feet shuffled again. This time his measured voice was aimed toward the door. "Maddox is a master of deception. He deceived you back in nineteen eighty-four, and he's deceiving you now, Mr. Buschke. He will *not* deceive me again." Dad walked toward the door. "Out of respect for your time, I'll take the note. And out of respect for us, why don't you wait a few months and see if Maddox's sudden conversion bears fruit."

CHAPTER TWENTY-EIGHT

"How thoughtful ... This one is from the Woodwards." Mum held up the multicolored greeting card and leaned in closer to the hospital bed. "Can you see it all right, sweetheart?"

Miah nodded despite her left eye only producing a shadowy image of everything in the gray and aqua-accented ICU room.

"It says, 'Praying you'll get well soon. May your every need be met through the encouraging gestures of friends, through the warm love and support of family, through the fine wisdom and knowledge of doctors and nurses ... And through the healing hand of God.' And then there's a verse down here. 'Put your trust in the LORD. Psalm 4:5.' They signed it, 'Dear Miah, you have been in our thoughts and prayers constantly.' Constantly is underlined. 'We're hoping God will fill your heart with peace, knowing you are loved and cared for deeply by your friends. Sincerely, Jack, Sue, Rylee, Macie, and Jackie Jr.' Oh, and look! Jackie made a picture on the back. He wrote, 'I love Miah. She plays the guitar real good.' He spelled guitar, g - e - t - a - r. And there's a picture of you playing your guitar. Isn't it just the cutest?" Mum smiled and held the picture so she could see it.

Mum was right. Childlike charm flowed from the purple stick girl with long yellow hair. The girl, who she assumed to be herself, held what looked like a giant, red banjo and stood in a patch of orange circles with blue stems. And what was the pink thing at the top? "What's the pink thing, Mum?"

"I believe it's supposed to be a heart." Mum giggled then pulled another card from her lap. "Let's see. This one is from ... Oh! This is from the man who found you, Miah. Ryan Ambrose and his son, Bailey. They stopped by to see you, only you were asleep. Did you know he goes to Open Door too?"

"Knock. Knock. Is eight o'clock too late for a visitor?"

"No, not for us." Mum mimicked the caller's whisper. "The nurse may have a little something to say about it, but come in. Come in."

It took too much effort to turn her sore, collared neck toward the door, so she didn't. Instead, she closed her eyes, enjoying the medicated peace while the visitor tiptoed in, came around to the other side of the bed, and stood next to where Mum sat.

"I would have been here sooner, but your husband was determined to get every last cow checked and treated for pink eye. How's she doing tonight?" The stranger's voice remained hushed.

"She's been sleeping *a lot*. Brandt, the flowers you brought are beautiful."

So, the quiet stranger wasn't a stranger after all. Ever since her first day of consciousness, Brandt had been a faithful, hovering presence. Never saying much, simply keeping watch over her like an angel—a beautiful, bronzed angel.

"You think she'll like 'em?" Doubt brushed over his whisper.

"Let's find out, shall we? Miah ... Brandt is here. Look, sweetheart."

She opened her eyes and tried to disguise the queasiness churning within her tender belly. Oh! The flowers *were* beautiful! Her friend stood at Mum's side, bearing a bouquet of the most delicate rosebuds she'd ever seen. Regretfully, all she could muster was a breathy, "hey."

"Hey, yourself." Concern tempered Brandt's lopsided smile as he slipped past Mum, bent close, and kissed her forehead—the only place on her face that didn't really hurt too much. "How you feelin'?"

She simply nodded and returned his smile. If she lay completely still, it seemed to keep the nausea to a minimum. "They're so pretty," she managed to squeak.

"Yeah? You like 'em? They made me think of you—pure, natural beauty."

Pure? Beauty? If a person had ever described her as beautiful, they surely couldn't now. Not anymore. Heartache over her loss welled up in her eyes, tightening her throat and momentarily hindering her ability to speak.

Brandt swallowed hard as if to keep his own feelings from seeping out. "There's a dozen here. Ten white and two yellow. The yellow are supposed to stand for me and you. The florist came up with the idea. I liked it. I hope you do too." He swallowed again then permitted a nervous cough to escape his mouth. Was her battered face triggering painful memories of Skye's premature death? Did the injustice of it all make him feel as if he'd been violated too? Yes, most definitely. She could see the grief simmering in his coal-colored eyes.

Mum must have seen it or at least sensed it too. She rose from her chair and patted Brandt's arm. "I'm going to step out for a few minutes to stretch my legs and get some fresh air. Will you two be all right?"

Brandt hid his face from Mum, clearing his throat of his telltale emotion. "You okay with that, Miah?"

She nodded.

"All right. I'll be back in fifteen or twenty minutes. Just going to grab a snack before the cafeteria closes."

"Take your time, Mrs. Brennan. I'll watch over her." He

followed Mum as far as the small, wheeled tray sitting against the wall. Then pulling it close to the bed, he placed the crystal-looking vase with its petite, white and yellow bouquet right where she could see it. "How's that, Miah?"

She gave him a weak thumbs up with her bandaged right hand, then turning, he snapped his fingers as if banishing sorrow from the room. "Oh! I almost forgot!"

He walked back toward the door and picked up the backpack he must have dropped when he first came in. "I worked at the farm today. With Mr. Ellison. What a great guy. He told me to tell you he likes what you did with the music studio. And when I left, Josh handed me these. He said you had asked for them."

Brandt reached into the pack and pulled out her spiral-bound journal and the black frame that held the object of all her hopes and dreams. He walked back over to the tray and placed both next to the flowers. "This pic is awesome, Miah. Where was it taken?"

Yes, it was awesome. And she hoped it would give her the inspiration to get beyond this ... this trial ... this tribulation—if that's what she dared call it.

Brandt stepped up to her bedside. "Where'd you snap it, Miah?"

"Wyoming."

As recognition sparked in his eyes, he snagged the photo again to take a closer look. "So, this is the picture of the cowboy you fell in love with? Which guy is it, Miah? The old cowpoke or the young wrangler?" He chuckled in spite of himself.

"Funny."

"How do you know he's not an ugly son of a gun? You can hardly see the dude's face. I'm still jealous though." He pulled a smug grin and placed the picture face down on the tray.

"Hey."

"You can look at it when I'm not here."

"It's my inspiration."

"Whatever ..." He turned and set the haunting, golden-hued portrait back up so she could see it. Then he drew close, his face looking all gentle breezes and quiet waters. "... whatever it takes to get you home. Are you comfortable?"

No, she wasn't. A brew of pain and hot bile boiled within her stomach. But she'd never tell him. She wanted him to stay. She wanted him to remain like an eternal mountain range, whispering of everything sure, everything strong.

"Do you want a drink of water?"

She closed her eyes, willing the nausea to subside. "I'm fine ... Actually, I ... I need the nurse. I'm going to be sick!"

Brandt fumbled with the call button as lemony reflux stung her throat, causing her to gag. Then to her embarrassment, he grabbed a small plastic tub and held it in front of her chest.

"She's gonna throw up!" he shouted at the rush of energy that burst into the room.

In one efficient motion, the nurse worked the bed controls while rearranging the plastic weave of I.V. lines, drainage tubes, and monitor wires. "Watch the tracheostomy, young man. And Miah, brace your incisions."

Like she'd done before, she pressed a pillow tight against her wounds, insulating herself from the serrating pain. It didn't help trying to mute her retching; the brownish evidence spewed into the pan, giving away her anguish, bringing with it a spasm of coughing. Tears, snot, and sweat broke out from every pore in her face, and all the while Brandt held the puke-colored pan, smoothing her back. Why did she let Mum leave? Why did Brandt have to see her like this? Surely her fit made his own stomach turn.

Once her coughing and heaving subsided, the nurse provided a warm, wet cloth and some encouraging words. "You're a trooper, Miah. The toughest patient I've ever had."

She nodded her thanks and wiped at her tears as Brandt

stepped away, spitting out a curse beneath his breath. Clearly, this had shaken him.

How could she have been so selfish? How could she have wanted Brandt to stay, to join in this ... this suffering? Hadn't he suffered enough already? She turned away from the lights and commotion and let shame close over her tears. If death came and swallowed her up, she wouldn't care. Not one bit.

She lay still as the tombstones in her cowboy's picture and remained motionless while the nurse listened to her lungs, checked the drainage tubes, and then hustled from the room, promising to return to suction the tracheostomy.

With nothing but the hum and click of machines to fill the silence, Brandt's presence loomed even larger, more infinitely rooted. This would not be easy. As much as she wanted Brandt to stay, the right thing would be to give him freedom from this sterile cage of painful memories.

"Miah?" He shuffled to the bed's edge, whispering her name as if it were magic. Then like the brush of an angel's wing, his touch drew rainbows across her skin. "Miah ..." No, he wasn't going to make this easy.

"Hey ... Are you okay?" He came around to the other side of the bed where she had no chance of avoiding his goodness. "Miah, you're doing it again. Don't push me away. Please, I want to help. I have to help. I ... I'm feeling responsible for all of this."

"What?" She forced herself to look into the unexpected wave of emotion in Brandt's dark eyes.

A surprising tear zigzagged its way down his cheek and fell to her arm.

"Brandt, you ... you don't have to stay. This is too much for you."

He leaned in even closer, licking a tear from his lip. "I ... I'm so sorry, Miah."

She watched in unbelief as an internal flame ignited everything that had kept Brandt stitched to her side the past four days.

"I should have walked you to the camper." He dropped into Mum's chair as his whole body rocked under the weight of his regret. "Oh my God. I could have prevented this ... this nightmare—everything Maddox did to you, everything you're going through now. I'm so, so sorry, Miah."

"No." She reached for his arm. "Brandt ... don't." Where did all this come from? How could he even think this? What happened to her simply happened. No one was to blame. No one but Duane himself.

"I've played Friday night over and over in my head. I had so many opportunities to stop Maddox. At the concert—if only I had known he'd been watching you. At the dance—I should have taken him out right then and there. And ... and I should have walked you all the way to your camper. If only I had walked you to your camper! I'm so sorry."

With every slow turn of his bowed head, Brandt's black braid wagged back and forth like the tail of a guilty puppy. But Brandt wasn't guilty—of anything.

He looked up, suddenly unashamed of his tears. "Miah, what happened ... after I left? How did he take you?"

She shook her head. No. She would never tell him. Already, he was paying a self-induced penance for a sin he didn't commit.

"Miah." He moved close, hovering above her like mist over stormy seas. "Tell me."

The memory began to stir the mire in her gut again.

"Have you told your mom, Miah?"

"Not everything."

"Your dad?"

She bit back the building grief and nausea.

"Drew?"

A tear slipped from the corner of her eye. "Leave me alone, Brandt."

"Have you told Bri? Miah, did you tell Bri?"

This time a whole stream of tears bubbled up from the murky waters of her soul. "She hasn't … I haven't seen her yet."

"Then tell me, Miah. Let me bear this with you. Maybe Bri's not strong enough right now. But I am. You need to get it out and … and I need to hear it. Miah, please. I want to walk through this mess with you. I care about you so much." When she didn't budge, Brandt bent and kissed the scabbed-over bump on her lip. "Okay then. Start with something small. Like, what happened here?" He ran a gentle fingertip over the tender wound.

She shook her head. "It's a secret."

"No secrets. If you want to heal, you have to let it all out."

Brandt's concern seemed so sincere, his kindness genuine, and his understanding deep. After all, he too knew what it was like to experience loss at the hands of injustice and evil.

"Tell me, Miah. What happened here?"

"He … he bit me."

Anger and confusion flashed across Brandt's face. "He bit you?"

For reasons she didn't understand and couldn't control, anger flared up within her too. "Yep. Right after he raped me!" There. Was he satisfied? Did that feed his need to know the awful, gruesome facts?

Brandt straightened then turned away, his braid swayed back and forth across his back, in sync with the shaking of his head. When he turned back around, his eyes were rimmed with tears and his voice was hushed and tight. "You are so beautiful, so brave, Miah."

Instead of backing down like she hoped he would, Brandt brushed her hair from her face and impelled her to go on. "Now, tell me. How did you get this?" He kissed the bruised brow above her purple, swollen eye.

Her anger melted into shameful grief. "I tried to run away."

"Good for you, Miah. I am so proud of you." He pressed his

cheek against hers, their tears mingling together. "Let it out. Can you tell me more?"

And so, she did. In breathy, painful sentences she spilled her secrets one by one, painting him a picture of what her hell had been like—from the foggy, frightening beginning to the terrible, desperate end.

When she finished, he surrounded her with his arms as if to protect her from any more evil. And they cried it all out, the two of them. They grieved her fear and suffering. They grieved the loss of her vitality and innocence, the loss of her sense of security, and the loss of her confidence in the future. Despite all her losses, they gained something new: a bond of understanding and a strengthened friendship, which could only come from sharing grief and pain together.

He smiled and wiped at her tears. "Are you all right? Did it help ... a little?"

She nodded. "I think so."

"I have something very special for you. Do you want it now, or would you like to rest?"

"Now."

CHAPTER TWENTY-NINE

randt stood, reached into his back pocket, and held out a small light-tan leather drawstring satchel.

"What's this?"

He widened the opening of the pouch. "It's my medicine bag. You can use it for a while. I put some nice things in there for you."

"A medicine bag?"

He nodded as if she should understand. "Yeah, to help with your healing." He pulled out a small baggie of light brown shavings. "This is tobacco. You can offer it every day, along with your thanksgiving, to Creator. It will put your heart and mind in a good space. I taped a short Bible verse on the bag. It's about giving thanks in all circumstances. I'm thankful you're alive."

"Thanks. Me too."

Next, he produced a finger-length bundle of dried, greenish-gray grass. "This is sweet grass. You can burn it before and when you pray. It will help calm and purify your thoughts. And this ..." He withdrew another Ziploc bag of thin, inch-long leaves. "This is sage. When you burn this, it will help release what is troubling your mind. And two more things. First ..." He pulled out a small sprig of cedar—something that finally looked familiar. "You can make a tea with cedar, or you can pour the brew in bathwater for healing and protection. And finally, I whittled a small cross out of cedar, to remind you Jesus is with you."

Brandt gathered the items, stuffed them back in the leather pouch, and placed it in her hand. "You can add things too. Things that will give you strength and courage, like maybe more bible verses or a song or poem—anything that will remind you that you are loved and not alone."

"Thank you, Brandt, for sharing this with me. I love it. When I get out of here, you'll have to show me how to make the tea."

"Of course."

As if he read her thoughts, Brandt reached for the Styrofoam cup and held the straw to her lips. "You'll probably think I'm crazy, but I'm gonna say it anyway." He waited for her to swallow before lowering the cup of water to the floor. "I'm going to marry you, Miah Joy Brennan. And when I do, I'm gonna help make your dreams come true. We'll move to Wyoming, and even though the land belonged to my people first, I'm going to buy back the biggest, best ranch in the Bighorn Mountains. We'll stock it with fifteen hundred head of cattle and one, two, three ..." He counted out the ten white rosebuds in the vase. "... ten kids who look just like their beautiful mom. And one day we'll be shopping or something with our little tribe in tow, and we'll come across the cowboy in that picture of yours. He'll see your beautiful self and wish he'd found you first. Then it'll be his turn to be jealous."

She grinned. "You *are* crazy."

"Crazy in love with the bravest, most beautiful girl in the world!" He stretched his broad chest across her own sore ribs and gave her a gentle squeeze. When he pushed back, his hand rested on the bed next to her hip, crushing the misplaced, but not forgotten, letter at her side. "Hey, what's this?"

"Oh ... it's a note." She slid the paper from his fingers.

"From a friend?"

"From Duane. His lawyer came here yesterday and gave it to my dad."

"Duane? Ronald *Duane* Maddox?" Lines of anger mixed with confusion etched Brandt's forehead.

When he motioned for her to hand over the letter, needles of apprehension poked through her body. What would Brandt do with Duane's very strange and outrageous request? Would he explode in anger or quietly weep as she had? "Brandt, the note wasn't meant for our eyes. I found it on the tray stuffed inside an empty disposable coffee cup along with a wadded-up napkin. I don't know what possessed me to read it, but I did. I wish I hadn't."

Despite her warning, Brandt sat on the edge of the bed and smoothed out the crumpled paper. As his eyes followed the words across the page, she watched the pattern of his emotion change from curiosity to disgust and back to curiosity. Then red rage flushed his face and his jaw pumped with anger before he dropped his hands and the paper in his lap. "He's manipulating you, Miah. You know that, don't you?"

She nodded. "I hope he is. Because ... if he truly is sorry, if he's honestly seeking forgiveness ..." She paused to catch her breath as a wave of sorrow battered her heart. "I can't forgive like Grandmother Jannali. I-I'm completely gutted by anger and fear. The deepest part of my soul is shattered, r-repulsed by what he did. I feel so hurt and betrayed." Her eyes burned with tears and a whimper squeezed from her constricted throat. "And I don't know who to point my anger at, God or Duane."

"Miah ..." Brandt grew quiet and stared at the wall behind her. When he spoke, he reached for her hand. "Your dad once told me to give my pain and my anger to God. I think he'd tell you the same. Cry out to Creator—He can handle it." With care, Brandt folded the paper, reached across the bed, and placed it between the photograph and the vase. When he sat back down, his hands fell open in his lap as if weighing his words. Releasing a sigh that sounded older and wiser than his nineteen years, Brandt looked her straight in the eye. "Could it have been just Friday night—only five nights ago—when a very smart girl told an angry young man to let go of his bitterness and work to make things better?"

He reached out and held her hand. "I think she said something like, 'it starts with a choice.' The girl was right, you know? Since then, she's had some horrific things happen to her. I hope she'll remember her words and know, while she can't always choose the things that happen to her or around her, she can choose what happens inside of her. I hope she chooses joy. If not now, then someday. Because if she doesn't, I'm afraid the man who hurt her will always have a grip on her."

Sniffing back her grief, she whispered, "At the end, I was resigned to death. God gave me such peace." She paused. "I know God promises to be near to the broken-hearted, and He was with me out there in the woods. But right now ... I don't feel Him." She closed her eyes to the torrent of tears that threatened to overwhelm and carry her away. "Where is He? Where is God, Brandt? I need him now more than ever."

Brandt tightened his grip on her hand. "He's here, Miah. But your pain and grief are raw—so thick and impenetrable, making it difficult for you to see Him right now. So ... maybe, for a while, you'll need to rely on me, on your family and friends to show you what's true and what's not." He leaned toward the tray, and with his other hand tugged a tissue from the box.

She took the tissue and wiped away her tears before another wave could cascade down her face. "I know nothing happens without God's permission. He knew this ... this tragedy was coming. And somewhere buried deep in my heart, I believe ... somehow God can use this for good, for His glory. But right now, I'm so angry and sad. It's unbearable." She pulled a pillow against her chest and buried her sobs within its white, sanitized folds. "How am I going to get through this? Will I ever be able to sort this all out—make sense of it?"

Brandt leaned forward, surrounding her as if he were a hiding place in which she could take refuge. And she couldn't stop her tears and fragile voice from exposing how far her doubt had traveled through her heart. "For the past three days, I've been lying here wondering why God would let this happen, especially when things were so promising with Smoky Mountain Media. Did He want to put an end to my dreams? Were my goals not in line with His will and somehow, I missed His cue?"

When she looked into Brandt's eyes, compassion and the willingness to understand blinked back at her, encouraging her to go on. "Brandt, I … I don't know how to explain it except that my brain feels paralyzed, stuck out there in those woods with Duane. And I'm afraid I'll never find my way out. I want to—for you, for my family. If and when I'm able to escape this nightmare playing over and over in my head, will I know what God expects of me? I mean, I'm not sure about anything anymore. Should I give it all up? My hopes? My dreams? What if God wants something different from me?"

PART II

I consider that our present sufferings are not worth
comparing with the glory that will be revealed in us.
- Romans 8:18

*"We never know the trials that await us in the days ahead. We may
not be able to see the light through our struggles, but we can believe
that those days, as in the life of Job, will be the most significant we
are called upon to live."* - Robert Collyer.

CHAPTER THIRTY

October 13, 2001

*D*id she have everything? Miah turned toward her bed and stared at the black carry-on bag as if she had x-ray vision. Tickets, passport, CD player, toothbrush, an extra change of clothes, Bible, journal ... No! How could she have forgotten to pack her Bible and journal?

She left her post at the window and moved to the nightstand, yanking too hard on the top drawer. It opened easier now that she'd cleaned it out. She grabbed the books and then paused to admire her work. The drawer looked so tidy—more organized than it had ever been. Mum would be so proud. In fact, she would be shocked. The whole room fairly echoed of order—like it had when they first moved into this old farmhouse.

But now, instead of moving in, she was moving out and ... Well, this was it. Goodbye room. Goodbye for now, at least. A sigh escaped her lips as she extended the handle of the carry-on bag and slid the overweight thing to the floor with a clunk. She gripped her Bible and the chronicle of her two-month, harrowing journey tight in her hand. Strange, she'd never noticed it before, but the books felt heavy, as weighty as the luggage she rolled across the wooden floor. It made sense, really. She'd stuffed all her hurt, all her questions, and all her anger within the margins of the ancient book and within her own contemporary, personal testament. With time, no doubt, they'd become even more chock-full.

It had been nine weeks since her ordeal, and although the stab wounds and bruises were healing, she continued to feel a vulnerability deep within her chest and a very real weakness in her stomach. Doctor Emily, her counselor, had warned her the road to recovery would be a long one. She just hadn't expected this ... detour. Maybe going home and doing what she knew she had to do would be the final leg on this unwanted odyssey—an odyssey in which the purpose and destination were still unknown.

She paused at the doorway and took a final look around the four yellow walls and the white feminine furniture Mum and Dad had purchased for her twelfth birthday. The tops of the pretty ensemble were no longer cluttered. They strictly displayed the essentials: her trophies from the state fair, pictures of family and friends living in Australia, and the picture of ... her cowboy. Leave it, Miah. After weeks of praying for direction, God has finally spoken, and now life has taken a decidedly different turn. But ... Perhaps God would eventually bring her full circle. It didn't hurt to hope, did it? Because without hope, despair would quickly fill the vacant space, and she certainly knew what the demon of despair could do.

Almost defiantly, she backtracked across the room to the small writing desk, scooped up the black-framed photo and slid it in the front pocket of her bag, next to her passport and airline tickets. Without looking back, she crossed the threshold and headed straight down the hallway, down the stairs, through the lounge room, turned the corner into the kitchen, and wheeled the bag to the back door.

Twelve fifteen. She had plenty of time. And it appeared as if Mum was ready to go too. Mum's burgundy luggage sat at the door, and the kitchen had been cleaned up from last night's going away party. Party? Is that what it should be remembered as? Maybe more of a send-off or farewell. Who knew? Who really knew? Only God. *God, I am so mixed up and afraid. Help me to trust you. Give me peace. A half day of peace is all I ask. Help me to get through the good-byes. Help my dad and my brothers. And when Brianna and Brandt hear the truth about my leaving, help them to understand. Help them to forgive me for my secrecy. I'm going to miss them so much.*

However, she wasn't going to miss all the awkwardness, especially at church. Where once she loved going to church, she had now come to almost dread it—not Pastor Bryce's teaching though. No, she held on to his every word, drew comfort and help from his practical explanations of the Bible. She would miss his sermons most.

What she wouldn't miss were the pitiful glances and whispered conversations from acquaintances and strangers alike. If they knew the truth ... Oh, they'd really have something to talk about. Yes, it would be good to get away. If only to give people time to forget and give her time to ... to what? Heal? A healthy heart and mind seemed so hard to imagine.

Like a ghost visiting old haunts, she returned to the lounge room and sat down at the sun-soaked baby grand. Her fingers brushed across the keyboard as if they were expecting some miraculous apparition of inspiration. Yet nothing came to her. Would the words and melodies ever flow from her heart again? So many unanswered questions requiring heaps of faith. *God, I believe. Help my unbelief. Help me to trust You'll work this all out for Your glory ... someday. Give me patience.*

The bright noontime sun glinted off the shiny, black-lacquered piano like fool's gold in a mountain stream. Its hopeful gleam enticed her to wander out into the autumn air that made the veranda feel like the inside of a fridge. All too soon winter would lock summer's freedom and glory in an ice box of gray skies and death-white, frozen landscapes. No, she wouldn't miss the long, dark days of winter. Pulling her hoodie over her head, she snuggled her Bible and journal close to her chest and settled down onto the wooden swing to wait for Brandt.

How many winters had she endured? Four, could it be? Yes, and endure is exactly what she had done. She'd never been able to acclimate herself to the frigid temperatures of Michigan. However, she had finally come to appreciate the crispness of the harvest season. If a girl opened her eyes to all the loveliness, she could find beauty in the vivid yellows, reds, and oranges of the sugar maple leaves; the spicy, sweet smell of apple pie and hot cider; and the fun of mustering fallen leaves, carving pumpkins, and roasting marshmallows around a bonfire. Yeah, she would miss autumn and the final harvest of Mum's prize-winning garden.

Although the diligently tended rows of produce were now yellowed and droopy, there were still some hearty summer squash, zucchini, and tomatoes waiting to be plucked from their vines. Mum had left them for someone else to pick. Maybe Dad? Or maybe Josh or Brad? Yeah, Brad would be the one to venture out to Mum's garden.

Like the dying garden, she pondered the books she'd lowered onto her lap. While she didn't feel especially inspired, she opened her journal to a blank page and began writing. October 11, 2001. Going home to Amaroo Station. Did this qualify as a happy face day or a sad face day? It was hard to say. Of course, she wanted to see her relatives and friends—especially Grandmother Jannali—because she would understand. However, her reason for going home seemed so ... awkward? Pretty much. Debatable? Yes, some people would love to give their two cents worth. Needed? Absolutely. The safe and quiet isolation of Amaroo Station would be essential to prepare her heart and mind for the decision that lie ahead. And anyway, being in the spotlight had become almost unbearable. Yes, indeed, going home would be in her best interest.

She only wished her whole family would go, especially in light of the terribly frightening terrorist attacks of September 11. But Dad said they couldn't just up and leave; it would put Mr. Ellison in a very inconvenient spot. So, she and Mum would go. First to Brisbane for a couple of weeks and then to Amaroo Station for the rest of the time. If all went well, she would return sometime next year. That is, if America was still standing.

The dreadful thought made going back to Australia even more difficult. How could she leave Dad and her brothers, all her friends, especially Brandt and Bri, when it seemed all of America might topple over? Between the threat of anthrax, the air strikes on Afghanistan, and President Bush's declaration of the "War on Terror," it seemed as if the whole world stood on the brink of self-destruction. *Are you there, God? Do you see us struggling down here? We are literally dying from all the evil!*

Trying to find some evidence of hope, Miah's eyes searched in and around the yard, the garden, and the soybean field across the dirt road in front of her. None of it seemed evil. In fact, it all looked peaceful, untouched by the brokenness of sin. *"Creation isn't completely broken, but it's broken enough to let us know something's definitely wrong."* Since the New York tragedy, Pastor Bryce had preached this repeatedly. He didn't mean for everyone to lose heart. No, he only meant to point people to the One who could redeem all the trouble and heartache—of which she'd had her fair share.

She sighed and looked down at her journal. What should she draw? A happy face or sad face? Maybe a blank expression, because really, her heart felt numb. She was curious though. How many days since the tenth of August had she rated as happy? She flipped back through the pages and started to count.

Tuesday, August 14. One. A psychologist, Dr. Emily Lanning,

came to talk with her and set up regular meetings. Her kindness canceled out the upsetting visit from Duane's attorney. Wednesday, August 15. Two. Brandt brought her flowers, (which they couldn't keep in the ICU), but their talk was healing in so many ways. Friday, August 17. Three. Brianna finally came for a visit—short and awkward as it was. Later in the day, C.J. visited. He had just returned from a three-day trip to Nashville and brought with him encouraging news from Smoky Mountain Media. Now, because of all the changes in her life, the record company would have to wait—indefinitely.

Saturday, August 18. Four. Her tracheostomy was removed, and she left the ICU. She couldn't believe it when Adam Chisholm walked into her new room on the Intermediate Care floor. He had been thoughtful enough to remove his scary makeup and spiked jewelry. And in his own strange way, he apologized for coming to the concert drunk and for provoking Brandt. Adam's humility opened the door for Dad to say his own apologies and regrets.

Sunday, August 19. Five. One happy face and one sad face defined the day. Her lung had collapsed again, forcing her to return to the ICU. And it all happened on Brad's twenty-first birthday. Monday, August 20. Six. She moved back to Intermediate Care. There'd been a downside, however. Joshua and Brandt left for another year at Michigan State University.

Tuesday, August 21. Seven. She started physical therapy for her arm and chest. And after preparing a statement for Ronald Maddox's sentencing hearing, the judge gave him seventy-five years. She couldn't have been more relieved. And now, Maddox wasn't even in the state. He'd been extradited to Texas. And once Texas had their time with him, he would move on to Oklahoma, Colorado, and then to Utah to receive sentencing on the other cases against him. While Dad seemed satisfied to think Duane would soon be a dead man, strangely, her heart and mind were wrestling with the seeming contradiction between

God's justice and grace and what He expected her to do with both.

There were only two happy faces from August 22 to August 27. Friday, August 24, she went home to her own bed, her own room. She and Drew had a talk like they hadn't had in a long time. He'd been devastated by what had happened. Then Sunday, August 27, after a busy day of visitors, (everyone from the band came again) it had been Brad's turn to bear his soul. Never in her life had she seen him cry, yet on August 27, he did. He apologized for all the times he'd teased and tormented her. As horrible as her whole ordeal had been, she would forever be grateful her relationship with her brothers had been enriched. Somehow, they all had a stronger sense of family.

From there it seemed like a long streak of sad faces, only in her journal though. Of course, on the outside, she tried to give the appearance of a girl who had the grit and determination to overcome her adversity, because that's how the news reporters portrayed her. That's what everyone wanted and expected her to do—especially Dad. On the inside, however, she'd felt like an implosion going to happen.

She'd done everything Dr. Emily told her to do: memorize scripture, journal her thoughts, spend time with family and outdoors with nature, and as her body permitted, she exercised faithfully. Yet despite everything she did, she had found herself being sucked into a black hole of hopelessness. She had begun to sense an elusiveness of God's Spirit, a terrible separation, until the pain in her belly became more than a discomfort, and every morning she had to force herself to get out of bed. Depression, despair, and post-traumatic stress disorder, call it what you will, it took her down a very ugly road. So ugly that ...

Her stomach lurched in her gut as her fingers rested on her journal entry for Saturday, September 15—the valley of the shadow of death day—exactly four days after the world had practically stopped turning. There were no happy faces drawn there.

None whatsoever. The morning of September 15, Dad literally pulled her out of bed and forced her to sit at the breakfast table with the family. When she'd proceeded to puke up her scrambled eggs and tomatoes, he cursed Ronald Maddox's name and stormed out of the house.

Her heart recoiled now to think how she'd retaliated against Dad's seeming rejection, to think of the added fear and grief she had put her family and friends through, especially Drew and Rob and Kylie's mum. Never again ... She promised.

While she'd meant Saturday, September 15 to be the final entry in her journal, the following Wednesday's entry had been filled with hope and purpose. Although the doctor's report had been so very hard to take, at least now, she knew she wasn't going crazy. Now, with understanding, she could endure the malaise and nausea and move forward. And with help from her family, she just might pull it off.

With a renewed sense of God's presence, she'd resolved in her heart to overcome, not only for herself but also for those who had sent cards of encouragement, saying how their lives had been changed because of the brave way in which she faced her ordeal. If they only knew how truly weak she often felt.

However, like them, she now had a fresh perspective. Despite her stumbling, she had to believe God had a reason for every-thing. She had to believe her suffering would not be wasted. She would trust in His will because really, she didn't have a choice. Since the setting of the sun on the tenth of August, He had pretty much determined the course of her life. God was in control, and the only way she could move forward was by following His steps and clinging to His promises as if her life depended on it.

Speaking of life and death ... Miah turned an ear to the distant, familiar whine of Brandt's motorcycle and envisioned him bent low over the machine as it sped around the curves of Clark Lake. Seconds later, the engine growled into a lower gear, making the turn onto Somerset. When the bike hit a screaming, death-defying speed, her body shuddered within itself. Why did he feel the need to push the outer limits of risk-taking? Just when she couldn't bear to listen any longer, the throttle cut back to a saner pace to complete the tree-lined, gravel portion of the journey. Even so, her heart raced at its own breakneck speed as she left the swing, tapped down the steps, and crossed the lawn to greet him.

CHAPTER THIRTY-ONE

Miah made it to the end of the driveway just as Brandt passed by the huge maple whose top leafy portion had turned a fiery red-orange. The tree looked remarkably glorious. So did Brandt's smile. He had raised the polarized face shield so she could see his beautiful face grinning back at her from fifty meters down the lane. At forty meters, the motorbike revved then bucked back on one wheel as if it were a wild bronc in a rodeo. He rode as far as the postbox before crashing back down on the front tire. Skidding to a halt, he motioned for her to join him.

Who could resist his smile? She rested her eyes in his and teased him with her own confident grin. Brandt's steady good-ness and trustworthiness the past few weeks had filled her with assurance. And in another time and place, she may have given in to his kindness, his strength, and his striking beauty. Perhaps God knew she would give in to temptation. Maybe God knew if tragedy hadn't struck, she may have compromised her pledge to remain chaste until marriage. Perhaps God had deliberately taken drastic measures to keep her and Brandt from falling into temptation. No, that was such a ridiculous thought, because despite her conscious effort to remain chaste, she now had to suffer the same consequence as someone who didn't try at all.

"Hey, beautiful. How you feelin'?" Brandt's gloved hand gently brushed the yellowish bruise on her left cheek.

"Besides you nearly giving me a heart attack, I'm fine."

"How's the eye?"

She closed her right eye, lifted the patch covering her injured eye, and then looked around. "Not much change. Everything's a gray haze."

"Give it more time. It's only been, what? Ten days or so since the surgery? It'll come."

She grinned and shrugged away her hope. "Argh, I'm not holding me breath, matey. If pirates can get along with one eye, I can too."

"Come here, you big toughie. I think you need a hug." He wrapped his leather-jacketed arms around her gray John Deere sweatshirt then pulled back and patted the seat behind him. "Let's go for a ride. I'll go slow over the bumps, I promise. Watch the muffler. It's hot."

Despite the tenderness in her chest, she climbed onto the seat, leaning close to Brandt's back. The pain didn't stop her from enjoying the feel of his strength. He was self-assured and comfortable—not afraid of her like Dad, like Bri. No, he seemed to understand her when no one else did. His friendship was a timely gift from God that kept her mind off her troubles.

"Ready?"

She gave him a thumbs up and squeezed his belly tight. To her surprise, instead of turning the bike around and heading back down the gravel lane, Brandt eased the machine forward and putted along until they reached the front of the big red barn. When he cut the engine, a huff of unbelief tumbled from her smile. "I thought we were going for a ride!"

"We did. And now it's done." He helped her off the bike then directed her toward the barn.

"Aren't you going to take off your helmet?" He didn't answer. Instead, he led her through the wide-open threshold, past the auction ring, which had been set up just last night. For months her family had been planning their annual livestock auction, and now she'd be missing out on all the festivities.

As if he could read her thoughts, Brandt tugged on her hand. "Don't worry, Miah. Your dad will make sure Battle Chief is sold to a rich rancher who'll pamper your project's prized genes. Come on."

"Where are we going?"

His answer came in the form of a hard push against the wide metal gate, then he drew her into the shadowy part of the A.I. barn. For a split-second dread seized her body immobile as memories abused her fragile mind. "Where ... where are we going, Brandt?"

He stopped at the stairway to the loft of the barn then settled his fawn-like eyes on her. "Come up to the hayloft with me?" He held out his hand as an offering.

What was he expecting? Surely he wasn't thinking they'd ... No, he probably only wanted a goodbye kiss—one to remember. She accepted his hand and climbed up the wooden stairs after him. "I thought after our manure fight and my dad's torture treatment you would have seen enough of this hayloft to last you a lifetime."

"Just the opposite. I think about it all the time, Miah."

When they reached the top of the stairs, he paused to let her catch her breath before ascending the grassy, stepped pyramid. The loft smelled of everything fresh and familiar, and the wide, prickly plateau spread out before them like a checkerboard tablecloth. Instead of moving to a secluded corner or to the safety of the center of the haystack, Brandt chose to sit on the reckless, dangling edge, which gave them a view of the rafters and the cement floor and stanchions below. Why didn't he take off his helmet?

"Brandt, don't you want to take off your helmet?"

He shrugged off a self-conscious chuckle, then sucking in the dusty air, he plucked a long stalk of dried grass from their stubbled chair. "Miah, I have something I want to give you. Three things, actually." Slipping the straw between his lips, he loosened the chin strap and lifted the helmet over his ears.

"Your hair! You cut your hair! Why, Brandt?" She couldn't believe it! Raising to her knees, she brushed her hands back and forth across the soft, spiky bristles that stood out straight from his lovely, brown head like soldiers standing at attention.

"Miah ..." He pulled her hands down to his chest as if her touch pained him.

"I ... I liked your hair the way it was." She settled in closer to him, hoping his eyes would give her a clue to the reason why he'd made such a drastic change, but they were fixed on the cement floor way below them.

When he finally looked her way, his hand clasped her knee, making it clear he wanted her to stay near. Then leaning away, he unzipped the side pocket of his thrift store leather jacket and produced a photo-sized envelope. "Since we're not going to see each other for a while, I thought you might need a more inspiring picture to put in that black frame of yours. I hope you'll find this photograph worthy of covering up your dumb ol' cowboy from Wyoming."

She turned the envelope over in her hand and stole another glance at his surprising new style. What had possessed him to do such a thing? A dare? Too much ribbing from his college mates?

"Aren't you going to open it?"

She couldn't stop staring at him. "I'm trying to get used to your hair."

"I'm still me!"

"Well, you don't look like you." She slipped her finger beneath the flap and pulled the five-by-seven photo from its envelope. "I forgot all about this ... It turned out so good. I love it! And the best part is, your hair is still long." Her eyes moved from the photo, back to his short, cropped cut, and then back to the picture again. Bri had snapped the photo of them that very first Sunday Dad had invited Brandt for tea—the day before her seventeenth birthday. "How did you get this?"

"Bri gave it to me."

"I wonder why she didn't give me one?"

He shrugged. "It's good, isn't it? Almost better than the picture of your cowboy."

She did have to admit, despite the subjects, the portrait looked quite artistic. The afternoon sun, sparkling off the ripples in the waterhole, gave the picture a heavenly appeal. And although her hair had curled in the hazy humidity, the blonde wisps had framed her face almost like a halo. Her eyes ... Oh, how embarrassing! It would be obvious to anyone who saw the photo that she was totally infatuated with the sweaty, dark-skinned fisherman who smiled back at her. But what could she say? "It's perfect. Thank you, Brandt. I'll put it in the frame straight away." She leaned over and kissed him on the cheek. "I'm going to miss you so much. I wish I didn't have to leave."

"Me too." He held up a finger, reminding her another gift awaited. Reaching into his left jacket pocket, he pulled out a small velvet-covered box. "Don't worry. I'm not asking you to marry me *yet*. So just ... open it."

"Oh, my word! It's beautiful!" Her giggles joined with his laughter.

"Here. Try it on." He took the ring from the box and pushed it on her left ring finger. "Is it too big?"

"No, it's perfect. I'm sure I'll gain my weight back soon enough. I love it!" She couldn't stop giggling. "It's ... It's so ... Is it real? The pearl and diamonds, are they real?"

A playful smirk softened his furrowed brow. "Of course they are! What do you take me for?"

"I'm sorry. That's really rude, isn't it? It's ... it's just so unbelievable. I mean ... I've never had anything so special. You've made me feel very loved. Thank you."

"Hey, are those tears? I've seen enough of those salty things to fill an ocean. Let's stick with laughter for a while, okay?"

She nodded and tucked beneath the strong beam of his arm that had supported her for the past nine weeks. "This is going to be so hard being away from you. I'm afraid you're going to forget how much I care about you, how much I've appreciated your patience with all my bumbling, and ... how much I ... love you." Slipping off the awkwardness, she sat up and fished around in her sweatshirt pocket. "I have a couple things for you too." She handed him the blue, sealed envelopes labeled with a number "one" and a number "two". "Now, you have to promise me you'll open them in order, and you can't open them until I'm gone."

His nod seemed almost somber. "I will—if you promise you'll never forget I love you too. No matter what happens."

No matter what happens? What could happen? September 11 ... Something like September 11 could happen again. It might spoil their plans and get in the way of their future. "Brandt, do you think America is in trouble? Do you think there will be more terrorist attacks?" When she looked into his eyes, she saw a brave resolve she hadn't noticed before.

"No. Not if I can help it."

"Not if *you* can help it?" She grinned and unzipped his jacket as if she were searching for a big red "S" on his chest. "I knew you were special, but I didn't know you were Superman."

"Miah, I don't know how to tell you this." He picked up her hands and stared at the ring, pushing it back and forth on her finger. "Sometimes there are things people have to do ... even when it doesn't make sense. Do ... do you know what I mean? From the outsider's perspective, it seems crazy, as if that person has lost his last ounce of reason. But if that person doesn't do what he's supposed to, he runs the risk of stalling out, losing all sense of purpose."

She tried to follow his thoughts.

"Miah, I guess it's like you going home to Australia. Only you know what you have to do to find healing for your grief and your pain. And even though I don't want you to go, even though to me it doesn't necessarily make sense, it's something you really feel compelled to do. You told me not to ask any questions, to trust you, remember?" He paused to collect his thoughts. "I need you to do the same for me—trust me. Support me in what I feel compelled to do."

CHAPTER THIRTY-TWO

"What are you going to you do?" The question quivered off her lips. Then rising to her knees, she brushed her fingers through Brandt's black, velour-like hair which only served to validate her wild imagination. "Please, tell me you're not thinking ..." The words stuck in her throat as she wrapped her arms around his beautiful head and brought it near her heart. Her chest ached, not from her stab wound, but from a deep sense of dread. "Why? Why, Brandt? What about school?" Her body swayed, rocking him back and forth as if he were already dead. "What about Wyoming? You told me you'd take me to Wyoming." He sat there wordlessly, letting her embalm him with her love. "Help me to understand. Please."

His big, strong hands reached up and pulled her down to his lap and the level of his smile. "I'll take you to Wyoming. Don't worry, Miah."

She searched his eyes for any hint of sanity. "You can't take me to Wyoming if you're dead! War has a tendency to kill people, Brandt."

He encircled her with his arms, surely trying to bring her comfort. "I didn't expect you to understand, Miah. That's why I asked you to trust me. I'm not going into this blindly. I've put a lot of thought into it."

"Did you pray about it, Brandt? Did you talk to my dad or Pastor Bryce about it?"

In answer to her question, he simply stared into the low-hanging trestles. It wasn't until she hid her disappointment and a lone tear in his neck that he finally spoke. "Miah ... I'm out of money." His long lashes flickered with humility. "I didn't know what to do. My options were to either enlist or go home, and I certainly don't want to go home. Not until I can show my dad I've become more of a man than he'll ever be. And since you're leaving for Australia, I figured it wouldn't really matter if I left too."

"If you're out of money, how could you have bought this ring? Take it back, Brandt."

"It won't matter, Miah. I only had money for books—not the classes. It's only four years of full-time active duty, and the GI bill will help pay for the rest of my education. You'll graduate from high school and jump into university or travel to Nashville with C.J. and negotiate the contract waiting for you. When I get back, I'll finish vet school. And once you finish your world tour, we'll have saved enough money for a down payment on a thousand-acre ranch in the Bighorn Mountains."

He grinned at her as if his plan would surely save the world. However, his scheme overlooked one thing. He would be lucky to save himself. There were no guarantees he would make it home alive. "Can't you get some help from your tribe or from the government? You're a Native. Your education should be free. And for what they did to your people, you should be exempt from military service. I hate your country!"

"Whoa! Settle down, girl. I did get help—from both. It's just ... the money spread thin because I chose an out-of-state school, and anyway ... I knew I'd find you here." He smiled and gave her a reassuring squeeze. "Miah, no one twisted my arm to join the

Marines. I enlisted. And I love this land—the land of my ancestors. Our families are here. Our future is here, and ... I'd kind of like to keep it that way. I can't stand by and let some Bin Laden guy kill thousands of innocent people and strike terror in the minds of our families and friends.

"Everything that's happened between me and my dad, with Skye, with you ... Miah, I've tried to deal with it the right way. I've tried to forgive. It's so hard to forget. And this attack is too much. I have to do something." He shrugged. "You forget I come from a long line of warriors. It's in me. And all I know is, I need to get it out of me. The only legal way I've found, is to go over to Afghanistan and kick some ugly Al-Qaeda ... butt. I'm going to kill one turbaned terrorist for all the times my dad hit me and my mom. And I'm going to kill another for the white supremacy discrimination that led Skye to take his life. Then I'm going to kill two of the bearded bas— baboons in memory of all the people who died in the Twin Towers, and—"

"Stop it."

"And the rest of the sons of you-know-what, I'm going to kill for the evil monster who scarred my beautiful girlfriend." He leaned in close and kissed the pink scar above her lip.

"Stop it, Brandt. You sound as mad as Maddox himself. Please, don't do this." She felt a tear trickle down her cheek and fall between their whispers. "I need you." *If only he knew how desperately.*

"It's already done, Miah."

"Why didn't you talk to my dad? He would have helped. Or ... Mr. Ellison. He could have found work for you."

"Four years, Miah. It's a blink of an eye."

Brandt's answer was final, his resolve firm. He had left her with no other option but ... prayer? Yes, perhaps God would watch over Brandt like He had watched over her. God had brought *her* home. Not safe. Not sound. Nonetheless, He brought her home. "When? When do you go?"

"I'll finish up this semester, and at the end of January—just when I'm getting sick of winter, I'll head to Parris Island, South Carolina for training. The U.S. Marine Corps is going to transform me into one of the few and the proud." He chuckled. "So, what's it gonna be, Miah. A cowboy from Wyoming or a Marine from South Dakota? The choice is yours."

No, she would not participate in his careless reverie. He obviously had not counted the costs of his decision. Didn't he know that if he went to war there would be a very real threat to his life and their dream? Well, she wouldn't—she couldn't be a part of this plan. Her fragile mind had been on a crazy, two-month-long rollercoaster ride, and he was asking her to have a go for another four years? She would end up in a straitjacket for sure.

With the silence between them growing, Brandt tugged at her crossed arms. "So, you're going to shut me out again?"

She shook her head not knowing what to say.

"Miah."

"I ... I don't think I can take it."

"The ring?"

Oh, she hadn't thought about the ring. "The worry ... the fear. You asked me to promise that I'd always remember you love me—no matter what happens. Do you think something is going to happen? Deep down, do you have a feeling something terrible is going to happen to you? Because if you do, you better stop and reckon with it. I am not as strong as you think I am. If anything happened to you, I don't know what I'd do. I can't imagine living without you. Who else could I trust? You're the only one who understands ... who knows everything." *Well, almost everything* ...

He shifted her weight off his knee and pulled her closer. "No, Miah. I don't think anything is going to happen. I'll probably never see combat. And if I do, I'll be fine. Out of the hundreds of thousands of troops that served in the Gulf War, only a few hundred died. War has changed. It's much more technical and precise. And hey, you never know. I could leave on my bike this afternoon and die in an accident on my way home. There are no guarantees. You of all people should know that, Miah.

"And anyway, I had this plan in my back pocket even before I met you. I knew the money would eventually run out. One thing I'm beginning to understand, Miah. God's ways are bigger than ours. For whatever reason, my summer internship fell through, which stunk financially. But if it hadn't fallen through, I wouldn't have met you or your family. I wouldn't have met the Creator in a personal, saving way. I wouldn't have been able to face the pain of my past with some semblance of grace. And I wouldn't have been able to help you in the way you needed."

He brushed a curl from her face. "Now, with you going home, what's left for me to do? Go back to the reservation and try to find work in a town that doesn't exactly value its Native neighbor? No, I'd rather die. I'm moving forward, Miah. You've got a dream. I've got a dream. They're big dreams, good dreams. And like I've heard you say: 'God holds the plan, so I'm walking forward in faith.' Isn't that what you always say, Miah?" He pressed his fingers into her sides. "Hmm? Am I right?"

"It's what I *used* to say."

"Oh, no. You can't get off so easy." He assaulted the ticklish part of her ribs again and kept on until she couldn't stand it any longer "Ready to admit I'm right?".

Her high-strung emotion came out in a cascade of uncontrollable giggles. "Yes! Yes! Ow! Don't make me laugh, Brandt!" He drew close and covered the remaining trail of her laughter with his smiling lips. His kisses were tender, and his dark eyes were pools of certainty.

"You go back to Australia, Miah. Go home and find the healing you need. And I'll go wherever the U.S. Marine Corps sends me. We'll meet back here in four years—you stronger and me with money in the bank. Then we'll discuss what's in these blue envelopes of yours." He turned away pretending to open them. "What are in these anyway?"

Dread flushed her face as she tried to snatch the envelopes from his hand. "I told you to wait until I'm gone. Give 'em away, you big ratbag!"

Laughing, he raised the envelopes high above his head, surely enjoying her discomfort. "You know the moment you leave the driveway, I'm going to open these, don't you?"

"I don't care. Just don't open them now." She couldn't bear to see his face when he read the truth about her leaving. Dad's reaction had been enough to send her into another downward spiral of doubt. Even so, he eventually came around. Hopefully, Brandt would too. And if he didn't? If he couldn't wrap his mind around the whole crazy thing? Well, she'd find out soon enough. His rejection would most likely come in the form of a long, sad silence. No letters. No phone calls. No e-mails. And then how would she deal with yet another loss?

A series of short, high-pitched whistles interrupted her thoughts, and she responded like any good cattle dog would. "My dad's calling. It must be time to go." Her sigh was filled with regret. "Promise you'll write?"

Brandt swallowed his emotion and nodded. "Every day."

"Every day?" She smiled and ran her hand across the soft spikes of his hair. "Don't make promises you can't keep, soldier. Just write when you can. My address is in envelope number one. But I won't be there for two weeks. We're going to Brisbane to visit my mum's family first."

He nodded again.

"And when you know your address in South Carolina, you'll send it to me, won't you?"

"Absolutely."

Their eyes met, and they paused to take a long, deep drink of one another. Brandt was good and brave. And when he leaned in close, his kiss lingered on her lips as if he were savoring every bit of her trusting, hopeful heart.

"You're the best thing in my life, Miah. You're strong and kind, and I'm going to miss you so much." His whisper spoke assurance in her ear and gave her the courage to respond with a kiss full of its own promises.

"I'll miss you too. The picture and ring ... Thank you. They're beautiful, Brandt. Every time I look at them, I'll think of you. I'll pray for you. Please ... be safe."

"I have one more thing for you, Miah." His left eyebrow arched high like a suspension bridge as he dug in his pocket and pulled out a clear plastic bag. "Would you be the keeper of my soul?"

"What?" She studied the bag he offered her.

"In case I die. Will you be the keeper of my soul?"

"What is this? What are you talking about? And you better not die."

Brandt's expression grew serious. He opened the bag and cradled a long black braid. "Miah, the Oglala believe our hair carries the spirit or essence of who we are as a person. So, I cut my hair before the Marines did—before they could sweep it up and throw it away. My spirit is much too special to be thrown away." He smiled and then went on. "We believe when someone dies, their soul needs to be purified before they go on to spend eternity with the Great Mystery, Wakan Tanka. So, a lock of hair is taken from the dead person and purified using smoke from sweet grass. Then it's wrapped in buckskin along with other meaningful possessions to make up a soul bundle."

He looked her way with a quiet grin. "This is where you come in, Miah. The soul bundle is kept by someone who agrees to live a harmonious life until the soul can be freed. After a time of mourning, the bundle is opened to release the soul to travel the Ghost Road ... the Milky Way. Then the bundle is burned."

For a split second his dark brown eyes exposed the innocent

little boy hiding behind his broad shoulders. "I thought since you liked my hair so much, you might want to hang onto it for me."

She cupped her hands to receive the glossy black gift. "I would be honored. Thank you." Her own smile faded, and her voice took on a reverent tone. "Is it true about the soul bundle, Brandt?"

Brandt nodded.

"Do ... do you believe it?"

"I believe in the Great Mystery, Miah. I believe in eternity. And ... I believe Jesus Christ is the one and only keeper of my soul."

She nodded, blinking away her tears. "I love your faith, Brandt. The Great Mystery. It's ... it's so beautiful, like you."

The metal gate screeched on its hinges and startled them from their quiet goodbyes. They both watched as Dad walked past the Bobcat and broken four-wheeler then systematically checked each stanchion.

"Daddy, we're up here."

He turned and searched the rafters. "It's time to go, sweetheart."

"One more minute?"

"Be quick smart now. G'day, Brandt."

"Good day, Mr. Brennan."

Obviously feeling the awkwardness of the moment, Daddy tipped his hat and quickly made his exit.

"Well, I guess this is it." She took Brandt's hands in her own and pressed them to her cheek. "I will love you forever. Beyond all time." The tears were scratching their way up her neck, into her throat. "I ... I better say goodbye to everyone else."

Nodding, he gave her hands a squeeze and then picked up the blue envelopes. "Toksa ake."

"What?"

"Lakota never say goodbye, Miah. Toksa ake. I'll see you again."

He looked down at the cement floor way below them. Longing lingered in his touch as he slid her off his lap and made a move to help her climb down from their high, grassy perch. He grasped her hand as if he would never let go, and once they reached ground level, he pulled her into the shadows and simply held her tight. Except for his breathing, he didn't move. When his hand moved to the curve of her back, drawing her even closer, a familiar wave of dread nearly consumed her.

"Miah ..." Brandt's words stalled in his throat and his breathing sounded almost strained. It wasn't until she felt his tear drop to her cheek that a dawning fell over her like the final, black curtain of a tragic play. This goodbye—this toksa ake—had to be so much more difficult for him. While she would travel home to the familiar, to those who would embrace and love her, he would be facing the unknown, where everything—the people, the land, the circumstances could potentially be very hostile. He truly was the most courageous person she had ever known.

While his brave heart pounded out a steady beat, hers nearly split wide open. *God, please protect Brandt. Love him and keep him. Bring him back to me.*

Once again, the gate screeched open, only this time Josh peeked his head around the corner. "Hey! Rattle your dags, you two. Miah, it's going to take you two hours to get through airport security!"

"I'll miss you too, Brad." Tears rolled down her cheeks as she made her way around the semicircle of family. "Rob ..."

Rob held out his arms to receive her next. A grateful lump grew in her throat when he pulled her tight and rocked her in his arms. "Hey, little sister." He had been such a pillar for them all. And for one more time, she rested against his chest and let him support her with his strength.

"Rob, thank you for everything. Thank you for … saving me. I'm sorry I put you and Drew through … Well, you know."

"I'm so glad we were there." He pat her back then gave her a final squeeze. "I love you, Miah."

"I love you too."

She made her hug for Amy sweet and sincere—like Amy herself. "Take care of yourself and my little niece or nephew. I'll be praying for a quick and easy delivery."

Amy's eyes were filled with emotion and although she tried to speak, she could only manage to nod her goodbyes.

"Hey, Miah." Josh stood by, ready with a big embrace. "You're my hero. I'm going to miss you."

"I'll miss you too, Josh. Good luck in school and watch over your mate." She dipped her head toward Brandt who stood quietly next to Mum.

And then came Drew. He held her for what seemed like forever and when he spoke, his words were barely a whisper. "I'm so sorry for everything, Miah. If I could, I'd take it all away."

"I … I know. Thank you, Drew. I'm so sorry for what I put you through. I … I just lost sight of the truth." Her gratefulness overflowed in the form of tears that she hid in the folds of Drew's shirt.

"No worries, Miah. That's what brothers are for, aye? But you owe me one."

Nodding, she pulled away and brushed at her face.

"So … can you give this to Kylie for me?" He slid a small mailing package into her hand.

"What is it?"

His smile didn't release any information. "You'll just have to wait and see." He wrapped his arm around her shoulder and gave her a final squeeze. "See you at Christmas, okay? Love you."

"I love you too."

"All right. Do you girls have everything?" Dad checked his phone. "It's twelve-fifty. We should have left five minutes ago."

She went through a quick mental list. "My journal and Bible! I left them on the veranda! Pull the truck to the front, Dad. I'll meet you and mum there. See you later, everybody!" Her family shouted out their final farewells as she grabbed Brandt's hand and took off in a careful trot for the front yard and the front porch.

Brandt took the veranda steps two at a time, snatched her books from the swing, and leaped to the sidewalk without hitting a single step. After a quick glance toward the driveway and her parents, he pulled her behind the pudgy Alberta spruce standing guard over the flower bed. His kiss felt strong and eternal—like she hoped his love would remain.

With the blue envelopes still in his hand, Brandt lifted her chin, inviting her to look into those shimmering brown pools of promise. "I love you, Miah Joy Brennan."

She could only nod. Her longing for things to turn out right gripped her voice in a tearful chokehold. If only they had more time. If only there wasn't this secret between them. If only she had the courage to tell him face to face, then ... then what? She'd know the limit of Brandt's love? She'd realize they'd just shared their last kiss? No. Her soul couldn't handle that. Not yet. Not here.

Like a pump being primed, her salty tears wet her lips, releasing a flow of courage that helped her echo her lover's vow. "I love you too, Brandt Traversie DuCharme. No matter what happens, I will always love you."

CHAPTER THIRTY-THREE

Amaroo Station, Queensland, Australia
October 28, 2001

Finally ... A few moments of solitude. Miah sipped the ice-cold apple juice and stepped out onto Granddad and Nana's veranda. She walked to the straight-backed wooden rocker then changing her mind, she eased herself onto the yellow cushioned settee. The endless plains stretched before her as she closed her tired eyes and welcomed the afternoon breeze to cool her freshly sun-kissed skin.

It had been two busy days of visiting aunties, uncles, and a road train full of cousins, and it hadn't necessarily been the fun kind of visiting. At times the family reunion had felt downright awkward, as she knew it would be. However, in the end, after all her relatives had a chance to voice their opinions and wrestle with her shocking decision, they'd all come to the same conclusion she had: that this would be the right thing—not an easy thing by any means—still, the right thing to do all the same. Hopefully, Brandt had come to the same conclusion too.

She sandwiched the white envelope between her prayerful

palms as if she could somehow sense the spirit of his letter. Would it be filled with angry words that had been penned under the influence of bitter tears, or would there simply be a sad, patient understanding? Hoping for the latter, she expected the former as she slid her finger beneath the mint-flavored flap, which surely had been close to Brandt's lips.

Dread trembled through her fingertips as she unfolded the note. Typewritten? One-and-a-half typewritten pages? Oh ... This was not going to be good. *God, please let me take the disappointment bravely—like an American soldier.*

Oct. 21, 2001
Dear Miah,

I am the luckiest fool alive to have someone as beautiful and forgiving as you, love me the way you do. I'm so thankful that despite all you've been through, you can still love "deep and wide" as you said in your letter. This tried-by-fire love is what helps you deal with your circumstances with so much grace.

You, of all people, have a right to be angry and vengeful. But like we've talked about, you have chosen a better way. And now after some time has passed, I've come to see you're making the right choice. I mean, where would any of us be without grace?

However, I'm embarrassed to say my first reaction to your news had been an immature fit of rage. Since Maddox was held up in some cell in Oklahoma, I had to pick a fight with a wall—and, well, the wall won. I got the consolation prize though—an awesome Michigan State green cast on my right hand. And lucky you, you get this Word doc instead of my messy handwriting. :-)

But honestly, it's probably a good thing you told me your plan in a letter. If you hadn't, I'm afraid our goodbye might not have been so hopeful. As you can see by the date at the top of this paper, it has taken me some time to get a grip on this whole thing and reply in a positive way.

Miah, I've tried a thousand times over (as I'm sure you have) to understand why Creator would allow such evil to happen to someone as good as you. And now He has the audacity to throw in this "detour", as you call it? I have to admit, that my view of God has been challenged. So much so, that I've found it hard to trust Him like I once did.

Your dad's been struggling with the same thing. Somehow C.J. sensed our inward battling, so yesterday, he, Pastor Bryce, and Dr. Bakhuysen stole us away (along with your brothers) for some guy time. We started at the West Michigan Gun Club where we shot off a couple hundred angry rounds. After we left the gun club, we went for a hike in the Barbour State Game area. While the whole scenario may send chills down your spine, the walk seemed to be exactly what we needed.

We found the shed, Miah. (Sense my hesitation.) And then we hiked to what the map called "God's Soup Bowl." I haven't settled in my mind whether it's an appropriate name or not. Anyway, right there in the stillness of that amphitheater, our "mates" explained that in our times of deepest trials, God gives supernatural strength to those who need it most. They said you hadn't gone stark-raving mad like I first suspected; instead, God has given you an added measure of His Spirit to help you deal with this unbelievable situation. They said it's a peace and strength we won't necessarily be given or understand.

When I consider your decision in light of this, I have to trust you know what you're doing, and God knows what He's doing too. I only wish I could be there to help you now. Which brings me to the contents of your blue envelope number two. :-) Girl, your surprises are killing me! I can't believe I'm going to the Australian Outback for Christmas!

When I set out to leave the rez, I never thought I'd end up on the other side of the world. Thank you for this incredible opportunity. And please thank your parents for sharing their frequent flyer miles.

I'm so excited to meet the rest of your family, especially Grandmother Jannali. Josh helped me fill out the passport application, and I started a countdown to December 20 on my calendar. Sixty more days 'til I see your beautiful face!

And thank you too for the ticket home. It will be good to see my mom and Jett before I head off to South Carolina. And for you, I'll do my best to patch things up with my dad.

Miah, if I'd known about the decision you were wrestling with, I never would have committed to the U.S. Marine Corps. I hope you believe me. With all my heart I want to stay and protect you from the judgment and pain you'll face.

The only way I'll be able to get through these next four years is to tell myself that in a very round-about, long-distance way, I will be protecting you—and I'll be praying for you too. I'll be praying God will strengthen you: body, mind, and soul, so you can do what you feel you have to do. I hope by your sacrifice, you'll find healing and closure for yourself.

This morning Pastor Bryce shared a verse that really stuck with me. It's from Joshua 1:9. "Have I not commanded you? Be strong and courageous! Do not tremble or be dismayed, for the Lord your God is with you wherever you go."

Miah, you've probably leaned on this truth a hundred times over, but it's new to me. Since the next four years are going to mean a lot of time apart, I'd like this to be "our verse." Let's hold onto the promise that God's watching over us, no matter where we are.

I love you, Miah Joy Brennan!

Very, very sincerely,
Brandt Traversie DuCharme

Thank you, God. She emptied her lungs of her bated breath and held the note close to her heart. *Thank you for Brandt's love and acceptance. Thank you for turning his anger to understanding. Please don't let him falter in his faith anymore. Keep him strong in his love for You. Keep my dad strong too. And wherever Brandt ends up, help him to trust in Your care and protection.*

"Miah, we should be getting along. It's two forty-five." Mum opened the screened door and peeked a kind smile beyond the worn wood. "Oh ... a letter from Brandt?" The bright blue in Mum's eyes fell to the note and then bounced back up, most likely checking for tears. "Good news? Bad news?"

"Good. He's good with it now. He struggled at first—like Dad. He understands though, and he's excited to come for Christmas."

"For your sake, I'm so glad." Mum walked over, delivering a hug. "So, are you up for one more visit?"

"I reckon." She took her time folding the note on its creases then tucked it back into the envelope. "Why do I feel so nervous to visit the Barcelows and Grandmother Jannali, Mum? I should be happy."

"I know. I'm a little apprehensive too." Smiling, Mum offered a hand up. "Come on. We can do this together."

Two fifty-five. They should be here any minute now. Anna Barcelow placed the lamington cake and apple pie in the center of the table then pressed a calming hand to her belly. How silly that her insides were fluttering about like anxious butterflies. After all, how long had she known Claire Brennan? Twenty?

Twenty-five years? Hadn't their friendship grown into something as comfortable as an old pair of sneakers?

Exhaling a heavy breath, she tried to rid herself of any hint of uneasiness. She wanted their time together to feel like a warm, loving embrace—a safe place where Claire and Miah could let down their guard and simply be cared for, be understood, and most importantly, be free to find some solace.

She turned an ear to the front door and listened as John Brennan's old Ute rambled up the red, gravel road. "Mother! Kylie! They're here!" After pulling the kettle off the stove and adding the tea to steep, she made her way to the front door. It looked like Claire was driving and ... Yes, Miah's yellow-white hair brightened the passenger-side window.

Miah ... The last time she'd seen Kylie's pretty best friend had been during the Christmas holiday. The fair-skinned girl had always been pleasing to the eye, but there on her sixteenth Christmas it seemed she'd been gifted with an added measure of womanly charm. And her loveliness had been enhanced because she wasn't aware of her head-turning beauty. Her innocence and carefree laughter made her even more intriguing to watch.

Now, however, it would be a miracle if her cheery, childlike disposition had survived the horrible trials of the past two, almost three months. A person couldn't go through the fire without being changed, could they? No, there would be scars— emotional and physical handicaps they'd have to politely overlook.

"Where are they?" Kylie stepped up beside her at the screened door while Mother took a spot at the front window.

"They're on the other side of the shed. They should be turning the corner any second now."

"I don't know why or how it could be, but my stomach feels all jittery, Mum."

"Mine too. Quick, let's say a prayer." She took Kylie's hand then turned and held out her hand to Jannali. "Mother, we're going to pray—for peace." When Mother joined them, they all bowed their heads. "Lord, thank you for bringing Claire and Miah home. Calm their nerves as well as ours. May your Holy Spirit be amongst us and give us your peace. Help us to love and care for Miah and Claire in a way that brings comfort to them. In Jesus' name we pray. Amen."

Kylie and Mother echoed their agreements, and then they all resumed their posts. They watched in silence while the tired utility vehicle made its way through the gate and finally stopped next to Caleb's just as spent pickup. Their visitors paused a long moment before opening the Ute's doors, but the moment their feet hit the gravel, Kylie bolted from the house like a racehorse out of the chute. With tears streaming down her cheeks, she caught Miah in a heartfelt embrace.

Anna wiped at her own tears and followed Mother across the yard to greet Claire with their own open-armed welcome.

"Claire ... Welcome home, sweet friend. I'm so, so sorry for all you've been through. I wish we could have been there for you ... for Miah."

"Oh, Anna, you were with us. In your prayers. In your cards. In the timely phone call that ... that saved Miah's life. You were with us in the way you and Thom helped with the station so John and Ella could come to us. We have always been aware of your love and support."

Without as much as a polite hesitation, Mother clasped Claire's hand and brought it to her cheek with an emotional pat. "Claire, dear girl."

"Jannali ... I've missed you so much. It's wonderful to be here with you now. You ... you've been a source of inspiration to Miah."

"Oh?" Mother suppressed a humble giggle. "How so?"

"Well, you somehow found it in your heart to overcome the pain of your past and forgive those who stole you from your family. Miah is trying so very hard to do the same."

"Oh, yes. Saying I forgive you is the easy part. Acting on it and meaning it in your heart is nearly impossible. However, with God, all things are possible."

"G' day, Mrs. Barcelow! Grandmother Jannali!"

"Miah ... Oh, bless your heart." Anna reached out and pulled the too thin girl into her arms. "It's so good to see you."

"You too." Miah reciprocated with a hug, tears pooling in her blue eyes. "It's good to be home. Thank you for having us over."

"Well, we couldn't wait one minute longer to see you. I hope your grandparents didn't mind that we nicked you away for a bit. How are you doing?"

Miah smiled through misty eyes. "Pretty good."

She appeared well, all things considered. Except for the five or so missing pounds and the pink scar on the edge of her lip and in the middle of her neck, she looked like the Miah they had always known and loved. Could it be her left eye was bruised and tracked a little slowly too? "Miah, I wish we could have been there for you. We prayed for you every day, every minute of every day."

"Thank you, Mrs. Barcelow. I felt your prayers. Except for that one ... most difficult day, I have experienced ... God's comfort." Miah wiped away a lone tear with a slightly trembling and scarred hand. When she tried to gain control of her building emotion, her chest heaved beneath her bejeweled, navy blue tank top, revealing the edge of an angry red scar.

So, the unthinkable had truly happened. Although she didn't want to believe it, the painful proof was there plain as day. This precious girl, who had once nursed at her own breast, really had been abducted and abused by a madman who left her fighting for her life. Unbelievable. And here she stood before them, able to smile and go on. "Miah, you're a walking miracle."

A breath huffed from the curve of Miah's upturned lips. "Yes, I am, and ... I have you to thank. Thank you for being sensitive to God's voice and for ringing our house. I was in a dark spot and thought there was no way out but to end it all. I ... I acted out in a moment of weakness." Shame colored her face a warm hue of pink.

"It's all right, child." Mother stepped forward and took Miah's scarred hand in hers. "God knows our frame. He is mindful we are but dust. When we are weak, His power is made perfect."

"My pastor said the same thing. He said it wasn't a coincidence that Mrs. Barcelow rang us and insisted Rob look for me. It was a miracle—God making the impossible, possible. And I've seen Him working all along the way."

"And you will find His power now as you seek to heal and overcome." Mother placed her hands on Miah's shoulders as if she were bestowing a blessing upon the beautiful, young woman. "What you are going to do will be difficult, my dear, but remember, in our weaknesses, God is strong, and so are your friends. We will help you through this, Miah."

In her strong and knowing way, Mother reached for Miah's hand. "Why don't you three get tea ready? Miah and I will be there soon."

***

"Come with me, love. Old Jannali wants to show you something."

Miah took Grandmother Jannali's extended hand and walked with her across the station yard toward the west paddock.

The dusty sunbaked earth and dried clumps of cow dung smelled of all things good and right. And yes, for today at least, the flies that rose from their resting places and buzzed around her face were welcomed too. She was home, safe, and among dear friends. Nothing could spoil her peace, not even a little fly.

They walked beyond the thick trunk of the lone bottle tree to the edge of the paddock and its gate that led to the endless western horizon. "Oh wow, Jannali! There's new fencing! So straight and clean. And three strands of electric wire instead of two. Did Mr. Barcelow and Caleb do this?"

Jannali kept her eyes trained on the hundred or so cows and calves grazing in full measure of peace. "Yes, with the help of your granddad and uncles. And do you know why the fence is there, dear one?"

Was this a trick question? "Well, as long as I've been on God's green earth, this fencing has always been used to protect the calves from dingos."

Her older friend chuckled, and her soft brown eyes were swallowed up by her abundant cheeks. "Ah ha! You are very bright, child. And what happens if a mob of dingoes does get through the fence?"

What was Jannali getting at? She turned and gave Jannali a sly grin before answering. "There would be lots of bawling, bellowing and running and kicking."

"Too right." Jannali smiled. "The cattle would certainly make a ruckus. And if one of those calves were being attacked, the cows wouldn't feel obligated to be neighborly to their enemy." Jannali stepped closer to the gold-colored, treated-wood fence. "The Creator, who cares for the sparrow, implanted this protective instinct within the beast. It was by His design."

Resting her weathered hand on top of one of the new posts, Jannali turned and looked her in the eyes. "Child, it's okay to keep your distance, to protect yourself from the man who hurt you. The Creator, who loves you deeply and intimately, made you to survive—*and* to thrive. He is the One who 'works righteousness and justice for *all* the oppressed'—for you and even for the man who hurt you. Let God do His work in your heart, and let Him do whatever work He chooses to do in the heart of your enemy. It's not up to you. If in time He gives you the grace to forgive, then forgive. But for now, your job is to heal and to trust God."

Holding back tears, Miah nodded her thanks. Of course,

Jannali knew her angry, blistered heart was struggling with Jesus' command to forgive. Her older friend had been stolen from her family and abused, not for a night, but for years. And miraculously, somehow, sometime along the way of her suffering, Grandmother Jannali's anger and sorrow had dulled enough so the muted hues of humility, joy, and yes, forgiveness could be seen in her life. Maybe someday down the road, all the wounds of her own heart would heal too. Maybe one day in the distance, hope and joy and ... forgiveness could be possible, could color her life too. "Thank you, Jannali."

Jannali stretched her soft, understanding arm around Miah's waist and gave it a loving squeeze. "I hope Anna, Kylie, and your mum saved us some tea and cake. Should we head back to the house?"

CHAPTER THIRTY-FOUR

iah pulled the black and white polka dot pillow into her arms and stretched out belly-down on Kylie's bed with a moan. "Oh, I ate too much."

"Too much? You had three tiny bites of Lamington cake." Kylie sat down on the other side of the bed and crossed her legs.

"Sheeze, Ky. Were you counting?"

"Not on purpose. You're just so bloomin' skinny, Miah."

"You noticed? It's my stomach. It hasn't been right ever since ... Well, you know."

Kylie pulled at a wild thread on the all-white quilt and nodded.

Of course, she knew. Kylie had probably spent the past thirty minutes of their teatime trying to picture the whole, terrible scenario in her head. And who could blame her? Kylie's only other option would be to come right out and ask for all the gory details and she'd never do that. No, Kylie would find it much more satisfying to let her imagination fill in the sordid gaps, and if by chance anyone offered a few details from reality, she'd consider that just dinky-di too.

"I-I don't reckon you want to see my scars, do you?"

Kylie uncrossed her legs and then shrugged as if it were neither here nor there. "If you feel like you want to show me. I mean ... if you think it might help you."

"It would. First, you have to open this." She leaned over the edge of the bed, pulled Drew's package from her handbag, and tossed it in Kylie's lap. "It's from Drew, and I'm dying to see what it is."

Friendly fire shot from Kylie's dark eyes. "Hey, that's not a fair trade. What goes on between me and Drew is none of your bizzo."

"Oh, yes it is. It's *all* of my bizzo! Open it."

"All right. Hang on." With her tongue rolling around in her cheek, Kylie pulled at the brown packaging and withdrew a pink envelope and small, light blue box.

Tiffany's? Drew bought Kylie something from Tiffany's? What about flying lessons?

"Miah, I'm already warning you. The letter is off-limits."

"Totally fine. I only want to see what's in the box."

"Fair enough." Kylie curled her lips in a cunning grin and began to loosen the trademark white bow at a cruel, snail-like pace. Then at the last moment, she yanked hard on the ribbon. "I can't stand the suspense either!" Giggling, Kylie pulled off the top of the small box and peered inside. Her gasp was worth the wait. "Miah, look! It's beautiful," she whispered, waving her closer.

The necklace did indeed shine. And Drew would be so delighted with Kylie's response. Her friend dangled the sterling silver heart pendant up in front of the sunlight then squeezed it tight in her hand as tears started to rise along the rim of her long, dark-brown lashes.

"Drew must care about you a lot. I mean, Tiffany's? Jingoes, Ky."

Kylie sniffed back her emotion and nodded. "I miss him so much."

"Obviously, he misses you too." And she missed Brandt with such a longing that her stomach felt as if it might turn inside out. Or ... maybe the Lamington wasn't settling right. She rolled on her side and pulled the pillow close to her belly.

"Miah? Are you all right?"

She nodded and sat up to help Kylie with the clasp. "So Ky, are you ever going to give me the oil about you and Drew?" They moved off the bed to admire the gift in the big mirror topping Kylie's dresser. Blimey! Compared to Kylie's perfect, genetically derived tan, her face looked green—as green as the bile rumbling in her belly.

"Are you sure you're all right, Miah?"

"Mmm hmm." She swallowed a flood of tangy salivation. "So, are you going to tell me what's going on? Drew's been talk-—I'll ... I'll be right back."

She covered her mouth, raced down the hallway, and made it to the toilet just as the chocolate and coconut-covered sponge cake retched from her belly. Her fingers clutched the porcelain bowl through the lurching ride, and when the spasms came to an end, she lay back on the coolness of the tile floor. *God, I'm trying to be obedient here. Couldn't you at least make things a little easier?*

"Miah?" A quiet knock pushed the door ajar then Kylie let herself in. "Are you okay?"

When she peeked her good eye opened, Kylie had crouched near with all kinds of concern on her face. Or was it shock? Had Kylie seen the ugly scar on the underside of her jaw?

"Do ... do you want me to get your mum, Miah?"

"No. I'm all right. I get this almost every day. Usually in the morning."

"Is it from being stabbed ... in your stomach?" Kylie's careful eyes landed where Duane had planted his knife.

"No, my wound is pretty much healed." Sighing, she levered herself up and leaned against the wall. Would she have to lay it all out for Kylie? No, Kylie's imagination was probably working overtime; she'd eventually put two and two together. And if her imagination didn't tip her off—Er ... maybe it already had.

Kylie's curious eyes had grown to the size of a twelve-sided fifty cent piece. "Miah ..." And her fingers came up, covering her gasp. "You're pregnant? How?"

If Kylie's unbelieving tears were brought on by the shock of her revelation, her own were the result of a growing, unexplainable anger. She knew what Kylie meant. It was an innocent question everyone asked—the same question she'd asked God a million times over. But for some reason, she couldn't stop the bitter exasperation from rising like vomit and spewing all over her beautiful friend's face. "For crying out loud, Kylie! What do you think? The monster raped me!" Her rage forced Kylie back against the unforgiving shower door.

The dense silence that threatened to swallow her up in a black hole of shame was broken only by Kylie's stuttering breaths and quiet sobs. And her own hot tears steamed their way down her cheeks, piling guilt on her stupid, miserable shoulders.

"Kylie ... I'm sorry. I don't know what got into me. I'm so, so sorry. It's just ... I-I've had to answer that question a hundred times, and like you—and everyone else—I'm stumped why God would allow a pregnancy. It's maddening all the way around. But I shouldn't take my anger out on you. Can you ever forgive me?"

A dripping faucet marked a slow tense beat, then finally, Kylie reached out with a forgiving embrace. "You don't have to be sorry, Miah. I ... I shouldn't have pried. I knew about the rape, but the pregnancy ... is such a surprise. I mean ... I thought the doctors would have ... given you something."

She nodded. "I know. It's shocking. And you didn't pry. I was going to tell you. I just didn't know how." She grabbed some toilet paper and wiped the tears from Kylie's face. "I am so, so sorry."

Kylie nodded her forgiveness. "It's okay. You have a right to be angry."

"I shouldn't take it out on my best friend." She wiped at her own tears as Kylie sighed heavily against the acoustical bathroom walls.

As difficult as it would be, she owed her friend an explanation.

CHAPTER THIRTY-FIVE

"Straight away they gave me two white pills and twelve hours later, two more pills—just in case. The doctor told me I hadn't been menstruating like I believed. The bleeding came from ... an injury. So, to prevent the possibility of a pregnancy, I took the bloomin' pills. And since the tests for a few STDs came back negative, I didn't give it another thought. I couldn't think about it. I needed to focus on getting better so I could go home."

Kylie's teary eyes blinked with gracious understanding.

"Once I came home from the hospital, I couldn't shake the nausea that came and went at will, and my energy level seemed slow in returning. Some mornings I had to force myself to get out of bed. The doctor blamed the nausea on the wound to my belly and the lack of energy on all the blood loss. All my other symptoms: the nightmares, fear of the dark and being alone, and shortness of breath, he accounted to Post Traumatic Stress Disorder.

"Part of my anxiety grew from the final test I knew I had to pass. Waiting for the HIV test and its results was like waiting for the electric chair. Because my general health didn't improve, I convinced myself I had AIDS. And then to top it off, I began to feel this very real separation from God. It felt as if the closeness of God's presence I'd experienced earlier had simply been in my imagination. I had serious doubts that God even existed. It felt like my prayers were hitting my bedroom ceiling, bouncing back, and slapping me in the face.

"It was the Saturday morning after the September 11 terrorist attacks when my dad burst into my room, 'fed up with my indolence and isolation.' He literally dragged me out of bed, down to the breakfast table, and forced me to eat. When I proceeded to puke it all up, he stormed out of the house, cursing Maddox's name all the way into the yard. It ... it seemed to me, not only had I been abandoned by God, but by my dad as well. So, I deceived myself into thinking death by an overdose of Vicodin would be better than facing life without the support of God and my dad—the two I needed most.

Kylie pulled her hair off her neck then settled back against the shower door again. "And that's when my mum rang? When Rob and Drew found you in the bath?"

She nodded. "I couldn't take the pain and loneliness anymore. Brandt was away at university, Bri had busied herself with a school production, and Alicia and the rest of the band ... Well, since I wasn't up to playing, they gave me space I didn't necessarily need."

"Bri hasn't been there for you?"

She shook her head. "I think I scare her or something. It's easy to understand—I'm not the same person she once knew." She shrugged. "But it was God's presence and my dad's love and understanding that I needed and craved. If they weren't able to meet me in my grief and confusion, I determined I couldn't, or wouldn't, endure AIDS without them."

"Miah, you ... you don't have AIDS, do you?"

"I hope not. The results from the first test came back negative, but I won't know for sure for another three and a half months. If the virus doesn't show up in six months, then I'm clear. Ronald Maddox's first test came back negative too." A little huff escaped her smile. "I suppose He can find some comfort knowing he'll be kept alive for at least another three and a half months."

"So, how did you find out you were pregnant?"

"After Rob and Drew found me, they rushed me to the hospital and when I woke up, my psychologist was there. After a bit of insistence on my part, she and I concluded something wasn't quite right. So, my physician ordered an upper GI test and some blood tests, and that's when I received the unbelievable results. My dad had a royal fit, privately ranting and threatening to sue the hospital for 'doling out dodgy pills'. The doctor explained the pills weren't faulty—it had to do with timing. The pills are effective to prevent eighty-five percent of pregnancies if taken within twenty-four to forty-eight hours of a rape, but then their effectiveness drops to fifty-eight percent after that. I took the pills three days after ...

My dad finally settled down when my mum reminded him the hospital's doctors saved my life. Then he turned his anger in the right direction—on Maddox. But me, I was simply glad to know I wasn't going crazy. It seemed once my fears were relieved, I could begin to open myself up to God and move forward toward healing. And that's why I'm here."

"To heal?"

She nodded then raised herself off the hard tile floor. "To heal and get away from people's stares, whispers, and expectations. Oh, my bum. It's so sore."

"It's so bony!"

She gave Kylie a smirk then turned on the faucet and helped herself to a washcloth. She ran the cloth under the cool water, rang it out, and tossed it to her friend. Soaking another cloth for herself, she covered her face and sucked a long drink from the folds of the soft cloth. Refreshment slid down her burnt throat like pure Michigan snow.

"Miah ..." Kylie interrupted her frosty holiday. "What are you going to do with the baby? Are you going to have it?"

She slid the washcloth off her face and gazed at her friend's wide, curious eyes. "Yes." Then turning, she caught the image of her tall, skinny self in the mirror. She didn't look pregnant. Instead of the magical glow she'd heard pregnant women get, she looked tired and beat up. Kylie stood and joined her at the mirror.

"Are you going to keep the baby, Miah?"

She watched herself shake her head. "No. I don't know. I go back and forth. Today I feel as if I'm leaning toward adoption. We asked my pastor and his wife if they wanted it because, for whatever reason, Celia can't carry her babies to full-term. But they think it would be too difficult a reminder for me—seeing Maddox's baby all the time." Tears blurred her vision. "It doesn't really matter. Either way, I'll be haunted. I am haunted." She sighed away her grief. "I just have to keep telling myself God has this figured out, and He'll make His way clear when it's time. Come on, let's go back to your room."

Kylie nodded at their reflection and then led the way. "Don't hate me, okay? You know you don't have to put yourself through this, right? Don't you think God understands your predicament? I mean ... you have options."

Oh no, here we go again. *God, give me grace ... and patience.* She settled back on Kylie's bed and tried to hide her threatening tears within the ruffles of the black and white pillow. "I-I know I have options—and I've been wrestling with them for the past four or five weeks." She tried to swallow the lump of sorrow building in her throat. "Should I end a life that God allowed—forced as it was—and viable even after I took the morning-after pills? If I truly believe in the goodness of God's will, why would I try to change it? And if I did change it, would it be as good? I'm trying to believe God has a million good reasons why I am pregnant with Ronald Maddox's baby. And I'm choosing to believe one of those reasons is to give me some hope and purpose, because …"

Hot emotion swelled until her words poured from her mouth in a grief-filled cry. "I-I'm literally hanging on by a thread, Ky." Tears burst over the rims of her eyes and rolled down her cheeks. "I so … so desperately need to know that God really is working this out for good, because right now, it … it hurts so bad, and I am so afraid." Fear and pain spilled from her heart as she hid her sobs in the softness of Kylie's pillow.

"Miah." Kylie walked to the edge of the bed, bent, and held her, smoothing her back. "He will. He is. God is working even now. Yes, we have to believe God is working through all this."

She nodded and let her tears flow down onto Kylie's shoulder. And it seemed as if all creation were grieving right along with her. A steady dirge of buzzing and chirping played through the bedroom window, accompanying her tears and sniffles. When she gathered her strength, she sat up and held her friend's hands within her own scarred hand. "I-I know this is going to sound weird, Ky, but I believe God had this whole thing in His sights long ago. I think He began preparing me when I was only eleven."

Kylie straightened too and didn't seem at all afraid of the scars, instead she caressed them as if they were sacred—something to be treasured. "What do you mean, Miah? How?"

"Do you remember when Brad and Josh stole my journal? I was so angry, I threatened them with a whip and knocked the breath out of Josh."

Kylie nodded. "You spooked a horse that injured Brad's hand and nearly trampled Josh."

"Aye. And after my dad rescued us all, he taught me about consequences and forgiveness and grace, and I … I made the choice to follow Jesus. My dad told me it wouldn't necessarily be easy—there would be costs. So … I knew there would be sacrifices to be made." She closed her eyes to the here and now. "I only hoped God wouldn't hold me to them."

"Kylie." She peered intently at her friend. "I guess what I'm saying is, maybe by having this baby—by being obedient—I'll eventually be glad I did something beyond myself. Maybe years down the road after Maddox is dead and gone, after my heart has experienced some measure of healing and is capable of giving grace, then maybe I'll be glad I gave life to his baby."

Kylie walked across the room and closed the door on the voices coming from the kitchen then sat on the edge of the bed. "You are the bravest person I know, Miah. And having this baby is the most sacrificial and grace-filled act I've ever heard of."

A refreshing breeze blew in the window and rolled across them like a breaking wave. "My pastor told me grace is like the wind, Ky. Although it's unseen, at times it's an incredible force. Receiving mercy when we don't deserve it has the power to soften the hardest, most broken hearts, like Maddox's. Like mine. She sighed away the shame that snuck in on the breeze. "And grace is what I need from you." She took Kylie's hand in hers. "I'm sorry for hurting you. Can you forgive me?"

"Miah, there's nothing to forgive. I'm sure I can't understand all you've gone through and all you're going to go through, but I want you to know I think you're very courageous and when you're feeling weak, I'll be here for you." The compassion in Kylie's eyes morphed into a twinkle of mischief. "But don't think for one second I'm gonna give you the oil on me and Drew."

"Hey! Come on now!"

"Consequences, consequences. There are consequences to our actions, Miah." Kylie's sing-song voice erupted into a chorus of giggles.

Thank you, God, for this laughter, for my friend Kylie, and for this time with her.

"Knock. Knock." The door creaked open without much of a

warning. "The ladies in the kitchen told us there's a little lost lamb in here who has finally found her way home." Kylie's dad peeked his fair, freckled face into the room, and then Caleb, a naturally tanned version of his dad, stepped in, opening the door wide. "'Ow ya doing, Miah?"

She jumped up from the bed and greeted her friends with the warm hug they deserved. "Mr. Barcelow! Caleb! It's so good to see you!" Mr. Barcelow's embrace felt as strong as her dad's.

He gave her back a hardy pat then held her away, wiping tears from his face. "You're a good girl, Miah." His mouth quivered as he struggled for words. "Very brave. I'm glad you've come home."

"My mum told you why I came home?"

Mr. Barcelow hesitated then nodded his flush-faced answer.

"Do you think I'm crazy?"

"Like I said, you're a very brave girl."

"Thanks." She couldn't hold back her tears either. Seeing the emotional responses of her friends and family always seemed to trigger a flood of her own. But Caleb wasn't crying. His dark eyes had been transfixed on her belly and were now glued to her chest. Which could only mean one thing. She quickly adjusted her tank top to cover the telltale scar. Then she held out her hands hoping to break the awkwardness of Caleb's trance. "Hey, Caleb. 'Ow've you been?"

He took her hands in his and lifted his eyes to a more comfortable place—the scars on her lip and neck. "Good. We've missed you ... and your family. We've been praying for you a lot." His sincere words worked to ease the tension warming her neck and cheeks.

She nodded and returned the smile. "Thanks. Your prayers meant more than anything and ..." She tugged on Caleb's calloused hands. "... just because I'm home doesn't mean you have to stop. I'm still going to need them."

"Hey, what's this, Miah?" Mr. Barcelow pulled her left hand

from Caleb's grasp and studied the pearl ring with the two tiny diamonds. "You're not engaged to the young man we've been hearing about, are you?"

"Mr. Barcelow, do you think my dad would allow that?" They all laughed at the truth of her statement. "Actually, it's a promise ring. Brandt gave it to me right before I left Michigan."

Caleb leaned in to take a closer look. "A promise of what?" His brow twisted into a disapproving scowl.

Slipping her hand from their scrutiny, she shrugged. She wasn't sure she wanted to divulge the details of the intimate conversation she'd had with Brandt. "He uh ... He promised me he would come home safe ... from the military."

"If he's in the military, how'd you meet him? And how old is he anyway? Is he older than me?" Caleb's voice deepened with wariness, and Mr. Barcelow looked concerned. If they were having trouble with her relationship with Brandt, how were they going to react when they learned of Kylie and Drew's budding romance?

"He's Josh's friend. They go to university together. And he's not exactly in the service yet. He just signed up—after the terrorist attacks. He wants to go to Afghanistan."

Caleb's tone grew even more judgmental. "He *just* signed up? Miah, if he cares about you, if he knows what you're about to go through, why would he go and do something stupid like enlisting?"

"I didn't tell him I was pregnant—not until he'd already joined. And it's not stupid." Her temper heightened with the tears rising in her eyes. "He has his reasons, Caleb. Very good reasons."

Although Caleb was a year older and a head taller, Kylie shoved him out of the small circle. "Don't listen to him, Miah. He's just jealous."

"Jealous of what?" Caleb scoffed.

"Miah's boyfriend!"

Caleb's dark eyes shot a quiver of flaming arrows. "Belt up, Kylie!"

"All right, you two."

Kylie ignored her dad's reprimand. "Well, it's true! He's had a crush on Miah ever since she was thirteen." Kylie kept her coy grin trained on the floor, avoiding Caleb's glare and her dad's disapproval.

"That's enough, Kylie."

Caleb's eyes held an apology when they looked her way. Despite shaking his head to refute Kylie's allegation, it was true. While he'd always tried to conceal his teenage infatuation, it continually showed up in the patient way he spoke with her. But even though he had always been much kinder to her than her brothers ever were, she'd been careful not to show any partiality. She'd discouraged his affections with the same sisterly disdain she reserved for her siblings. It kept things less awkward.

Caleb stepped back into the circle. "Miah, I don't want to see you getting hurt again. You've been through enough already."

She nodded, accepting his kindness. "I know. Thank you. Truly, Brandt would never hurt me. He's as trustworthy and caring as you. And ... You'll be able to see for yourself. He's coming here for Christmas. With my dad and brothers."

CHAPTER THIRTY-SIX

Amaroo Station, Queensland, Australia
December 2001

"It's fifty-seven for four in eighteen overs!" With her voice raised to the cloudless sky, one of Miah's younger cousins shouted across the playing field.

Another clapped his hands together. "Come on, mate, you can do this!"

Brandt held the paddle-shaped bat like they told him and focused all his attention on the ball in Josh's hand. Hold the bat steady, connect with the ball, then run to the three wooden posts, or wickets, at the other end of the rectangle pitch. That's all he had to do. It couldn't be too hard, could it? "Bring it, dude!" he taunted.

Josh took a final glance around the field then with all the finesse of a professional cricket player, he let the ball fly with a funny-looking run-hop wind up.

Brandt's hand tensed around the bat, and when the ball bounced on the red ground before him, he took his best shot.

"Dang!" The ball flew beneath the bat and smacked hard into the wickets behind him. A polite moan of disappointment rose from his teammates and the spectators who were sitting under the shade of the front porch, or veranda as they called it.

Kylie, who played wicket keeper, retrieved the ball and stepped up with a consoling pat on his back. "Good try, Brandt. Sorry to say, you're bowled."

If the truth be known, he didn't care. Now he could get some relief from the hot sun and join Miah and the rest of her "rellies" in the shelter of her grandparents' porch. As he lumbered up the steps, her family members were kind to pepper his deflated ego with a chorus of "good try, mate." But where had Miah disappeared to?

Not wanting to appear lost without her, he took a seat next to Caleb, but only after the dude gave him an icy glare then reluctantly scooted over on the wooden bench.

"Sorry I let the team down, bro. It's a lot harder than it looks," He motioned toward the yard where another of Miah's many cousins took his turn to bat. When Caleb didn't respond, he gave it another shot. "Josh is a good pitcher. I never knew. I mean, back home we usually play basketball."

Caleb kept his black eyes trained on the game in front of them, acting like he hadn't heard. Then perhaps out of guilt, he managed an obligatory reply, condescending as it was. "Bowler. I think you meant to say, Josh is a good bowler."

"Oh, uh ... right." He chuckled. "Lots of new terms to learn. Cricket's a great game though. Don't know why it's not played in the States."

Shifting his weight on the bench, Caleb smacked hard at a fly as if the prospect of friendship and conversation was something to be squashed.

What was the guy's problem? And where in the heck did Miah run off to? He surveyed the functional station yard with its collection of trucks and outbuildings, and then his eyes ran down the lineup of people to his right who were gathered on the white-washed porch. Miah was nowhere to be found.

"Hey, Caleb, do you know where Miah went?"

Miah's friend snapped with all the hospitality of a hermit crab. "Nope. Not a clue."

"I hope she's feeling all right."

The dude coughed a comment into his shoulder that sounded a lot like "bull."

"What'd you say?"

"Nothing. Nothing at all." Caleb stood and walked down the wide steps. His boots scuffed up a cloud of dust all the way to the red water hydrant that was planted by one of the larger outbuildings. He pulled up the handle and let the water run over his hands into the trough below.

He decided to let Caleb and his bad attitude go. The dude obviously had feelings for Miah, and in the morning, he'd have her all to himself again. Not that Miah would want the rude son of a gun; nor would her family let them be alone anyway. They hoarded her attention like squirrels hoarding acorns in autumn, and once again someone must have snatched her away.

"I hope you can forgive my grandson."

He looked up to see Jannali intent on taking Caleb's place on the bench. He steadied the old woman's hand as she lowered her soft, ample self to the seat with a sigh.

"The boy hasn't experienced the depth of loss you and I have." She kept her tender gaze on Caleb who'd just immersed his dark, wavy hair beneath a thick stream of water.

"He cares for Miah, you know." Jannali turned her kind eyes toward his own. "So ... this letting go will be difficult for Caleb."

He nodded in reply. "I understand, Jannali. I'll let Miah work things out with Caleb."

"You're a wise young man. A good man."

"I'm learning ... from people like you, the Brennans, from Miah herself."

As if Miah's name were her cue, the screen door squeaked open behind them, and Miah emerged from her grandparents' house looking as fresh as a tall glass of pink lemonade. Yellow hair, pink lips, and eyes sparkling like ice cubes. He could just about drink her up.

With a lunch cooler, tote bag, and water bottle occupying her hands, she squinted in the afternoon sun, her blue eyes scanning the playing field. "Did Brandt bat yet?"

Her Uncle Quinn, the clown of the bunch, leaned behind her and gave him a wink to play along. "Aye, he did, love. Josh bowled him out. Your man's got a temper, he does. He fairly spit the dummy out there. Threw the bat and took off runnin' through the west paddock, swearin' like a trooper."

She turned toward her uncle, shaking her head. "Too funny, Uncle Quinn. Where is he?"

Brandt tugged on the water bottle hanging from her left hand.

"Hey! How did I miss you sitting there?" Her giggle joined in with the flock of happy budgies twittering in a nearby gum tree. "Because you're sitting on my dodgy eye side, that's why!" She nudged aside the tragic truth of the matter with another brave chuckle.

Her granddad stood, wobbling a little as he stepped around one of the little "knee biters" playing at his feet. "Miah, the keys should be in the Ute. Be back before dark now and keep the radio on channel 27. Call if you run into trouble."

"Thanks, Granddad. We'll be fine."

Everyone's eyes popped with questions, but only Miah's Uncle Quinn had the audacity to poke around for the answer they were looking for. "Where you goin', Miah? Can we come too?"

The air sparked with mischief as she responded to her uncle's childlike plea with a patronizing, motherly tone. "I need one hour of peace from all of you. So no, you may not go." She laughed again then handed off the cooler. "Come on, Brandt. The sun's sinking fast. Hooroo, everyone!"

***

"You didn't tell me where we're going."

"It's a surprise." Miah's smile widened, and the corner of her eyes turned up behind her sunglasses.

The strange, exotic landscape spread before them like an IMAX film; even so, he couldn't keep from studying the beauty of Miah's soft features. This might be the last chance he'd get to take her all in without interruption.

The warm wind made her blonde curls dance across her cheeks and down her bare shoulders, drawing his gaze to the full length of her long, tanned arms. Her left arm reached forward to meet the steering wheel, while the right stretched out the window, surfing the breeze. And in between both, her white buttoned-up blouse veiled the mystery of her womanly curves.

She turned, sliding a grin toward him. "What?"

"N-nothing." He'd been caught. "Uh, can I hold your hand?"

"I'd like that." Her right hand abandoned the warm wind and took over the wheel, freeing the rose-pink of her fingertips to slide between his own like a key in a lock. They were a perfect match.

"So, how much longer?" He asked.

"Almost there. See the bridge up ahead?"

He peered through the bug-speckled windshield. Where moments ago the flat, grayish-green scrubland had fought to keep some semblance of life, the vegetation had now become taller, thicker, and taken on the decidedly viable color of spring-time green. And from it all, rose a wooden bridge, looking much too big for the stream bed it spanned.

"The Maneroo Creek runs beneath the bridge and eventually joins the Thomson River south and west of Longreach. Usually by this time of the year, its banks are brimming. And believe it or not, sometimes during The Wet this whole area gets flooded. Then of course, the bridge is useless. And today, we're not going to use it either!" With a "yahoo!" Miah jerked the truck to the left, bouncing over the lip of the two-track and onto the rough plain of prairie grasses. "Hang on!" She gunned the engine, and her whole beautiful self bubbled over with laughter.

He gripped the dash and yelled above the rattling and coughing of the old pickup. "Are you sure you can handle this thing? You don't even have a driver's license!"

"Oh, I can handle it all right. The question is, can you?"

The truck hammered along hitting bump after jarring bump for what seemed like forever. Dang ... and his arms were aching from hanging on for dear life. Suddenly the truck crested a small rise and lurched across a watery ditch before crashing down into the middle of a green oasis with a wheeze.

"You're a maniac, girl!"

"I may be a maniac, but I got us here in once piece, didn't I?"

"We're here?"

"Aye."

Miah cut the truck's engine, and it seemed as if all sight and sound had been digitally enhanced. Beneath the transparent blue light of the seamless heavens, a plethora of winged wildlife chirped and buzzed amidst a wonderland of small-leaved trees and bushes somehow thriving in the reddish, sandy earth. And babbling up from the thirsty-looking ground, a large pool of dark water gave eternal depth to the unlikely spot.

"Wow ... This is incredible." He glanced around, indulging his senses. But Miah jumped from the sweltry cab eager to move the afternoon's agenda along—whatever *it* was.

From the moment his plane had touched down in Longreach six days ago, Miah kept him on a frenetic touring schedule. She'd carried this off under the guise of wanting to give him a full Outback experience. Sure, he'd enjoyed every minute because he'd been with her *and* an entourage of family and friends. Still, what if all these activities were Miah's attempt to ignore the proverbial baby elephant trumpeting his or her presence through every building, across every paddock—over every inch of the three-thousand-square-mile cattle station? Was busyness Miah's way of forgetting the tiny reason that had barely begun to round her belly? He hoped not. It wasn't healthy.

By the time he reached the other side of the pickup, she'd already pulled her gear from the bed of the truck and had begun hiking in the direction of the water.

"Come on, you bludger!" She tossed the words over her shoulder as if playing a friendly game of catch.

"Bludger?" He trotted past a rocky outcropping and some squatty trees before catching up to her and relieving her arms of the weight of the cooler. "What's a bludger?"

"It's a layabout. You know, someone who relies on other people to do all the work."

"What? Give me those things!" He pulled the tote off her shoulder then grabbed a kiss from her smile as he bent to take the water bottle from her hand. "So, what do you call this place?" He swung the tote and water bottle in a wide gesture that included the whole living, breathing sanctuary.

"The Spring." She stopped beneath a thick eucalyptus tree whose gray, peeling branches hugged the sandy bank and black water like a lover's embrace.

"Well, that's original, if not confusing. You call springtime 'The Wet' and this waterhole 'The Spring.' It's a little backwards, don't you think?"

A sudden seriousness stroked her crooked smile. "Actually, The Wet and The Spring are closely connected." She took the tote from his hand and began unfolding its contents: a large grass mat and two beach towels. "And it's the reason I brought you here today. Before we say goodbye tomorrow, I wanted you to know the secret about this place and the secret in my heart.

She reached for the bend of his arm and led him to the water's edge. "I reckon you didn't know we're standing on top of an ancient sea. It's called the Great Artesian Basin, and it lies beneath a huge part of Australia. Scientists say the water's been trapped underground for two million years." She crouched down and ran her hands through the dark pool as if it were sacred. "Because of the Great Artesian Basin, people are able to survive way out here in the back of beyond. Boremen, like my dad, drill down through the sandstone, and when the water bubbles up, it's capped and piped. In some places, the water flows from the ground free, without coaxing, like this faithful spring."

She stood and with her eyes, she took a slow walk around the perimeter of the oasis. "It's during The Wet that the state-sized aquifers are replenished. And then I come to The Spring to get filled up too. This is my second most favorite place on Earth."

"Let me guess. Your most favorite place is the Big Horn Mountains."

When Miah turned to face him, emotion made the blue of her eyes look all shimmery like the water before them, and her voice was just a whisper. "Yes ... and anywhere you are."

Is that how Miah truly felt? If so, how could he be so lucky? He wanted to kiss her again, but she bent to spread the beach mat then began to unbutton her top.

"Come in the water with me? It's a perfect twenty-five degrees. Or, uh ... about seventy-five Fahrenheit." She stepped out of her flip-flops and jean shorts then tossed them on the mat with her blouse.

Her beauty left him immobile, unable to breathe. He could only stand there like a doofus and watch her bikini-clad body step closer to the kick-drumming in his heart.

"What are you waiting for? Are you afraid of the snakes?"

"Snakes?" He pulled off his T-shirt.

"Don't worry. The hospital in Longreach has antivenom—if you get there in time, that is."

"You're not making me feel any better."

Giggles tumbled from her smile and trailed her tan, mile-long legs as they took three running strides then dove into the deep water.

Although creation's ticks, hums, and tweets filled the hole Miah's absence left, its glory couldn't compare with the wonder of her beauty. And come tomorrow afternoon, he'd be missing her laugh, her voice, her heart-stopping smile so much. The flight home would begin the loneliest four years of his life. *Creator God, please make the time go by quickly. Keep Miah safe. Keep me safe too.*

Miah's fair skin and golden hair finally broke through the surface of the water, and her smile was aimed right at him. *God, thank You for the incredible gift of Miah and her love. Thank you for the hope you've given me.* He dove in headfirst and swam in the direction of Miah's welcoming grin.

Beneath the cool waters, her hands reached out and pulled him close. When he came up for a breath, her eyes, her smile, her arms all wrapped in his, said yes to their hopeful future. Her skin smelled of fruit and flowers freshly washed by a summer rain. If only he could peel away the space between them. "Miah, I love you so much."

Her lips were dotted with diamonds of water, and she dropped words of assurance into his ears. "I love you too. More than you'll ever know." Her kiss was filled with such confidence. How did she expect him to keep his mind from moving to things meant only for a time to come?

"Miah ..."

When her finger drew a quieting line across his jaw and onto his lips, he couldn't stop his hand from rising through the water and touching the safe, soft skin above her breast.

And in a flash, the magic ended. Like the hammer on a mouse trap, her fingers clamped down on his hand and pushed it back into the water. "Jingoes, Brandt! Can't we pretend for just one day that August ten didn't happen? That Ronald Maddox didn't happen? I ... I hate these stupid scars!"

"What? Miah ... I didn't mean-—"

"Just forget it." She pushed away, turned, and dove deep under the water.

CHAPTER THIRTY-SEVEN

In what seemed like forever, Miah re-entered the land
of the breathing without her usual enthusiasm for
life. He watched her troll through the water, her nose barely
breaking the surface, her eyes closed on the sting of her
memories.

"Miah?" Brandt quietly paddled near, circling her like one of
the cautious butterflies bobbing at the water's edge. "Hey ... I'm
sorry. Your beauty moves me so much, and I forget. I forget how
close the pain is. You act so strong sometimes."

When he reached for her, she dipped her tears beneath the
water and allowed him to pull her into his arms. He was hardly
ready for the flood of emotion that gushed from Miah's heart as
her face broke through the water and pressed against his chest.

"I only wanted to show you how much I love you! I wanted
to take your hand, swim with you to the bottom of the spring,
and have you feel the rush of water." She swiped at her tears. "I
wanted to tell you my love for you is as unending as the ancient
water flowing up from the bottom of this spring. But Maddox got
in the way. He gets in the way of everything!" Her sobs echoed
off the banks of the hushed, reflective pool. "And now all I want

to do is sink to the bottom of this waterhole and stay there 'til my breath runs out. I hate him! I hate what he's done to me. I hate what he's making me do!"

What could he say to comfort her? What could he do to give her peace? *Creator God, please be here. Help her.* He held her close, letting her cry away her pain and disappointment. "Miah, I know you love me. Thank you. Thank you for bringing me here. It's incredible. And this time is not wasted or ruined. You can still show me the spring. We can redeem the moment. With Creator, don't you believe everything can be redeemed? Isn't that why you're doing what you're doing—giving life to Maddox's baby?"

She lifted her head enough to wipe her tears again. "I don't want to. I ... I'm so afraid. And now you're leaving. I want to disappear too."

He touched the soft, scarred skin beneath her chin and tilted her face toward him, searching her eyes for the despair that almost took her life before. "I'm not disappearing, and you're not going to disappear either, do you hear me? You have to swear you'll do everything you can to keep your mind and your body healthy—if not for yourself, then for your family. For me."

Sniffing back her emotion, Miah nodded her promise. "I'll try." She turned in his arms, lay back, and rested her head on his chest until her tears subsided. The warmth of the sun settled on the still water, warming their skin, quieting their thoughts. Finally, Miah broke the silence with a careful sigh. "I ... I felt the baby a couple of days ago." She paused as if to muster the courage to go on. "It felt like a tiny pebble tumbling inside my belly."

"Did it scare you?"

"Not so much as it finally registered in my mind there's no turning back. This is real. I'm going to have a baby."

Miah squeezed his arms tight across her chest, and the

lowering sun made the pearl ring on her finger glow pale yellow. "Caleb thinks your enlistment into the marines is poor timing."

As much as he hated to admit it, Miah's friend was probably right. "Well, what do *you* think, Miah?"

"I think Caleb is wise beyond his years."

"Do you want to know what I think? I think he's in love with you." When she didn't deny it, he held her even tighter and continued. "Miah, if I could find a better way to pay for school, I would. I hope you believe me. I think if you could see where I came from, you'd understand why I need to fight what I feel is a great injustice. And you'd understand why an education is a must for me. It's my only way out of a dead-end life. I want to build a better future. A future for us."

"A future for us? You and me? Or you, me, and this baby? What happens if when this baby is born, I can't let it go? I can't imagine that happening, but what if in the end, my heart says yes? Do you trust me to make the choice on my own? I mean, if this ring means anything, and if you can't be here, are you okay with me making the choice for you? For us?"

He released his hold on her and turned her to face him. "You're not seriously thinking about keeping the baby, are you?"

Her gaze dropped to the water with a shrug. "Not seriously, but I have allowed my mind to wander there a couple of times."

"Miah, you're seventeen! What about your goals, your dreams, your music?"

"My music?" She scoffed. "Brandt, I haven't written a new song since before the fair. I've got nothing. Nada."

When the fight drained from her spirits, he bolstered her body in his arms. "Then sing the old stuff. Get inspired again."

She looked annoyed then turned away. When she faced him once again, a big sigh escaped her lips. "It's not as easy as you think, Brandt."

"So, you're just going to hang it up?" How in the world could she throw all her talent away? He could hardly believe his ears.

"Miah, you can't! You have a recording contract waiting for you. Isn't that what you've always wanted? And ... and if you don't want it, didn't Smoky Mountain Media offer to buy your songs? At least sell them your songs. Let someone else sing them. You've got to get your songs out there. They're awesome."

She bit at the scar on her lip, contemplating his words. "Yeah, I ... I guess I could do that." Her pout spread into a sly grin. "Maybe I could set up a college fund for my boyfriend or something."

"No, your boyfriend will do just fine on his own. In fact, your boyfriend now has some frequent flyer miles and is pretty sure recruit training will finish up just about the time his girlfriend's baby is due. The best part is he might get a little time off before he has to report for infantry training."

A shimmer of hope made Miah's sapphire eyes sparkle. "Are you serious?"

CHAPTER THIRTY-EIGHT

Queensland, Australia
May, 2002

If it hadn't been for the olive-colored, marine-issued duffle bag, she wouldn't have recognized Brandt. His face was hidden beneath the shadow of a navy-blue ball cap, and he'd become taller, broader—a strong beam of a man.

Of course, all their letters and phone calls during the difficult months of separation couldn't reveal the changes. One thing remained the same; he still had the power to throw off the rhythm of her breathing. Miah gulped the dry air then linked arms with Mum and Nana to steady herself.

They watched from behind the large viewing window as Brandt walked across the tarmac. And when he entered the airport terminal, his eyes, earth-colored and serious, searched the smattering of people waiting in the arrival lounge. Would he recognize her right away, or would it take him a minute? After all, she'd changed too. Not a year older. Not yet. But five months stronger, a lifetime wiser, an eternity more in love.

Nana caught his eye first, and he responded with a shy smile and a nod. And Nana's breath caught too. She held her hand to her chest and released a whispered oath. "Oh, my beating heart. He's so handsome, Miah."

Brandt's beauty left them all dumbstruck. They stood there like idiots, making him come to them. And on his way, the entire chatty lounge seemed to stop and turn as to be graced by his presence and upright dignity. A U.S. Marine had come to Longreach? Surely, the people all wondered why. She herself had trouble understanding what kept drawing him back to her. Fate had left her tattered and used up. What hopeful thing could Brandt possibly see in her?

Ever respectful, he dropped his bag, removed his hat, and greeted Nana first with a hug. He then turned to hug Mum, his lips brushing her cheeks with a quick kiss. His greetings were wordless as if everything good and familiar had overwhelmed him. When he finally turned to her, all the pent-up thoughts and emotions leaked out in a trickle of quiet tears, and his mouth quivered like a crumbling fortress. "I missed you so much, Miah."

She nodded her agreement as his thick arms wrapped her in an embrace of love and relief. Relief? Yes, a deep feeling of comfort is exactly what sighed from her lungs—a feeling of reassurance after all the distress of the past thirteen weeks. Could relief be what Brandt felt too? Is that what made the tears flow free? "I missed you too, Brandt. It's so good to see you."

"I'm sorry I couldn't be here for you, Miah."

Her tears and hushed words blended into the folds of his thick hooded sweatshirt. "It wasn't your burden to bear."

"I'm sorry I couldn't help you decide what to do. Are you all right?"

Nodding again, she squeezed him even tighter until her arms began to ache. "I am now. I'm so glad you're here. But ... How are you?" She drew away from the strong tower of his chest, searching for truth in his eyes. His letters had spoken of long days of brutal training, hours of being pushed beyond his physical limits, and nights where only sheer exhaustion brought sleep and relief from the battles being fought in his mind.

He looked down at her, smiling. "I'm fine. I'm just glad I made it through the training." Then he pulled her close again, the heat of his body radiating a sense of satisfaction. "We made it, Miah. With everyone's prayers and support, we made it through. I'm an official U.S. Marine, and you finished what you set out to do too. I'm so proud of you."

"And we're proud of you too." With her usual grace, Mum stepped into their private reunion. "Congratulations on your graduation, Brandt. I wish we could have been there."

"Thanks, Mrs. Brennan. I still can't believe Josh and Mr. Brennan came all the way down to South Carolina to support me. So kind of them. Did they tell you my family, even my dad, came too?"

Mum nodded. "Yes, I'm so glad for you."

"Yeah, My dad and I, we've ..." He shrugged. "Well, ever since Miah sent me home before recruit training, my dad and I have learned we can actually be in the same room together without fighting." He shrugged again. "It's hard to admit, but my attitude had been a big part of our problem. I was pretty cocky before I left for college." He adjusted his hat then gave a humbled dip of his head. "A little respect goes a long way. Things seem to be getting better, all the way around."

"I'm so glad to hear it. I do wish I could have met your parents. Trace said they're very gracious people." Mum turned to Nana then back to Brandt. "Well, Nana has a roast in the oven, and we have an hour's drive ahead of us. Shall we continue our conversation in the truck?"

"Sounds good to me." Brandt offered his arm to Mum then grabbed his bag as Nana led the way out to the car park.

"Hey! Wait up, you guys!"

Miah sipped the last drop of tea in her cup while Granddad gathered the remaining crumbs of his chocolate pavlova onto his fork. He paused then lifted the treat to his mouth. "Well, Brandt, do you know what's next for you?"

"Yes, sir. I'll be heading to North Carolina to complete Infantry Training at Camp Lejeune." Brandt pushed his scraped-clean plate away then leaned back in his chair, folding his hands across his belly, which had to be aching from all the food he'd eaten. He had seconds of everything and thirds of the roast and gravy. And who knows how many slices of Nana's homemade bread he'd devoured. She'd lost count after four.

"What will you do there?"

"More training—to prepare for what may come."

Before glancing Brandt's way, Nana poured herself some more tea. "Is there any risk of you going to Afghanistan?"

"There's a risk, but ..." He raised his shoulders as if the chance of injury or death could simply be shrugged away. "That's one of the reasons why I enlisted. I want to help remove the threat of any more terrorist attacks."

Nana added a little cream and sugar. "Well, I hope you don't have to go."

"Thanks, Nana."

A cooling breeze swirled through the screened door, stirring the quiet thoughtfulness settling over the big mahogany table. Then, as if he were fighting the sleepiness a large meal and twenty-four hours of traveling brings, Brandt sat up with a start. "Oh! I almost forgot! Mr. Brennan wanted me to give you some new pictures of Rob and Amy's baby. They're in my bag. Should I get them?"

A warm light clicked on in the window of Mum's faraway eyes. "I'd love to see them."

Brandt thanked Mum and Nana for the meal, then tossing his

napkin on the table, he pushed back his chair with a promise to return.

When he hustled through the doorway and down the hall leading to the other side of the house, she stood and began clearing the table. Mum and Nana joined her. And all the while Granddad sat forward, elbows on the table, sipping his coffee, ruminating on his sage thoughts.

Did Granddad think her too young to be in such a serious relationship, especially after all she'd been through? Like Caleb, did Granddad think Brandt a fool for choosing a risky path, all in the hopes of a free education?

If indeed those were the thoughts churning within Granddad's mind, she didn't want to know. After nine months of dwelling in an emotional storm, it seemed unhealthy to occupy herself with another uncomfortable situation. While she wanted to be honoring to Granddad, she had to believe God had brought Brandt into her life for a specific reason—to be her help in time of need, to help her look beyond all the pain toward the future— whatever the future might bring.

When the hallway floor creaked beneath the weight of Brandt's footsteps, Mum and Nana stopped their work and returned to their seats. She, however, found rinsing the dishes a bit more therapeutic than looking at baby pictures.

It wasn't that she didn't care about her new niece, but it was just too soon. Her soul still felt scraped raw after delivering her own baby girl into the hands of two childless strangers. Even now, the thought of her little girl made her body respond in a very physical way. Although Mum assured her the natural reflex would eventually subside, it hadn't yet. And so, she could only hope God would give her strength to get through this difficult time of transition.

God, thank You for my niece, Charlotte. Thank You for a home for my little Aleah Grace. Please keep her safe. May she grow up to know You and love You.

"Aww ... She's perfect. Absolutely adorable. Such a sweet smile." Mum purred.

"Aye, and Rob and Amy are nearly bursting with pride." Nana cooed.

She couldn't stand it any longer. She had to join the picture show. Hang the ache in her heart. She would be the best auntie Charlotte would ever have. Stepping to the table, she leaned over the back of Mum's chair and took a peek at the photos too. Charlotte's beauty certainly deserved all the praise Mum and her grandparents were dishing out. What a difference three months could make. Compared to Aleah, Charlotte looked huge. "She's so big already."

Mum flipped to the next photo, then glanced over her shoulder. "Babies grow fast, Miah. But remember, Charlotte started out four pounds bigger than Aleah."

Mum was right. Where Rob and Amy's baby had arrived six days late at eight pounds, seven ounces, Aleah came two weeks early and weighed just under six pounds. She'd fairly disappeared in the pink blanket Nana had embroidered with Isaiah 49:15 and 16.

"Can a mother forget the baby at her breast and have no compassion on the child she has borne? ... I will not forget you. See, I have engraved you on the palms of My hands." Neither I nor God will ever forget you, Aleah Grace.

Mum meandered through the small stack of photos then suddenly stopped when the picture before them looked surprisingly familiar. "Oh ... Miah. It's you and Aleah."

Brandt leaned into their huddle to take a closer look. "Uh, Mr. Brennan gave me a copy. I must have mixed it up with the others." He reached out to retrieve it. "Miah, do you mind if I keep it? I wanted to take it with me to Georgia."

"Why?"

"You look so beautiful and ... and it's a good reminder to pray for her. You asked me to, remember?"

As a matter of fact, she had. And when she'd mailed Aleah's picture and a short note to Maddox's attorney and friend, she'd requested everyone pray for God's purposes to be fulfilled. Truth be known, she couldn't bring herself to whisper a single prayer for Maddox. After she and Granddad had driven to Longreach and closed the postbox door on the letter, she had literally washed her hands of Maddox forever—as if that were even possible.

Nana leaned over to see the picture too. "Miah, I can't get over how much Aleah resembles you when you were a baby. Except for her dark hair, she's an exact replica. You were a tiny mite too."

Mum agreed. "Drew didn't give you any room to grow. He and his seven pounds took up all the space."

Nana chuckled then sat back in her chair. "We have a lot to be thankful for: two healthy great grandbabies and a mob of strong, bright, grandchildren." Nana's smiling eyes moved from the pictures and settled across the table on Brandt. It was just like Nana to embrace every living soul who crossed her path.

"Thank you, Nana."

"For what, Miah?"

"For loving Aleah and ... for loving Brandt."

"They're easy to love, my dear. *You're* easy to love." Nana reached out and patted her hand. "We're going to miss you and your mum when you go back to America. I don't know what we'll do with ourselves!"

In keeping with his no-nonsense, disciplined character, Granddad gave an affirming nod. Then instead of reaching for the Bible like he usually did, he stood and walked across the room.

Granddad stepped through the darkened breakfast nook and then disappeared into the veranda. Returning seconds later, he carried his guitar back across the kitchen to the place where she sat. "I thought instead of reading the Bible tonight, you could lead us in a song, Miah. Seeing how God has helped us all through some trying times, I reckon *Great is Thy Faithfulness* would be appropriate."

"Granddad, I ... I haven't ... My callouses—they're gone." She held up her left hand as if that would convince him to put the guitar back.

"God has been faithful, hasn't He?"

"Yes, of course, but ...." She shook her head in denial. "I ... I haven't worked my voice since before ..." When she looked to Mum for help, she only received an encouraging nod. She didn't want to be disrespectful, but truly, she didn't feel like singing, let alone leading her family in worship. She didn't know when or if she'd ever feel like singing again.

Lowering his guitar, Granddad's blue eyes dimmed in disappointment. "I don't mean to pressure you, love. God has given you a gift. I hope you won't continue to keep it buried."

With her throat too choked up to talk, she and Brandt walked along hand in hand until the wooden fence of the west paddock blocked their aimless path. Brandt stopped and turned her to face the horse-shaped silhouettes nodding and swaying beneath the silver light of the first quarter moon. He wrapped his arms around her, and she leaned into the strength of his body. Somehow his nearness could help calm the stormy emotions buffeting her heart. Where no one else understood her, it seemed Brandt knew what she needed: time to be quiet, time to think. Unlike Granddad, Brandt would never try to make her do anything she wasn't ready for.

She leaned her head back against his chest, stared into the hazy light of the Milky Way, and listened to Earth's eternal hum. While there was something holy about witnessing the land and its beasts finally at rest beneath the protective canopy of the heavens, she didn't necessarily feel reverent. Instead, she felt judged—wrongly judged.

Brandt brushed the curls from her face, then touched his lips to her cheek. "Are you all right?"

She looked up to meet his lips with her own kiss then nodded. "In all my seventeen years, not once has my granddad had to reprimand me. I've always had so much respect for him— I never wanted to disappoint him, you know? He's been like God to me. So yeah, this kind of stings."

She sighed and swallowed her shame. "No, it stings a lot. I mean, how can he possibly understand what I've been through? Has he ever been attacked? Been violated in ... in the most personal way? Has he given birth to a baby only to give it away? Is his sleep disturbed by nightmares? When he looks in the mirror with his one good eye, does he see a handful of ugly scars? How could he possibly expect me to just bounce back from all this trouble?" Her heart swelled, releasing a couple of teardrops. "It's not that I don't want to get past all this crap. It's ... It's just harder than I thought it would be.

"I-I don't know how to explain how I feel, except ... Try to imagine a paralytic trying to walk. It's impossible without miraculous intervention. My heart and my brain are paralyzed, Brandt. They are stuck on August 10, and I need a miracle to move my brain beyond my trauma to tomorrow, to something better and hopeful."

She rested more of her weight into Brandt's chest as the bright lights of the winter constellations grew blurry through the lens of her tears. "I don't know, maybe I am being a baby about this. Maybe I should pick up my guitar and play until my fingers bleed. Maybe I should sing until I don't have a voice. Maybe it's exactly the therapy I need."

When Brandt remained silent, she pulled his arms tighter across her chest and breathed deep of the night air that had cooled to a chill. "Do you think I'm being too sensitive?"

He shrugged. "No, not really. Your granddad's getting old, Miah. Old people sometimes say things others only think."

"So, *you* think I'm burying my talents too?"

"I don't think you'll keep them hidden forever. In time, when you're ready—when you realize the worst is behind you, you'll dig them back up. I don't doubt it."

He sighed then kissed the top of her head. "You do realize the hardest part is behind you, don't you? We have to believe that."

A shiver of dread ran up her spine and joined with the rising vapor of Brandt's hope-filled breath.

PART III

Consider it pure joy, my brothers and sisters,
whenever you face trials of many kinds, because you know that
the testing of your faith produces perseverance. – James 1:2-3

*"The education of our faith is incomplete if we have yet to learn
that God's providence works through loss, that there is a ministry to
us through failure and the fading of things, and that He gives the
gift of emptiness".* - F.B. Meyer

*"And emptiness itself can birth the fullness of grace
because in the emptiness we have the opportunity to turn to
God, the only Begetter of grace, and there find all the
fullness of joy."* - Ann Voskamp

CHAPTER THIRTY-NINE

Michigan, United States of America
May 2003

*E*ven through the driving rain she heard it. The cry screamed of absolute anger. Such a ferocious wail for a newborn. Or was it anguish? Could it be the tiny thing had been hurt? Whatever the circumstance, the infant sounded distressed beyond patience. She would find her. Yes, she'd find the helpless babe and somehow comfort her.

Rain poured down in thick, unearthly glass sheets, obscuring her vision and making her steps unsure. Still, she stumbled on, searching for the elusive cry behind every boulder, under every fern, and around every tree in the dense, green forest that seemed to be under an evil curse.

"Miah ..." The familiar hiss slithered down from a low-hanging branch and stopped her in her tracks. Before she could react, he beckoned her with the sticky sweetness of insincerity. "Miah. Come here, love."

"Maddox! No. Oh, please. I ... I have to find the baby. Can't you hear her crying?"

"No worries, dear." Brandishing a bloodied knife in front of her face, the serpent-man's eyes flashed an evil yellow. "She's not crying. Not anymore." His mocking laughter thundered through the forest, and his lips smacked in satisfaction as he licked the knife clean with his forked tongue. "Come here, little mother. I'm still hungry!" He yanked her close, his grip searing into her wrist like brimstone. Oddly, even before the burnished blade plunged into her chest, her last breath wheezed from her desperate lungs. And as the stormy otherworldliness faded into the twinkling grayness of death, another voice called out to her just beyond a distant, glorious beam of glittery light.

"Don't be afraid, Miah. Run! Run to me!"

"Brandt?"

While her breaths came in very real, short gasps, Miah shook the nightmare from her head then slammed the alarm off with a heavy, shaking hand. *Please, God, cleanse my mind of the memory of this dream. Give me Your peace today—especially today. I need to feel Your presence. And wherever Aleah and Brandt are, please, keep them in Your care.*

As she clicked on the lamp and pulled her Bible and journal from the nightstand, Brandt's most recent and treasured letter fluttered to the floor, landing out of reach. Oh, Brandt ... three more years ... so far away, so out of reach. Come home safe, love.

She flipped back the covers, retrieved the folded note, and placed it in her lap for safekeeping. While she knew each beautiful word by heart, she'd read the note again; it had become part of her morning ritual. But first things first.

She opened her Bible to the book of James and then grabbed her glasses from the nightstand. Just like her glasses were essential to protect and strengthen her good eye, her counselor told her she needed to also put on the corrective lens of God's word every morning. If she didn't, Satan's lies would have her vision warped by noon. He'd have her believing she'd been made a pawn in God's game, that God was the offender, and He'd cruelly cheated and ruined her. Her counselor suggested memorizing special portions of scripture to render the deceiver powerless. This week she'd been making slow progress on the first chapter of James.

Closing her eyes, she held the Bible close to her chest and willed the first few verses to beat from her needy heart.

"James, a servant of God and of the Lord Jesus Christ, to the twelve tribes scattered among the nations: Greetings! Consider it pure joy, my brothers, whenever you face trials of many kinds, because you know that the testing of your faith develops perseverance. Perseverance must finish its work so that you may be mature and complete, not lacking anything. If any of you lacks wisdom, he should ask God, who gives generously to all without finding fault, and it will be given to him. But when he asks, he must believe and not doubt, because he who doubts is like a wave of the sea, blown and tossed by the wind.

She lowered her Bible to her lap and searched through chapter one. Verse one through six memorized! Practice makes perfect. She read through verse eleven then stopped at twelve, her favorite. *"Blessed is the man who perseveres under trial, because when he has stood the test, he will receive the crown of life that God has promised to those who love Him."*

Lord, be the strength of my life. Opening her journal, she wrote out the rest of her prayer.

Lord, help us all to persevere in our trials ...
Brandt, me, Mum and Dad, my family, my friends,

Bri, Kylie, Alicia—the whole band. And in our perse-vering, help us to find joy. Please guide us and give us Your wisdom. Help us to be faithful so in the end we can lay the crown of life at Your feet. Thank You for Your word that gives me peace. And ... Be with Brandt. Please keep him safe.

Now for the best part of the day. She pulled Brandt's note from the folds of her blanket and opened the paper for what must have been the hundredth time. Even so, she never got tired of seeing his handwriting. And she never got tired of envisioning his kind eyes searching for words while the Middle Eastern sun beat on his broad, camouflaged shoulders. *God, let Brandt know I love him. Let him feel your love too.*

> *Dear Miah,* March 10, 2003
>
> *I hope this letter finds you better than I'm doing. Actually, I'm fine. I just miss you beyond what I ever could have imag-ined. So, I spend a lot of time revisiting our moments together. Like a song, I play them over again in my mind. The memories keep me going—and so do your letters. Thanks for writing so often. It helps a lot.*
>
> *I'm sorry for the mental struggles you are having. The nightmares and all the fear and doubt are not surprising to me at all—they're probably normal. You are not a "kook." And no, Miah, I don't think it's weird that you are troubled by the death sentences Maddox received in Texas and Utah. It kind of haunts me too. After what I've experienced, I agree. Every death is tragic—the evil and the innocent alike. Maybe he'll find peace in the waiting.*
>
> *I hope you'll find some peace too. I'm sure I can't under-stand what it's like to feel a little life move and grow within you and then give her into the care of the Creator. She's in good*

hands though. Still, I'm so sorry you've had to walk this most difficult path. I'm sorry for all the pain you're experiencing. Unfortunately, it will probably hurt for a very long time. Oh, how I wish I could be there for you.

I believe you're right, Miah. Putting it down on paper can help. I know your letters help me. I'm grateful you feel free to share your thoughts with me. It helps me face my past with honesty and grace. But hey, I'm not going to live back there anymore. You and me, we have to keep looking forward to the future—a much better future!

Is it really only two more months until you finish your freshman year at community college? I'm so proud of you for keeping up with your schoolwork through all the troubles. And can you believe it? I've already racked up a year of active duty! See, didn't I tell you it'd go fast? A blink of an eye.

So, have you made a decision about a major? I hope you'll choose music and consider transferring to Michigan State University. They have the best music program. Even so, I understand your need to live at home and commute. I want you to feel safe.

And I don't think C.J. or Alicia and the band really means to pressure you. Just like your granddad, they simply know talent when they see it, and they don't want it to go to waste. Miah, even if the new songs aren't coming, pick up the guitar and start singing the old ones. It's worth a try, isn't it?

Perhaps Brandt was right. She eyed the dusty guitars hanging on the wall between her dresser and the window. What would it hurt to pick them up? Maybe music is what she'd been missing. It had been such a big part of her life—the only part really. Then the fair had happened. Then she'd been forced to give up so much.

Well, it's almost lights out, so I better sign off. Unfortu-

nately, this may be my last letter for a while. Things are shaking up a bit around here, and I have a feeling I won't be here long—in Kuwait, I mean. Wherever I go, please know, I'm thinking of you and praying God will be your strength. Don't forget Joshua 1:9. "Be strong and courageous! Do not tremble or be dismayed, for the Lord your God is with you wherever you go!" You have my heart, beautiful!

Love,

LCpl Brandt Traversie DuCharme
(Notice the fancy letters in front of my name? I just earned myself a promotion to Lance Corporal!)

I love you too, Lance Corporal Brandt Traversie DuCharme. She laid the note within the pages of her Bible, pushed back the covers, and traded her U.S. Marine-issued, camouflage T-shirt for her running clothes. Maybe she'd take Brandt's advice and give Alicia a call to see if the band might want to get together sometime—to try it on and see how it feels.

She stepped over to her Taylor and gave it a half-hearted strum. Its out-of-tune strain followed her over to the window where dawn's early light didn't look very bright. In fact, those heavy clouds were full of cold spring showers. And since she didn't feel particularly brave today—not with the nightmare she'd had—she would play it safe and run on the treadmill. No need to take any unnecessary risks.

She pulled on her socks and running shoes. Were Mum and Dad awake too? She opened her bedroom door and listened. Sure enough, their voices percolated up the stairs along with the smell of coffee. Most likely, they were talking about the exciting day ahead.

After twenty-one months and fifteen thousand kilometers had left an awkward canyon in their relationship, Bri had accepted her invitation to join them for a special dinner. Mr. and

338

Mrs. Ellison were flying in today, and they were bringing a big operations rancher with them. He had bought Dad's prized bull and just happened to be from Ranchester, Wyoming, the little town where she'd snapped the picture of her cowboy in that overgrown cemetery so very long ago.

She walked over to her small writing table and considered the black-framed photograph Brandt had given her the day she left for Amaroo Station a year and a half ago. The portrait had served its purpose. Her warrior's come-and-get-me grin had most assuredly inspired her to keep looking forward to their hopeful future. But now, with someone so close who might know the people of Ranchester intimately, how could she not take a step back into her past?

She opened the back of the frame and slid the photo of her cowboy out from behind the portrait of herself and Brandt. While the young stockman's picture may have been hidden through two winters and a spring, he had never been forgotten. And now, after all she'd been through, she felt more connected with him than ever. She held the picture closer and ran her fingers over the image of the boy and the man and the golden-hued cemetery. The cowboy's brave acceptance of the loss of his loved ones still had the power to bolster her resolve and sense of hope. Yes, to be sure, she still held him close to her heart.

"Jonas and Linda, these are our kids." Dad started the introductions on the right side of the crowded semi-circle, whose numbers, hopefully, didn't intimidate the kind-eyed gentleman and his pretty wife. "This is Rob and his wife, Amy, and their little girl, Charlotte. And this is Brianna Bakhuysen, a friend of the family." He skipped around Ben and Maddie Ellison. "Then there's Bradley, Andrew, and finally our daughter, Miah."

Their guests were gracious and attentive as they offered their hands to each of them. "Good to meet you all. Ben told the truth when he said you're a respectable bunch." Polite chuckles filled in the conversation, and then Mr. Sherland turned back to Dad. "What a fine family you have, Trace."

"Thanks Jonas. Claire and I have been very blessed."

"You have another son, don't you?"

"Aye. Our son, Joshua, is working on his degree at Michigan State. He'll be here Sunday and is looking forward to meeting you both."

"Oh, and likewise. We will count it a privilege to meet him." The gray-haired man let out a humble chuckle and met her smile with a quick wink of his warm, brown eyes.

She liked him. The bloke seemed true blue. And she couldn't wait to pull him aside and ask him the question she'd waited years to ask.

"So, Jonas and Linda, 'ow bout you? You have a family?" Dad crossed his arms, giving the couple his full attention.

As if it were a custom, Mr. Sherland folded his arms across his chest too. "Well, you know, Trace, Linda and I never had children of our own. However, the good Lord saw fit for us to raise our nephew. Back in nineteen eighty-four, we lost Linda's sister, her husband, and their one-year-old daughter in an auto accident."

Nineteen eighty-four—the same year she and Drew were born. The same year Maddox met Ava ... Stop. Take every thought captive.

"They left behind a three-year-old son who we've been blessed to raise as our own. And we are so very proud of him. That's one of the reasons we're here. Besides checking out your operation, we've come to visit our nephew." Mr. Sherland turned to his wife who mirrored his smile. "He just graduated from the University of Michigan and has been accepted to their medical school. He hopes to be a missionary someday."

No way. It couldn't be, could it? If she were eleven when she snapped the photo, and her cowboy looked to be thirteen or maybe fourteen at the time, he would be twenty-one or twenty-two now—old enough to graduate from university. But honestly, what were the odds Mr. Sherland and his nephew were the American cowboys in her picture? She studied the man's hair, the shape of his head, and the curve of his shoulders. No, there's no way she could really tell without asking him straight up and showing him the photo.

Her heart pounded in her chest as Dad replied in his own kind way.

"Is that so, Jonas? Your nephew must be a special young man to have risen above his sad circumstances. I'm sure he couldn't have done it without your love and care. It's so inspiring to hear stories of people, like your nephew, turning trials into triumphs." Dad's gaze had a faraway, ponderous look as it settled on the wall just behind her. "Jonas, you and Linda have every reason to be proud of your nephew."

"Thank you, Trace."

Finally, a break in the conversation. She took a small step forward and spoke up. "Mr. Sherland?" Her face began to heat up like a tea kettle and her heart began to pound in her chest. Could her search really be over before it had even begun?

"Yes, Miah." The corners of the pastoralist's mouth turned up in a sincere grin.

"When we first came to America, Mr. Ellison took us to his station—I mean ranch, near your town. And while we were there, I took a photo of a man and a boy who were visiting a cemetery. They had come on horseback and although the sun had just risen, I imagined the two had traveled a long way. So, it seemed to me, whoever was laid to rest there, must have been very special to the man and the boy. The two stood there looking so sad, yet so strong, and it fairly broke my heart." She paused to steady her anxious breath. "I fell in love with the green, rolling hills of the Big Horn Mountains, and I vowed that someday I would live there. And when I did, I would find the man and the boy. Is there a chance the man and the boy in the picture are you and your nephew?"

A tiny breath of unbelief puffed from Mr. Sherland's smile while curious amusement lit up his brown eyes. "Well, I'd be happy to take a look, dear. Do you have the picture?"

She nodded. "It's in my room."

"Miah, we're ready to eat." Mum entered the dining room and placed a steaming bowl of her home-canned, green beans on the table. "Could you show Mr. Sherland the photo after tea?"

Despite nodding politely, her insides were nearly boiling over with excitement. After six years of wondering, the mystery of her cowboy might soon be solved—she could feel it! Bri must have sensed it too. Her head wagged in amazement when their eyes met from across the semi-circle.

They all gathered around the table and after taking a seat and bowing their heads, it seemed like Dad's offering of thanks would never end. The procession of food around the table was even longer and slower because everyone was distracted by the question of whether President Bush's decision to invade Iraq could really be justified. The only interesting part was speculating whether Brandt had taken part in the lightning-fast, search and destroy mission. She seriously hoped not.

"Don't you kind of get sick of all the media play?" Drew swallowed another bite of salad. "I don't know, it's all too dramatic for me. I'd rather listen to my music." He shook his head as if to dismiss the whole war thing from his thoughts, and when the phone rang, he looked happy to have a reason to change the subject. "Got it!" He popped up only to have Dad hold him back.

"Let it go, Drew."

"Dad ... It might be the airport. I never heard back if I could use a plane to take Mr. Ellison for a ride."

Dad nodded his permission.

Drew bounded over to the counter that separated the kitchen

from the dining room and picked up the phone. "Hello!" When his eyes met hers, he raised his brow in a hopeful arc. His excitement fairly matched her own, and who could blame him? All Drew's hard work had paid off, and now he could finally show Mr. Ellison that his money had been well invested. Intent on listening to the phone conversation, Mr. Ellison looked excited too. In fact, they all were curious.

Her twin grinned while the gaze of his bright blue eyes danced around the long, stretched-out table. Then like a balloon with a slow leak, his hope dwindled to disappointment. "Which Mr. Brennan would you like to speak with? Trace, Rob, Brad, or Drew?" He let out a huff and raised the phone toward Dad. "The bloke wants to speak with 'Miah's father'." Drew looked her way and gave a clueless shrug while Dad waved the call away.

"Take a message, Drew." Then Dad moved his chair closer to the table and addressed their guests. "My apologies for the interruption."

"Trace isn't available right now. Could I take a message?" Drew paused to listen and then his eyes shot her way. "Oh, hey, Jett. Of course I know who you are. Brandt's told us all about you. Have you heard from him lately?"

Jett? Why would he be calling here? *Unless ... No, God. Please, no.*

"Sure, okay. One moment." Drew avoided her questioning eyes as he walked toward Dad and handed off the phone. "I think you should take this. It's Jett ... DuCharme, Brandt's brother."

Turn, Drew. Turn around and look at me. Please, look at me! He didn't though. Instead, he stood guard while Dad pushed back his chair and excused himself from the table.

"Daddy?" When all she received was a motion to remain quiet, her face flushed with flaming dread, and her stomach squeezed in tight on her first few bites of dinner.

"Hello, Jett. This is Trace, Miah's dad. How are you?" Even

when Dad looked her way, his posture remained intent on the voice at the other end of the line. "Uh, yes, she is." Turning his back to her, Dad's shoulders dropped as he moved further into the semi-privacy of the kitchen. "I ... I see."

What? What do you see, Daddy? The silence became as palpable as the anxious glances being tossed around the table like a hot potato. And though the worst surely ran through each of their minds, no one wanted to be caught thinking it.

And then it came. Exactly what she didn't want to see. Dad pulled his hand through his thinning curls and held them tight. "Jett, I ... I'm so... so sorry." And then Dad's broad shoulders heaved in grief.

"No! Daddy!" She tried to rise from her chair, except Rob pulled her back and Mum moved to her side, hemming her in as if she were a young child again. *O God, it must be bad! So very, very bad!*

"Daddy!" She tried to stand again, and still Rob held her back. "Rob! Please! Let me go!"

"Your brother was such ... such a strong, confident leader— so very brave."

Was? Was?

"You ... you and your parents can be proud of his accomplishments." Dad's emotion stalled his ability to speak, and when he finally spoke again, his voice was full of anguish. "I know ... I know ... He added so much good to our family too, Jett. He ... he really seemed to be the only one who knew how to comfort and encourage Miah. He meant everything to her—to us too."

This is not happening! God, didn't I give enough? Didn't I try to trust you and obey you? Now you take away my one love? My hope and future? This is too much. I am undone—so utterly undone! She pushed back hard in her chair and ran from the unbearable scrutiny of her judgment seat.

"Miah!"

CHAPTER FORTY

*B*olting out the back door, she took off across the north pasture. God was not going to abuse her anymore!

Miah, I AM your hope and your future. Whoever believes in me will not be disappointed!

Oh really? Then what is this I'm feeling, God? Are You engaging me in a word game here? Is it disillusionment, confusion, disenchantment? What is it? She stumbled, caught herself, and when Rob called out to her, she ran even harder for the woods. *Lord, what complaint do You have against me? Does it give You pleasure to punish me?*

Her heart pounded in her chest and her lungs burned for air. If only they would both give out or explode. *How much do You really think I can take? I am not that strong, Lord. So why don't You just ... get it over with and take me now!*

She hid beneath the shadowy cover of the forest and collapsed onto the brown, musky earth. *My death is what you wanted all along, isn't it? Why do you prolong my agony?* She tore at her clothes and heaped herself with the gritty compost of the woodsy floor. *Return me to what I once was! Dirt and ash!*

No, My beloved. My intent has never been to bring about your demise. It has always been to fill you with My glory and grace, to transform your life into something beautiful—just like I did for Jannali and Brandt.

Well, God, I'm sorry to tell You this, but Your little plan is failing—miserably! She tossed another handful of dirt onto her head.

Miah, I didn't mastermind all the pain you're experiencing. Trust Me, I do know how you feel. I have the scars to prove it, and I grieve right along with you. Because I love you so much, I will never leave you to suffer alone.

If You love me, why didn't You protect Brandt? Why didn't You protect me? Her heart thrummed an angry beat and tears burned a hot path down her cheeks. *I don't understand! What horrible sin did I commit to deserve this?*

A patient silence passed through the forest, and then like a sigh, a light breeze rustled the dry leaves around her. *Daughter, you misunderstand My ways. This is not a punishment. Because of My love for you, I already paid your debt with My death on the cross, remember? The work is complete. The debt paid in full. If you choose to trust Me, I can help you fashion this suffering into something meaningful. However, it's not necessarily an easy path for those who surrender to this transformation. Whoever wants to save his life will lose it; but whoever loses his life for Me will find it.*

How many times, Lord? How many times must I lose it? She pulled at her hair. *I don't believe I can do this again.*

Miah, since the day I saved your soul with the blood of My Son, the way has always been before you. Put your hope in Me—in Me, Miah. Not in your friends. Not in your dreams. If I didn't withhold My Son from you, will I withhold anything you need—strength, comfort, hope, a future? Put your hope in Me and choose to say yes to everything that comes your way—even the losses. Because in Me, is anything really lost? My daughter, everything belonging to Me is yours also. This is not Brandt's end. This is not your end. You have My Spirit as a guarantee of your future glory in eternity.

My glory? She dug her fingers deep into the black humus, packing her nails with the rich matter of things that had once lived. *There could never be anything glorious about me, Lord. I am wretched, broken, ruined.* She lay face down in the bed of decaying leaves and moss, watering the litter with her tears.

Even your brokenness I can use, beloved. Didn't you know that grief prepares the soil of the heart to receive what falls from heaven? The humble are those who I water with grace.

Flood me then, until I drown! Until I drown in my grief ... and ... and yes, in Your grace. Oh, God! ... Her tears flowed like the small stream weaving amongst the woods all the way to the waterhole. *I-I can't do this. I can't do this on my own. Please, Father, help me. Teach me the way of surrender.*

She released all the air in her lungs, and somehow her tears slowed as if they had finally run their silent course. Then strangely, a calm resignation flowed through her veins embalming her mind and body. *And still, I will trust in Your unfailing love.* She pressed her body further into the earth. *Oh, God, I surrender my hopes, my dreams. My everything. Take it all. Because even in this, You will work everything out according to Your perfect plan. For You are always good and I am always loved.* She wiped at her doubt-filled tears. "I believe, Lord. Help my unbelief."

The words brushed past her lips in a hushed prayer she lifted to heaven as an offering. If only it were possible, she'd will her spirit to follow her prayer up through the tarnished silver clouds to its destination somewhere beyond the Milky Way, up where

....

Hey, beautiful!

Could it be? Sniffing back her sorrow, she lifted her head off the pungent pillow of leaves and scanned the woodlands for her warrior's face. "Brandt?" In reply, a silent gust swooped down from the tops of the trees, rustling the dry leaves around her and teasing her cheeks with an airy kiss. *Oh, Brandt, could you really be gone?* The thought became too much, so she lay back down and let the breeze sweep across her body like eternal winds rolling across the Great Plains. *If only I could see you one more time, feel your arms around me.*

This time his voice came like a gently flowing river. *I'm here, Miah. Don't despair. Keep believing for the day when all the good God has for you is realized. His grace will be made complete, and your joy restored.*

Are you really here, Brandt, or am I simply wishing, simply imagining you are near? No, his presence was as sure as her tears. She could sense, without a doubt, her friend dancing close on the wind, looking down upon her as he made the celestial journey to his bright, new home.

And then in a breath, he vanished, and the only thing remaining was a soul-moving melody that dispelled any uncertainty of their encounter. It played in and around the highest branches of the trees, singing a new song over her. Time seemed to slow and then stop. She lay there long enough to memorize each word, every measure of the requiem that captured the essence of her strong, free-spirited friend joining in the frolic of the prairie winds. *Thank You, God, for remembering me, for giving me this tribute to Brandt's short but well-lived life. He did his very best with what You gave him, didn't he, Father?*

"Miah?" A twig snapped behind her, letting her know the voice calling out this time had a very physical quality. "Miah, are you okay?"

She buried her face further into the acrid blanket of matter. "Go away, Bri. Please, I want to be alone." Bri didn't budge. She stood there while a paradoxical twitter of birdsong surrounded them. The mocking song continued, and Bri crouched down. "Miah, I'm so sorry," she sniffed.

Strangely, Bri's tears were welcomed, almost gratifying. So Miah simply lay there on the cold, damp ground and let Bri do all the grieving for a while. It felt good to release the pain and burden to someone else, to have someone care that leaves and twigs were stuck in her mop of filthy, tangled hair.

"Miah ..." Bri removed another tiny twig then shifted in her crouched position. "I ... I don't know what to say or do. I'm so sorry. I'm sorry I let you down."

"What?" She raised her eyes enough to see unchecked tears erupt from somewhere deep within Bri's heart.

"I'm sorry I wasn't there for you when you needed me most." Liquid remorse ran down the apple of Bri's cheek and landed amongst the organic refuse of the forest floor. "I ... I didn't know how to help. And Brandt ... He seemed to know exactly what you needed."

"You did what you could, Bri." She pulled herself up from the ground.

Her friend choked on fresh tears. "No, Miah. I failed you. At first my fear kept me from helping you, and when I saw how perfectly Brandt related to you, I became envious. I blamed him for the distance between us. And now ... and now he's ... I'm so sorry for all your pain—for the pain I caused you. Will you forgive me?"

"Yes. I ... I mean, it's okay, Bri. This whole thing has been difficult for everyone. We've all had things to work through. There's really nothing to forgive."

"I could have helped. I should have helped."

"It worked out all right, Bri." She shrugged and wiped at her tears. "God provided." *Yes God, You provided ... And I can't believe You'd take him away.* The memory of Brandt's kind smile brought on a fresh flood of emotion. "B-brandt gave me the freedom to ... grieve like I had to grieve. H-his boldness gave me the strength and courage to do what I had to do. Bri, it was a gift you weren't meant to give. So, don't blame yourself. Just ... Be with me now. I think I'm going to need you more than ever." She reached out and pulled her friend close as another presence stepped up and joined them in their embrace.

"Rob! Oh, Rob ..." One look at Rob's face and she knew. She knew. Even so, she had to hear it. She rose to her knees and emptied her tears on his shoulders. "He's gone, isn't he?"

Rob held her tight, confirming the reason for her broken, grieving heart. And then Dad pushed through the brush, offering his own comfort. "He didn't suffer, Miah."

She left the strength of Rob's arms and fell against Dad's chest. "Oh, Daddy!" Like a drenching, spring downpour, tears burst from her heart in a torrential, sad flow. "How? How did it happen?"

"Miah, it doesn't really matter, does it?"

"Yes. I need to know."

He brushed her cheek with his hand and wiped the dirt on his trousers.

"Tell me, Daddy. Please."

The reluctance in his light blue eyes told the whole, tragic story. "His unit was under heavy fire, sweetheart." Dad's tears slid down his cheeks, joining hers on the ground. "He fought bravely. Rescued many wounded, but ..." He looked beyond her as if visualizing the whole tragic scene.

"But what? What, Daddy? How?"

Dad only looked at her and shook his head. "No. No more, Miah. It's already too much for your imagination to handle. Take comfort in the fact that Brandt went quickly, and he's with the Lord."

Dad was right. If she knew too much, she'd replay Brandt's final moments over and over in her head, imagining his fear, his pain, and his last thoughts. No, for now she would let it be. Sorrow escaped her soul through a tired, stuttered breath, "Oh, why? Why did he have to die? We had so many hopes, so many dreams. What will I do without him?"

She rested her spent body against Dad's strong chest, not expecting him to reply, but perhaps in his own struggle to understand, he forced an answer from his trembling lips. "You'll trust

God, Miah—just like you've done every step of this … this unbe-lievably harsh … journey." Grief heaved from his chest and in his fight to gain control, his body shook against hers.

"Daddy?" She turned to Rob for help, but his own eyes had welled up at the sight of Dad's brokenness. "Daddy, It's okay. We'll get through this together."

His head wagged in sorrow. "My brave little girl. I'm so sorry for all this pain—for what I've put you through. If I would have known what was going to happen, I never would have brought you here." He made a swipe at his tears. "You believe me, don't you?"

"Of course, I do." Sniffing back her tears, she dabbed at the dirt smeared across his weathered cheek. "If it wasn't for you, I don't know where I'd be. You showed me the way to Jesus, the way to hope. Don't you remember?" She searched for the light of recognition in his tapering tears as Rob and Bri stood and quietly stepped away. "Without Jesus' love and mercy and His Word to give me strength, I would have given up long ago."

Mum crept up and crouched beside her as Dad settled back against a wide oak. He looked to Mum and then back at her. "Yes, but you tried to give up. How can I … How can Mum and I know you won't do anything like that again?"

Miah pushed further into his arms and rested her head against the steady beat of his heart. "I won't. As long as I know you love me, I won't."

"I have always loved you, Miah. I know I didn't navigate the pregnancy and your healing with patience and understanding, but I have always loved you."

"I know that now. Hold me, Daddy."

CHAPTER FORTY-ONE

The water looked as bleak and heavy as her heart felt. She tried to count the dark ripples lapping against the edge of the fishing dock, but every time she reached ten or so, she'd get distracted by the truth of her all-consuming grief. As hard as she tried to control her thoughts, they kept going back to the horrible reality of it all. *Lord, be my solid rock, my firm foundation.*

She raised her bowed head and tapped Bri's elbow, giving her release. "Bri, you don't need to stay here. Why don't you go back up to the house? Get something to eat. I'm fine, really."

Her friend skimmed a bare toe across the water, seemingly determined to keep vigil with her at the end of the dock—the same dock where Brandt had entrusted his life to Jesus with Josh, Dad, and Pastor Bryce by his side.

"Miah, are you hungry? If you want, I could get you something? Some tea, at least?"

The spring breeze felt cool against her face and brought with it the sickening smell of Easter lilies, death-white funeral lilies. "No, thanks. I'm not hungry. But you go. You need to eat."

Bri's dark brown eyes were steadfast like the weeping willows bowing low over the small lake. "I'll stay until you're ready."

Ready? Ready for what? To face the Ellisons, the Sherlands, her family—that's what. How did Bri know her inner struggle? How could her friend, who had gone through life unscathed, possibly understand the difficulty of plastering on a brave smile through the polite condolences and promises of prayer that were sure to come. Still, she did. Somehow, she understood. "Thanks, Bri."

Bri gave a compassionate nod then turned her gaze to the destination of their quiet prayers. The gray of the overcast sky had lifted, making way for sail-white clouds to roll across an azurite sea, so they both sat content, watching the silent parade pass before them.

"I see a horse." Miah's words came out in a whisper, absent of any emotion.

"Where?" A pair of dragonflies danced around the tips of Bri's pink-polished toes as she searched the sky.

"Just above the tallest tree over there."

"Oh, yeah. It looks like a unicorn." Bri nodded.

"A fat unicorn."

"Then ... Wouldn't it be a rhinoceros?" When a quiet giggle escaped Bri's dimpled smile, she couldn't help but join in. But then, as if it were a sin to dabble in joy, a six-foot wave of grief loomed above her head and smacked her down under its suffocating weight. All her pain and disappointment roiled over her, dragging her along the gritty floor of despair, leaving her gasping for breath as if she'd been stabbed all over again.

Where a feeble cry of mercy should have been forming, a curse burned in her throat and threatened to spew from her mouth. It would feel so good to let it fly, to let it ricochet off the water with her sobs and hit God square between the eyes, because in His angry retaliation, maybe He'd finish her off.

Before she could utter a single oath, the loving arms of

Pastor Bryce and his wife Celia reached out from behind her and enfolded her like an eiderdown comforter. Their embrace absorbed her tears, muffled her cries, softened her fall. Pastor Bryce's prayer flowed past her ear, whispering a gentle fountain of God's love to her. "God, You are the One who sees, who hears our cries. Like one lost in the desert, we have come to our end. Our souls are empty. If we don't get some relief to our lips and down our parched throats, we will die. Open our eyes to the abundant well of healing we are trusting You to provide."

A well of healing? *Yes, Lord, heal us. Open our eyes to the healing hidden somewhere within this moment. Help us to see ... You.*

"May we have the strength to do the deep-drinking of Your mercy, to taste the refreshment of Your presence in the midst of our sorrow." Pastor Bryce whispered his final plea as their bodies rocked to the sad cadence of their tears.

Bri hushed an agreeing amen while Pastor Bryce's wife choked out her own difficult "yes, Lord". Lovely Celia Harrison, whose countenance reflected a miraculous inner contentment, had buried not one or two, but three, almost full-term babies in a garden watered with tears. This dear woman had nearly died of thirst waiting for God's mercy. Although she'd surely choked on the dry, gravely dust of unfulfilled dreams, she didn't stop believing in the goodness of God.

Miah reached out and clung to the strength of the friend who'd been refined by holy fire three times over. "Oh, Celia, Pastor Bryce, thank you for coming. I ... I didn't hear you drive up. How did you know?"

Empathy welled up in their eyes. "Your mom called us. She's very concerned for you, Miah."

Her sweet, sensitive mum who'd willingly joined her in this long, emotional roller-coaster ride had probably become sick with anxiety, fearing a replay of September 15, 2001 and being on suicide watch for a month. She wouldn't put Mum through that again.

"Celia, how do you do it? How do you keep looking forward when life continues to slam your fingers in the door? I need to know."

Celia moved from a kneeling position and sat down on the dock. With her eyes still brimming with tears, she spoke carefully as one who'd been offered well-intentioned words of ready-made comfort too many times. "Some days we do better than others, Miah. However, Bryce and I try to dull the pain by counting the joys, giving thanks for the small blessings from above. Like this holy time with you and Bri right now. Like this unbelievably blue sky and warm, sunny afternoon. Whenever we choose to open our eyes to God's graces, He always shows up in amazing and affirming ways."

Celia paused as if seeking permission to continue. "Miah, giving thanks doesn't deny the tragedy or that our hearts have been rent completely top to bottom. Giving thanks merely opens the door for God to do His most refining work in us, to heal us. It's a choice though. Sometimes a very hard choice."

A choice? Hadn't she known that all along? Hadn't Grandmother Jannali once urged her to choose joy? Hadn't she and Brandt encouraged one another with this very same challenge? Yes. And just this morning, hadn't she been reminded in the book of James to consider her trials all joy?

Celia's quiet voice gathered strength. "I find whenever I begin to thank God for *all* things at *all* times simply because He is *always* good, then miraculously, I am blessed by the holy presence of God Himself. I find healing for my hurting soul in God's presence, in His word ... in the thanksgiving."

"But how, Celia? How can I possibly learn to trust God in all things, even in the pain? I want to, but I know the minute I'm left to myself, I'll fail."

"This time ..." Celia looked to Bri with a knowing smile. "We won't let you fail. We won't let you down, sweetheart. Choosing joy over this kind of deep pain may take a team effort and a lot of determined discipline to trust God and His word. Just like a girl who's intentional about finding the perfect lyric and melody that will reach down and touch a listener's heart, choosing joy is going to take an immovable mountain of resolve and the collaborative support of your friends. Nevertheless, you said it yourself, Miah: 'how can I possibly learn?' Because you're a musician, I think you know the answer to your own question."

She knew the answer, all right. She'd only heard Pastor Bryce repeat the mantra over and over in his teaching. "Practice?"

"Yes, exactly. The apostle Paul wrote to the Philippians, 'For I have *learned* to be content'. This kind of learning takes a lifetime of practice." Celia took Miah's hands in her own. "Until-your-fingers-bleed kind of practice."

Miah considered her unutilized and softened fingertips resting in Celia's hands. Perhaps that's why she had never learned to give thanks in all things. While God had been relentlessly teaching her the song of surrender, she'd never really practiced it. And she certainly knew the importance of practice. Practice until the song became second nature, until she could sing and play the piano at the same time, until she could sing while strumming a syncopated rhythm.

At one time in her life, hadn't practice been the most important thing? Then tragedy had stepped in, and with one swipe of its cruel hand, it had smashed her hard work and dreams to the ground. *Thank you, God? How can I thank You when it seems my entire world, my whole purpose for living has been wiped out? Where is the joy? It's so very difficult to see beyond this ... this emptying.*

"Celia, can you help me to see the joy in this? Can you show me how to give thanks even in the sorrow? I want to give it a try. I ... I need to give it a try."

Celia smiled and wrapped a loving arm around her side

while Pastor Bryce moved to hem Bri in on the left. "Sweetheart, Bryce and I have found suffering has the potential to produce two different kinds of sorrows but serves one purpose—to draw us into a closer relationship of trust with God. Second Corinthians 7:10 tells us that Godly sorrow—the kind of sorrow God wants us to experience—leads us away from sin and doubt and results in salvation. There's no regret for Godly sorrow. But worldly sorrow, which lacks faith and repentance, results in spiritual death ... and despair. You and I have been down that destructive road, where the thoughts get scary and desperate, haven't we?"

Their eyes met in understanding. "They're not scary to God. In fact, if we invite Him, He'll meet us right there in all the ugly, broken places of our lives. If we allow Him, God will shape our hurt and disappointment into something new and better. The key word here is *if*.

"Miah, our reaction to trouble has a huge effect on our future and who we're becoming. We can choose to waste away in bitterness or self-pity or we can continue to do what God has called us to do—to bear fruit, to reflect His essence, to be loving and faithful and honorable so others might be attracted to His goodness. It's for this reason we're here, isn't it? To love others because God first loved us? To serve because He serves?

"Miah, you yourself, are an example of the miracle poured out when we choose to recognize the graces God extends to us in the midst of our trials. In our thanksgiving, such a rich generosity can well up within us until we feel compelled to share God's grace with others.

Celia looked out across the rippled lake and then continued. "For those who are devoted to following Christ, their lives take on a continuous, natural rhythm: enduring trials, receiving grace, offering thanks, extending generosity, experiencing joy. Over and over, grace upon grace. It's a cadence that keeps us abiding and growing in Him."

She understood. She truly did, but why did it seem her trials were far beyond what her brothers or Bri or Kylie had ever suffered? Why her? Why the Harrisons? Why Brandt? Why did it seem some people slid through life without as much as a broken toe? Was her sin so much greater? *Father, help me to understand.* Her tears slipped from her eyes, quietly landing in her lap.

"Miah?"

How should she respond? With the truth of her questions? Her doubts? Her sin? No, she couldn't.

"Miah, don't withdraw from us. Please."

She planted her elbows on her crossed legs and stared into the dark water that reflected her grief. "Celia, is it a sin to say I'm terribly disappointed? I mean, it's not fair my brothers seem to get off scot-free. And deep down, all I ever really wanted was to please God—bring Him glory with my music and by keeping my relationship with Brandt pure. I don't get it. Why wouldn't God accept my offering?"

"Oh darling, He did accept it." Celia's arms stretched across her shoulders, swaddling her in comfort. "I'm sure He thinks it's the most beautiful thing He's ever received from you. But God is relentless in the refining of His children. Don't you worry, He's working on your brothers, on Bri, on your mom and dad, on me, on Pastor Bryce. And He'll continue to work on you too. I don't think there's a single doubt in any of our minds—God is going to use you, Miah. In His perfect time, God is going to use your music and your devotion for His glory."

Pastor Bryce reached over and squeezed her hand. "And even if He doesn't, Miah. Even if He writes your story differently from what you had planned, it will be a good one, because God writes with our best interest in mind—with an eternal perspective. And it's for this reason we need to keep our focus on eternal things. When we begin to expect too much from this life and way too little from the next, we start to stumble. Someday you'll see Brandt again. And Celia and I will see our children again."

At the thought of their babies, Pastor Bryce struggled to gain control of his emotions. "If we ... try to remember there's a reward at the end of all our suffering, somehow it takes the horrible sting away from our ... losses." He wiped at a runaway tear.

"The Bible is filled with reminders of the future glory promised to us in eternity. Look at the splendor all around us. If a sin-tainted, broken earth can be this breathtaking and afford us infinite opportunities to explore and learn, how much more wonderful will heaven be?

"Our tears will be wiped away and we will meet Jesus just as He is—Jesus!" Once again, a flood of emotion hindered Pastor Bryce's ability to speak. He apologized with a helpless smile then continued in a whisper. "Jesus ... The One who loves us beyond what we can imagine, the One who bought us with His own precious blood so we might know real joy, right now, and live in it forever.

"Scripture leads us to believe that the death of a follower of Christ, is actually a victory and eagerly expected. Because the price of our ransom was so costly, there's a joyful urgency in the way God opens His arms to welcome His beloved into the mystery and beauty of His presence. Can't you just imagine the Father's joy in the delight of His children as they experience all the good He has in store for them? I'm sure it must be a precious sight to Him."

Brandt's entrance into heaven was anticipated and cele-brated by God Himself? Could it be true? She lifted her eyes to the brilliant blue light of the heavens and tried to envision her love's first few moments in eternity—unburdened, jubilant. Like a stolen, battered girl being reunited with her family, surely Brandt experienced an overwhelming measure of relief ... bliss. Yes, she could almost imagine it. *Thank You, God. Thank You for saving me, for bringing me home.* She drew in a deliberate breath as one embarking on a difficult mission. *And*

Lord, thank You for saving Brandt ... for taking him ... home ... to be with You.

There. She did it—offered her thanks, meager as it was, but willingly just the same. Her tears bubbled up from a well, hidden deep within, with a force as unstoppable as the Great Artesian Basin. They flowed silent and free like a cleansing fount, washing away doubt from the muddied banks of her soul. And when her tears were emptied, the assurance of God's presence sang over her with a quiet anthem. allowing her the hopeful expectation of joy. One day. Yes, one bright and glorious day. *Thank You, God. Thank You.*

POSTLUDE

Labor Day, September 2003

Three to four-foot swells crashed over the sand bar, and like the relentless waves, her friends and family wouldn't let up.

"Come on, Miah! It's buckets of fun!"

"You're gonna miss out on the best waves of the summer!"

"The water won't get any better than this!"

They spoke the truth. Even though autumn lurked around the corner, today the sunshine beamed bright, the air sizzled hot, and the water of Lake Michigan sparkled with exceptional beauty. If she didn't dive in now, it would be another year before she'd be able to enjoy the clear, fresh surf of Pentwater, Michigan. Then again, this happy feeling didn't come around every day either. One quick journal entry and then she'd join her friends in the red-flag waves. She had to capture this joy on paper before it blew away with the breeze.

While she'd been diligent to count the small blessings God brought her way, it had been three months since she'd felt free to participate in the robust living happening all around her. Each time she'd been tempted to join in, she was stopped short by the reality that something was missing—the soul-to-soul friendship with the young man who shared her dreams and knew her best.

Every good thing reminded her of the joys she and Brandt would never experience together, and it always made her feel ... guilty. How could she dare consider the future when her love's had been cut short? How could she even think to look for inspiration in the golden-hued photograph Drew had retrieved from the wastebasket and placed on her nightstand? "When you're ready to hope," is what he'd said.

Hope. That's what Dr. Emily, her therapist, had been working to instill in her. And her family and friends had joined in too, urging her to remember Brandt's life had not ended, and neither had hers. "Brandt is living in the very real presence of God's light and love, and you are here to complete the tasks God has given you," Pastor Bryce had counseled. He said, "despite beatings, imprisonment, shipwrecks and snakebites, the apostle Paul never gave up on his mission and you shouldn't either." He explained how a person's ability to bounce back from trouble seemed to be in direct correlation to the size of their vision and goals.

At one time her dreams had been mountainous, but now she wasn't even sure they were meant to be conquered. Still, her pastor urged her to follow the proverbial carrot on the end of the string in order to keep moving forward. Whether the "carrot" should be her music, missions, attending university, teaching, writing, or working at the farm, she simply didn't know.

If it wasn't for the troublesome and irrational fear that plagued her from time to time, she had half a mind to run away to the beautiful hills of South Dakota to commune with the beauty of God's creation and spend some time with Brandt's family—to get to know them better. Jett had stayed true to his promise to keep in touch, and he never failed to end their phone conversations with a generous Lakota invitation. He had even offered to explore the Bighorn Mountains with her, to help her find the cowboy who had eluded her on the terrible, fateful day she received the news about Brandt.

Although she had never found out if Mr. Sherland and his nephew were indeed the cowboys in the golden photograph, she had a strong sense the boy was attending medical school one hundred kilometers away in Ann Arbor, but she wasn't ready to have her bubble burst. She still wanted to imagine him riding a lonesome Wyoming range, searching for purpose, existing beneath the looming shadow of death ... just like she'd been doing.

As hard as she tried to fight it, mortality's curse had an insidious way of penetrating the protective walls she had worked so hard to build. At unsuspecting times, the curse would show up in the form of a disturbing thought, a nightmare, or fear so real it took her breath away. Even the strings C.J. had pulled in Nashville worked to accuse her. The unsigned recording contract collecting dust on her dresser was a cruel reminder of what could have been, of what was stolen from her.

Then there were the ever-present, eager blue eyes of her niece. Rob and Amy's daughter, Charlotte, was only three months older than her own brown-eyed flesh and blood. While Charlotte's beauty and innocence delighted them all, Miah couldn't help wondering what charms Aleah would have entertained them with. At sixteen months, would Aleah merely toddle, or would she be steady enough on her feet to run around in the sand with her cousin, Charlotte, and C.J. and Teá's little girl, Aspen, or ....

Or would she pursue them with a bitter glare in her brown eyes, just like her daddy? What do you think, Miah?

Stop it! Stop it! Get away from me, Satan!

Lord Jesus, please protect my thoughts from the evil one. Please don't let him spoil this beautiful day. Help me to remember You are stronger than any dart of doubt he can throw my way.

"Miah! Are you coming or not?"

"Aye! Give me a minute, Drew, will ya?" She smiled as her brother dove headfirst into a four-foot whitecap then popped up with an exuberant shout. Shaking the water from his blonde curls, he looked unaware of the surprise creeping up behind him. With a mighty whoop, Josh lunged toward Drew, dragging their laughter beneath a thunderous, crashing wave. Her own laughter bubbled with the foaming surf, and it felt good, and for the moment, even right. A thoughtful smile lingered on her face as she rolled her pen between her fingers and began to write.

Monday, Labor Day, September 1, 2003

Here it is, already the final day of the second annual, small group campout. I needed this so very much. I think we all did. When I look back and see how far I've come, I'm overwhelmed with the knowledge of God's power and presence in my life. And He is here today. I'm so sure of it. What a glorious day! All creation shouts and sings of His grace and His perfect peace. The heavens declare the works of Your hands O, LORD! Yes, indeed they do! The sky is such a deep, infinite blue today...

... the same deep, infinite blue that colored the sky when the U.S. Marines buried one of their bravest—her warrior. And who knew what color the sky reflected before then? For three days prior to his burial, she and her family and Pastor Bryce and Celia, along with Brandt's family, friends, and even strangers, had kept constant vigil over Brandt's beautiful soul before finally committing it to eternity. And after the thirty-eight-hour wake, they left the school and followed the military motorcade two hours north where they laid her love's body to rest in the green, forested mountains of the Black Hills National Cemetery. The Black Hills ... where the Creator imparted His sacred song to the Sioux Nation, where He spoke them into existence eons ago.

But Brandt hadn't simply existed. No, he lived big and strong and courageously. In his short life, he brought honor to his God, his people, and to his country. And he was highly regarded, even by people who didn't know him. Before the wake, hundreds of Native American people joined in the seven-kilometer-long procession down a remote dirt road in the middle of nowhere, South Dakota. They came from communities all around the state to pay tribute to one they called Standing Rock.

When the long, military motorcade finally crunched to a stop in the gravel road, those closest had gathered in silence to watch. With precision, six men in uniform transferred the simple, flag-draped box from the back of a black, Cadillac hearse onto a horse-drawn wagon. Four tribal chiefs in traditional headdress and regalia had reined their horses behind the wagon, followed by marines marching in blocked formation. Finally, the residents of one of the poorest counties in the United States had taken up the rear. Most were in cars and trucks, but some were on horseback. And many came on foot, bringing star quilts and generous gifts meant to keep the memory of Standing Rock—LCpl Brandt Traversie DuCharme alive.

The solemn procession ended at the Prairie View High School gymnasium where Brandt had once learned to box and play basketball. In perfect synchronization, the marines transported the adorned casket to the front of a ceiling-high tipi that ennobled one end of the basketball court. And all the while, someone kept a sad, steady drumbeat. There wasn't a dry eye in the bleachers as Brandt's family took their places of honor and two marines stood guard at the tipi's entrance.

Then offering a prayer in the Lakota language, a tall man with long, black hair purified the air with a bundle of smoking sage grass as another pair of marines opened the casket. It was then all her grief rushed her senses like the waves crashing before her now. Brandt's hair had been shaved clean to his head and the resolute face she'd kissed goodbye after his furlough in November, appeared ... vacant, completely void of the brave soul she'd fallen in love with.

Brandt's body, shrouded in a decorated, marine-blue dress uniform, no longer contained the selfless spirit that had made her life more purposeful and hopeful. His soul had departed and now resided somewhere ... somewhere else, with someone ... *Someone.*

She had watched through thick tears as Brandt's great-uncle, a veteran himself, stood and placed a gift in Brandt's unmoving, folded hands—an eagle feather—the highest honor for bravery a Lakota warrior could receive. The tearful, broken man then turned and bid the people to come.

The first to rise were the elders, many of whom bore the distinctive, single eagle feather, signifying they too were warriors who once served the land and its people. They placed their gifts within and around the box and then gave their condolences to Brandt's mother and father, and to Jett. Jett had looked to be her age—simply a younger version of Brandt, maybe less tame, but still so incredibly handsome and terribly painful to look at. For an instant, his eyes had met hers, and he gave a nod of recognition as his lips mouthed her name. Before she could wonder what he was doing, he stood, walked toward the first row of bleachers, and invited her and her family and the rest of the Michigan entourage to come next.

"Jett, we ... didn't know of your tradition. We didn't bring a gift."

Though his eyes brimmed with grief, he had smiled. "It's okay, Miah. We will give you one."

"No ... No." A storm of regret, embarrassment, and grief swirled within her being as she reached into her purse and pulled out the gold-colored fabric bag protecting the lock of smooth black hair she'd had professionally bound and kept with her wherever she went. "Jett ..." Tears kept her words locked inside her heart. She unzipped the bag and cupped Brandt's hair in her hand like the treasured offering it was. "For the soul bundle."

As if Brandt's hair was the talisman that could heal all his inward pain, Jett took the gift in his hands and ran it across his tear-stained cheeks. "He gave this to you?"

She'd nodded. "The day he cut his hair."

"Do ... do you think he knew he was going to die?"

"No. He promised me he'd come back. I think he was simply doing the responsible thing—for all of us. And I-I think he understood how special and how loved he was by you and your family, me and my family, and the Creator."

Jett nodded as if he understood. "Thank you." Then he dismissed himself with the raise of his brother's hair. "I'll give this to my dad. Thank you. Please, all of you, come."

So they did, and she'd never known such grief. She didn't know whether to cling to Brandt's still body and hope by some miracle to be taken up high past the Milky Way too or if she should run until her broken heart bled out. However, she did neither. Instead, she leaned against her family and friends and simply wept. She wept for Brandt's smile that would never touch her lips again, for his strong hands that would never lead her again. She wept for the wedding they would never have, the babies they would never hold, and the land they would never homestead.

Then she let the memory of Brandt's growing faith, his courage, and his kindness be her strength. Surely heaven's door had opened wide to receive his sincere and faith-filled spirit.

Brandt's parents wordlessly received her with a warm loving embrace and for a moment they quietly grieved their great loss together. Then somehow her voice made its way through her tears. "Brandt was a gift to me ... to all of us from the Creator. He ... he stood by me through a very difficult time. His love and kindness gave me strength and hope to look ahead to the future. He was so confident and brave. It gave me courage too."

His mum nodded in understanding and held a tissue to her eyes, trying to soak up all her sorrow.

"Brandt loved you all so very much and wanted to make you proud of him."

Brandt's father couldn't hold it together. He broke down and held her tight. "Thank you ... Thank you, Miah. Your words are healing to me. He was such a good boy. And I was not always a good father."

She leaned her head against his heaving chest. "Brandt loved you. And he knew you loved him too."

He nodded and wiped his eyes. "Thank you."

When she turned to Jett, once again she was taken back by his resemblance to Brandt and found it so very difficult to look at the dark pools in his eyes. She closed her own eyes on her tears and reached out to hold him. "Jett, I'm so very sorry for your pain."

"I'm s-sorry for yours too," he stuttered in her ear.

"What will we do without our Standing Rock?"

He shook his head and tried to hold back his sorrow. "I ... I don't know. I going to miss him so much. First Skye and now ... I feel so all alone." He brushed away the heavy tears that flooded his eyes. "He was my hero, you know?"

Bitter emotion swelled in her throat as she nodded in agreement.

Jett looked toward the casket, and then his tear-filled eyes skimmed across the gym before resting on her. "We ... we should stay in touch. I think he'd want us to."

She smiled despite the salty grief burning her cheeks. "Yeah. I think so too."

After her parents and Pastor Bryce and Celia gave their

condolences to Brandt's family, they all returned to the bleachers where she let Mum rock and rock and rock her as if she were a child again.

The minutes turned into hours and by the twenty-fourth hour of the wake, clothes began to sag, eyes became bloodshot, and dark shadows covered the faces of the men. Even so, the care and compassion remained strong. People continued to bring their gifts. They cried together, ate buffalo soup and fry bread together, and while drums pounded out an ageless rhythm, everyone listened to story after story of how Brandt's life had honored the Lakota traditional values and the Seven Directions: North (wisdom), East (fortitude), South (generosity), West (courage), Up (honor), Down (respect), and most importantly, Inward (humility).

Then Brandt's great-uncle stood again and explained the connection between humility and Brandt's sacrifice for the country. "Recognizing that only Creator is sacred and perfect, our son, Standing Rock, tried to live with humility toward and for the well-being of all living things. For this reason, Standing Rock died to protect our safety."

The emotional tribute prompted even more stories and more giving of gifts. It wasn't until she'd listened to the Lakota warrior songs and watched the photographs of Brandt's life up on a large screen that she finally knew what gift she could bring.

Two marines helped her find a piano and quietly rolled it to the end of the gymnasium, nearest Brandt's body. With her heart thumping in her chest, she too gave testimony of the young man who'd given her courage to look ahead, who'd made her smile despite her pain and fears, and whose love inspired the two new songs she shared with his family and friends. And when she finished singing, she softly played on to the beat of the drums while mourners continued to bring their generous gifts: elaborate, handmade star quilts, beadwork, dream catchers, gold and silver jewelry, photographs, artwork, letters, and flowers.

However, two hours before midnight, thirty-six hours from the beginning of the wake, the giving truly became sacrificial.

Quilt by expensive quilt, gift by thoughtful gift, Brandt's family gave them all away—first to the marines who had taken part in planning the ceremony, and then to close friends and family who had faithfully stood by their side. In the end, Brandt's family had given away thousands of dollars' worth of items that could have been used to make their life easier. But community and sacrificial love—that is the Lakota way.

Their generosity had continued into the next day. For delivering a heart-felt eulogy and offering words of hope at Brandt's burial, Pastor Bryce and Celia were the blessed recipients of one of the beautiful star quilts. And she had been deemed worthy to receive one of the invaluable quilts too. With tears betraying their brave smiles, Jett and his parents had chosen a private moment to present the gift. They explained the pattern represented the morning star, which guides all people with the light of knowledge to travel the holy path—a path, despite her stumbling, she was still determined to follow.

The colorful quilt now hung on her bedroom wall to help her remember ... Remember Brandt? She could never forget. Remember the lessons learned from Brandt's family and friends? Yes. Through all their poverty, suffering, and losses, somehow the Lakota people had discovered the way of joy, and slowly she too was realizing it was through giving that joy and healing are found. Giving away life-sustaining gifts, giving one's life for the safety of others, giving hope to a hopeless man, giving a baby to a childless couple, giving thanks even when your heart is breaking ... Miraculously, it could all amount to joy.

When a girl gives up, when she surrenders her plans and desires, it's there in the struggling and pain where she might get a tiny glimpse of what it could look like for God to take her hurt and disappointment and turn them into something else, some-

AUTHOR'S NOTE

*In gratitude and honor of the 73 Native American men and
women who gave their lives in Operation Enduring
Freedom (Afghanistan, 2001-2014) and Operation Iraqi
Freedom (2003-2010).*

Despite experiencing immense suffering, loss of life and land,
forced assimilation, and the destruction of their cultures, Native
Americans have participated in every major U.S. military
encounter from the Revolutionary War to the twenty-first-
century conflicts in the Middle East. Historically, they have the
highest record of military service per capita when compared to
other ethnic groups.

In the twentieth century, more than 12,000 Native Americans
served in World War I, and 10,000 Native women joined the Red
Cross. During World War II, over 44,000 Native Americans
served, including nearly 800 women. (You may have heard of the
Code Talkers of World War I and II.)

Since World War II, Native Alaskans and Hawaiians have
also served in great numbers and with distinction. Service

continued at a high rate throughout the twentieth century, in peacetime and war.

Today, Native Americans and Alaska Natives serve at five times the national average. There are more than 24,000 Native American men and women on active duty, and more than 183,000 veterans identify as American Indian or Alaska Native.

During Operation Enduring Freedom (Afghanistan, 2001-2014), some 30 Native American and Alaska Natives were killed and 188 wounded. And in Operation Iraqi Freedom (2003-2010), 43 Native Americans died, while 344 were injured.

For more information on the history of Native Americans in military service, check out these helpful links:

1. https://americanindian.si.edu/static/why-we-serve/topics/conflicts-in-the-middle-east/

2. https://www.usar.army.mil/NativeAmericanHeritage/#:~:text=Historically%2C%20American%20Indians%20have%20the,serve%20in%20the%20Total%20Force.

3. https://www.nicoa.org/american-indian-veterans-have-highest-record-of-military-service/

4. Understanding America: The Legacy of Native American Military Service - United States Department of State

5. A History of Military Service: Native Americans in the U.S. Military Yesterday and Today · United Service Organizations (uso.org)

THANK YOU FOR READING EVEN IN THIS

If you were impacted by Miah and Brandt's story, you are invited to continue your experience at dianna.l.lanser.com where you can:

- Share how you feel about *Even in This* and read what others are saying.
- Learn about and communicate with the author.
- Purchase additional copies.
- Download bonus chapters.
- Follow the Author on social media.

If you would like to support this project:

- Share or mention the book on your social media platforms.
- Write a book review on your blog or on a retailer site. If you know of authors or speakers who have a voice to the wider culture, ask them if they would review the book and make some comments in their website, newsletters, etc.

- Pick up a copy for friends, family, women's shelters, prisons, rehabilitation homes, and the like where people might be encouraged or challenged by its message.
- Recommend this book for your church, workplace, book club, or small group.

AUSSIE GLOSSARY

Back of beyond: Far away in the outback

Battler: A hard trier or struggler

Belt up!: Shut up

Bloody: All-purpose intensifying adjective

Bludger: Lazy person

Bullyrag: Intimidate by bullying

Come good: It will turn out all right

Cow cocky: Small-scale cattle farmer

Cuppa: A cup of tea or coffee

Daks: Trousers

Dinky-di: The real thing, genuine, honest, on the level

Droving: Rounding up or driving cattle

Fossicking: Searching or rummaging around for something

Fridge: Refrigerator

Good on ya!: Well done!

Gum tree: Eucalyptus tree

Hooroo: Goodbye

In full feather: In good health

Joe Bloggs: An average person

Jumped-up: Full of self-importance; arrogant
Kerfuffle: A noisy argument or commotion
Layabout: A lazy person
Madder than a cut snake: Very angry
Nick: To steal
No-hoper: A hopeless case
Jingoes!: Exclamation of wonder or surprise
Rattle your dags: Hurry up
Spit the dummy: To get very upset or overreact in an angry and childish manner
Lamingtons: Sponge cake cut into squares, covered in chocolate and coconut
Loo: Lavatory or toilet
Oil: True or reliable facts; information
Owyergoin: How are you going?
Paddock: Field or meadow
Pashing: Kissing passionately
Pommy: An English person
Rack off: Go away
Ratbag: Someone who does not behave properly
Road Train: A diesel truck pulling two or more trailers or semi-trailers.
Station: A large farm or grazing property
Swag: Bedroll used in the outback or for camping
Quid: Money
Tack: Hard work
Tea: Evening meal
Thingo: Thing, whatchmacallit
Ute: Utility truck or vehicle
Wet, the: Rainy season in northern Australia
Yakka: Hard work
Yobbo: Uncouth, aggressive person

ACKNOWLEDGMENTS

How does a person happen to write a novel, and why would they?

In 2006, I was forty-five years old. My husband Brent and I had five children, ranging in age from fourteen to three. We were in the "thick of things".

While my greatest joy was being a mom and wife, our marriage was strained by the stress of supporting a large family —strained to the point that we needed intervention. That's when **Greg and Joni Henry**, dear friends from our small group at Ada Bible Church, came alongside us and helped guide us toward surrender, unity, and healing. Thank you, Greg and Joni!

During this time, I began a discipline of walking several miles every day to listen to Christian music, pray, and think. One song in particular, "Praise You in This Storm", by Casting Crowns, stirred my memory and my imagination. That's when Miah's story began to form in my mind. However, guilt also began to grow. Instead of using my precious time away from the responsibilities at home to commune with God, the story kept occupying my imagination.

I confessed this shortcoming to my sister-in-law, **Jamie**

Lanser, and instead of counseling me to "take every thought captive", she encouraged me to write the story down. Thank you, Jamie! I'm glad I listened to your advice.

Several months later, my mother-in-law, **Janet Lanser,** gifted me with a ticket to Calvin University's Festival of Faith and Writing (Thank you, Mom!) where a few of my chapters received special recognition from the late **Lawrence Dorr**, a Pulitzer Prize Nominee. His kind encouragement fueled my resolve to continue writing and complete the story.

I joined a writer's group made up of a few people I met in Lawrence Dorr's private critique class. Author and ghost writer, **Lisa Burgess** was the first person to read the entire manuscript, and she blessed me with her time and helpful feedback. Thank you, Lisa!

For Christmas that year, my sister-in-law, **Sheryl Casey**, gave me a copy of *The Shack* by William P. Young. It caused an avalanche of emotion and grief as my soul wrestled with the paradox of God's goodness and tragedy. My parents had died when I was in my early twenties, and although God had blessed me with great faith and peace, *The Shack* revealed within me a latent desire for answers—a need for reckoning. What I learned about God's love from this book impacted the rest of my life and shaped Miah's life. Thank you, Sheryl.

Somewhere along the line, I hired my husband's cousin, **Lindsey Winsemius**, to edit the manuscript. Her insight and help were invaluable. Thank you, Lindsey! After making the necessary edits, I submitted several chapters to Authonomy, an online writer's community facilitated by Harper Collins. After nearly a year online and through the support of friends and family, the book earned the number one spot on the "editor's desk" and a review from an editor from Zondervan. The editor offered helpful suggestions to make my writing and the story stronger.

After more revisions, I had the book edited by **Kirsten**

Brink, a graduate from Calvin University who went to work for Baker Publishing. Kirsten, I'm sorry I lost track of you, I hope you're making it in the publishing world. Thank you for your help.

Once again, the story underwent changes, and after that, I shelved the book—out of reach and out of my thoughts. I wanted to be fully present in my children's lives. The writing process and the story had served a great purpose. I gained an understanding of myself and the God who loves me, who foreknew the tragic losses I would face in my early twenties and yet, He allowed them. I learned there is peace and joy in surrendering, in saying yes to the losses, and trusting God with the future.

During the hiatus from my make-believe world, the Lord took his chisel and sandpaper to my heart through a devotional by Ann Voskamp, which I received from another sister-in-law, **Jane Lanser**. Thank you, Jane! I read the book twenty-six times, and when I finally set it down, God had transformed me, made me anew.

Then, just like the Creator who promised to never leave me or forsake me, I couldn't forget the girl from the outback. And when the time was right, I blew the dust away and breathed life back into her story. But Miah needed chiseling and sanding too, and so did her boyfriend.

When the last rough spots were smoothed, it was time for another edit. Years earlier I had heard author **Lorilee Craker** speak at a local writer's conference. I had been so impressed with her that I kept her name in my file all those years. When I reached out to her, it was a long shot launched by prayer, but to my surprise, she kindly accepted my request for an edit. Thank you, Lorilee.

I loved all her suggestions—they were spot on, and we had a mutual love and respect for our Native American "relatives". It has taken two years (maybe three) to refine Miah and Brandt's story to what it is today. I'm so grateful for each person who has helped me in the process, and for the gracious God who put them in my life.

Here are a few more names I need to thank and recognize:

- **Kim Karr:** Thank you for allowing my son and me to observe a Kent County Search and Rescue team training. Thank you for your heart to serve and to save.
- **Joni Henry, Sheryl Thompson, Val Adrianse, and my husband Brent Lanser:** Thank you for upholding this project in prayer. You are my most favorite and treasured friends.
- My children, **Alicia Betts, Brandt Lanser, Andrew Lanser, Amy Schultz**, and **Nicole Lanser:** Thank you for letting me borrow your names. Thank you for letting me carry my pencil and paper to your games, track meets and play practices. Thank you for letting me read "just a paragraph" to you every now and again. You are my joy.
- **Grand Rapids North Word Weaver Friends** – Thank you for sharing your writing knowledge and incredible giftedness with me.
- **Lorilee Craker** – Thank you for your kindness and the final edit. Your imagination and creativity amaze me.
- **Hannah Linder** – Thank you for using your artistic talents to create a captivating and beautiful cover. You are patient, kind, gifted, and appreciated.
- **Catherine Posey** – Thank you for presenting all 111,627 words, from cover to cover, in an organized and appealing way.
- And finally, special thanks to **Dr. Casey Church** – Thank you for taking time away from your busy travel

and speaking schedule to read my manuscript and serve as the cultural consultant on this book. May the Lord bless and expand your efforts to share a hope-filled, Indigenous expression of the Gospel among Native communities in North America.

<h1 style="text-align:center">DISCUSSION QUESTIONS:</h1>

Spoilers ahead!

1. Miah had some pretty big dreams. What are some of your dreams? How are you trusting God to help you move forward? What scriptures do you utilize for inspiration? What steps can you take this week to help move you closer to your goal?

2. What do you think Miah and Brandt's initial attraction and relationship was built on? What did Miah value in Brandt? And what did Brandt value in Miah? How did it change over time?

3. The Brennan family was freely welcomed into the fellowship at Open Door Bible Church; however, it seems Trace quickly judges and dismisses Adam Chisholm (devil boy). How did this make you feel about Trace? After Trace repented, how did you feel? Is there someone who needs your apology or forgiveness? What is keeping you from withholding either? How can we develop an open heart toward others, especially those who are different from us?

4. How would you describe Trace's relationship with Miah before the attack and after? If you or a loved one has ever walked through a crisis, did you find yourself withdrawing or did you lean into your loved ones? What were the reasons for your reaction?

5. How did Miah's faith in God help her in her ordeal? Where in her story did you see evidence of strong faith? When did you see her stumble? What part did scripture play in her ability to remain clear-minded? In the last six to twelve months, what situations and circumstances have challenged your faith in God? Do you currently feel strengthened or weakened in your faith? How has scripture helped or encouraged you?

6. The Brennan family had a close circle of friends from their church. What role did their friends play during Miah's abduction and in the aftermath and after Brandt's death? List all the benefits you can think of for surrounding yourself with a small group of friends.

7. What was your favorite scene in the book? What scene did you dislike?

8. Grandmother Jannali and Brandt DuCharme are representative of Indigenous people who have suffered under or been disrupted by colonialism. What are some ways you can learn more about the culture, the current struggles and hopes of the Native people whose land you live on? How can you be an advocate for their healing?

9. What do you think was the cause of Duane Maddox's murderous bitterness? Do you think he was capable of true repentance?

10. Miah had many people in her life who cared for her and supported her after her ordeal. And both she and Brandt had some difficult relationships to navigate.

What do you value most about your friends and family? What would you like to improve about your relationship? What steps can you take to build a healthier relationship with them?

11. Jesus tells us to forgive our enemy and pray for those who persecute us. If you have experienced deep hurt from someone, have you been able to forgive the person who harmed you? How has that ability or inability to forgive affected you? Have you ever been forgiven of something or been given grace? How did this make you feel?

12. Merriam-Webster dictionary defines a miracle as "an extraordinary event manifesting divine intervention in human affairs." What miracles did you see in Miah's story? What miracles have you experienced in your own story?

13. What character do you most identify with? Why?

14. After Miah learns of Brandt's death, she believes God takes delight in abusing her. She wrestles with the paradox of God's goodness and her and Brandt's suffering. In chapter thirty-nine, she asks God, *"If You love me, why didn't You protect Brandt? Why didn't You protect me?"* How does God reply? What difficult situations or painful circumstances is God asking you to trust Him with? What portions of your life need to be surrendered so the Lord can begin to do His redemptive and restorative work? When in the past have you seen God create beauty and goodness from something painful or tragic in your life?

15. In the postlude, Miah reflects on her journey through grief and her inability to move forward with hope. Pastor Bryce had explained to Miah that a person's ability to bounce back from trouble seemed to be in direct correlation to the size of their vision and goals.

If you find yourself paralyzed by fear or grief, what would it take to name and move toward the goals and dreams you once had? Who might keep you accountable?

16. Both Miah and her dad, Trace, lean on James 1:2-4 for strength during the story. Those verses tell us to count all our trials as joy. What benefits of counting joys does James list in the first chapter of his letter? How might counting three blessing each day change your perspective of God? How might this counting increase your joy and faith and help you on the path of healing?

MEET DIANNA

diannalanser.com